NEW CUMBERLAND
PUBLIC LIBRARY

D1156305

In Memory of

Betty Lee Blando

Presented by

Judith Bank

to

New Cumberland Public Library
2011

Heart Language

THE PENNSYLVANIA GERMAN SOCIETY

The Pennsylvania German Society is a nonprofit educational and literary organization. Its purpose is to preserve, disseminate, and advance knowledge of the history and culture of the Pennsylvania German people and their three-hundred-year history in America, including their contributions to the development of American society. To accomplish these purposes, the Society promotes scholarly research, publishes in print and other media, and offers educational programs of interest to the membership and the general public.

www.pgs.org

EXECUTIVE BOARD OF DIRECTORS

President: David L. Valuska, PhD
Vice President: Ronald S. Treichler
Secretary: William Donner, PhD
Treasurer: George F. Spotts

DIRECTORS

Veronica Backenstoe
Rev. Wallace J. Bieber
Troy Boyer
Daniel Breidegam
James A. Dibert
John B. Frantz, PhD
Norman Hoffman

Robert M. Kline, MD
Daniel N. Schwalm
Michael Showalter
Carl D. Snyder
Eugene S. Stine, EdD
Lee Thierwechter
Carolyn C. Wenger

Editor: Simon J. Bronner, PhD
Executive Director: Erik Fasick

SUSAN COLESTOCK HILL

Heart Language

Elsie Singmaster and
Her Pennsylvania German Writings

THE PENNSYLVANIA STATE UNIVERSITY PRESS
UNIVERSITY PARK, PENNSYLVANIA

NEW CUMBERLAND
PUBLIC LIBRARY

801784223

"A Sound in the Night," "The Courier of the Czar," and
"The Amishman" from *Bred in the Bone, and Other Stories*
by Elsie Singmaster. Copyright © 1925, and renewed 1953
by Elsie Singmaster. Reprinted by permission of Houghton
Mifflin Company. All rights reserved.

LIBRARY OF CONGRESS CATALOGING-IN-PUBLICATION DATA

Singmaster, Elsie, 1879–1958.
  Heart language : Elsie Singmaster and her Pennsylvania
  German writings / [edited by] Susan Colestock Hill.
      p.   cm. — (Pennsylvania German history and culture)
Includes bibliographical references and index.
Summary: "A selection of short stories by Elsie Singmaster
that focus on the Pennsylvania-German experience.
Includes commentary framing them in historical, cultural,
and literary contexts"—Provided by publisher.
ISBN 978-0-271-03543-7 (cloth : alk. paper)
  1. German Americans—Pennsylvania—Fiction.
  2. Pennsylvania Dutch—Fiction.
  3. Short stories, American.
  I. Hill, Susan Colestock, 1945– .
  II. Title.

PS3537.I867H43   2009
813'.52—dc22
2009001847

Copyright © 2009 The Pennsylvania German Society
All rights reserved
Printed in the United States of America
Published by The Pennsylvania State University Press,
University Park, PA 16802-1003

The Pennsylvania State University Press is a member of the
Association of American University Presses.

It is the policy of The Pennsylvania State University Press
to use acid-free paper. This book is printed on Nature's
Natural, containing 50% post-consumer waste and meets
the minimum requirements of American National Standard for Information Sciences—Permanence of Paper for
Printed Library Material, ANSI Z39.48–1992.

Contents

List of Illustrations   vii

Foreword by Charles H. Glatfelter   ix

Preface   xv

Acknowledgments   xvii

A Sketch of Elsie Singmaster   I

SELECTED PENNSYLVANIA GERMAN SHORT STORIES
BY ELSIE SINGMASTER

Big Thursday   79

The Vacillation of Benjamin Gaumer   96

The County Seat   116

The Old Régime   125

The Eternal Feminine   135

The Squire   143

The Belsnickel   152

The Suffrage in Millerstown   161

Zion Church   170

A Sound in the Night   177

The Courier of the Czar   190

The Amishman   206

Frau Nolte   222

Wildfire   233

Settled Out of Court   243

Thanksgiving Is n't Christmas   253

Bibliography of Elsie Singmaster's Works   265

Index   277

Illustrations

1 Elsie Singmaster, formal portrait at approximately age forty. Courtesy of the Macungie Historical Society, Macungie, Pennsylvania.

2 Singmaster Tannery, Macungie (formerly Millerstown), Pennsylvania. Photo by William Mickley Weaver, April 1889. Courtesy of the Macungie Historical Society, Macungie, Pennsylvania.

3 Singmaster family homestead, Macungie, Pennsylvania. Photo by William Mickley Weaver, 1889. Courtesy of the Macungie Historical Society, Macungie, Pennsylvania.

4 Singmaster family farm, Cotton Street, Macungie, Pennsylvania. Photo by William Mickley Weaver, c. 1887. Courtesy of the Macungie Historical Society, Macungie, Pennsylvania.

5 Elsie Singmaster with her cousin, Edna Mae Weaver. Photo by William Mickley Weaver, 1887. Courtesy of the Macungie Historical Society, Macungie, Pennsylvania.

6 Singmaster family portrait, c. 1895–96. Photo by Lindenmuth Studio, Allentown. Courtesy of the Macungie Historical Society, Macungie, Pennsylvania.

7 Singmaster/Lewars wedding announcement, 1912. Courtesy of the Macungie Historical Society, Macungie, Pennsylvania.

8 Elsie Singmaster, formal portrait at approximately age sixteen, c. 1895–96. Courtesy of the Macungie Historical Society, Macungie, Pennsylvania.

9 Elsie Singmaster in front of the Adams County library, 1948. Courtesy of the Macungie Historical Society, Macungie, Pennsylvania.

10 Allentown-Emmaus-Macungie trolley, Macungie, c. 1902. Courtesy of the Macungie Historical Society, Macungie, Pennsylvania.

11 Leon Guipon, *Pennsylvania Germans, Century* magazine, January 1906. Courtesy of the Macungie Historical Society, Macungie, Pennsylvania.

12 Elizabeth Shippen Green, drawing of the Amish man Martin Ebersole accompanying Singmaster's story "The Amishman," in Elsie Singmaster, *Bred in the Bone, and Other Stories* (Boston: Houghton Mifflin, 1925). Reprinted by permission of the Houghton Mifflin Company. All rights reserved.

13 A scene from Pennsylvania German village life outside the H. G. Readinger General Store, Macungie, c. 1904. Courtesy of the Macungie Historical Society, Macungie, Pennsylvania.

14 Elizabeth Shippen Green, drawing that accompanied "A Sound in the Night," collected in *Bred in the Bone, and Other Stories* (Boston: Houghton Mifflin, 1925). Reprinted by permission of Houghton Mifflin Company. All rights reserved.

15 Elsie Singmaster, formal portrait at approximately age sixty-five, c. 1944. Courtesy of the Macungie Historical Society, Macungie, Pennsylvania.

16 Violet Oakley, sketch of Elsie Singmaster, 1924. Houghton Library, Correspondence and Records of the Houghton Mifflin Company, bMS Am 1925 (1656), folder 32. Reprinted by permission of the Houghton Library, Harvard University.

Foreword

Susan Hill deserves credit for bringing to our attention the use of Pennsylvania Germans as characters in American literature and the role and vision of Pennsylvania German authors writing on "their people" for outsiders. Elsie Singmaster was often hailed for giving a "true-to-life" account in fiction of the Pennsylvania Germans in the early twentieth century and was widely read in her time. With the twenty-first-century interest in cultural identity, the representation of America's regional ethnic groups, and women as interpreters of local and social experience, Hill's literary biography of Singmaster and her selection of Singmaster's stories are appealing and important for the present day. Let me set the stage for Hill's masterly book by offering some historical context.

The first noteworthy attempts to describe and explain to a national audience the characteristics and achievements of the Pennsylvania Germans occurred only after the Civil War. Although large numbers of these people had lived in Pennsylvania for more than a century and a half, they were members of several ethnic groups that historians had largely ignored. Admittedly, the first Speaker of the U.S. House of Representatives, in 1789, and seven of the first fifteen governors of Pennsylvania between that date and 1865 were Pennsylvania Germans, but none had ranked with John Adams and Thomas Jefferson as statesmen, or with James Fenimore Cooper and Ralph Waldo Emerson as literary figures.

The call to the first meeting of the Pennsylvania German Society in 1891 declared that the new organization was intended both to honor the memory of the forebears who were said to have turned the Pennsylvania wilderness into a veritable garden and to demonstrate to other ethnic groups that the Pennsylvania Germans ranked with the best of them in producing good and useful citizens. Four years later the society committed itself to preparing and publishing what it called a badly needed complete and connected history of the Pennsylvania Germans. In 1897 the society began publishing volumes in a series it called *Pennsylvania: The German Influence in Its Settlement and Development, a Narrative and Critical History*. The first five volumes dealt with the period before 1740. Four dealt with the history of several German churches in Pennsylvania. A few reprinted primary sources. While this series included much valuable information, it was far from the complete and connected history that its promoters intended.

In 1901 Oscar Kuhns (1856–1929) published *The German and Swiss Settlements of Colonial Pennsylvania: A Study of the So-Called Pennsylvania Dutch*. A native of Lancaster County, Kuhns was a graduate of Wesleyan University who had later studied at the University of Berlin and elsewhere. In 1890 he returned to Wesleyan as professor of Romance languages. In his preface he explained that while there were many books on the early settlements in New England and the South, as well as on the Dutch in New York, there was almost nothing on "the so-called Pennsylvania Dutch," who he believed were moved by the same spirit as the Pilgrims had been in coming to the New World. Although he dedicated the book to two forebears who were pioneer settlers of Lancaster County, Kuhns insisted that he had tried to be strictly impartial in preparing his work. Here was a connected account, but one limited largely to the eighteenth century. A new edition appeared in 1914. The work has since been reprinted.

In 1909 Dr. Albert Bernhardt Faust (1870–1951) published a work entitled *The German Element in the United States: With Special Reference to Its Political, Moral, Social, and Educational Influence*. A native of Baltimore, Faust had earned his bachelor's degree and doctorate at Johns Hopkins University. After study abroad and membership on the faculties of several American institutions, in 1904 he began his long professional career in the German Department of Cornell University. In that year the German Department of the University of Chicago awarded his monograph on the assigned subject (which became the basis for his later book) the Conrad Seipp Memorial Prize. Taking time for further research, he published his two volumes, consisting of some 1,150 pages, in 1909.

Faust believed that Germans had played a major role in the country's development and that, from the beginning in 1683, the Pennsylvania Germans were an integral part of that development. His work was closer than anything that had yet appeared to being the complete and connected history the Pennsylvania German Society had envisioned in 1895. It is regrettable that it was not more widely read and studied. Had it been, few would have been justified in claiming that they did not know who the Pennsylvania Germans were or what they had done.

Faust claimed that what he called German American literature began with the writings of Francis Daniel Pastorius, the founder of Germantown, Pennsylvania. He praised the dialect literature that had recently begun to appear in print, especially the work of Henry Harbaugh (1817–1867) and Henry L. Fisher (1822–1909), whose poems were inspired by their personal knowledge of the daily lives of Pennsylvania German farmers. He considered their work "one of the few original notes in American lyrical poetry" and ranked it in importance with southern plantation lyrics.

Faust's comments on the contemporary work of two women writers were confined to a footnote. He noted that Helen Reimensnyder Martin was the author of the novel *Tillie: A Mennonite Maid*, published in 1904. "The short stories of Elsie Singmaster," he wrote, "appearing in the *Atlantic, Lippincott's, Century, Scribner's, Youth's Companion*, etc., are mostly concerned with the Pennsylvania German folk."

Elsie Singmaster was born in 1879 at Schuylkill Haven, Schuylkill County, the second child and only daughter of Reverend John Alden Singmaster (1852–1926), a young Lutheran pastor then serving in his first parish. He was a native of Millerstown, in Lehigh County, whose family had arrived in Pennsylvania from Germany in 1749.

After completing his work in the college and seminary at Gettysburg, Singmaster was ordained in 1876. During the next quarter-century he served four parishes: Schuylkill Haven (1876–82), Macungie (1882–86), Brooklyn, New York (1887–90), and Allentown (1890–1900). In the fall of 1900 he returned to Gettysburg, first as a professor at the seminary and then, beginning in 1906, as its president. He died in office, unexpectedly, in 1926.

Singmaster quickly established himself as a leader in the Lutheran Church and in the communities in which he lived. He was, for example, a chief founder of a hospital in Allentown and later of one in Gettysburg. He wrote more than a thousand articles that appeared in Lutheran periodicals.

Although influenced by her residence in the country, town, and city, Singmaster was perhaps most deeply shaped by her close relationship with her father. She moved with her family into a house on the seminary campus in the fall of 1900. Except for brief periods thereafter, that house, and later the one her father built on the campus, remained her residences for the rest of her life. After brief periods of study at West Chester State Teachers' College and Cornell University, she enrolled at Radcliffe College and received her undergraduate degree in 1907, at which time she was elected to Phi Beta Kappa, an honor she shared with Oscar Kuhns and Albert B. Faust. After three years of marriage to Harold S. Lewars, she was widowed in 1915 and lost her only child at birth two months later.

Years later, Singmaster said that she had always wanted to be a writer. Her literary career began in 1905, when she was twenty-six years old, still a Radcliffe student, and listed in the Gettysburg directory as a resident of

Confederate Avenue on the seminary campus. Between then and 1950 she published more than three hundred articles and about forty books. After 1912 she was always known as Mrs. Lewars in Gettysburg, but as an author she was Elsie Singmaster.

She became part of what is known as the local color school in American literature, which flourished for about half a century after the Civil War. In both prose and verse, these writers used fiction to describe what they saw as the distinctive cultural lives of various ethnic groups. Among the members of this school were Bret Harte, George Washington Cable, Hamlin Garland, Joel Chandler Harris, Sarah Orne Jewett, and James Whitcomb Riley.

Not surprisingly, Elsie Singmaster chose to present the Pennsylvania Germans to the public, using the model of Henry Harbaugh and Henry L. Fisher rather than that of Oscar Kuhns and Albert B. Faust. She knew she was one of them, a sixth- or seventh-generation descendant of eighteenth-century immigrants. There were fewer than fifty miles between Schuylkill Haven on the west and Allentown on the east, with Macungie somewhere in between. Singmaster wrote about residents of Millerstown, a town that dates from the late eighteenth century; its name was changed to Macungie in 1875 to distinguish it from another Millerstown in Pennsylvania.

Possibly Singmaster took from her father, but if so she certainly adopted as her own, a desire to understand the Pennsylvania Germans on their own terms and represent them fairly, whether she was describing the Lutherans and Reformed of Lehigh County or, later, the sect people of Lancaster County. Although she could be critical, she was reluctant to pass judgment. In any event, she wrote only after first using methods of research similar to those being used in universities. Macungie maintained a strong hold on Singmaster and her family. Although they lived in Gettysburg for many years, she, her parents, and her husband were all buried in Macungie.

In 1913 Singmaster published the first of several books dealing with the Battle of Gettysburg. In 1917 she published two on the four-hundredth anniversary of the Protestant Reformation. In the mid-1920s three were occasioned by the 150th anniversary of the American Revolution. The last four books dealt with topics in Pennsylvania history. All but ten of her works were classified as fiction. By 1950 Singmaster's health was failing. In 1952 she entered a Gettysburg convalescent home, where she died in 1958, after being bedfast for two years.

During most of Elsie Singmaster's literary career, a contemporary named Helen Reimensnyder Martin (1868–1939) was also contributing to the growing body of Pennsylvania German literature, but from quite a different perspective. Born in Lancaster in 1868, and thus eleven years older than Elsie, she was the daughter and granddaughter of Lutheran pastors. Her father, Reverend Cornelius Reimensnyder, served a number of brief pastorates in five states before leaving the parish ministry in 1865 to become an agent of the American Sunday School Union. From his residence in Lancaster, he traveled widely for a quarter-century, preaching, delivering Bibles, and organizing Sunday schools.

Helen Reimensnyder attended Swarthmore and Radcliffe colleges but did not graduate from either. In 1899 she married Frederic C. Martin and moved to Harrisburg. By this time she had already adopted certain strong beliefs that guided the rest of her life. She held that women had long been dominated, even brutalized, by men. Capitalism and the church were culpable, she contended, for sanctioning this arrangement. She advocated women's suffrage as a first step in righting this wrong. These beliefs were reflected in her first novels, published in the late 1890s.

By her own account, an interest in the Pennsylvania Germans, of whom Martin was certainly one, developed only after a friend asked her to investigate his family history for him. She later used this new interest in three articles published in 1902 and 1903, and in *Tillie: A Mennonite Maid* (1904). Tillie was a woman dominated by an ignorant father, but she eventually escaped his clutches. The book was well received and was reprinted often over the next thirty years.

Between 1904 and 1937 Martin published some thirty novels and numerous articles. Several of the books were dramatized and made into movies. In her *New York Times* obituary in 1939 she was described as a "novelist who won fame with stories of Pennsylvania Dutch life." Undoubtedly her works appealed to many readers and continued to sell after her death. Her biographical sketch first appeared in the 1906–7 edition of *Who's Who in America,* six years before the first entry for Elsie Singmaster. Testimony to Singmaster's lasting literary influence, however, appears in recent editions of the *Oxford Companion to American Literature,* in which Singmaster is highlighted but Martin is not.

In a 1910 assessment of Martin's work to that date, which appeared in *Pennsylvania-German* magazine, Harriet C. Long concluded that, while they were indeed widely popular, Martin's books did not portray Pennsylvania German life accurately or fairly. Martin did not seem to understand the people she wrote about, to all of whom she attributed "mean and undesirable traits," never balanced by a "redeeming touch nor an admirable characteristic." This was the evaluation reached by many members of the

Pennsylvania German Society and reaffirmed by Homer T. Rosenberger in his history of the society, published in 1966.

By the 1920s the local color school of which Elsie Singmaster had been a member was eclipsed by one in which different settings and their problems reflected the dawning of a new era. Industrialization and urbanization, along with what has been called American homogenization, resulted in new, urban Millerstowns whose problems were no longer those of farmers and small towns.

If Elsie Singmaster's work had been narrowly antiquarian in nature, there might be little reason to return to it now except as a historical source. Her contemporaries agreed almost unanimously that her care in research, breadth of vision, and clear style of writing enabled her to create accounts that were true to life. Despite the differences between the Millerstowns of then and now, there is thus still purpose in seeking what remains of lasting value in the Millerstown Elsie Singmaster described so faithfully for her readers.

Hill's account of Singmaster took form as research for the master of arts in religion degree at the Lutheran Theological Seminary at Gettysburg. Her completed thesis, "Seeking Fruitfulness: Elsie Singmaster Lewars, Victorian Woman in Ministry," came to my attention when Hill submitted a copy to the Adams County Historical Society after graduating in 1999. I remembered Elsie Singmaster Lewars as a longtime member and officer of the board of directors of that organization. Since that time, I have encouraged Hill's continued interest in Singmaster's Pennsylvania German stories and books. At her request, I have read and reviewed her text in detail and recommend it now to those who continue to seek a greater understanding of Elsie Singmaster's people and of her place in the development of the American literary tradition.

Charles H. Glatfelter
Gettysburg, Pennsylvania

Preface

I became interested in Elsie Singmaster when I was a student at the Lutheran Theological Seminary at Gettysburg (1996–99). My master's thesis, "Seeking Fruitfulness: Elsie Singmaster Lewars, Victorian Woman in Ministry," contextualized the story of Singmaster's life in the church as it was influenced by the social and cultural standards of the Victorian era in America. It also examined the ways in which Singmaster was able to affect her community and her readers through civic and church work and through writing both fiction and nonfiction. Although Singmaster was a successful author and a woman of some stature in the church, she sought to influence others subtly from the sidelines rather than from a designated office. She was at once a woman with limited access to power and one who used her place and her gifts to voice her strong ideals and beliefs. Singmaster's personal story is valuable to historians who seek to recover part of the past through women's stories to present a broader, more inclusive account of the American experience.

Singmaster's relationship to the Pennsylvania German community became apparent early in my research, but it was the Pennsylvania German Society's interest in Singmaster as a regional storyteller that led me to produce this volume. The stories included here recall much about Pennsylvania German people and traditions through fiction. At the same time, in combination with information about Singmaster's life and times, they illustrate important elements of women's literary history and social, cultural, economic, and political trends. When published in national magazines, these stories not only entertained subscribers but also constructed an ideal vision of America, embodied by Singmaster's Pennsylvania Germans, that many citizens believed had made their young country successful. Singmaster hoped that Pennsylvania Germans would never change, but she wrote stories that recorded social and cultural transitions within the Pennsylvania German community. Singmaster's work can be enjoyed as regional literature, as Pennsylvania German literature, and as a resource for telling a larger American story.

Singmaster's publications extend beyond the parameters of this collection. She wrote books as well as stories, and I have thus included a bibliography of her work in this volume. Pennsylvania German characters and places occupied pride of place of her literature, but she also wrote extensively about Gettysburg, her home for nearly sixty years. One Civil War work, *Swords of Steel,* was a 1934 Newbery Award honor book. Some of Singmaster's Civil War stories have been reprinted in the recent past. It is fitting that we should have a new volume of Elsie Singmaster Pennsylvania German stories available at a time of renewed interest in, and scholarship on, Pennsylvania German studies, arts, language, festivals, and folklore. Elsie Singmaster and her work on Pennsylvania Germans deserve to be remembered and reexamined for their artistic, ethnic, and historical contributions to American life.

Acknowledgments

Many people with interests in Pennsylvania German studies, literature, local and church histories, and the Singmaster legacy have contributed to the making of this book. It is with great pleasure and appreciation that I acknowledge those who have encouraged, prodded, and inspired me during its writing and publication. Dr. Susan Karen Hedahl of the Lutheran Theological Seminary at Gettysburg originally proposed Elsie Singmaster Lewars as the subject for my master's thesis in church history, and she worked with me on a January-term project about Singmaster while I was a student at the seminary. Dr. Gerald Christianson, also of the Gettysburg Seminary, advised me on matters of church history and theology and was instrumental in developing the concept for this anthology. Peter Stitt of the *Gettysburg Review* and Dr. Janet Powers of the Gettysburg College English Department both read a sampling of Singmaster's stories and encouraged me to have them reprinted.

Dale Eck, director of the Macungie Historical Society and my sometime research partner for nearly ten years, worked diligently to help compile the attached bibliography, pictures, and photographic commentary. He also helped to verify factual information. The Macungie Historical Society's growing collection of Singmaster artifacts, memorabilia, photographs, and literary samples has been a rich source for research. The Adams County Historical Society, Wentz Library at the Lutheran Theological Seminary at Gettysburg, the Adams County Public Library, and the Houghton Library at Harvard University all shared important archival materials, and their staffs provided valuable research assistance. The Houghton Library's Elsie Singmaster collection houses more than five hundred letters exchanged between the author and her publisher. Susan Roach of the Gettysburg College Library and Susan Kerr of the Adams County Public Library located copies of many articles that are out of print and borrowed academic sources from other libraries for my use. Gettysburg College Library has been a rich source of scholarly works, magazine collections, and microfilm, and its research librarians were eager to assist me.

I am especially grateful to members of the Singmaster family who have shared memories, correspondence, and memorabilia with me. Elizabeth

Moatz of Macungie, Pennsylvania, Alan Singmaster of Devon, Pennsylvania, and Isabelle and James Flander of Iowa have been wonderfully supportive. James Arthur Singmaster Jr., Alan's father, now deceased, was ninety years old when I interviewed him, and his contribution of memories and materials was priceless. Friends of Elsie Singmaster Lewars—Harold and Elizabeth Dunkelberger, Robert Fischer, Elizabeth Gifford, Robert Koons, Mary Lou Schwartz, Herman Stuempfle, Charlotte Swope, and Frederick Wentz—all searched their memories and personal collections for critical information. All of these folks were generous with their recollections and impressions of Elsie Singmaster Lewars, and I am in their debt.

Dr. Charles Glatfelter, professor emeritus of history at Gettysburg College, served as a member of the Board of Directors of the Pennsylvania German Society, president of the Pennsylvania Historical Association, and director of the Adams County Historical Society. He not only expressed interest in my work on Elsie Singmaster but also related memories of Singmaster from early associations at the Historical Society. He encouraged me to pursue further study of Singmaster's Pennsylvania German writing and reviewed my manuscript. I am very grateful for Dr. Glatfelter's support, evidenced in the Foreword.

Finally, Dr. Simon Bronner's vision to include *Heart Language: Elsie Singmaster and Her Pennsylvania German Writings* in the Pennsylvania German Society's series made this volume possible. His guidance and critical review have been essential to the project, and his patience and kindness have been greatly appreciated. Thank you, Dr. Bronner, and members of the Pennsylvania German Society, for the opportunity to share Elsie Singmaster's life and stories for the benefit of today's readers.

A SKETCH OF ELSIE SINGMASTER

While studying writing at Cornell University as the nineteenth century came to a close, Elsie Singmaster submitted a story about the Pennsylvania Germans that elicited an animated response from her professor, Clark Northrup. "Who are these queer, unreal people?" he exclaimed. "They're NOT queer! And they're *very* real," she protested. "They are my people living in the traditional ways of their ancestors!"

He shot back, "Then write more about them!"[1]

Unaware that her fictional characters of Millerstown, Lanesville, and the surrounding Pennsylvania valleys and villages would fuel a publishing career stretching nearly half a century, Singmaster at first put her stories to paper to fulfill a daily writing requirement. Like the character Jesse Hummer in her Pennsylvania German novel *The Magic Mirror,* she wrote "about persons and scenes with which he [Jesse] was familiar . . . persons at hand whom he could understand . . . not about people two centuries away and on the other side of the world."[2] Always a careful observer of her environment and the personalities that surrounded her, Singmaster adapted her experience with Pennsylvania Germans into a local color literature that drew national attention.

A small, stocky woman of strong will and determination, Elsie Singmaster possessed many of the physical and emotional qualities often associated with Pennsylvania Germans. Of all the different strains in her heritage, the industry, order, and common sense attributed to the Pennsylvania Germans appealed to her most. She knew the Pennsylvania German dialect, the language of her family's village and her earliest school years. Like the stalwart characters in her stories, she was family- and community-minded. She felt a strong religious commitment to her German Lutheran faith. Esther Forbes commented on Singmaster's Pennsylvania German ancestry in an article in the *Boston Evening Transcript:*

Miss Elsie Singmaster came of stock mentally sturdy and self-respecting. Her father's family were all of Dutch and German extraction. . . . On her mother's side she inherits English, Irish, and French traditions and blood. . . . I asked her which of these contrasting stocks she believed herself most to resemble. Spiritually at least she thinks she belongs with the Pennsylvania Germans. . . . The facial type with the broad cheek bones and square jaw and forehead would suggest Germanic strain. . . . She is short, squarely built and looks capable of great physical or nervous endurance. The courage and honesty, the sympathy and flashes of humor she finds in her books are all present in this woman.[3]

Singmaster's adoption of Pennsylvania German ways was not without obstacles. Elsie's mother, Caroline Hoopes Singmaster, insisted that her children speak English at home, even though they lived among the Pennsylvania Germans in the eastern Pennsylvania towns of Schuylkill Haven and Macungie during the early years of their lives. In keeping with Caroline's tradition, Elsie's parents used the Quaker pronouns "thee" and "thou" in private conversation. Elsie's father, John Alden Singmaster, was a Lutheran clergyman, and his ministries ranged beyond the environs of eastern Pennsylvania to Brooklyn, New York, and then to Gettysburg, exposing the family to environments outside the Pennsylvania German.

Elsie did well in school and dreamed of a writing career from an early age. Encouraged by her parents, she studied at West Chester Normal School in Pennsylvania, Cornell University in Ithaca, New York, and Radcliffe College in Cambridge, Massachusetts. By the time she studied writing at Cornell, American literary taste had begun to embrace ethnic and regional differences. Folk culture and ways of speech became a prominent theme in post–Civil War local color literature and eventually defined a genre and readership for Singmaster's Pennsylvania German work. This fortunate pairing of opportunity and preference fulfilled a lifelong dream for Singmaster. "In my early acquaintance with the Pennsylvania Germans," she wrote, "I was extremely fortunate. My teachers at Cornell pointed out to me the valuable ore in this almost untouched field, and the 'local color,' then greatly sought after, buoyed, I suspect, many [of my] stories into port which had not a great deal to recommend them." Always an avid reader, Singmaster recounted that at age eleven she "already dreamed of becoming an author."[4] Now, at age twenty, this student of "brilliant scholarship,"[5] eager to write and convinced that she had gleaned all she could from the Cornell writing courses, left school and returned to her family home in Gettysburg to pursue a literary career. The year was 1900.

Elsie Singmaster's self-deprecating remark belies the influence of her contribution to American literature, and specifically to the record of Pennsylvania German life in America. In her stories and books Singmaster adapted for popular literary consumption the daily lives of an often belittled ethnic population. She tied their values to the American ideals of peace, justice, and individual opportunity. In the wake of industrialization, she asked how the young nation might benefit from the strong values of Pennsylvania German culture.

Educated in New England, Singmaster spoke the language and embraced the ideals typical of educated upper-class Americans of her time, but she also believed that her Pennsylvania German farmers and villagers embodied the highest possible standards of character, physical stamina, religious faith, and civic values, despite the views of the larger society. The high esteem in which the nation held its founding fathers and defenders of American freedom also applied to the descendants of America's Pennsylvania German settlers, in Singmaster's view.

While Pennsylvania German culture was very popular during the heyday of local color writing in the early twentieth century, Singmaster found its popularity in decline after the Great Depression. She refused to change her approach, however, with the result that modern critics found her work out of touch. For many years, her story and the value of her work have thus been all but forgotten.

This book reexamines Elsie Singmaster's legacy and brings part of her significant body of literature back into print for contemporary readers. Before presenting her stories themselves, some background is in order on three significant forces in Singmaster's life and work: her Pennsylvania German family heritage; her German Lutheran background and close ties to the Lutheran Church in America; and the social and cultural environment of the late Victorian era in the United States. A brief account of Pennsylvania German literature and the growth of national interest in the local color genre will also help provide the context for Singmaster's story. What follows, then, is a discussion of these factors and of Singmaster's work and its place in the literary marketplace.

ELSIE SINGMASTER'S PENNSYLVANIA GERMAN BACKGROUND

Singmaster genealogical records confirm the arrival in Philadelphia, on Sunday, September 19, 1749, of the "Ship Patience, Hugh Steel, Captain, from Rotterdam, last from Cowes," bearing among her passengers both

Fig. 1 This formal portrait of Elsie Singmaster was used by Mary Rice Hess in her 1929 Pennsylvania State University master's thesis, "Elsie Singmaster." The thesis was published serially in Preston Barba's column, 'S Pennsylvaanisch Deitsch Eck, in the *Allentown Morning Call* between June 16 and August 25, 1956.

Johann Adam and his son, Georg Friederich Zangmeister (1725–1811).[6] The *Patience* carried on that voyage approximately 270 persons from the German Palatinate and the Duchy of Württemberg. Johann Adam and Georg Friederich settled near Trumbauersville, Bucks County, Pennsylvania. Georg Friederich fathered John Adam (August 7, 1766–July 28, 1820), who became a tanner in Millerstown, Pennsylvania.[7] A grandson of John Adam, James Singmaster (1823–1896), and his wife, Sarah Ann Mattern (1824–

1894), parented John Alden Singmaster (1852–1926). John Alden (Alden) and Caroline (Carrie) Hoopes Singmaster (1852–1931), married on November 1, 1877, and had five children, four boys and a girl, Elsie, born second in sequence after James Arthur and before John Howard, Edmund Hoopes, and Paul. John Alden Singmaster was a Lutheran pastor in Schuylkill Haven, Pennsylvania, when Elsie was born on August 29, 1879. Although Caroline was of English Quaker descent, John Alden's background bound him tightly to eastern Pennsylvania, where he too was born, in Millerstown (now Macungie), into a family of successful business and community leaders of German descent.[8]

John Adam Singmaster, who served in the Revolutionary War, moved from his first Pennsylvania home in Bucks County to Millerstown in the Lehigh Valley, where he found employment at a local tannery. He married Lydia van Buskirk (1779–1865) there in 1794 and eventually bought a 105-acre farm, the acreage of which currently makes up a large portion of downtown Macungie as well as Kalmbach and Macungie memorial parks. In 1810 Adam (as he was known) bought the tannery once owned by his

Fig. 2 The Singmaster Tannery is the oldest documented industry in the original village of Macungie (formerly Millerstown). The enterprise was founded by the Reverend Jacob van Buskirk but was later owned by his son-in-law, John Adam Singmaster. Singmaster family members owned and operated the business until the 1890s. Solomon's Lutheran and Reformed Union Church, visible in the background, is the burial place of Lydia van Buskirk, who married John Adam Singmaster in 1794.

Fig. 3 This stone structure, still standing at 165 East Main Street in Macungie, is believed to have been the home of John Adam and Lydia van Buskirk Singmaster. The earliest part of the structure (rear) was probably erected in the early nineteenth century. At least two additions were added by Singmaster family descendants.

father-in-law, the Reverend Jacob van Buskirk, a Lutheran pastor in Macungie from 1769 to 1793 and again from 1795 to 1800. Family genealogical records show that John Adam's sons, including John, great-grandfather of John Alden Singmaster, were engaged in farming, tanning, and in some cases the iron business. John Alden's father, James, an economically successful Pennsylvania German citizen, owned half a dozen farms. According to his obituary, he was also a bank president, a tanner, and a merchant in leather, coal, lumber, and iron, as well as Macungie's first burgess.[9]

Pennsylvania German immigrants like the Zangmeisters and their descendants established new homes and communities in an area still considered the frontier. It was this period of national and regional development that fascinated Elsie Singmaster. The Pennsylvania Germans' language, work ethic, farming methods, building styles, ethnic background, and social practices set them apart from settlers of English background, but also grounded them in common values, shared experience, and strong belief. The Singmaster forefathers and -mothers, Adam, Lydia, and their ancestors, and the members of the Millerstown (Macungie) community were prototypes for the Pennsylvania Germans depicted in Singmaster's stories. Singmaster's fictional characters, based on the real people and circumstances of her experience, are farmers, businessmen, homemakers, and members of tightly knit communities whose lives are intimate and affirming within their neighborhoods yet insular in the context of the broader culture. They are members of families dominated, yet also loved and sustained, by their fathers and nurtured by the vitality and wisdom of their mothers. Singmaster's Pennsylvania Germans are hardworking and upwardly mobile against many odds, including their penchant for introversion and their seeming lack of respect for education. They are a faithful people who encompass a rich variety of religious expressions. Struggling to hold on to who they are while yielding to change, their ambivalence demonstrates, from Singmaster's point of view, an important dynamic of transitional immigrant culture.

ELSIE SINGMASTER'S GERMAN LUTHERAN HERITAGE

Dr. John Alden Singmaster, a graduate of Pennsylvania (now Gettysburg) College (1873) and Gettysburg Lutheran Theological Seminary (1876), served, in addition to Schuylkill Haven (1876–82), Lutheran parishes at Macungie/Lyons (1882–86), Pennsylvania; Brooklyn, New York (1887–90); and Allentown, Pennsylvania (1890–1900). Although they followed Dr. Singmaster to these other parishes, Elsie and her family returned to Macungie for the summers. The town represented love and magic for Elsie and her brothers. "When I was four years old," she wrote,

> my father became pastor of a charge comprising six churches lying between Allentown and Reading, and we lived for several years in Macungie, the Pennsylvania German village where he was born and where many of his kinsfolk lived. It was quiet and tree-shaded, lying at the foot of a wooded hill we called "the mountain." Because of my father's affection for his home and because it was a safe place for children, we returned there for many summers, leaving first Brooklyn, New York, then Allentown, Pennsylvania, with rapture the instant school closed on the last day in June and returning with drooping heads on the first day in September. . . . It was a perfect period of our lives—the fields and streams were ours, affection and good will surrounded us.[10]

The Singmasters had religious ties to German Reformation history and to the development of the Lutheran Church in America. A Singmaster genealogy, *Ein Jahrhundert aus der Geschichte der Familie Zangemeister*, connects the Millerstown/Macungie Singmasters to sixteenth-century Zangmeister ancestors in Memmingen, Germany, from whom Adam and Friederich descended, and to the Lutheran Reformation.[11] The medieval German Zangmeisters were tradesmen who became prosperous and held responsible positions at St. Martin Church in Memmingen before, during, and after the Reformation. Günther Bayer's descriptive booklet, *St. Martin, Memmingen* (August 1967), includes information about a Singmaster ancestor, Eberhard Zangmeister, an influential Burgermeister in Memmingen. A reference to Eberhart Zangmaister appears in *Luther's Correspondence*.[12] According to Bayer, Zangmeister was a church leader who "advanced the cause of the Gospel between 1522 and 1555 by firmness and courage."[13] Even today, St. Martin Church contains a Zangmeister chapel, established by Eberhard between 1505 and 1510. At that time he managed a trust established at St. Martin by his uncle, Magnus Zangmeister, for the purpose of financing prayers offered by parish priests in the Zangmeister side chapel on behalf of departed souls from that family. The Zangmeister family crest, bearing an image of the tongs of the ironmaster's trade, appears in a stained-glass window in this chapel.

In keeping with their German heritage, the newly established American Singmaster family's religion remained firmly Lutheran. As mentioned above, Adam Singmaster's wife, Lydia, was the daughter of Reverend

Fig. 4 The weather-boarded home pictured in the center of this photograph is the former Wescoe Meeting House (razed c. 1959), once the summer home of Elsie Singmaster and her family in Macungie. It is likely that Singmaster, as a young girl, first witnessed Pennsylvania German sectarian immersion baptism on this property. Today the farm is known as Kalmbach Memorial Park.

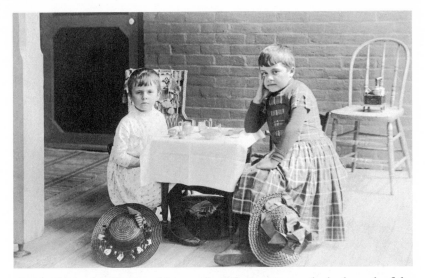

Fig. 5 Young Elsie (*right*) and her cousin (*left*) share tea on the back porch of the home of William M. Weaver, 10 East Main Street, Millerstown. The home was originally built by Elsie's grandfather, James, the first burgess of Millerstown (now Macungie). Millerstown was incorporated in 1857; its name was changed to Macungie in 1875.

Jacob van Buskirk, "the first native-born Lutheran in the Pennsylvania field to study for the ministry to be ordained."[14] Henry Melchior Muhlenberg, known today as the father of Lutheranism in America, was van Buskirk's teacher and colleague. Continuing a close affiliation with the Lutheran Church, Dr. Singmaster's father, James, helped organize St. Matthew's Evangelical Lutheran parish in Macungie and donated land for the new church building when members separated from Solomon's Lutheran and Reformed Church in 1868. John Alden Singmaster later served as pastor at St. Matthew's parish (Macungie) from November 15, 1882, to July 4, 1886.

The Singmaster family moved to Brooklyn, New York, in 1887, when Dr. Singmaster became pastor of St. Matthew's Evangelical Lutheran Church, located at the corner of Clinton and Amity streets. Elsie, eight years old at the time, heard her father preach his inaugural sermon on John 15:5. That sermon not only set the tone for his ministry there but also articulated a metaphor of faith, the vine and the branches, that became significant in the life of his young daughter. This critical text, which imagines an eternal connection between Christ and his followers, was part of Elsie's Christian formation and remained a foundation of her theology. Sixty years later, in 1947, when she was sixty-eight years old, she told her friend Luther Gotwald that

Fig. 6 Seated (*left to right*): Caroline Hoopes Singmaster, Reverend John Alden Singmaster, Edmund Hoopes Singmaster. Standing (*left to right*): Paul Singmaster, James Arthur Singmaster, John Howard Singmaster, and Elsie Singmaster.

she wished to hear him preach a sermon on John 15:5 because it was her favorite text.[15]

In 1900 Dr. Singmaster accepted a position as professor of biblical theology at the Gettysburg seminary, where in 1903 he became the fifth chairman of the faculty, a title changed to president in 1906. He also served as president of the East Pennsylvania Synod from 1897 to 1899 and as president of the General Synod from 1915 to 1917. Elsie's correspondence expresses pride in her distinguished Lutheran past. She wrote her cousin Julia, "Several years ago some Singmaster descendants in the west called our attention to a genealogical tree of the family, and we were able to get a copy from Germany. There was a record back to 1415. One of our ancestors—yours and mine—was a pupil of Martin Luther and lived in the family of Melanchthon. The first girl recorded was 'Else.'"[16] To her cousin Sadie she later wrote, "I am writing so promptly to announce that I am sending you a present. Some years before his death, Father was able to secure copies of the Zangemeister book from Germany, which traces the family back to 1415—few families can do better than that."[17]

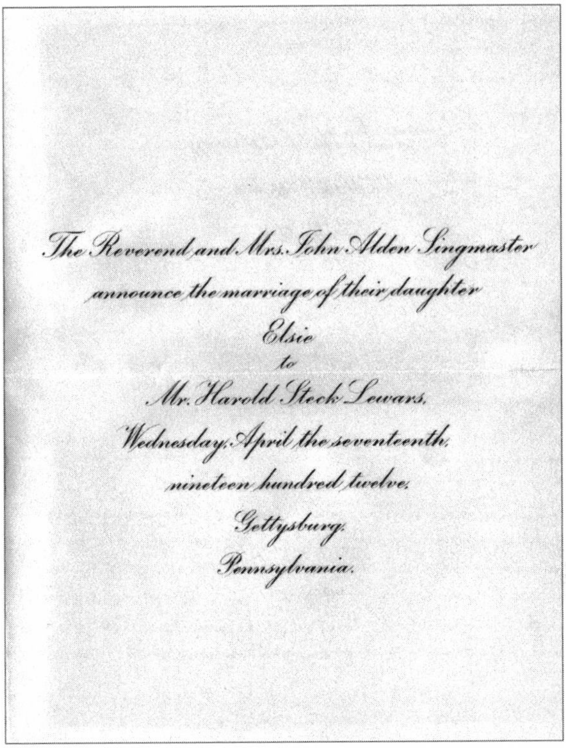

The Reverend and Mrs. John Alden Singmaster
announce the marriage of their daughter
Elsie
to
Mr. Harold Steck Lewars,
Wednesday, April the seventeenth,
nineteen hundred twelve,
Gettysburg,
Pennsylvania.

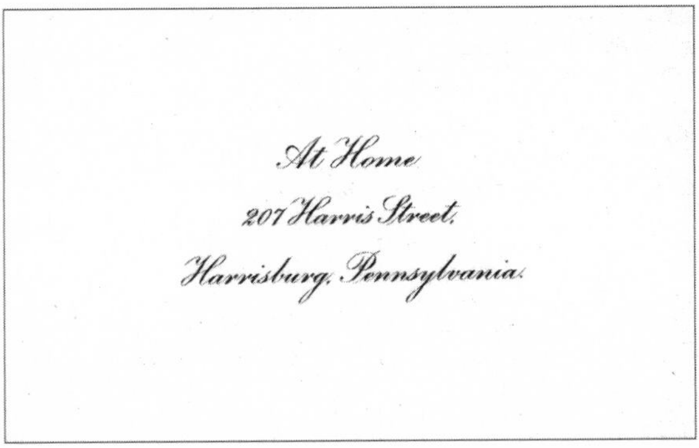

At Home
207 Harris Street,
Harrisburg, Pennsylvania.

Fig. 7 Elsie Singmaster and Harold Lewars had been married nearly three years when Harold died, on March 14, 1915, at Gettysburg. Elsie Singmaster Lewars remained a widow until her death on September 30, 1958. The couple's only child, Harold Singmaster Lewars, died at birth, May 10, 1915.

When Elsie Singmaster married Harold Steck Lewars on April 17, 1912, she became part of a family with a similar German Lutheran background. Harold Lewars, himself a church musician and hymn writer, was the son and grandson of Lutheran clergy.[18] The Lewars family believed they were descendants of the famous Pennsylvania German Conrad Weiser.[19] Singmaster wrote about Weiser, a German Lutheran immigrant during the time of the earliest European settlements in colonial Pennsylvania's Tulpehocken region.[20] More than a dozen German immigrant families, including members of the Conrad Weiser family, came to the Tulpehocken area after first settling in New York's Schoharie region. The group resettled near the present-day location of Womelsdorf, Pennsylvania. Weiser, who had lived with the Iroquois, or Long House tribe, as a young man, served as negotiator and peacekeeper between the Native Americans and the European newcomers to the land. Elsie Singmaster's historical fiction *The Long Journey* and *A High Wind Rising* follow the Weiser family's emigration to America and Conrad's role in early American history. Weiser's daughter, Anna Maria, married Henry Melchior Muhlenberg. Reflecting on the descendants of the Weiser and Muhlenberg families who served as leaders in early American religion and politics, Elsie Singmaster wrote proudly to her publisher, "Weiser became thus one of the founders of a long line of distinguished American Lutheran clergymen and patriots."[21]

Henry Melchior Muhlenberg was an emissary from the Old World Lutheran Church in Halle, Germany, and helped build up the German-affiliated Lutheran Church in America during the eighteenth century. By the early nineteenth century, American Lutherans wanted to relax ties with Germany and form closer relationships with fellow American Protestants. The ensuing interdenominational dialogue gave voice to the Pennsylvania German view that Lutheran Reformation history, imported into the New World by German immigrants, was one important source for the ideal of American liberty. Lutherans believed that the doctrinal Lutheran respect for local authority rather than distant rulers, and the church's emphasis on the doctrine of *sola scriptura,* or the authority of scripture alone rather than clerical hierarchy, linked Martin Luther's Reformation theology and the American principles of independence and political representation.[22] This connection strengthened Pennsylvania Germans' sense of their participation in and contribution to America's formation and of their identities as sons and daughters of the new Republic.

In 1917 the Singmasters participated in the four-hundredth anniversary celebration of Luther's challenge to the Roman Catholic Church. Lutheran institutions continued to emphasize the connection between the Reformation and the American principle of freedom. The Joint Committee on the Celebration of the Quadricentennial, of which Dr. Singmaster was a member, was appointed by the General Synod, the Lutheran organization that encompassed the Gettysburg Lutherans. The General Synod hoped to unite American Lutherans through the shared responsibility and remembrance associated with this project, and it planned to publicize basic Lutheran history and beliefs throughout the four-hundredth year with special worship, papers, songs, books, stamps, and medals. In May of the same year, Dr. Singmaster addressed the ecumenical convention of the Women's Home and Foreign Missionary Society. "Things that are transpiring today in this unparalleled war," he told his audience, "can only be settled permanently in the application of the Reformation—a return to primitive Christianity. The Reformation, history proves to us, was an event of such importance that no sect can claim to be sole heirs to its blessings. . . . But the Lutheran Church, we feel, has a special blessing and a special duty in the Reformation . . . and has conserved its ideas just a little better than have any of our brethren."[23] Using familiar Lutheran rhetoric in the context of war with the German fatherland, Dr. Singmaster believed that Reformation religious doctrine could play a role in the resolution of present-day problems, and that the Lutheran Church should take an active part in keeping that tradition alive in both the United States and the wider world.

The Lutheran quadricentennial committee turned to Elsie Singmaster for a short, broadly popular version of Martin Luther's life.[24] She wrote *Martin Luther, the Story of His Life,* in response and asked Houghton Mifflin to publish it, as the committee had agreed to read, approve, and advertise but not to publish the book.[25] In this biography Singmaster argues that Luther's historical stature is second only to that of Jesus and that, like Jesus, Luther belongs to the whole world, not merely to one geographical region. The significance of Singmaster's biography was twofold. First, it allowed her to participate in a cooperative project among several Lutheran synods that contributed mightily to the 1918 merger of the General Synod, the General Council, and the Synod of the South to become the United Lutheran Church in America.[26] Second, at a time when tensions associated with World War I were putting enormous pressure on German Americans, it allowed the joint committee and Singmaster to map out historical, religious, and philosophical common ground between Germany and the United States.

Elsie Singmaster's Pennsylvania German characters are portrayed as religious people. Ecclesial buildings and characters abound in her stories, as they did in Pennsylvania's Lehigh Valley. Among Singmaster's characters we find pastors, church members, organists, choir singers, and even members of church quilting groups. They proclaim their faith according to their various Pennsylvania German religious denominations. Cross-cultural encounters often confound those who wish to remain faithful to their particular churches and beliefs, but others convert from one denomination to another. Piety is the center of the lives of sect people in particular.

The reader can see the centrality of church and religious faith in the life of the author as well as in her subjects. Singmaster loved the church and its traditions. She wrote Esther Forbes at Houghton Mifflin, "What impressed me most in Allentown? I think the old, old German churches with their fine ancient hymns—such as Bach used for his cantata, 'Sleepers Awake.'"[27] Indeed, Zion Church, in a story by the same name (*Atlantic Monthly*, March 1913), dominates the landscape in Singmaster's Zion Valley and becomes the center of tragedy and the hope for redemption in the life of Pennsylvania German Matthias Lucas. The Moravian church in "The Chimes of St. Peter's" (*Pennsylvania-German*, February 1908) is the setting for a magnificent traditional Christmas Eve service. In *The Magic Mirror*, set in Allentown in the 1890s, Mrs. Hummer takes strength from simply being present in her church, where the design and ornaments are dearer to her than those in her own home. Sarah Ann Mohr, in "The Covered Basket" (*Pennsylvania-German*, July 1909), carefully guards the church record book her pastor father gives her for safekeeping.

Katy Gaumer, the subject of a novel by the same name (1915), becomes embroiled in a mystery surrounding missing communion ware at the Millerstown Lutheran Church. A German Lutheran named Hannes emigrates from war-torn Germany to colonial America in the novel *I Heard of a River: The Story of the Germans in Pennsylvania* (1948). In Singmaster's short story "The Persistence of Coonie Schnable" (*Reader*, September 1906), the author playfully considers differences between Millertown's "Luseran" and "Efangelical" churches. In the story "Frau Nolte" (*Century*, December 1925), the protagonist, struggling with depression, is renewed by the gospel as presented in Bach's magnificent Mass in B Minor. Frau Nolte "was a Lutheran," Singmaster writes, "and churchly architecture and appointments pleased her. Bach had been a Lutheran, too, and he realized man's need for ceremonial beauty." Singmaster and many of her characters were connected indelibly to the church in the deepest part of their souls.

It was in Macungie that Singmaster first encountered Pennsylvania German members of a regional religious sect who baptized by immersion in the millrace near her Macungie home and who later inspired stories like "Bred in the Bone," "A Sound in the Night," "The Courier of the Czar," and many others. As a child, Elsie was amazed to learn of the strange sectarian ways, but she credited her father with teaching her to respect regional religious differences.[28] Later, when stories about Pennsylvania sect people were taking shape in her mind, Singmaster wrote to Ferris Greenslet at Houghton Mifflin, "You New Englanders simply would not believe your eyes if you could see some of our Amish and Mennonite people."[29] Nevertheless, embracing freedom of religious choice as well as her father's counsel, she portrayed the Pennsylvania sectarians as real people who approach life from a traditional point of view. Singmaster's sectarians, like their Pennsylvania German brother and sister church people, were religious Americans challenged by the modernity of the wider culture.

In "The Courier of the Czar," winner of a 1924 O. Henry Short Story Award, Singmaster presents the pious Improved Mennonite sisters, Tilly and Betsey Shindledecker, with a dilemma. Singmaster describes the sisters as "members not of the main body of the Mennonites but of a small and very strict offshoot called the Improved Mennonites." They are deeply shy and live a private, religious life seldom disturbed by the outside world. They quilt, paint dower chests, and make and raise by hand everything they need for subsistence. They read only the Bible, the Martyr Book, the hymnal, and the almanac.[30] The balance of their existence is compromised, however, when Tilly's eyes begin to fail as she is sewing her fifty-eighth quilt. Doctor Landis, a "worldly Lutheran," comes to treat Tilly and absentmindedly leaves behind his copy of Jules Verne's book *The Courier of the Czar*. Unbeknownst to Betsey, Tilly is immediately drawn to the book's bloody illustrations and is desperate to read it. Should Betsey read the book to Tilly to help relieve her suffering and boredom, or is such a book the devil's work, tempting the sisters beyond their sanctified way of life? Betsey gives in, and reading the book causes the Shindledecker sisters both guilt and delight. It takes the entire Improved Mennonite congregation, to whom Betsey reads a part of the book during her meetinghouse confession, to find redeeming aspects of Betsey's decision and settle the matter.

Singmaster draws her readers into the lives of this unfamiliar Pennsylvania German religious sect to tell a story of temptation by forbidden fruit. While her story informs the reader about the unusual dress, homes, meetinghouses, and practices of these religiously centered people, it also depicts them battling with the universal tensions involved in living a disciplined religious life. Singmaster mediates their strangeness by portraying the commonness of their circumstances. At the same time, the pious devotion of the Improved Mennonites, compromised only by extreme circumstances, reflects the distinctive ethical standards of this Pennsylvania German sect.

ELSIE SINGMASTER AS WRITER AND VICTORIAN

The "cult of true womanhood," a term used by the historian Barbara Welter, helps us to contextualize the Victorian social convention about wom-
en's nature in the culture in which Singmaster operated. The idea originated
in the culturally dominant Northeast, and it guided American women's activities throughout the Victorian period. "True womanhood" describes
four "cardinal virtues" of the authentic Victorian woman: piety, purity,
submissiveness, and domesticity.[31] Women were held to be moral and religious in nature, sexually pure, outwardly submissive to their husbands
though influential in private, and happy only within the context of the
home. Women's domestic sphere was defined by traditional moral and
religious values, and Victorian women generally conformed to the roles
expected of them.

The male sphere, by contrast, was the workplace, which the Victorians
viewed as tainted by competition and politics. Naturally pure and protected
from contamination by the boundaries of their homes, women were ele-
vated to positions of moral superiority over males. Devoting herself to service and subservience while giving final authority to the man of the house,
the Victorian woman nevertheless asserted herself within the home, where
she was trusted to guide and nurture family members through her God-
given generous and loving spirit. She raised her children to become contributing citizens of the United States, God's newest creation.[32] Entrusted
with molding the young for devotion and citizenship, motherhood was
both a religious and a patriotic calling.

Born just prior to the late Victorian period (1880–1901), Singmaster
might have been expected to find fulfillment within the environs of home
and family, but it is here that she departed from the norm. After just three
years of marriage (April 1912–March 1915), Singmaster's husband, Harold
Lewars, died after an extended illness. Singmaster was pregnant at the
time, and she suffered the double tragedy of losing her newborn, Harold
Singmaster Lewars, just two months later. Already a successful author and
now a childless widow, she was forced to reexamine her femininity and her
long-term goals. Ironically, Singmaster's literary work granted her a part to
play in the socially defined role of mothering.

Victorian American children, naturally innocent and teachable according to Enlightenment philosophy, needed their virtuous mothers to guide
them to citizenship. Since the early Victorian era, women writers, working
in the privacy of their homes, had found a public voice in their edifying
stories and novels for the improvement of their readers. Victorian mothers

often used gentle stories like Elsie Singmaster's as teaching aids in place of the strict Calvinistic catechetical materials used formerly, which they believed might frighten rather than nurture their children.

Singmaster traced her early interest in writing to the use of good English at home, her love of reading, and long exposure to storytelling.[33] She read voraciously and broadly as a child, including in her repertoire her brothers' Rider Haggard and Jules Verne volumes and her father's collections of Scott, Dickens, Hawthorne, and Hugo. She liked the classics and theology but also devoured popular novels like the *Duchess* and Mrs. Humphry Ward's *Robert Elsmere,* casually left behind by others in railway stations.[34] As she matured, Elsie absorbed the stories with which her father delighted his listeners. It was reported that Dr. Singmaster could "tell a better story in three sentences than most people can in many pages!"[35]

In 1890, at age eleven, Elsie wrote a story about a paper doll. "The plot was not wholly original," she later confessed. "When the story was printed in a teachers' journal my conscience began to trouble me and has ever since."[36] As a young teenager she submitted household hints to a monthly women's magazine that offered $50 rewards for the best entries. To her delight, she won, and she announced her intention to buy a typewriter with the prize money. Her father demurred. "Elsie, thou shalt not buy thee a typewriter! I will buy the typewriter for thee."[37]

Elsie's father saw his daughter's potential and supported her in her goal to pursue higher education and become a writer. After graduating from Allentown High School in 1894, Singmaster continued her studies at her father's alma mater, West Chester Normal School, from 1894 to 1896. She entered Cornell in 1898. "It was at Cornell, in the Freshman English course, and the following year in a daily theme course, that I set out upon the long, arduous, and blissful path of the writer," she recalled. "A daily theme course is an almost intolerable affliction to the student who is interested only in science or languages or history but happy the would-be writer who is compelled each day to find something to write about and to present it clearly."[38] Singmaster remained at Cornell until 1900 but then took a five-year break from school during which she wrote stories and studied English, history, French, and German at home. Later, feeling the need to strengthen her writing with a stronger academic background, she applied and was admitted to Radcliffe College in Cambridge, where she graduated in 1907 at age twenty-seven.

Singmaster's novel *Bennett Malin* describes the personal journey of Miss Anna Gleason, a gifted and successful teacher in early twentieth-century America. "I was brought up in an age and in a family where it was the cus-

Fig. 8 This photograph may have marked Elsie Singmaster's graduation from West Chester Normal School,
c. 1895–96. She attended Allentown High School until
1894 and in 1898 enrolled at Cornell University, where
she studied until 1900. She graduated Phi Beta Kappa
from Radcliffe College in 1907.

tom to take care of the girls and not expect them to take care of themselves
or to do professional work," says Miss Gleason. "My family was willing that
I should be an amateur painter, but that was all; they did n't realize that I
was good for nothing else but painting. Nor did I for that matter. Finally we
got to understand each other."[39] Like Miss Gleason, Singmaster chose a
socially acceptable female profession but repudiated some of the constraints
of women's sphere. Ironically, Victorian society's effort to contain women
also enabled them to advance from within. In Singmaster's case, the merg-
ing of education, writing, mothering, and ministry created a safe way to
affect the world legitimately from women's designated place.

Between 1905 and 1950 Elsie Singmaster published some 350 short stories and articles and more than forty books. The first story, "The Lèse-

Majesté of Hans Heckendorn," appeared in the November 1905 issue of *Scribner's* magazine and set her on the path of her forty-five-year literary career. Pennsylvania German themes and characters dominate her early writing, and she returned to stories about "her people" throughout her life. In October 1932, nearly thirty years after publishing her first story, she wrote Ira Rich Kent, her editor at Houghton Mifflin, that she had returned to Lancaster County to collect new ideas for stories.[40] It was after this visit that she wrote about powwow doctoring, at one time an established part of the folk medicine of Pennsylvania Germans. Indeed, stories published as late as 1942 are peopled by characters of Pennsylvania German heritage.

Singmaster's stories imagine a feminine journey for her Pennsylvania German women characters that was similar to her own. She portrays these women in traditional roles but also creates situations that challenge their customary ways and social limitations. Many of her women prosper within the Pennsylvania German community, but others find a way out through ambition and education and become successful in the wider world. It is in their struggles for self-determination that these women become most interesting; Singmaster draws them into the mainstream experience of American women while also commenting on the circumscribed status of women in American society.

"The Eternal Feminine" (*Lippincott's Monthly*, July 1910) features the character Susan Ehrhart, the wife of the parsimonious Samuel Ehrhart. Within the context of Pennsylvania German Millerstown, Singmaster questions a wife's social obligation to facilitate her husband's moral development. Susan attempts to leave her mean husband, but her resolve weakens and she decides to stay. "I can't help it!" she whines. "I like him." Susan's weakness disappoints the feminist reader, who wants Susan to stand up to her nasty husband. In fact, however, Singmaster uses Susan's spinelessness to comment on the nineteenth-century concept of the "eternal feminine." According to this romantic archetype (a classic example is Goethe's Margaret in *Faust*), a woman finds fulfillment in loving those unworthy of her love and thus offers the possibility of redemption for the undeserving beloved. In Samuel's case, however, there is little hope for redemption. He wants Susan for her good cooking and for the extra money her hard work will bring him. He "looked forward to the day when she would become as much of a wage-earner as himself." The question of Samuel's redemption is left open. In her depiction of his deep-seated miserliness, Singmaster turns the concept of the "eternal feminine" upside down.

In another story, "The High Constable: A Millerstown Burglar Story" (*Outlook*, April 28, 1915), Susannah Kuhns fulfills the expectations of her

Pennsylvania German community. "By day Susannah washed and ironed and scrubbed and cooked and trained her children and managed her husband. Susannah, judged by Millerstown's standards, was a success." But Susannah realizes that she is unsatisfied in the domestic sphere. "I want to do something myself!" she says. "If the Presidency of the United States had been open to her sex," the narrator tells us, "she would have beheld herself occupying that high office."[41] Susannah suffers the frustration of a woman constrained by domestic responsibilities that thwart her ambition to "be somebody." How she resolves her feelings makes for delightful reading, as we watch Singmaster question gender roles and affirm women's public ambitions.

In "The Suffrage in Millerstown" (*Saturday Evening Post,* March 16, 1912), Singmaster describes the life of Lizzie Kerr, a typical Pennsylvania German housewife and mother.

> There are few women in Millerstown who take naps or who lie down in the daytime. It is safe to say that no woman, unless she was seriously ill, ever lay down for a whole afternoon. . . . When one has a husband and seven children, the youngest less than a year old, and when one is the only woman on a farm where there are fourteen cows, twenty pigs, and a few hundred chickens that need constant attention, one should be busy every moment. . . . An hour ago she had been standing by her kitchen table working her bread, an entirely suitable and becoming occupation for the mother of seven.

The glue that holds Lizzie's life together is her cooperative relationship with her husband, Alfie. Lizzie owns the Kerr farm through her family inheritance, but she and Alfie share economic and familial responsibilities. On this day, however, Lizzie and Alfie become engaged in a power struggle over Alfie's upcoming vote on temperance. Alfie refuses to honor Lizzie's deep allegiance to temperance, which she sees as a vote not only for liquor but against her. Lizzie reacts in the only way she knows how: to protect her children's future, she locks Alfie in the cellar on Election Day. This action so empowers Lizzie that Alfie worries she will parade in the streets like the suffragettes of London! Lizzie, "a stranger to herself" in her newfound power, tells her husband, "I do not know yet what I will do." The reader is left to imagine the final outcome, and to appreciate the impact of the suffrage issue on the small Pennsylvania village.

In "The Amishman" (*Ladies' Home Journal,* April 1925), Singmaster's female sectarians propose a more conventional social response than their

Millerstown forebears. "The Amishman" is a post–World War I story that appeared at a time when the nation was torn between traditional and modern values. The story's protagonists, Mahala Ebersole and Sallie Funk, provide quiet stability at home, while Mahala's son, Martin, romantically pursues an unprincipled "worldly" girl outside their community. Mahala and Sallie are Pennsylvania Germans whose deep roots go back to the first generation of German immigrants in America. They work the same farms as their forefathers and maintain an orderly, albeit old-fashioned, Amish lifestyle. Singmaster paints them in favorable contrast to the story's modern but undisciplined "Ladies of Gibraltar" and to Martin's beautiful but deceitful blonde city girl. In writing about the tensions that arise when the Amish live and work side by side with modern Americans, Singmaster raises questions about what is ageless and worthy within Amish culture. Amid the cross-cultural chaos created by Martin's impulsiveness, Singmaster's Amish women stand firm in their convictions. In having Martin return to his Pennsylvania farm and Amish community, newly convinced of the value of sectarian ways, Singmaster seems to honor long-accepted Pennsylvania German principles. In response to a changing national environment, she affirms the old ways.

Like Mahala Ebersole, Sallie Funk, Susannah Kuhns, Lizzie Kerr, and other Singmaster female characters, the author was an ambitious woman who wanted to make a difference. Successful and respected in her own right, Singmaster also possessed the social advantages that flowed from being the daughter of a knowledgeable and influential Lutheran pastor well connected to the religious elite. In her story "The Christmas Guest" (*Pictorial Review*, December 1926), Singmaster describes the social status of her character Mrs. Eline: "as the daughter of a minister and the widow of a teacher she occupied a social position second to none."[42] Singmaster felt a responsibility to both national and local citizens. Her typical daily schedule included writing, visiting, and helping within the Gettysburg community. In these ways she used her talent for personal development and Christian charity and also cemented her social standing. Cognizant of Singmaster's position and contributions, residents of Gettysburg often referred to her as "Gettysburg's First Lady."[43]

During World War I, the patriotic Singmaster stopped writing for two years in order to contribute to the war effort. She became active in the Adams County chapter of the American Red Cross and served that organization for the rest of her life. In 1921 she contributed an essay on the local Red Cross organization to Percy S. Eichelberger's *Adams County in the World War* (Harrisburg: Evangelical Press, 1921). Singmaster was also a leader in the Gettysburg Civic Nursing Association, an organization her father started before leading the effort to establish Gettysburg's hospital. She was an officer on the Adams County Historical Society's board of directors from 1939 to 1942 and served as vice president of the organization from 1943 to 1956. In 1946, as spokesperson for a select community group, she solicited the Adams County commissioners for permission and funding to start a public library. She helped lead the organization through its early searches for a location, book acquisition, and staffing and served as president of the board of directors from 1947 to 1949. In January 1950, after the library moved to a new location in the former county prison, Singmaster wrote the library's story, "It Was Once a Jail," for a Sunday edition of the *Philadelphia Inquirer.*

In keeping with her Pennsylvania German ancestry and with expectations for Victorian women, Singmaster refined her leadership skills within the safe and familiar setting of her church. She wrote nonfiction essays, articles, books, and stories relating to the work of church groups. These works reflect the evangelizing efforts of the various denominational groups and Singmaster's dedication to their causes. Though she held no official leadership position in the Lutheran Church, church officials sometimes invited her to participate in the work of the church. Singmaster also had an enduring relationship with the Gettysburg seminary. Her "Centennial Hymn," later revised and renamed "The Seminary Hymn," was first sung at the seminary's celebratory hundredth-anniversary worship service on September 21, 1926. Her lecture "The Practice of Writing" was delivered to seminary students and was first published in the *Lutheran Quarterly* in April 1912. It was reprinted posthumously in the August 1959 Elsie Singmaster Lewars commemorative issue of the *Gettysburg Seminary Bulletin.*

Singmaster dedicated her time and talent to women's church organizations as well. She joined the Women's Missionary Society at Christ Lutheran Church, Gettysburg, in 1901 and remained a member for the rest of her life. The society hoped to convert the world's non-Christians to Christianity and to build up the church worldwide through the efforts of self-sacrificing, educated church women.[44] Singmaster contributed to these efforts through her leadership in the local organization and her literary contributions at the national level. The United Lutheran Church in America (ULCA) Women's Missionary Society published and sold her historical study books, pamphlets, and plays for local program use throughout the country. Her fictional story "The Unconquerable Hope," published in the January 1908 issue of the *Atlantic Monthly,* promoted missionary recruitment and service to a national audience. Another story, "The Golden Mountain," featuring

Fig. 9 A committed public servant, Elsie Singmaster Lewars petitioned the Adams County commissioners to establish a public library in Gettysburg for the benefit of local youth and returning World War II veterans. In 1944 Singmaster became a founding member of the Adams County Public Library Board of Directors.

fictional Congo missionary Daniel Hazlett, appeared in the December 1918 edition of *Harper's* magazine.

The Lutheran Deaconess Movement was founded in Germany by Theodore and Zelia Fleidner and was brought to America in 1846 by a Lutheran pastor named William Passavant. This was a women's social ministry that responded to the poverty and homelessness created by the Industrial Revolution. Beginning in October 1934 Singmaster served as a member of the ULCA's Board of Deaconess Work. At the invitation of the board she presided at the first Council of Women in full-time service to the church, sanctioned by the ULCA at its 1942 Louisville convention. Under Singmaster's leadership, the council provided a forum for the study of the status of women workers in the Lutheran Church. For the first time, Lutheran women officially and self-consciously asked questions about their equality as employees of the church. The council looked at women as valuable resources in the church and the world, and it provided Singmaster an opportunity to exercise her ability to "[make] certain that the best method of help was discovered and followed." She wrote afterward to the Philadelphia Motherhouse director, Sister Anna Ebert, "I was very anxious to do well, and I hope I did not do *too* badly. I am much afraid of not recognizing thin ice until I hear it cracking beneath me!"[45] Although she lacked a clerical position, Singmaster was a skillful leader and communicator, and her voice was heard within the broader institutional community. Sister Mildred Winter, the first female field worker in the ULCA diaconate and the first female executive secretary of the ULCA's board, claimed that even men listened to Singmaster, as they recognized her value as a "thinker."[46]

In the 1929–30 school year, after a decade of discussion, the Lutheran-affiliated Gettysburg College enforced its 1926 decision to discontinue its practice of allowing women students to attend classes at the all-male institution.[47] Singmaster was a leading force in rallying public opinion against the move. Accustomed to Singmaster's normally reserved behavior, friends remember her reaction to the college's decision as a rare instance of her anger. She had first argued against the trustees' decision in "Women's Co-Education at Gettysburg College: A Plea for Its Continuance," an article published in the April 15, 1926, issue of the *Lutheran*. Now, several years later, she asked local service organizations to support women's enrollment. County schools, at her encouragement, wrote letters to the college urging the continuation of co-education for the benefit of their female scholars. She was also instrumental in getting a town meeting committee to provide a public forum for discussion of the question, but she again gained a wider audience for her cause with an article entitled "The Case for Co-Education," which appeared in the *Lutheran* magazine on February 27, 1930. Finally, Singmaster helped raise $8,500 from local contributors, which she offered to the Women's General League of Gettysburg College as seed money for a new women's dormitory.[48]

Elsie Singmaster had been the first woman to receive an honorary degree, a doctor of literature (1916), from Gettysburg College. In her view, the exclusion of women from the degree program at Gettysburg College was a step backward not only for women's education but also for the freedom of humankind. The college president and board of directors eventually reconsidered their decision and voted in 1935 to readmit women to the student body. As her friend Mary Lou Schwartz observed of Singmaster, "She was a determined tiger, fearless when she thought she was right."[49]

LITERARY MOVEMENTS

Singmaster applied her legendary determination to both civic service and literary efforts. She was passionate but disciplined and even-tempered in her work. Donald McPherson, a family friend, described "her wise judgment . . . calm personality, her incisive mind, her energy," and the "deep impact" of her character upon those who knew and worked with her.[50] In her focus on Pennsylvania German life and culture, Singmaster sought to "explain a group of people whom she thought misunderstood," in the words of another observer.[51] Her goal was to counter the stereotypical image of Pennsylvania Germans as unfriendly, miserly, and superstitious.[52]

Singmaster's project of letting the Pennsylvania Germans tell their own story from within, as it were, through her characters and stories, was impeded by the tendency toward ethnic isolation in many communities. Singmaster's story "The Old Régime" (*Atlantic Monthly,* October 1908) suggests that nineteenth-century Pennsylvania German schools may have sacrificed the intellectual progress of their students in favor of ethnic preservation. The 1834 *Act to Establish a General System of Education by Common Schools* provided an opportunity, but not a requirement, for individual Pennsylvania German communities to choose public English-speaking schools. Offering the potential to make connections to the world outside the Pennsylvania German village, this was an important development in educational and social growth for the village children and youth. At the same time, exposure to mainstream people, places, and institutions threatened the established ways that had so long identified Pennsylvania Germans. When the law was passed, only twenty-six of one hundred school districts in Lehigh, Berks, Lancaster, Lebanon, and York counties favored public school systems, but by 1865, roughly a generation later, 99 percent of all Pennsylvania districts voted to accept them.[53]

In the mid-nineteenth century, a growing fear of eroding identity and culture inspired Pennsylvania Germans to collect literature in the traditional dialect. Letters and columns in Pennsylvania German dialect appeared in mainstream eastern Pennsylvania newspapers as well. *Harbaugh's Harfe,* a serious collection of ethnic poetry written by Reverend Henry Harbaugh (1817–1867) to help preserve the Pennsylvania German dialect, was published in 1870.[54] In 1891 the Pennsylvania German Society was formed by a group of "thirty-one persons, including the state librarian, former Governor James Beaver, and future Governor Samuel Pennypacker."[55] The organization had among its goals the preservation of the Pennsylvania German language.

This literary preservation project paralleled the community's acceptance of public education. By the turn of the century, *Pennsylvania-German* magazine offered both poetry written in dialect and English-language articles, stories, and commentary about Pennsylvania German life. Economic and political interaction between Pennsylvania Germans and the "English" continued to open doors to cultural exchange. It was difficult, however, for outsiders to penetrate or correctly represent the tightly integrated Pennsylvania German community and its language. Writers from national magazines and newspapers made clumsy efforts to study the ethnic group and publish their observations and conclusions. Singmaster's story "The Man Who Was Nice and Common" (*Harper's,* November 1911) is a humorous depiction of one such attempt. During a lengthy summer stay, an "English" storyteller tries but fails to win Millerstown's trust while gathering and recording Pennsylvania German lore. The townspeople have their fun with the man by telling him a lot of tall tales. The tables are turned on the capricious Millerstonians when their guest publishes their tales as empirical fact.

In "Pennsylvania Dutch," an 1869 article in the *Atlantic Monthly,* Phoebe Earle Gibbons, who lived among the Pennsylvania Germans for twenty years, tried to capture and record the group's character and customs. "[The] Pennsylvania Dutch . . . people . . . have much that is peculiar in their language, customs, and beliefs," she wrote, "[but] I have learned heartily to esteem . . . their native good sense, friendly feeling, and religious character." Gibbons focused on the Mennonites and Amish, who made up only a small percentage of the total Pennsylvania German population. Even so, she incorrectly equated sectarian ways with "Dutch" ways, failing to capture the complexity of the Pennsylvania German population. She also misrepresented the Pennsylvania German dialect, calling it "mixed and corrupt" and angering those who spoke and prized it.[56]

At the turn of the century, Pennsylvania Germans came to national attention in the local color work of Helen Reimensnyder Martin (1868–1939) and Elsie Singmaster. Both women were daughters of German American

Lutheran clergymen and both had been students at Radcliffe College. Martin wrote novels and stories about the Pennsylvania Germans, but, though of Pennsylvania German heritage herself—she was born in Lancaster—she found little to redeem their "bovine dulness [sic]," and her work is marred by stereotypes and melodrama. "I have been obliged to select, for the purposes of fiction, their worst, rather than their best, side," she wrote, "the best being too unheroic, too tame, to be at all interesting."[57] Martin was a socialist who rejected conservative Pennsylvania German culture and maligned her kin in order to make political statements about gender and economic inequality in America. Her work failed to reflect her social concerns, however, because her overwhelmingly pessimistic Pennsylvania German portraits undermined her intentions.[58] In a review of Singmaster's novel *Katy Gaumer,* a writer for the *Nation* found a "convincing fidelity" in Singmaster's depiction of the Pennsylvania Germans. By contrast, Martin's "urban point of view" in *Martha of the Mennonite Country* diminished "the simple people [who] appear through the spectacles of a sophistication which largely distorts them."[59] When a Mennonite minister once mistook Martin's work for nonfiction, Martin explained to him that she wrote fictional stories for profit. Amazed that she would do such a thing, he exclaimed, "So then you write lies for lucre!"[60] Martin's harshness provided an unintended but striking foil for Singmaster's gentler point of view.

In the words of the literary historian Fred Lewis Pattee, local color (1880–1920) was an American regional literary genre that portrayed the lives and people of America's "border lands . . . [and] new-found nooks and corners."[61] In short story format, local color sought to capture authentic American identity amid the rapid social and demographic changes that followed the Civil War. By focusing on places where people took their identity and character from interactions with their local surroundings rather than from European traditions, local color literature celebrated America's geographic and multicultural differences. The California writings of Bret Harte (1836–1902) and the stories of New England life by Harriet Beecher Stowe (1811–1896) are early examples of local color writing. Late nineteenth- and early twentieth-century regional writers like Hamlin Garland (1860–1940), Frank Norris (1870–1902), Sarah Orne Jewett (1849–1909), and Edward Eggleston (1837–1902) wrote about place and culture in the American West, California, New England, and Indiana, recording distinct landscapes and their inhabitants. William Dean Howells (1837–1920), editor of *The Atlantic* and *Harper's* and a proponent of local color writing, wrote, "no one writer, no one book, represents [America] for that is not possible, our social and political decentralization forbids this. . . . But a great number of very good writers are instinctively striving to make each part of the country and each phase of our civilization known to all the other parts."[62] Local color authors wrote about places they knew from personal experience. Using place, dialect, humor, and the narrative of everyday experiences, they hoped to show their readers a picture of America shaped by its "timeless" rural folk population.[63]

Local color writers used the literary device of an educated narrator who responded to lower-class members of a rural or frontier community. The characters in local color fiction are unsophisticated but entertaining, exotic in their racial or ethnic particularities but at the same time fully American. Local color stories, with their heavy use of regional dialect, convey the impression of being part of an oral tradition that has been passed down from generation to generation. These stories connected modern Americans to the homespun wisdom of past generations and conveyed to their readers a sense of "native" American heritage.[64]

Approximately twenty-eight million immigrants from diverse homelands entered the United States between 1880 and 1920; by 1920 half the nation's population was first- and second-generation immigrants. American business and government were most interested in the labor provided by the newcomers and wanted to absorb them as quickly as possible into the industrial workforce.[65] America's population had always been racially and culturally diverse, but the massive influx of immigrants from southern and eastern Europe at the turn of the century, and the migration of blacks from the South into northern cities, increased racial and ethnic tensions. Earlier waves of immigrants from northern Europe had been assimilated easily enough, but the Jews, Catholics, and African Americans who flowed into America's cities and factories became the targets of an elitist establishment that saw them as a threat to America's bloodlines.[66] Economic inequality heightened class divisions and contributed to urban decay in immigrant communities. The popular concept of an American "melting pot" envisioned the fusion of different ethnicities into an English-speaking, hardworking Protestant community. The local color literary genre expressed growing popular nostalgia for the "old stock" believed to embody America's colonial standard, and sought to preserve it.[67]

Local color's emphasis on regional themes and people grew out of popular anxiety about the divisive impact on traditional American identity of massive waves of new immigrants, industrialization, domestic migration, and growing racial tension. The literary marketplace provided an outlet for this anxiety, as the country tried to frame these cultural and socioeconomic changes within the context of earlier times and simpler folk. Writers searched for common ground that could connect America's past and present by identifying homogeneous national traits in folk cultures capable of uniting all citizens and empowering them with a great common vision for the country's future.[68] The work of local color writers, empowered by the authenticity of their locally informed prose, was both celebratory and constructive. Their stories, though regionally specific, expressed a vision of America rooted in New England tradition, while they also acquainted readers across the country with immigrant practices that fell outside that norm.[69] The growth of newspaper and magazine subscriptions and interconnecting railroad lines exposed a national audience to ethnic American cultures and challenged readers to examine and embrace America's changing identity.

The genre's popularity grew as local color stories began appearing regularly in elite literary magazines at the turn of the century. The literary critic Fred Lewis Pattee and others saw these stories as polite and diminutive rather than as socially and culturally formative. By around 1920, however, the popularity of the genre had declined significantly, as readers saw the seemingly small, insignificant events in the lives of unusual people as increasingly anachronistic and irrelevant in a nation that was making vast and rapid economic advances. Because women writers were prominent in the local color field, the genre was associated with domesticity and was seen increasingly as "the literary version of the housework of realism, [and] its cultural work [was] reduced to mere preservation," according to the literary critic Stephanie Foote.[70] In recent years, however, literary theorists like Josephine Donovan, Elizabeth Ammons, Marjorie Pryse, and Judith Fetterly have reevaluated local color literature as the narrative expression of important cultural anxieties.

There is no consensus among modern literary critics on a "single local color or regionalist tradition," as many places, cultures, and writers are represented in the long history of American regional work.[71] In the last quarter of the nineteenth century, though, when the genre became popular, local color and regional fiction were understood synonymously. The intimate detail of local color fiction gave it an aura of truth. It was "a new kind of realism" that Hamlin Garland dubbed "veritism."[72] According to Garland, veritist writing embodied not only the facts about a place or people but the author's hopes and dreams. It came from the author's heart, and his or her life experience was deeply implicated in the story—"endur[ed]," in Hamlin Garland's words, sometimes brutally—rather than briefly observed by a passing visitor and recorded objectively.[73]

Published widely in short story format, regionalist writing both captured the American imagination and lent a sense of reality to its content. The profound social and economic changes that followed the Civil War, World War I, the Great Depression, and the New Deal all required reflection and gave rise to new perspectives. Literary regionalists engaged readers in creative dialogue about these historical junctures. They looked for national meaning and human interest in areas and people they knew well, and their local characters and circumstances created a new place for public involvement in literary forums. Regionalist authors were among the first American writers to augment the nation's "official" foundational myths with unofficial folk experiences.[74] They wrote with humor but also with purpose about their unique environments, hoping to inform their countrymen and -women and to mediate between their white Protestant culture and America's ever-changing character and identity.

The relatively unknown rural Pennsylvania Germans, with their peculiar ways and dialect, became a ready source for the local color genre. Earl Robacker, the author of *Pennsylvania German Literature: Changing Trends from 1683–1942*, was one of the first to acknowledge Elsie Singmaster's talent and her contribution to Pennsylvania German literature; he compared her "restrained" style of writing favorably with the turn-of-the-century "sentimental novel" and "rococo romance."[75] Indeed, the popularity of the local color genre catapulted Singmaster to prominence on the American literary scene.

Singmaster explained her long-term relationship with the Pennsylvania German people who populated her stories. "I knew in my childhood the Pennsylvania Germans of Allentown . . . and its neighborhood, members of the Lutheran and Reformed churches, thrifty, ambitious and still devoted to many German ways; later I became acquainted with those of the so-called 'sects'—the Mennonites, Dunkers, Seventh-Dayers and Amish, whose fine farms, great barns and religious garb give Lancaster County its unique character."[76] Set in the remote villages of Millerstown and Lanesville and the nearby Pennsylvania countryside, Singmaster's stories conform to a definition of local color in which place itself is treated like a character as it forms, motivates, and unifies the human characters. As the narrator of her story, Singmaster painted informed word pictures of Pennsylvania German homes, relationships, institutions, and rituals that recount incidents in the lives of her people as they encounter and interpret the familiar and the unfamiliar. The traditional cooperative values common to the small Pennsylvania village contrast with the competitive environment of industrialized cities.

Most of Singmaster's Millerstown stories appeared between 1905 and 1920, during the heyday of local color literature. An educated narrator tells tales of local folk that capture the look of their surroundings accurately. Dialect, courtship and marriage customs, ethnic foods, housekeeping traditions, religious life, holidays, and Pennsylvania German superstitions characterize Millerstown's communal life. Singmaster's short stories and her novel *Katy Gaumer*, also set in Millerstown, feature recurring characters: the Gaumers, the Kuhns, Sarah Ann Mohr, the Fackenthals, the Knerrs, the Weygandts, and others. Millerstown's citizens are influenced daily by both German and American traditions, and the resulting conflicts offer rich literary themes. According to Millerstown's paternalistic political leader, Squire Gaumer, in "The Squire" (*Atlantic Monthly*, September 1910), some old Pennsylvania German traditions are worth more than gold. And, indeed, Squire Gaumer sacrifices his savings and lifelong dream of travel to prevent Adam and Sula Myers's divorce. The squire reflects, "There had never been a divorce in Millerstown," and then announces, "there is to be no divorcing in Millerstown yet a while." The story expresses the give-and-take between established values and new social realities that underlies the whole Millerstown series. "Neither Millerstown nor the squire, English as they had become, was yet entirely of the world." Millerstown's honorable squire represents characteristic Pennsylvania German leadership as he mediates between old and new and the unfolding of an altered Pennsylvania German reality.

Millerstown's whole populace, often depicted as one shared living being in Singmaster's stories, acts upon, responds to, and forms the town's habits and attitudes. In "The Vacillation of Benjamin Gaumer" (*Century*, March 1906), all of Millerstown is focused on Ben Gaumer's indecisiveness about whom to marry. When Ben finally decides to elope with Jovina Neuweiler, the two sneak away in the early morning hours, before Millerstown can become aware of their plans. Responding to Millerstown's collective meddling, Ben "decided not to notify the men at the shop that he was not coming, but to let his mother send the boss word after he had gone. It would be a good joke on Millerstown." Millerstown is inhabited almost entirely by Pennsylvania Germans. It is independent and somewhat isolated from other Pennsylvania villages and towns—especially those of the "English." For its residents and for those who have left to live elsewhere, Millerstown's traditional Pennsylvania German lifestyle demonstrates a predictable norm against which their actions compare and contrast.

Mary Kuhns is the heroine of "Big Thursday," the first story Singmaster sold. Her native Millerstown is surrounded by countryside that "lay like a vast garden, well watered, well tilled, fertile." The land represents the hardworking, earthy Pennsylvania Germans whose farming methods and family life have enriched the country since colonial times. Mary resists some of her village's conventions. Refusing to attend a family funeral with her fiancé, John Weimer, she decides to leave tradition behind and go to the Lehigh County Fair unaccompanied. She is exhilarated by her newfound independence.

The fair, held in Allentown, is the antithesis of Millerstown's community and the well-ordered Pennsylvania German countryside. Mass transportation brings people together from different backgrounds, occupations, and locations, throwing them into a noisy, crowded urban environment. There Mary encounters "miners from Mahanoy City, Shenandoah, Centralia, and riot-stained McAdoo, . . . city reporters who had quarreled among themselves for the privilege of reporting the 'Dutch fair,' and . . . sportingmen who came to see the races." On one hand, the fair acts as a leveling agent for all who attend. Everyone can participate in the fair in the "finest State" of Pennsylvania and in the "great and glorious country," America. Mary senses the freedom afforded her as an American; at the same time, people at the fair treat her, a young woman alone, without Millerstown's affection. Men drink alcohol at the fair and speak to her rudely. Mary feels lonely and frightened. "Her taste of independence, at first sweet, had turned bitter." Soaked by a sudden thunderstorm and weighed down with disappointment, Mary returns to the arms of her fiancé, "Chohn," and vows that she will "nefer, nefer" leave Millerstown again.

Mary's language, a blend of German and English, is a metaphor for her dual cultural experience. While she has a firm foothold in her beloved but predictable Pennsylvania German village, she takes tentative steps into the thriving American mainstream. Her assimilation of American ways, like her use of America's dominant language, is uneven. Though her speech marks her as a Pennsylvania German, Mary has lived beyond Millerstown, if ever so briefly, and has been included in the larger American mainstream by her participation at the fair. Singmaster asks her readers to ponder what's at stake when an ethnic American, a female, no less, enters the larger American mix. She suggests that Millerstown's orderly, productive traits have not only contributed to the American experience but may also be a useful stabilizing force in the dizzying blending of the masses in modern American culture. What American traits, she asks, embodied in the Pennsylvania Germans, who used to "[be] the fair" but are now just one part of it, are threatened but worth guarding as the country adjusts to its ever-changing identity?

During the post–World War I years, Singmaster created new literary characters and situations, using the Pennsylvania German Mennonite,

Fig. 10   This "St. Louie"-style trolley connected Allentown, Emmaus, and Macungie. It is pictured at the terminus in front of the Continental Hotel, 39 Main Street, Macungie. Singmaster first referred to this trolley in her story "Big Thursday."

Dunker, and Amish religious sects centered in rural Lancaster County just outside the fictitious town of Lanesville. These independent groups separated themselves physically from "English" and "worldly" parts of the population, living simply but strictly according to their Christian principles and pieties. Most of these stories originally appeared in popular magazines and were reprinted in her collection of stories, *Bred in the Bone* (1925).

The unmarried sisters Betsey and Tilly Shindledecker appear in several *Bred in the Bone* stories and are among Singmaster's most lovable characters. They and William Hershey, Thomas Bashore, Eleazer Herr, and other characters in Singmaster's collection are members of the Improved Mennonite sect whose meetinghouse is just across the road from Betsey and Tilly's home. Singmaster portrays the Improved Mennonites and other religious Pennsylvania Germans as "a most interesting, unworldly, unusual, and worthy people."[77] In fact, she and illustrator Elizabeth Shippen Green offered to forego profit from the sale of *Bred in the Bone* if Houghton Mifflin would publish the volume. The stories highlight the peace, beauty, and simplicity of sectarian religious lifestyles as well as the risks of opting out

Fig. 11 Leon Guipon's drawing of Pennsylvania Germans in traditional attire arriving at the Lehigh County Fair accompanied Elsie Singmaster's story "Big Thursday," which appeared in the January 1906 issue of *Century* magazine. Singmaster praised Guipon's "art and accuracy" in an article entitled "Our Illustrators," *Atlantic Monthly*, February 1917.

of the larger, complicated, sophisticated, and sometimes dangerous world. Singmaster suggests through setting, plot, and character that rural sectarian ways have something of value to contribute to America.

Singmaster differentiated carefully among the various Pennsylvania German religious sects, using details of dress and worship practices to

Fig. 12 Elsie Singmaster and famed illustrator Elizabeth Shippen Green offered their work for free if the Houghton Mifflin Company would publish *Bred in the Bone* (1925), an illustrated collection of Singmaster's short stories about Pennsylvania German sectarians. They hoped their work would correct inaccurate and unkind public misconceptions of these Pennsylvania Germans. Green's drawing portrays Martin Ebersole according to Singmaster's careful description in "The Amishman."

distinguish them. In "The Amishman," for instance, the Amish Martin Ebersole manages a market stall in Lanesville, where the people of many Pennsylvania sects gather under one roof to sell their farm products.

> Beyond him was stall after stall, presided over by Amish and Men-nonite, Conservative or Progressive, Dunker or River Brother, each with his distinctive garb, or more worldly Lutheran or Reformed, all thrifty, shrewd, substantial . . . Martin . . . had a thick, curling silky beard . . . his hair, cut square across his forehead, waved almost to his shoulders. . . . His suit of thick gray wool, worn to a beautiful soft-ness, was home-made, the short coat held close round his body with hooks and eyes, the high-waisted trousers fastened after the fashion of sailors' trousers.

In "The Golden Rug," the Mennonite Mrs. Erlenbaugh and her daughters Sally, Minerva, Hester, and Lizzie wear the "gray Mennonite costume . . . caps, like infants caps in shape, with narrow ribbons left open and hanging upon their bosoms."[78] The scene inside Daniel Stolz's father's barn near Sorrel Horse, in "Settled Out of Court," describes the look of the members of an Old Order Amish congregation: "The bearded men, if they looked straight ahead, saw placid faces, heads coifed in transparent white, white organdie neckerchiefs and aprons. The dresses of the older women were dark gray or black; those of the younger women dark blue or purple or red." Mrs. Eichelberger, in "Thanksgiving Is n't Christmas," "was a Mennonite, but not an Amish Mennonite, and the rule of her meeting did not forbid her rolling her hair a little over each ear." Singmaster introduces these Pennsylvania Germans respectfully to the American mainstream as par-ticipants in the multicultural experience of the nation but also as variant strains in the Pennsylvania German community.

With the advent of local color writing in the late nineteenth and early twentieth centuries, Pennsylvania German and other dialects went public. The print media circulated stories punctuated by ethnic words and phrases that not only catalogued the country's regional people but also challenged the literary establishment's sole use of cultured English. Influenced espe-cially by Mark Twain's work, writers in the local color tradition used dialect to heighten the reality of their stories and to promote democracy by validat-ing language differences. At the same time, contemporary critics argued that the vulgarity of overused dialect suggested the growing use of "hybrid" English among America's middle class. They feared that this bastard Eng-lish threatened the public intellect and the country's ability to progress.[79]

The question of language in the industrializing nation added, ironically, to the polarization of the masses of non-English-speaking immigrants who made up the industrial workforce. In the factories, language differences between bosses and workers created and enforced socioeconomic boundaries. Differences were accentuated as city neighborhoods divided along lines of ethnic identity. Working-class families sought to share their lives there with people who spoke their native languages and understood their customs. One of the social problems of urban immigrant neighborhoods, dialect became representative of lower-class industrial workers, while high English was associated with the upper class.[80]

These divisions are obvious in Singmaster's stories, as industrialization invades the Pennsylvania German region's iron trade. Murphy, the boss in "In Defiance of the Occult" (*Booklover's Magazine*, February 1906), is an English-speaking "Irishman" (what Millerstown called the English speakers). Ollie Kuhns, the slag man in Millerstown's noisy, dirty iron furnace, speaks dialect. He fears that Murphy, with his proper English, will steal his sweetheart, Susannah. In another story, "A Millerstown Prodigal," Addison Miller's Pennsylvania German speech is a source of humiliation. When Addison's boss asks him to find a missing shovel, Addison says, "She is over by the wall. . . . The shovel, she is there." The Irish "scornfully . . . laughed at Addison's good Pennsylvania German."[81] In these stories, dialect signals the social and economic naiveté of its speakers, but it also isolates Singmaster's Pennsylvania German characters from the taint of the debased values associated with modernization.

Singmaster showed concern for the erosion of the purity of the Pennsylvania German dialect. In "Zion Hill," Peter Arndt Jr. anticipates the disappearance of the language of his forefathers. "He answered . . . the lawyer's questions, which were put and responded to in the uncorrupted German which had been since the days of the Indian almost the only speech in Zion Valley, but which was soon to degenerate into a hybrid 'Pennsylvania Dutch' and then to vanish. Even now the change was imminent, since nearer and nearer came the capitalists and engineers who sought the iron ore for great blast furnaces that were being built and for others that were planned."[82] There is a sense in this story that the author wishes not only to preserve a fading language but also to define Pennsylvania Germanness on the basis, in part, of the use of that language. Characters who speak the mother tongue of Germany are professional people who use high German only in formal circumstances. The evolution of Pennsylvania German culture, according to Singmaster's story, not only follows the development of Pennsylvania German dialect but also links the group to America's history from its earliest colonial days. Pennsylvania Germans like the Singmaster family distinguished themselves from the midwestern post–Revolutionary War German immigrants, the *Deitchlenners*, or "Germany-Germans." When the Pennsylvania German Society was founded in 1891, it formally defined Pennsylvania Germanness when it limited membership to descendants of these earliest Pennsylvania German immigrants.[83] Elsie Singmaster applied for membership on October 18, 1934.[84]

Singmaster incorporated dialect into her early local color work and into her later Pennsylvania German fiction by degrees. She rendered dialect as it sounded in the give-and-take of farm and village life. To capture that sound, Singmaster at first misspelled words, used idioms and German words in dialogue, and reversed the order of words to correspond to German grammatical rules. "The Vacillation of Benjamin Gaumer" provides a good example of dialect in Singmaster's early Millerstown stories. "'When I wass young,' Sarah Arndt went on,—'and dat was n't so many years back as when *you* wass young, Pit Gaumer,—de girls had more spunk as dey haf nowadays. Nobody would 'a' taken it from a fellar dat he went one Saturday wis one girl and de next wis anoder girl.'" By 1911, perhaps influenced by the use of English in the public schools, Singmaster had begun using only a few Pennsylvania German word clues to create the impression of dialect. An occasional "Ach" or "I thank myself" or "Yes, well" conveyed the sound of the dialect without overdoing it and trying the patience of the readers. "If I should ever compile my earlier stories, I would eliminate almost all dialect," she told an interviewer. "Much more can be effected by one word or expression here and there." Quoting Galsworthy, she added humorously that dialect, like sex, "is such a great strain that a little of it goes a long way."[85] Indeed, Singmaster was concerned about overburdening her stories with too much dialect, but her striking reversal after around 1911 also suggests that the political, economic, and social problems associated with immigration left an impression on her.

Singmaster was the only author of Pennsylvania German fiction in her time able to distinguish among the various dialect strains in the Pennsylvania German community and use them correctly.[86] In *The Magic Mirror* she delineates four varieties employed in the Allentown area: the formal language of the Lutheran Church, which can be traced to sixteenth-century Germany (High German); the academic English adopted by Pennsylvania German professionals; the language of Palatine immigrants passed down and preserved by daily familial usage (Pennsylvania German dialect); and Pennsylvania English, or English modified by the German Palatinate dialect.[87]

In an address before the Institute of German Studies in Philadelphia on contemporary fiction on Pennsylvania Germans shortly after the publication of Singmaster's novel *A High Wind Rising* (1942), Donald Radcliffe Shenton claimed that Elsie Singmaster understood and used dialect in her writing because she was an ethnic insider. He distinguished between the "Heart" and "Head" languages of the Pennsylvania German community and said that the dialect, the "Heart" language, protected the Pennsylvania German value system and way of life from the outside world. Its general unintelligibility in the English world created an intentional and effective cultural barrier, slowing the assimilation of Pennsylvania Germans into the English mainstream. At the same time, as Singmaster illustrated in "The Man Who Was Nice and Common," the same wall of protection prevented outsiders from appreciating their worthy neighbors, Shenton claimed.

Fig. 13 Characters much like these real Pennsylvania German villagers are central to Singmaster's regional stories. Gathered for conversation outside H. G. Reading-er's General Store (Macungie, c. 1904), they convey the sense of community evident in Singmaster's stories.

Shenton called Singmaster a pioneer in rendering dialect correctly and recommended her work as a model for others who wished to create credible Pennsylvania German fiction. And, again, he pointed out that her skill in this area, and moreover her ability to render dialect without denigrating the Pennsylvania Germans, depended on her intimate knowledge of their speech and culture.

> How easily she achieves the effect, the impression, of dialect in English narrative. No misspellings, but an occasional interjection or phrase such as "Nix kumm raus!" inverted and transposed word order, and many idioms. By these devices, she carries over the flavor and philosophy of the dialect without disturbing the prevailing emotion of the scene. . . . Elsie Singmaster translates the Heart Language across the barrier of dialect. And this, I maintain, can be achieved not by mastery of their idiom alone but only by the instinctive knowledge of one who has shared childhood with these people.[88]

Shenton understood the potential divisiveness of dialect writing and argued that Singmaster was able to avoid this pitfall because she was at home in both the Pennsylvania German and the English literary cultures.

Singmaster was motivated by more than a desire to record and preserve Pennsylvania German language and culture. By her own account, she did not choose the local color genre; it chose her, by recognizing the value of her stories early on and "buoy[ing] them to port." Singmaster continued writing Pennsylvania German stories into the 1930s, long after the local color genre had fallen from critical favor. In 1947, toward the end of her career, the literary critic and regional writer Dayton Kohler (1907–1972) called Singmaster a Pennsylvania regionalist, a writer whose "view is outward, less concerned with local differences than with those deeper qualities which make [her] men and women a part of the common race of man."[89] Kohler also acknowledged that Singmaster's local color realism distinguished her work. The Pennsylvania landscape provided a familiar backdrop in which the author's real men and women encountered real life.

Kohler's discovery of Singmaster as a regionalist foreshadowed feminist interpretations of women's local color writing in the 1960s and later. Feminist commentaries on the genre shed additional light on Singmaster's work. During the heyday of local color writing, male writers like Stephen Crane, Theodore Dreiser, and Jack London began to write romantic adventure stories. They wrote action-packed tales of conquest, starring chivalrous knights and other virile male heroes, set in the Wild West, on the high seas, and in other exotic locales. Claiming to capture the vitality of America's rapid expansion, these stories attempted to portray, in the words of the literary historian Charles Crow, "big slam-bang national themes of exploration, adventure, and conquest" that contrasted with the graceful, refined, and gentle writing typical of the local color genre, seen increasingly as the preserve of women.[90] Men's and women's literary expression became more and more divergent. No longer considered "high art" or "high culture" because of its association with the "passive" female world, local color lost its prominence in elite journals and became part of mass culture in popular magazines.[91] Female local color writers were consequently removed from the literary mainstream. In the early years of her career, Elsie Singmaster's stories appeared almost exclusively in highbrow American magazines like *Scribner's, Harper's, Century, Atlantic Monthly,* and others. After the 1920s, her stories appeared more frequently in popular magazines like the *Saturday Evening Post, Ladies' Home Journal, Youth's Companion, Woman's Home Companion,* and the like.

In *American Women Regionalists, 1850–1910* (1992), Judith Fetterly and Marjorie Pryse, according to Crow, raised awareness of women regional writers' artistic achievement and suggested that the merit of these writers has been underappreciated and deserves serious reconsideration.[92] From the safety of their subsidiary worlds, the women writers of Singmaster's era layered their seemingly innocuous local color stories with universal themes and appealing characterizations to make a point about social and cultural issues. As Josephine Donovan points out, women regionalists wrote about women characters living, like them, "at the margins" of their societies, where their opinions and activities transcended the prevailing patriarchal social structure and offered an alternative vision based on women's perspective.[93] Their stories often use comic irony to imply that men's reality is incomplete without the balance of women's judgment. Sarah Orne Jewett, whom Singmaster admired, was at the center of this writing tradition. It is reasonable to assume that Singmaster was influenced by Jewett's tradition and, like her, used her stories to affirm women's world and women's social impact.

Singmaster's Improved Mennonites Tilly and Betsey Shindledecker, mentioned above, are quintessential regional heroines: rural, close to nature, self-sacrificing, and utopian, yet challenged by people and concerns outside their sectarian world. They keep farm and domestic animals, grow their own food, sew their simple clothing and linens, and entertain themselves by quilting, cooking, reading, and singing. They attend nearby Improved Mennonite meetings, and the small congregation completes their

Fig. 14   Elizabeth Shippen Green's drawing, which accompanied "A Sound in the Night," depicts Improved Mennonite sisters Betsey and Tilly Shindledecker on their farmstead near Singmaster's fictional town of Lanesville. Green conveys the sisters' alarm when they hear an uninvited vehicle approaching their property. Betsey and Tilly are central characters in several of Singmaster's stories.

social circle. From the quiet fringes of American life, these shy female characters represent an alternative lifestyle. Their old-fashioned feminine ways and judgments provide a contrast to modern man's ways and question the wisdom of society's acceptance of male standards.

In "A Sound in the Night," male bootleggers hide a truck loaded with liquor on the Shindledeckers' rural Pennsylvania property. Singmaster uses the story to raise critical questions about both sectarian life and Prohibition. Improved Mennonites are forbidden to vote, so the sisters are unable to publicly declare their opposition to alcohol. Betsey, who equates liquor with the devil, nonetheless votes with her feet. She finds the rum-laden truck hidden by their sinkhole and pushes it and its devilish load into the depths. Singmaster's father was a member of the Prohibition Party, and her youngest brother, Paul, suffered from alcoholism. She wrote about the issue in an essay called "The Bird with the Broken Pinion" (*Atlantic Monthly*, December 1911) and again in "The Suffrage in Millerstown," reprinted in this volume. Betsey and Tilly Shindledecker confront social ills in several Singmaster stories and manage all their affairs without male presence or protection. In "A Man in the House" the sisters accept a stray male dog into their home. "He's fine company," says Tilly. "He'll take care of us. We have now a man in the house." Betsey responds, "He's better than a man. . . . He takes up less room, and he can't talk and he'll do as he's told." Living as separatists and being "crowd-shy" does not mean that the unmarried sisters lack confidence or strength of purpose.[94]

In the 1930s, Americans expressed renewed interest in the rural regions of their country through extensive travel and the appreciation of folk art and folk life. The abundant farmland of Lancaster County, Pennsylvania, located near Philadelphia and its bustling marketplace, became a cultural icon for the coexistence of "rurality and progress."[95] The sectarian Pennsylvania farmers still lived simply there compared to the progressive urbanites, yet they participated in urban life by selling their products to the city dwellers. In "Thanksgiving Is n't Christmas" (*Atlantic Monthly*, November 1937), Singmaster brings a Mennonite farmwoman, Mrs. Eichelberger, to the center of the cultural discussion. She prepares a Pennsylvania German Thanksgiving feast of turkey, ham, mashed potatoes, gravy, corn pudding, tomatoes, buttered beets, sauerkraut, bread, chow ("not a dog but a pickle"), piccalilli, hot slaw, spreads, pies, and cherry custard, all raised, gathered, and preserved on her fertile Pennsylvania farm. Mrs. Eichelberger and her husband share the festive meal with their nonsectarian "English" neighbors. The rich potential of Mrs. Eichelberger's land parallels the openhearted, hospitable character of the Pennsylvania German woman. As the stirrings of Nazism began to be felt in Germany, the Pennsylvania German woman's personality and productivity emphasized her American traits and the contributions of her forebears. On this national day of Thanksgiving, Singmaster invites her modern readers to remember Pennsylvania's and America's ideal origins, which welcomed difference, promoted tolerance, and provided economic opportunity.

Singmaster's Pennsylvania German stories feature both male and female protagonists, of course. Whereas her female characters use their influence from the sidelines, their male counterparts exercise power comically or tragically from their leadership positions within the community. The squire of Millerstown in "The Squire," discussed above, is an example of strong-willed, patriarchal Pennsylvania German leadership. In "Settled Out of Court," Singmaster depicts the alternative administration of law in the Old Order Amish community, led by male bishops. Singmaster's protagonist, twenty-year-old Daniel Stolz, is an Old Order Amish man in Lancaster County. His wife and baby have been killed by a reckless drunk driver, a young man named Rebbert who slammed his car into their buggy one night. Singmaster sets up an interesting contrast between Daniel and Rebbert: Rebbert is worldly and disrespectful but never intended to kill, while Daniel, the peaceful religious separatist, is overcome by grief and wants to murder Rebbert. Rebbert escapes legal punishment because he is a minor. "I had an awful accident once," he tells Daniel, who has found him by the side of the road after yet another accident caused by his carelessness, but "luckily, the victims were Conservative Dunkers, or Unimproved Amish, or Old Order Mennonites or something, or my father'd had an awful lot to pay. They don't go to law. He was sore enough as it was—I made mincemeat of the car." Daniel beats Rebbert unconscious and leaves him to die. The punishment he anticipates for breaching the unwritten law of his people will also be settled "out of court," meted out by his elders, who rely on God's law, not the human system of justice. Singmaster's young male characters possess the cultural and religious complexity of the Pennsylvania German community, which employs old methods of community justice that Singmaster portrays as healing, in contrast to the shallow, inadequate standards that guide Rebbert.

Matthias Lucas, the central character in "Zion Church," is Singmaster's most powerful male figure. He is a proud man whose family established and maintained Zion Church over three generations. Matthias dominates Zion Church as the church's stone edifice dominates the view of Zion Valley. "Devoted, generous, stubborn, Matthias Lucas might have said with conviction, 'I am Zion Church.'" When the members of the church prove that they and their church can thrive without his money and direction, Matthias surrenders to anger and violence and burns the church down. Singmaster concludes the story deftly, refraining from judging Matthias. His confession suggests God's forgiveness, but the author never assures the reader of Matthias's repentance. Matthias is a Pennsylvania German, but his pride and hardness are deeply human.

By 1906, when Singmaster published her first story, "Big Thursday," in *Century* magazine, subscriptions to American monthly magazines had increased from the post–Civil War figure of four million to sixty-four million. National magazines were a significant form of entertainment and influence among the American public. Monthly magazines outsold newspapers and weekly publications in the early part of the twentieth century, becoming the "major form of repeated cultural experience for the people of the United States," according to the historian and cultural critic Richard Ohmann.[96] During the Progressive Era, magazine editors used their freedom of expression, considerable journalistic independence, and increased capital to "penetrate to the power centers of the world"[97] and to influence the public according to their beliefs and hopes for America. Monthly magazines explored social, political, moral, economic, scientific, educational, national, and international issues, and their editorial views shaped public opinion. Through magazine subscriptions, Americans shared ideas with journalistic reporters and writers of fiction from the comfort of home. In 1906 Theodore Roosevelt told Edward Bok, the influential editor of the *Ladies' Home Journal* (1899–1919), that he "envied his power over the public."[98]

Side by side with nonfiction articles, periodical fiction commented on national leaders, politics, business, and personal life. According to Jan Cohn, the author of *Creating America: George Horace Lorimer and the Saturday Evening Post*, fiction writers unified the community of readers behind a national ideal as they told stories that depicted success-oriented, hardworking, thrifty, progressive, honest American citizens.[99] Exposing America's new class of uncultured industrial managers and their families to fine art and literature, the church, and domestic ideals, magazine editors helped define a middle-class sensibility of refinement and upward social mobility. Ohmann claims that these ideals, in combination with the consumerist values conveyed in the advertisements alongside the fiction in national magazines, created a new, profit-based "mass culture" in America. Magazines' literary content defined the national standard, while ads provided ideas and visual trappings for how to look and behave.[100]

Elsie Singmaster's early Pennsylvania German fiction appeared most frequently in the *Atlantic Monthly, Youth's Companion, Century,* and *Lippincott's Monthly.* The *Atlantic Monthly,* founded in 1857 as a New England literary magazine of high culture, first published local color stories under the editorship of William Dean Howells (1871–81).[101] Moving away from romantic sentimentalism toward literary realism, the magazine published stories and articles that appealed to growing public interest in cultural differences among the nation's new immigrant population. It helped standardize the content and style of regional writing according to the taste and desire of its culturally elite readers. The format of Singmaster's stories matched the magazine's literary definition of regional writing, which included the village setting, the educated visitor, local wisdom, dialect, and elegiac tone. Moreover, Singmaster's regional characters and their immigrant culture, evoking a "traditional" American character in contrast to growing capitalist trends, became part of an "elite press" participating in cultural work that could easily be read as "conservative."[102]

The *Century* magazine, originally known as *Scribner's Monthly*, was founded in 1881. Like the *Atlantic Monthly*, it was a highbrow literary magazine that published more English than American literature. Typical of literary journals of its time, *Century* in its early years remained aloof from social or political topics that might offend its refined readers. By the turn of the century, however, in response to maturing public tastes, *Century* began to include not only journalistic articles but also local color stories set in various American landscapes. In 1911 it published Singmaster's Pennsylvania German story "The Belsnickel," which told a unique part of the American story in rich detail. Somewhat surprisingly, it depicted the provincial ethnic village of Millerstown as a crucible for change and progress, showing the town's Pennsylvania Germans enacting one of their Christmas rituals in English for the first time. In this way they preserve their cultural traditions while at the same time evolving for the benefit of present and future generations. In this story's portrayal of the American dream of progress and assimilation, Singmaster considers the implications of ethnicity, gender, education, and public life. Her point of view is optimistic and progressive, and she envisions Pennsylvania Germans as ideal Americans.

It was Singmaster's combination of literary art and idealism that probably interested her in the *Youth's Companion*. First published in 1827, the magazine had evolved by the turn of the century into the most widely circulated family periodical in the United States. Featuring famous authors such as Emily Dickinson, Willa Cather, William Dean Howells, and Bret Harte, its reputation for excellence was already well established when Singmaster's stories first appeared in the early 1900s. According to Ohmann, "family" meant "respectable" in the magazine industry. Intending to provide an entertaining but instructive aid to upwardly mobile American families, the magazine vowed to print only what was good and proper.[103] The owner and editor, Daniel Ford, was a leader in innovative magazine advertising and marketing, but no tobacco or alcohol advertisements or controversial topics threatened families' moral sensibilities. Stories like "The Chimes at St. Peter's," "The Organ at Zion Church," and "The Supply at St. James the Less" all consider Pennsylvania German church life. "When Grampap Voted" champions the American ideal that each citizen's vote is precious. "The Reichards' Boarder," "The Device of Miss Betsey," "The 'Rose-and-Lily' Quilt," and other Singmaster stories paint sympathetic portraits of kind, earthy, but determined and contributing Pennsylvania Germans. Revealing a journalistic philosophy similar to that of the *Youth's Companion,* Singmaster's essay "Does It Pay?" reminds her young readers that worthwhile magazines enliven the mind, tell the truth, and use good English, while "silly" ones corrupt through "rascality and evil and sentimentality. . . . A boy or girl may be reminded of a passage in a great Book," Singmaster adds, "which says that if we wish to be clean we must think about clean things."[104]

Popular magazines like the *Saturday Evening Post,* the *Ladies' Home Journal, Woman's Home Companion,* and *Collier's* provided an alternative to the more intellectual literary journals, and were designed to attract a wider, less educated audience. They cost less than their literary counterparts, and their practicality and variety of stories, pictures, and advertisements appealed to a large body of both male and female middle-class subscribers. Though more journalistic than the literary magazines, the popular magazines attracted good fiction writers and advertised their names on the cover. *Saturday Evening Post* editor George Horace Lorimer, nicknamed "The Boss" by his writers, personally approved every story published in his magazine. He believed the *Post* had the power to shape society by articulating traditional values in fiction. A self-appointed "guardian" of American society, Lorimer printed stories that were "safe . . . conventional . . . clean . . . wholesome . . . fit reading for a clean and wholesome people."[105] During the 1920s and 1930s, he approved more than twenty Singmaster stories for publication, and her name appeared on the cover several times. Singmaster also believed in the power of a story to illustrate a point. In the preface to her book *A Cloud of Witnesses,* she wrote, "The pointing of a moral by means of a parable is as convincing to intelligent adults as it is effective with youth."[106] In this popular magazine forum, Singmaster's stories reached a wide readership. In 1929, just before the stock market crash and the onset of the Great Depression, the Curtis Publishing Company, owner of both the *Saturday Evening Post* and the *Ladies' Home Journal* as well as the *Country Gentleman* and *Jack and Jill,* reported net earnings of $21,534,265, more than any other publishing company before that time.[107]

The *Ladies' Home Journal* and *Woman's Home Companion* appealed mainly to female readers. Both magazines sought to entertain and inform women whose opportunities and education had increased since the dawn of the twentieth century. Gertrude Battles Lane, editor of *Woman's Home*

Companion, wrote, "In editing . . . , I keep constantly in mind a picture of the housewife of today as I see her. . . . She is intelligent and clear-headed; I must tell her the truth. . . . Her horizon is ever extending, her interest broadening."[108] Through story selection and advertising, the *Journal* appealed to an ideal American woman reader, seen as economically comfortable, naturally and internally beautiful, ageless, self-controlled, optimistic, and well-mannered.[109] At the same time, publishers and editors believed in the power of the American housewife to make a difference in society and aimed to encourage her participation and self-improvement.[110] In Singmaster's story "A Student of Languages," the Pennsylvania German Victoria Wagonseller acknowledges the importance of manners and magazines in the up-and-coming ethnic American home. Victoria introduces her teacher to her father. "'This is Mr. Mather,' she said. 'Mr. Mather, this is my father.' Yesterday Victoria would have said 'Meet my father'; but last evening in an advertisement of a book of etiquette on the back of a magazine she had read that this was an abominable form of introduction. Victoria needed but one hint."[111] In "The Golden Rug," Mrs. Landon, a wealthy, cultured New Yorker, discovers Mennonite Sally Erlenbaugh's artistic hooked rugs while visiting the farmers' market in Lanesville. Sally is grief-stricken because she has recently been jilted by her lover, but Mrs. Landon's offer to sponsor Sally in a domestic rug-making business gives her a new and productive focus. Writing about both sectarian and secular Pennsylvania German women, Singmaster's stories often supported popular magazines' view of the developing American woman.

Singmaster's stories held the greatest national appeal during the economic boom of the 1920s, an era in which American city dwellers outnumbered rural people for the first time and it became impossible to ignore urban influences on traditional American culture and society. Those who migrated to cities for economic reasons left their extended families and heritage behind and forged independent identities in new surroundings. Fiction like that of Helen R. Martin began to depict country folk as backward, unsophisticated, and out of date. The historian Ann Douglas has described the appeal of the city to artists and writers. "What drew writers and performers to New York was precisely what dismayed the more conventionally minded: the chance it offered to be *un*cared for, *un*tended. Artists of the Jazz Age . . . wanted 'to remain orphaned from the smothering arms of society.' America itself was an orphan of sorts. Severed by its own act from its mother country, long disdained and disowned by its European forebears, America was proving just how powerful orphans could be."[112] Rather than deny communal or familial influences, Singmaster's stories emphasize the freedom to grow within the imperfect but familiar environs of the Pennsylvania German ethnic village. Singmaster's villagers participate in public life. They venture beyond the territorial and cultural perimeters of their villages but remain connected to their homes through language, art, religion, and moral ideals. They keep what is meaningful in their ethnic heritage but seek a sense of belonging in their new country as well. Their assimilation to what Steven Nolt calls "their own ethnic advantage" is an exercise in constitutionally guaranteed autonomy and opportunity for self-improvement, without the parallel negation of the positive things in their backgrounds.[113]

Singmaster sometimes used encounters with city folk to illustrate Pennsylvania German cultural transformation through the "exposure of their German language and culture to their new surroundings," in Carmen Birkle's words. This cultural phenomenon, which Birkle calls "transculturation," acknowledges that ethnic subcultures can maintain their distinctiveness while living within a dominant culture, and can forge a new identity through interaction with that larger culture.[114] Singmaster portrayed a society she knew firsthand, in which Pennsylvania German culture was evolving in response to this kind of exposure and interaction. She rejected the prevalent popular image of Pennsylvania Germans as isolated and backward. Instead, her writing captures the dynamics of cultural mixing, as Pennsylvania Germans adjust to changing times and surroundings. Steven Nolt's scholarship on the development of Pennsylvania German ethnic identity supports Singmaster's point of view. According to Nolt, the designation of German-speaking colonial immigrants in Pennsylvania as "Pennsylvania Germans" rather than "Palatines" was a first step in their becoming ethnic Americans. The term identified a transitioning group that was neither German nor Pennsylvanian but an ethnic blending of both cultures. Moreover, Nolt observes, the Pennsylvania Germans and other German immigrants from Maryland and the Appalachian backcountry were "the first major group to experience this sort of ethnicization-as-Americanization."[115]

In "The County Seat," Susannah Kuhns insists that her family move from Millerstown, which she finds "too slow and too dumb and too Dutch," to the city of Allentown. Susannah is economically ambitious, and she is sick and tired of traditional, predictable Pennsylvania German life. The Kuhns family's move to Allentown illustrates the ongoing interaction between the Pennsylvania German village population and urban culture, with predictable results. Disillusioned by the false sophistication of the city, and hurt by its rejection of the honest, unpretentious villagers, Susannah and her family return to the peace and quiet of Millerstown and its close-knit community. Singmaster is not specific about the effects of their disappointed venture and leaves it to her readers to imagine how the Kuhns have changed as a result of the experience. Susannah reemerges a few years later, as rebellious and forthright as ever, in "The Eight Hour Day" (*Country Gentleman*, October 31, 1914) and "The High Constable," in which she attempts to change long-standing Pennsylvania German tradition from within her home and the village structure.

In "Frau Nolte," Singmaster depicts a German American New Yorker who returns to Bethlehem, Pennsylvania, after World War I to attend the local Bach Festival.[116] Nolte, once a famous soloist and music teacher, prefers "Frau" to the customary American title for voice teachers, "Madame." Unlike Pennsylvania Germans who claim American citizenship, Frau Nolte has resisted assimilation and has preserved her German identity throughout her distinguished prewar musical career in America's cultural capital. The defeat of Germany in the war, however, and widespread anti-German prejudice in its aftermath have robbed her of her artistic success, her religious faith, and her pride in her German heritage. Her presence at this ritualistic performance in the small Pennsylvania city sets the proud, urbane Frau Nolte to rights. In a surprising reversal, she is transformed by the small-town performance of Bach's great Mass, which humbles her, restoring her faith and promising her redemption. In the beauty of Bach's Mass Singmaster finds common ground with Americans of all stripes. "Frau Nolte" appeared in *Century* magazine in 1925, and the story's reconciliation of the German and American languages and the two countries' shared traditions underscored the hope of international reconciliation for the magazine's readership.

Remembered as a realist in the local color and regional traditions, Singmaster was also an outspoken idealist. In a review of her first book, *When Sarah Saved the Day,* a reviewer for *Pennsylvania-German* magazine expressed his hope that Sarah's noble ideals would inspire America's young readers to similar courage and heroism. Singmaster continued to affirm ideal Pennsylvania German qualities throughout her writing career. In a speech entitled "The Pennsylvania Germans," she catalogued the traits that she believed ennobled her people: their bravery and tenacity in seeking economic opportunity, autonomy, and religious and political freedom in a new land; their resiliency and rise to responsible and loyal citizenship in the face of prejudice and persecution; their inherent kindness and decency; their commitment to hard work; their sense of humor; their artistry; their frugality; their intelligence; and their honorable Christian character.[117] Singmaster not only admired these qualities in her ethnic community but encouraged them in other Americans. In his review of Singmaster's *I Speak for Thaddeus Stevens* (1947), Richard Current commented on Singmaster's "partisan" idealism in her treatment of Stevens, a Civil War–era politician who had once lived in Gettysburg.[118] As in her assessment of the stereotyping of Pennsylvania Germans, Singmaster believed that Stevens had been unfairly maligned by the public and the media and wanted to set the historical record straight. She emphasized Stevens's kindness and generosity to the poor, the troubled, and the slave, and hoped that his example in fighting for the oppressed would inspire all Americans.

Elsie Singmaster's upbringing in a religious household, her early life among the Pennsylvania Germans, and her immersion in the Gettysburg seminary community encouraged her beliefs, her vision for a better America, and her sense of duty to the development of her great country. Dayton Kohler of the *Bookman* commented, "She has maintained an uncompromising attitude toward the beliefs she held when she began to write. There is a quality austerely Lutheran in her nature which has bred in her a lasting dislike for anything cheap or trivial. Fundamental principles regarding the home, the State and the Church have been stressed again and again in the speech and actions of her self-respecting, God-fearing men and intelligent, devoted women."[119] Kohler's description captures the connection between Singmaster's essential beliefs and her work. She understood life in terms of her abiding relationship to Christ, the vine grower, the life giver, but also the pruner and disciplinarian. The interrelatedness between Christ and the believer in the Christian life, according to her book on Martin Luther, encourages service to others in loving response to one's personal salvation. Surely speaking for both sexes, Singmaster wrote: "the Christian man . . . has still before him his earthly life, wherein he must do good works, . . . so that his body may be purified and be made a fit vessel to hold the new man which he has become . . . a servant to all."[120] This call to discipleship through service was manifested in the faithfulness of Singmaster's characters and stories.

Singmaster fulfilled her Christian calling, in Lutheran Church historian Frederick Wentz's words, "where church and society, the Gospel and the world meet."[121] She believed that writing that lacked the purpose of improving the reader and the world was mere entertainment and unworthy of the calling. She could readily weave lighthearted plots, but her core beliefs, and her desire to express them creatively for the benefit of others, informed all of her work. In *The Book of the United States* (1926), for instance, Singmaster characterizes liberty as a "sacred fire" handed down from generation to generation to treasure and perpetuate. "My book is useless if you do not realize this," she told her young readers.[122] She likewise infused her Pennsylvania German characters with serious social purpose. They became examples of immigrant American citizens strengthened by the basic goodness of their cultural and religious backgrounds to rise to moral and ethical challenges, whether public or private. Their circumstances invited readers to ponder the stories' broad ethical themes.

THE CRITICAL RESPONSE TO ELSIE SINGMASTER'S BOOKS

Houghton Mifflin was Singmaster's primary publisher, from *When Sarah Saved the Day* (1909) to *I Speak for Thaddeus Stevens* (1947). In the beginning she wrote so prolifically that the company asked her to slow down until publication could catch up with her. The editors at Houghton Mifflin believed that the American literary market had a place for Singmaster books. When she submitted *The Hidden Road* (1923), Ferris Greenslet responded that Houghton Mifflin was "prepared to make a strong offer" based on the "soundness and richness [that her] work deserves."[123] Ira Rich Kent recommended illustrations and "an important promotion campaign"[124] for Singmaster's *Rifles for Washington* (1938). By 1940 Houghton Mifflin had completed seventeen printings of *When Sarah Saved the Day*.[125] Singmaster maintained a steady correspondence throughout her professional career with Greenslet and Kent, discussing royalties, book signings, contracts, and ideas for future projects.

The editors and the outside readers Houghton Mifflin hired to comment on Singmaster's submissions credited her "great historical research" and respect for "place and proper name";[126] one called her "mistress of the material she chooses to work with."[127] In recommending the publication of *Bred in the Bone* (1925), one reader noted that Singmaster's local color stories were "not greatly inferior to Miss Jewett's *Country of the Pointed Firs*."[128] Sarah Orne Jewett was recognized for her humorous local color writing about Maine and its simple inhabitants. Willa Cather, who dedicated *O Pioneers!* to Jewett, wrote, "It is that kind of honesty, that earnest endeavor to tell truly the thing that haunts the mind, that I love in Miss Jewett's own work."[129] "D. B. W." of the *New Republic* found a similar straightforwardness in Singmaster's *Bred in the Bone* stories about Pennsylvania German sectarians. "These dwellers in an austere Arcady know pain and triumph, passion and despair—but not confusion," D. B. W. wrote. "Their darkest hours—some of which Miss Singmaster has depicted with tragic and even sinister skill—are simple suffering, endured with a dignity of undistracted souls. There are tales, too, of quiet humor, some even with a satiric quirk. But the real achievement of the artist is in presenting the lives of the saints as credible—and, in some strange manner, successful."[130]

Singmaster told friends that she began preparing her books with meticulously gathered facts and real people, and then built fictional characters and stories from these beginnings. *Rifles for Washington,* illustrated by Frank Schoonover, told a fictional story based on the first rifle militia of Pennsylvania in the Revolutionary War. Schoonover also illustrated *I Heard of a River,* published in 1948. The novel *The Isle of Que* (1948) took place along Pennsylvania's Susquehanna River, and Singmaster's last book, *Pennsylvania's Susquehanna* (1950), brought together fact and legend about the great meandering river that winds its way through the center of the state. Singmaster wrote factual but interpretive American history for juveniles in *The Book of the Constitution* and *The Book of the United States.* Her *Stories of Pennsylvania* recounted history through individual stories in four volumes.[131] In 1942, the same year Houghton Mifflin published *A High Wind Rising,* Singmaster informed her publishers that all her books had been included in a statewide library listing entitled "What to Read on Pennsylvania."[132]

Reflecting the changing times and developing literary tastes of the public, the critical reception of Singmaster's books was mixed. As we have seen, critics like Dayton Kohler admired Singmaster's work and believed that her place in the American canon would endure. Singmaster's Pennsylvania German novels were highly acclaimed by those who shared the moralistic perspective of the Progressive Era. The *New York Times* called *Katy Gaumer* "natural and simple, vigorous in its healthful, normal life."[133] Singleton, writing for the *New Republic,* commented on the unspoiled insight of *The Hidden Road,* admiring "the air which blows through this refreshing book . . . an air . . . for gathering what Miss Singmaster has gathered here, the harvest of a quiet eye."[134] The *Saturday Review of Literature* called *Keller's Anna Ruth* "a story which has not been spoiled by pessimism or morbid detail,"[135] and the *New York Times Book Review and Magazine* remarked, "*Ellen Levis* shows an admirable insight into the true nature of man's enjoyment of life and of his ability to find happiness even though the thing upon which he depended to provide it proves him false."[136] The *Bookman* praised Singmaster's record of the Pennsylvania German way of life and suggested that she "must eventually be considered one of our finest writers."[137] The Columbia University Alumni Club recognized Singmaster's significance in Pennsylvania German literature in March 1936 by honoring her with an award for "contributions in the fields of the historical novel and short story and as an interpreter of the Pennsylvania Dutch life."[138]

Throughout Singmaster's career, Pennsylvania Germans responded enthusiastically to her work about their culture and history. Editorials, book reviews, and newspaper articles from the Allentown and Macungie areas testify to the warmth and appreciation local readers felt for Singmaster. Early in her career the *Pennsylvania-German* magazine heralded the publication of *When Sarah Saved the Day,* writing, "It is . . . the first time that the Pennsylvania-German people have been presented in a decent way and in a manner that does them justice."[139] In 1947 the Pennsylvania German journalist Preston Barba, of the *Allentown Morning Call* wrote, "Elsie Singmaster has long ago won for herself an abiding place in the hearts of the Pennsylvania German people, for she has looked deeply into their lifeways and delineated them with sympathetic understanding."[140] At the time of Singmaster's death in 1958, one editor of the *Morning Call* claimed that "none refined the ore [of the Pennsylvania German experience] and brought out its precious metal more effectively than she did."[141] Seven years after her death, Albert Hofammann of the *Allentown Sunday Call-Chronicle* recalled Elsie Singmaster and her work to the people of the Lehigh Valley, claiming that Singmaster's fictional portraits formed the "bed rock" for all others who write about Pennsylvania Germans.[142]

Singmaster maintained a personal relationship with the people of Lehigh County. She returned to her original home region for speaking engagements and book signings and always openly declared her devotion to the Pennsylvania German people and their way of life. In a speech in Allentown she told the people of Lehigh County she hoped they would never change.[143] When she published *The Magic Mirror* in 1934, Allentown residents welcomed Singmaster back home for a personal appearance at the H. Leh and Company Lending Library. A newspaper account reported that interest in Singmaster's book was so great that the library had to purchase twenty-four copies.[144] A letter of appreciation from Grace K. Nadig of Temple University reveals the importance of *The Magic Mirror's* contribution to Pennsylvania German families and histories: "My father was born and reared in Allentown. His father built a home in the vicinity of some of the scenes in your book at 4th and Linden Streets more than sixty years ago. . . . We, particularly my parents, remembered so many of the sections of Allentown mentioned by you. . . . I had to let you know how much the book has meant to us."[145]

In 1947, when national critics condemned Singmaster's book *I Speak for Thaddeus Stevens* because it was not historical enough, Preston Barba defended it, claiming that her treatment of Stevens created a rare intimacy between Stevens and her readers that academic historians had been unable

Fig. 15 This portrait was made around 1944. In 1945 Henry Borneman, then president of the Pennsylvania German Society, presented Singmaster with the organization's Citation for Distinguished Service in recognition of her literary interpretation of the early history of Pennsylvania German settlers.

to achieve. Barba also pointed out the antislavery connection that Singmaster established between Stevens and the Pennsylvania German Edward Rauch, better known as "Pit Schweffelbrenner," a writer of Pennsylvania German newspaper columns. Barba considered Singmaster an outstanding contributor to Pennsylvania German culture and literature.[146] From June 16 until August 25, 1956, just two years before Singmaster's death, Barba's column in the *Allentown Morning Call*, 'S Pennsylvaanisch Deitsch Eck, published, in eleven consecutive issues, Mary Rice Hess's 1929 Pennsylvania State University master's thesis, "Elsie Singmaster," in its entirety. The eleven installments appeared side by side with Pennsylvania German dialect selections by Ralph S. Funk (1889–1969), Louise Weitzel (1862–1934), Boonastiel (T. H. Harter, 1854–1933), and others, connecting Singmaster's English language stories with the dialect tradition. "No other writer of fiction has portrayed the Pennsylvania Germans," wrote Barba, "with so much integrity and art over so long a period of time as Elsie Singmaster."[147] In this way, Barba's readership became acquainted or reacquainted with the life and work of one of their own.

Ideas for a new Pennsylvania German book were forming in Singmaster's mind, and in February 1940 Ira Rich Kent approved an "important history" that Singmaster planned to complete by 1941.[148] She considered telling the story of Pennsylvania Germans beyond the picturesque life of the Amish and other sects; she wanted, she wrote to Kent, to emphasize "the enlightened contributors to our way of life . . . the makers of pottery and glass, the printers of noble texts, the Bach singers, the scholars, the Conrad Richters and Thomas Wolfes, the Herbert Hoovers and General Pershings, the Milton S. Hershey's et al."[149] In the end, Singmaster wrote *A High Wind Rising* to illuminate the story of Pennsylvania's earliest German immigrants. In 1941, while she and her publishers were pondering the name of her new book, Henry S. Borneman, the president of the Pennsylvania German Society, remarked to Singmaster that he "deplored the lack of a [Pennsylvania German] novel that was neither 'hexy, sexy, nor unkind'" in its description of Pennsylvania German subjects.[150] Singmaster told Borneman about her new book and solicited his help in advertising it. He obliged by providing her with the six hundred names on the society's mailing list. Published in June 1942, *A High Wind Rising* met with significant critical and popular approval. Now president of the society, Borneman wrote to Singmaster, "You have presented a most graphic picture of the Pennsylvania German pioneer [and] you have made a real contribution to the portrayal of early Pennsylvania German history."[151] At the society's 1945 meeting in Waynesboro, Pennsylvania, Borneman presented Singmaster with the society's Citation for Distinguished Service for her interpretation of the life and character of the Pennsylvania Germans. Her speech at that event, unfortunately, was not published.

A High Wind Rising was acclaimed outside the Pennsylvania German community as well. Virginia Kirkus, editor of *Harper's,* and authors Bruce Lancaster and Dorothy Canfield Fisher, in reviews and personal letters, praised Singmaster's novel, which Fisher called "rich, exciting, deep-rooted."[152] The *New York Times* and *New York Herald Tribune* gave the book good reviews, citing the author's ability to create balanced characters who contributed to the growth and development of the early Republic. The reviewers agreed that Singmaster's simplicity of style, restrained action, and lack of sentimentality combined to make a convincing and satisfying tale of Pennsylvania's early settlers.

Singmaster attracted the attention of other prominent writers and illustrators of her time. Pearl Buck, Mary Roberts Rinehart, Stephen Vincent Bénet, and Edwin Markham all visited her at her home in Gettysburg. Violet Oakley sketched a portrait of Singmaster that was used in promotional material in the 1920s. A scene in Oakley's enduring mural *Lincoln at Gettysburg,* now hanging in the senate chamber in the Capitol Building in Harrisburg, was inspired by Singmaster's story "The Battleground." Marguerite de Angeli followed Singmaster's suggestion when she wrote *Skippack School,* a book about the Pennsylvania educator Christopher Dock. For some, Singmaster became a representative of the principled, accurate, and purposeful regional literature of Pennsylvania. Esther Forbes summed up the respect for Singmaster in her "Literary Pilgrimage to Elsie Singmaster," a front-page biographical article in the book section of the *Boston Evening Transcript* on July 3, 1926. Forbes was a member of the editorial staff at Houghton Mifflin and traveled to Gettysburg to interview Singmaster. Later in her career, Forbes won the Pulitzer Prize for her biography *Paul Revere and the World He Lived In* (1943) and the Newbery Medal for *Johnny Tremain* (1943). In 1950 Pennsylvania governor James H. Duff recognized Elsie Singmaster's contributions to Pennsylvania literature by naming her a Distinguished Daughter of Pennsylvania, along with her friends Pearl Buck and Violet Oakley and nine other productive women who claimed Pennsylvania as their home.

Joseph Wood Krutch reviewed Singmaster's novel *Bennett Malin* for the *Nation* in 1922. He lamented that too few readers would pursue her fine new novel because of its old-fashioned point of view.

> There is some slight Jane Austen in Miss Singmaster's sharp delineation of society which has for her no illusions but against which she does not definitely rebel. . . . She seems thoroughly detached from the stream of contemporary thought and fiction. There is nothing in this book's manner of expression or in the ethical standards and values

ELSIE SINGMASTER

Fig. 16 Violet Oakley drew this sketch of Elsie Singmaster, which was used in advertisements of her publications in the mid-1920s. Oakley, the well-known Philadelphia mural painter, was inspired by Singmaster's story "The Battleground," which appeared in *Gettysburg: Stories of the Red Harvest and the Aftermath* (Boston: Houghton Mifflin, 1913), while she was painting the mural *Lincoln at Gettysburg*. Oakley's finished painting hangs in the senate chamber of Pennsylvania's Capitol Building in Harrisburg.

which it assumes which might not have been as readily employed fifty years ago as today. . . . It is old-fashioned New England but it is also vivid and real . . . an example of the vitality still possible in older methods and views, of the excellence which inevitably results from the sincere portrayal of character from any standpoint, be it the iconoclastic or the traditional.[153]

Krutch admired both Singmaster's sincerity of purpose and her literary merit, but he feared that her work would ultimately lose out to the preferred "revolutionary art and ethics" of the post–World War I period.

In 1936 the literary critic Malcolm Cowley characterized the "genteel" Howellsian literature of the 1880s and 1890s as a combination of English Victorianism and American Puritanism. He claimed that its staid, refined tone and circumscribed viewpoint adopted learned European conventions of the mind but denied the practical experience of middle-class Americans. Indeed, local color literature, rejected by Cowley, had begun to lose its literary supremacy by the early years of the twentieth century, when naturalist writers associated "feminine" Victorian attributes with regional writing.[154] Frank Norris, Stephen Crane, Theodore Dreiser, and other naturalist writers of the early years of the new century expressed their belief that the limited scope and overwrought emotion of regional writing could not encompass the hard facts of life in modern industrial America. Regionalism's "insularity . . . confinement . . . attention to detail . . . and . . . moral vision"[155] marked it as feminine, in historian Donna Campbell's assessment, and that designation distinguished it from the broad, passionate masculine style and themes of naturalist writing. "Realism is minute," wrote Norris, "it . . . bows upon the doormat and goes away and says to me, as we link arms on the sidewalk: 'That is life.' And I say it is not."[156] The new generation accused the polite Victorians of ignoring the here and now, "the beauty-in-ugliness of the American empire as it is today," in favor of an idealized past.[157] Rebelling against the perceived timidity and life-denying attributes of "women's writing," the naturalists established a "counter-tradition" and a gendered literary identity that separated them from women's literature.[158]

Campbell suggests that Americans in the first two decades of the twentieth century felt confined by the limits of regional literature and rebelled against them. The expanding magazine industry challenged publishers to print fiction that satisfied a larger but less educated audience than the cultured, protected female audience of the Victorian period. Readers expressed a new appreciation for the sensational and the romantic. "Lurid realism" described the underside of life and stood in contrast to Howellsian realism, where the bad and good in life were more balanced.[159] While local color artists like Singmaster wrote stories that exemplified the strength and integrity of their regional forebears during hard times, naturalist writers pitted characters against their inherently brutish human nature. Naturalist writing commented critically on the harshness and inequalities of industrial society; it described in grotesque detail the extremes of human experience. Utterly unlike local color writers, the naturalists were interested in the alienation and loss of individuality they saw as the consequences of urban industrialism. Both realism and naturalism influenced American writing into the 1920s, but realism's dominance had given way.[160]

The experience of World War I further separated young writers like Hemingway and Fitzgerald from the meaning and order portrayed in genteel fiction and echoed by these writers' Victorian mothers. During the 1920s, the persistent concept of the "Mother God of the Victorian Era" was challenged anew by returning veterans whose appetite for excitement had been kindled by the horrors of war.[161] The resistance of Jazz Age sons and daughters to the overprotective mothering associated with genteel writing diminished the appeal of Singmaster's type of writing. Like Singmaster's beloved nephew's depiction of his attentive aunt, perhaps, they felt that women of their mothers' generation were like bossy governesses, "in the wings pulling the strings."[162] They sought the freedom to script their own stories.

A writer for the *Nation* who reviewed Singmaster's novel *Ellen Levis* (1921) regretted the book's restraint and artificial contrivances, charging that Singmaster lacked the courage to venture beyond the genteel parameters of a bygone era. "There can be no question in regard to Miss Elsie Singmaster's talent, honesty of purpose, and knowledge," he wrote, but she "will not exhaust her situations . . . for any deeper searching of her people's hearts and minds. . . . She is tied to a notion of 'plot,' of a pattern of action invented and imposed from without. . . . This is more to be regretted since only a strong imagination and a firm hand could have described the progress of the flabby Amos toward sin and change and communicated the pathos of the old 'Kloster's' desertion and decay."[163]

A *New York Times* review of *The Hidden Road* (1923) commented similarly that the novel was "based upon a theme that is not particularly new or well worked out, but this is a secondary matter when the reader becomes acquainted with the slightly foreign, quaint, amusing, white-minded town people who drift through the chapters of the book."[164] And a *New Republic* review of *Keller's Anna Ruth* (1926) read, "The skill with which characters and situation are presented, the careful reticence of style, the strength and delicacy of draughtsmanship, only serve to emphasize a trite and sentimental story."[165] In the last of these, the Pennsylvania German character Anna Ruth Keller overcomes the miserliness she has learned during her lifelong servitude at her father's small-town grocery store. A spiritual awakening and an inheritance from her father help Anna Ruth achieve her dreams. The progressive *New Republic* dealt largely with national issues relating to industrialization. Despite the reviewer's apparent admiration for Singmaster's style and characterization, he saw Anna Ruth's story as contrived and simplistic when viewed against the complex circumstances in which America's urban immigrants found themselves.

SINGMASTER'S RESPONSE TO CRITICISM

Singmaster did not try to adapt her style to changing literary tastes. She remained steadfast in her aim of improving the minds and hearts of her readers through her work. She had commented early in her career on the lack of popular appreciation of highbrow literature and music in her humorous yet poignant essay "My Adventures in Criticism" (1912), written for the *Atlantic Monthly*'s "Contributor's Club." The world's citizens "are contented with poorer things when they might have better, they will not read Browning or listen to Bach," she lamented, but she knew she was powerless to change public taste. "I am ceasing to criticize," she continued, "except from the safe shelter of anonymity . . . because my complaints have not been productive of one iota of good. Moreover, they have always been ungraciously received either by the person whose good I sought or by the person upon whose sympathy I was depending. Those whose good I sought have not listened to me."[166] Still, Singmaster was clearheaded about her personal standards and held to them, whether she could influence others by her good example or not.

Dayton Kohler aptly summed up Singmaster's attitude. "As sturdily independent as one of her own characters, she follows no literary fads or fashions. . . . Her pages are as uncluttered with psychological or sociological documentation as her style is free from affectation. . . . She does not care for raw passions or fellow travelers in her own life, and she has seen no reason to put them into her books."[167] In novels like *Basil Everman, Ellen Levis,* and *Bennett Malin,* in which Singmaster's characters confront dark human impulses, the treatment of place, style, and plot typical of her local color stories was not adequate to express the heightened emotional turmoil. The *Nation*'s review of *Ellen Levis* complained that Singmaster was more concerned with the "picturesqueness and charm" of her story rather than with the satisfactory resolution of its plot.[168] Another *Nation* review of *Basil Everman* commented on the "warm and charming picture of her little college town . . . the external characteristics and harmless little oddities of her people," but regretted that "Basil Everman . . . comes out . . . not strong and impassioned and magnanimous, but only pure and clean and straight."[169]

Perhaps Singmaster suffered from the same difficulty that had plagued earlier local colorists like Sarah Orne Jewett and Mary Wilkins Freeman, who had written romance novels merely to satisfy their public but whose lack of deep interest in the project made the books less than convincing. In response to Jewett's novel *The Tory Lover* (1901), Henry James begged her, "Go back to the dear *Country of the Pointed Firs,* come back to the palpable present-*intimate* that throbs responsive, and that wants, misses, needs you, God knows, and that suffers woefully in you absence."[170] The *New Republic*'s D. B. W. wrote similarly, "One can only hope that Miss Singmaster's genre pictures of Pennsylvania may return to their former vigorous composition and sturdy structure."[171]

The Victorian concept of women and motherhood continued to shape Singmaster's viewpoint, and her work, over the years. As in her own case, the concept of motherhood was more that of shared femininity than of biological reality. It was expansive, theoretically, seeing women not as confined to the home but as empowered to assume broader moral leadership through social and religious programs and organizations. The female moral prerogative involved the sacred responsibility to treat the world as their household, the arena in which their influence was traditionally unquestioned. Organizations like the Women's Missionary Society (WMS) embodied the concept of educating members not to compete in the male-dominated arenas of church, academia, politics, and commerce but to be better "mothers" and thus bring to bear on the wider world a positive influence.[172] Singmaster belonged to the WMS for fifty years and worked faithfully with others to bring the Christian Word to less fortunate "heathen" peoples.[173] In her "Seminary Hymn," mentioned above, Singmaster describes a serene yet strong and enduring feminine presence—the institutional mother who first taught and then replenished her world-embattled graduates with the "oil of wisdom."[174] This was the same type of powerful feminine image that publishers and fathers of the early era of realism both promoted and protected by guiding their daughters' refined tastes and sensibilities. Naturalists and postwar authors and critics, by contrast, cast Victorian women writers aside, declaring them unfit for real life and therefore for real literature.

Records from the 1943 ULCA Board of Deaconess Work's Council of Women, over which Singmaster presided, illustrate the predominant view of women's social and spiritual influence during this era. According to the council's speakers, women's feminine nature was nurturing, comforting, and inspired by God's spirit. They assured the female audience that their gender alone gave them the power to promote world peace in a way that men, presumably, could not. Mrs. Bertram Pickard, a lecturer from the Women's Clubs of America, asked the professional Lutheran women to follow the example of the Chicago reformer Jane Addams, to "carry home values into the larger world," and she reminded them that "the law of love which turns a house into a home will turn the world into a home."[175] Dr. F. Eppling Reinartz, a Lutheran pastor, told the council, "Women have a unique task, and unique contribution in war time. They have the task of rearing babies, teaching youth, strengthening maturity and comforting old age, in a way that shows they are God's contact with persons."[176] And Dr. Bertha Paulssen, a German-born social theologian from the Gettysburg seminary, claimed that women's work during World War II had the power to connect the mechanized, technical male world to the eternal and the "Spirit Sphere."[177]

The new generation of the 1920s refused to acknowledge women's special, God-given prerogative. Influenced by Sigmund Freud's psychological theory, America's young urban population equated the feminine with weakness rather than with God. Young artists in the Jazz Age turned away from the sacred assumptions of their Victorian mothers' world.[178] In holding on to her strong ideals and rejecting the ideas and methods of the moderns, Singmaster saw her popularity diminish. The Lutheran pastor Robert Koons remembers with sadness that one day in the 1940s, while he and Singmaster were sitting together on the porch of the seminary refectory waiting to go in to dinner together, students passed by without greeting them. Singmaster looked at her friend and said, "You know, Bob, these young men act as if they don't know who I am."[179] The successful woman writer whose home was situated just next door to the refectory, once the daughter of the seminary president and the author of the seminary hymn, had ceased to be honored for her social place, her professional achievements, or her wisdom. This loss of status grieved Singmaster. While writing *Pennsylvania's Susquehanna* in the late 1940s, Singmaster confessed to having difficulty finishing the manuscript. She was seventy-one years old when this final work was published, bringing a long career to a close.

Singmaster couldn't have known that the twenty-first century would offer an opportunity for a revival of her work. Like her characters, many Americans in today's world are mobile, living in transitional surroundings that support their need for "information and capital."[180] Though they know little about their new communities, they express a longing to settle into a place they can call home. In response, local historical, cultural, artistic, and literary projects throughout the country reveal America's expansive interest in regional projects that help define local and national identities. As part of the ongoing discussion of home, anthologies such as Elizabeth Ammons and Valerie Rohy's *American Local Color Writing, 1880–1920* (1998) have reprinted regional stories of the nineteenth and twentieth centuries and have analyzed local color's early efforts to capture the essence of America. Interest in women's local color writing since the 1960s has encouraged a renewed appreciation of that marginalized genre in the traditional canon of American literature. Singmaster's Pennsylvania German fiction shares the common concern of citizens and scholars today who ask how America's identity can be widely inclusive while also retaining the rich cultural variety of its population. Carmen Birkle's essay "Home Away from Home: The Construction of Germany and America in Elsie Singmaster's 'The Lèse-Majesté of Hans Heckendorn'" (2005) has brought Elsie Singmaster's writing into the current discussion of ethnic American cultural transition and identity.

In recent years, Julia Kasdorf's *Fixing Tradition: Joseph W. Yoder, Amish American* (2002) and David Weaver-Zercher's *The Amish in the American Imagination* (2001) have studied sectarian Pennsylvania Germans in the context of mainstream culture. Both books suggest that Pennsylvania Germans continue to capture the imagination of Americans who try to comprehend the ever-growing complexity of their country's population in historical and cultural context. Both Kasdorf's and Weaver-Zercher's discussions and Beverly Seaton's essay, "Helen Reimensnyder Martin's 'Caricatures' of the Pennsylvania Germans" (1980), have given considerable attention to Martin's popular but controversial writing, but the value of Singmaster's more sympathetic Pennsylvania German fiction is acknowledged only in an occasional footnote. To appreciate the full value of Pennsylvania German literature and its impact on the ever-changing American scene, it is necessary to revisit Singmaster's contribution to it. It is my hope that readers of the stories reprinted in this volume will recognize that Singmaster has earned a place in the local color canon and in Pennsylvania German studies.

HER FINAL YEARS

The routine of work, community and church activities, public engagements, and family and social relationships constituted the essence of Elsie Singmaster's adult life. After 1950, health complications interrupted her established routine. One evening she became terribly alarmed when she lost her train of thought during a speaking engagement. After that incident, she refused invitations for public addresses. Some time later, Singmaster fell down the stairs at the Lewars House, which frightened her sister-in-law and housemate, Ethyle Singmaster.[181] Ethyle feared she could no longer take care of Elsie, and in 1952 the seventy-three-year-old left Ethyle behind in her beloved home and moved into Pape's Convalescent Home in Gettysburg. After an extended illness, Elsie Singmaster died at Pape's on September 30, 1958. In his funeral sermon at Christ Lutheran Church in Gettysburg, Herman Stuempfle commented: "The time for mourning has been a span of years during which we have watched a stricken body becoming an increasingly poor instrument for the keen mind and gracious spirit which it housed. None who knew the Elsie Singmaster Lewars of former years has been untouched by the long sad ending of a life so rich in talent and so generous in expending it."[182] Singmaster was buried near her husband, Harold, their infant son, her parents, and other family members in the Singmaster/Lewars plot in Fairview Cemetery in Macungie. Her estate was distributed according to her last will and testament, filed June 19, 1951. The final distribution of her earthly possessions revealed Singmaster's lifelong loyalties to faithful friends and helpers, to family, and to the Gettysburg seminary.

CONCLUSION

Singmaster's friends agree that she would most prefer to be remembered for her literary accomplishments. She was indeed part of the upper echelon of writers in the first half of the twentieth century, and it is fitting that attention once again be drawn to her work. In 1931 and again in 1947 Dayton Kohler predicted that Elsie Singmaster would be credited as one of the best writers of her time. In 1936 Anne T. Eaton wrote in the *New York Times Book Review* that Elsie Singmaster stories and books appealed to both adults and children through "characters whose . . . personality and reality . . . will endure."[183] When Simon and Schuster published *The Saturday Evening Post Treasury*, a volume including "what is probably the upper one fourth of the Post's contents" from 1897 to 1936, Elsie Singmaster's "Wildfire" was chosen for the anthology, along with stories by Edgar Allan Poe, Stephen Crane, O. Henry, William Faulkner, Stephen Vincent Benét, Mary Roberts Rinehart, and other renowned American writers.[184] Singmaster's story "The Survivors" was included in Martha Foley's *50 Best American Short Stories*, a collection of "the finest works of short fiction that appeared in American periodicals between 1915 and 1964." In recent years Singmaster stories have appeared in anthologies of Civil War fiction. *Civil War Women* (1988) includes the Gettysburg story "The Battleground," and *Civil War Women II* (1997) includes "Mary Bowman." *Gettysburg: Stories of Memory, Grief, and Greatness* is a reprint of Singmaster's *Gettysburg: Stories of the Red Harvest and the Aftermath* (1913). Other books and stories have been reprinted, but many of Singmaster's Pennsylvania German stories are available today only in used book stores, old magazine sales, or library special collections.[185]

Singmaster's fiction is filled with the humor, challenges, and dangers of living a particular lifestyle at variance with the social and cultural norm of one's adopted country. While they establish a historical record of Pennsylvania German life and identity, her stories may also represent the ongoing reality of cultural pluralism in twenty-first-century America. Singmaster's patient and sympathetic focus on tolerance and understanding can encourage today's Americans to encounter with equal forbearance those new and different Americans who attempt to balance the familiar and the unfamiliar in their journeys toward inclusion without cultural self-abnegation. Sectarian subgroups like the Amish continue to be a viable part of America's population, and Singmaster's stories call our attention to their continuing efforts to enmesh their old German American ways in the wider society to create a sense of belonging for their people.

Singmaster, like other women regional writers in early twentieth-century America, tested her role in life from the margins, in the belief that she, like her people, would find a place and a voice. Though her outlook was optimistic, Singmaster's stories reveal her familiarity with the social underbelly of racial, gender, and class differences that isolate outsiders from mainstream American life. She was a realist, but she believed in God's providence on earth and hoped to cooperate with God's unfolding plan for good. Her stories also reveal her faith in the strength of the committed human spirit to press ahead toward acceptance and inclusion despite differences. Under God, America and its great state of Pennsylvania, in Singmaster's view, were lively environments for the development and personification of the individual freedoms protected under the U.S. Constitution. Though the achievement of equality was experienced unevenly by the various groups of Pennsylvania Germans and by American women, Singmaster gave voice to the promise and the dream of American opportunity for all.

As Singmaster's long career progressed, some readers believed that her voice, tone, and themes promoted the status quo or even a return to old ways that no longer applied to new circumstances. Her conservative point of view, the habit of looking back to reflect on the past while moving ahead, was mistaken for retrogression by more radical modernists. But Singmaster, to the contrary, looked forward to a better America, and she encouraged her readers to get ahead through hard work, promoting women's rights, and seeking a fairer and more equal definition of American citizenship. Singmaster envisioned American progress within the context of the ideals of the country's forefathers. She felt compelled to honor the past and its lessons amid ongoing discussions of America's present and future. The difference between popular and critical reception of Singmaster's work provides an interesting insight into the interchange of ideas between America's readers and writers in the first half of the twentieth century, as well as a historical reference point for divergent literary opinions on identity and equality.

Elsie Singmaster's treatment of women perhaps best illustrates her desire to challenge limits without upsetting tradition. By the standards of neither early feminists nor their modern counterparts would Singmaster be labeled a radical feminist. She was forthright, but she rejected the outright rebellion of feminist forebears like Elizabeth Cady Stanton or Matilda Gage, who wanted to separate Christianity from the cause of uplifting women. Singmaster continued to value and to work within existing male-dominated structures like the church and the publishing industry. She adapted her voice to the expectations for women of her time. Similarly, her Pennsylvania German women characters tested and expanded their limits, but they often retreated again behind the borders of a gendered existence for the sake of familiarity, loved ones, or valued tradition. Best seen as "reformist" feminism, this one-step-forward, one-step-back dance that often characterizes women's journeys toward equality typified both Elsie Singmaster and her Pennsylvania German women, as they moved selectively and unevenly toward full inclusion in American life.[186]

American society changed dramatically during the course of Singmaster's lifetime, as cultural norms evolved and the national Christian identity gave way to religious pluralism. Individual differences protected by the Constitution preempted the seemingly cohesive views of earlier American society. Protestantism no longer dominated American religious life. The Victorian ideal of noblesse oblige no longer structured American society or allowed an elite class to define American norms. Elsie Singmaster, however, continued to define herself through her literature and public service, dedicating herself to the ideal of the Christian Victorian woman writer. While Singmaster's tenacious consistency helped define her integrity, it also separated her from the social and literary mainstream of her day and denied her enduring prominence in American literary history. Her legacy must now be reclaimed from the margins so that Singmaster may once again be appreciated on the merits of her life and work, and for her contribution to the preservation of the American experience.

A memo from one Houghton Mifflin staff member to another noted that Singmaster was "very cut up" about the negative review of *I Speak for Thaddeus Stevens* that appeared in the *Boston Herald Tribune* in May 1947.[187] She experienced this kind of criticism, like her loss of status at Gettysburg seminary, as painful rejection. Her steadfast perseverance in the face of such rejection only underscores her commitment to the high standards and ideals she set for herself and encouraged in her readers. It also exemplifies her resolute character, molded in the community of her Pennsylvania German people. It was this kind of perseverance amid change and loss, the essence of the Pennsylvania German legacy as she understood it, that she hoped to preserve and pass along. When read in the context of both American history and Elsie Singmaster's personal experience, the Pennsylvania German stories reprinted here preserve not only the author's excellent prose but her insight into the ever-evolving American dream, of which her Pennsylvania Germans were—and are—a valuable part. The fiction, the reality from which it was imagined, and the writer's craft all have earned a place in the telling of the American story.

Notes

1. Quoted in Richard T. Sutcliffe, "Meet Elsie Singmaster!" *Lutheran,* June 8, 1949, 21.

2. Singmaster, *The Magic Mirror* (Boston: Houghton Mifflin, 1934), 270.

3. Esther Forbes, "A Literary Pilgrimage to Elsie Singmaster: The Home and Scenes of a Chronicler of the Life of the Pennsylvania Countryside," *Boston Evening Transcript,* book section, July 3, 1926, 1.

4. Quoted in Harry R. Warfel, *American Novelists of Today* (New York: American Book Co., 1951), 620.

5. Clark S. Northrup, assistant professor of English, Cornell University, to chairman of the Committee on Admission from Other Colleges, Radcliffe College, Cambridge, November 17, 1904, RG XXI (student files), series 1, box 110, Radcliffe Archives, Schlesinger Library, Radcliffe Institute, Harvard University, Cambridge, Massachusetts.

6. David Singmaster, "Genealogical Newsletter Number 2," January 1976, copy in author's possession. The arrival of the *Patience* is also documented in Ralph Beaver Strassburger, *Pennsylvania German Pioneers,* 2 vols. (Norristown: Pennsylvania German Society, 1934), 1:408.

7. According to David Singmaster, the name Zangmeister was changed to Singmaster sometime between the Revolutionary War and the War of 1812. George and Phillip Zangmeister served in the Revolutionary War and Jacob Singmaster (son of George) in the War of 1812. In addition, the family is mentioned in the *Pennsylvania Archives,* 3d ser., vol. 13, *Provincial Papers: Proprietary and Other Tax Lists of the County of Bucks for the years 1779, 1781, 1782, 1783,*

1784, 1785, 1786, ed. William Henry Egle (Harrisburg: Wm. Stanley Ray, State Printer, 1897), where we find a 1784 reference to one George Singmaster, who registered sixty acres of land, one house, one outhouse, and seven people, and another reference, also in 1784, to Phillip Singmaster, who registered fifty acres of land, one house, and four people. A German fraktur birth/baptismal certificate for Carolus, born in 1801, spells the family name Singmeister.

8. The name of Millerstown was changed to Macungie on November 8, 1875, because the town was often confused with another Millerstown in Perry County, Pennsylvania.

9. James Singmaster obituary, Singmaster family scrapbook, Macungie Historical Society, Macungie, Pennsylvania.

10. Quoted in Warfel, *American Novelists of Today,* 619.

11. Dr. Ascan Westermann, *Ein Jahrhundert aus der Geschichte der Familie Zangemeister, 1415–1521* (Heidelberg: Heidelberger Verlagsanstalt und Druckerei, 1911). Note the addition of an "e" to the spelling "Zangemeister" in the German title.

12. *Luther's Correspondence,* critical ed., 127 vols. (Weimar: Hof-Buehdruckerei und Derlagsbuchhandlung, 1935), 6:525. The Zangmaister in the index of this volume refers to Eberhart, the mayor of Memmingen in 1533, when the Reformation was introduced in that city. Another variation in the spelling of the family name occurs in this source.

13. Günther Bayer, *St. Martin, Memmingen* (Memmingen: Evang.-Luth. Stadtpfarramt, St. Martin, 1967), 6.

14. Charles H. Glatfelter, *Pastors and People: German Lutheran and Reformed Churches in the Pennsylvania Field, 1717–1793,* 2 vols. (Breinigsville, Pa.: Pennsylvania German Society, 1980–81), 1:25.

15. Luther A. Gotwald Jr., Davidsville, Pennsylvania, to Susan C. Hill, Gettysburg, March 7, 1998.

16. Elsie Singmaster Lewars, Gettysburg, to Julia, Keota, December 3, 1923, copy in author's possession.

17. Elsie Singmaster Lewars, Gettysburg, to Sadie, Keota, January 31, 1940, copy in author's possession.

18. Harold S. Lewars wrote the music for hymn numbers 48, 65, 84, 91, 537, and 563 in the *Common Service Book of the Lutheran Church* (United Lutheran Church in America, 1918). He published *Hymns and Songs for the Sunday School* in 1914 (Lutheran Publication Society) and *The Primary Hymnal: Hymns and Songs for Little Children* in 1915 (Lutheran Publication Society).

19. In Singmaster's book *The Long Journey,* the author wrote a dedication "to William Black Lewars, a descendant of John Conrad Weiser and Conrad Weiser." William Black Lewars (1910–1984) was most probably the son of Ralph P. Lewars, brother to Singmaster's husband, Harold Lewars. In a letter of November 17, 2005, from Frederick S. Weiser to the author, however, Weiser (the general editor of *Weiser Families in America* [New Oxford, Pa.: Penobscot Press, 1997]) wrote that the Lewars family was not in fact descended from Conrad Weiser. "Conrad's great granddaughter, Eva Weiser, 1788–1880, married . . . Henry Lewars who had only a daughter Adelaide Lewars before he died. Thus the surname Lewars disappeared from Weiser progeny probably before Harold Lewars' father was born."

20. See the Web site of the Conrad Weiser Homestead, at http://www.conradweiserhomestead.org/history.htm. Tulpehocken is an area of Pennsylvania named for its proximity to the Tulpehocken Creek, which runs through parts of Berks and Lebanon counties.

21. E. S. Lewars, Gettysburg, to Ferris Greenslet, New York, July 17, 1916, folder 2, bMS Am 1925 (1656), Houghton Library, Harvard University, Cambridge, Massachusetts (hereafter Houghton Library).

22. Steven M. Nolt, *Foreigners in Their Own Land: Pennsylvania Germans in the Early Republic* (University Park: Pennsylvania State University Press, 2002), 115.

23. John Alden Singmaster, "Big National Convention of Women's H.& F. Missionaries," MS box 3, A. R. Wentz Library, Lutheran Theological Seminary, Gettysburg, Pennsylvania.

24. "Fourth Meeting of the Sub-committee on Literature and Publicity, March 17, 1916," United Lutheran Church in America, old box 8, old folder 30, Quadricentennial Celebration of the Reformation, Literature Committee file, ibid.

25. E. S. Lewars, Gettysburg, to Ferris Greenslet, New York, March 18, 1917, folder 2, bMS Am 1925 (1656), Houghton Library.

26. E. Clifford Nelson, ed., *The Lutherans in North America* (Philadelphia: Fortress Press, 1980), 292–93. The United Lutheran Church in America merged with other Lutheran bodies to become the Lutheran Church in America in 1962. In 1987 the Lutheran Church in America joined with the American Lutheran Church and the American Evangelical Lutheran Church to form today's Evangelical Lutheran Church in America.

27. Forbes, "Literary Pilgrimage to Elsie Singmaster," 1.

28. Mary R. Hess, "Elsie Singmaster" (master's thesis, Pennsylvania State University, 1929), Elsie Singmaster Special Collections, file 1000, folder H, p. 5, Adams County Historical Society, Gettysburg, Pennsylvania.

29. Lewars to Greenslet, April 11, 1921, folder 5, Houghton Library.

30. The "Martyr Book" refers to the traditional Mennonite *Martyr's Mirror* (1660), a book that describes the persecution of Anabaptist martyrs between 1524 and 1600. The "almanac" is probably the popular Pennsylvania German almanac published by Johann Bär and Sons, Lancaster, Pennsylvania.

31. Susan Hill Lindley, *You Have Stepped Out of Your Place: A History of Women and Religion in America* (Louisville: Westminster John Knox Press, 1996), 52.

32. Ibid., 54.

33. Hess, "Elsie Singmaster," 3–5.

34. Forbes, "Literary Pilgrimage to Elsie Singmaster," 1.

35. Sutcliffe, "Meet Elsie Singmaster!" 20.

36. Quoted in Warfel, *American Novelists of Today*, 619.

37. James Arthur Singmaster Jr., interview by author, Gettysburg, July 24, 1998.

38. Quoted in Warfel, *American Novelists of Today*, 619.

39. Singmaster, *Bennett Malin* (Boston: Houghton Mifflin, 1922), 254.

40. Elsie Singmaster Lewars, Gettysburg, to Ira Rich Kent, New York, October 4, 1932, folder 12, Houghton Library.

41. Singmaster, "The High Constable: A Millerstown Burglar Story," *Outlook*, April 28, 1915, 1026.

42. Singmaster, "The Christmas Guest," in *Stories to Read at Christmas* (Boston: Houghton Mifflin, 1940), 133.

43. Charlotte W. Swope, interview by author, Gettysburg, July 1998.

44. Patricia R. Hill, *The World Their Household: An American Woman's Foreign Mission Movement and Cultural Transformation* (Ann Arbor: University of Michigan Press, 1985), 42.

45. Elsie Singmaster Lewars, Gettysburg, to Sister Anna Ebert, Philadelphia, March 14, 1943, United Lutheran Church in America, Deaconess Collection, archives of the Evangelical Lutheran Church in America, Chicago.

46. Sister Mildred Winter, interview by author, tape recording, Philadelphia, 1999.

47. For more information, see Charles H. Glatfelter, *A Salutary Influence: Gettysburg College, 1932–1985*, 2 vols. (Gettysburg: Gettysburg College, 1987), 2:586–92.

48. "History of the First 25 Years of the Women's General League of Gettysburg College," 1936, Special Collections, Musselman Library, Gettysburg College. Although direct reference to Singmaster's gift is not mentioned in this history, the organization as a whole raised and contributed $20,000 from its endowment fund to reconvert the former Gettysburg Academy building (now Huber Hall) into a women's dormitory. Before the dormitory was built, there were no housing facilities for female students at Gettysburg College.

49. Mary Lou Schwartz, interview by author, Gettysburg, September 1998.

50. Donald P. McPherson Jr., "Mrs. Lewars' Service to the Community," *Gettysburg Seminary Bulletin* 39 (August 1959): 4–5.

51. Dayton Kohler, "Elsie Singmaster and the Regional Tradition," *Commonwealth: The Magazine for Pennsylvania*, September 1947, 16.

52. Singmaster, "The Pennsylvania Germans," folder P, p. 7, Adams County Historical Society.

53. Charles H. Glatfelter, *The Pennsylvania Germans: A Brief Account of Their Influence on Pennsylvania*, Pennsylvania Historical Studies no. 20 (University Park: Pennsylvania Historical Association, 1990), 39–41.

54. Singmaster's character Katy Gaumer recites Henry Harbaugh's poem "Das alt Schulhaus an der Krick" in "The Belsnickel."

55. Glatfelter, *Pennsylvania Germans*, 58.

56. Phoebe Earle Gibbons, "Pennsylvania Dutch," *Atlantic Monthly*, October 1869, 473.

57. Helen R. Martin, "American Backgrounds for Fiction: The Pennsylvania German," *Bookman*, November 1913, 244–45.

58. Beverly Seaton, "Helen Reimensnyder Martin's 'Caricatures' of the Pennsylvania Germans," *Pennsylvania Magazine of History and Biography* 104 (January 1980): 94–95.

59. Review of *Kitty [sic] Gaumer*, by Elsie Singmaster, and *Martha of the Mennonite Country*, by Helen Reimensnyder Martin, *Nation*, March 4, 1915, 250.

60. Quoted in Julia Kasdorf, *Fixing Tradition: Joseph W. Yoder, Amish American* (Telford, Pa.: Pandora Press; Scottsdale Ariz.: Herald Press, 2002), 153.

61. Fred Lewis Pattee, *A History of American Literature Since 1870* (New York: Century, 1915), 23.

62. William Dean Howells, "Editor's Study Columns," in *Editor's Study*, ed. J. W. Simpson Troy (New York: Whitson, 1983), 98, quoted in Stephanie Foote, "The Cultural Work of American Regionalism," in *A Companion to the Regional Literatures of America*, ed. Charles L. Crow (Malden, Mass.: Blackwell, 2003), 32.

63. Donna M. Campbell, "Realism and Regionalism," in Crow, *Companion to the Regional Literatures of America*, 94.

64. Ibid., 100–101.

65. Ann Douglas, *Terrible Honesty: Mongrel Manhattan in the 1920s* (New York: Noonday Press, 1995), 304.

66. Elizabeth Ammons and Valerie Rohy, "Introduction," in *American Local Color Writing, 1880–1920*, ed. Elizabeth Ammons and Valerie Rohy (New York: Penguin Books, 1998), xv.

67. Donna M. Campbell, "In Search of Local Color: Context, Controversy, and 'The Country of the Pointed Firs,'" in *Jewett and Her Contemporaries: Reshaping the Canon*, ed. Karen L. Kilcup and Thomas S. Edwards (Gainesville: University Press of Florida, 1999), 72.

68. Simon J. Bronner, *Folk Nation: Folklore in the Creation of American Tradition*, American Visions Readings in American Culture no. 6 (Wilmington, Del.: Scholarly Resources, 2002), 3–8.

69. Ammons and Rohy, "Introduction," vii, x–xi.

70. Foote, "Cultural Work of American Regionalism," 33.

71. Ammons and Rohy, "Introduction," vii.

72. Campbell, "Realism and Regionalism," 93.

73. Garland quoted in Pattee, *History of American Literature*, 375.

74. Foote, "Cultural Work of American Regionalism," 38.

75. Earl F. Robacker, *Pennsylvania German Literature: Changing Trends from 1683–1942* (Philadelphia: University of Pennsylvania Press, 1943), 126.

76. Quoted in Warfel, *American Novelists of Today*, 620.

77. Reader's notes on *Bred in the Bone*, March 13, 1924, bMS Am 2030 (C 1952), Houghton Library.

78. Singmaster, "The Golden Rug," *Woman's Home Companion*, January 1929, 15.

79. Gavin Jones, *Strange Talk: The Politics of Dialect Literature in Gilded Age America* (Berkeley and Los Angeles: University of California Press, 2004), 16–34, 94.

80. Ibid., 10.

81. Singmaster, "A Millerstown Prodigal," *Outlook*, February 28, 1914, 493.

82. Singmaster, "Zion Hill," *Country Gentleman*, December 22, 1917, 12.

83. Russell A. Kazal, *Becoming Old Stock: The Paradox of German-American Identity* (Princeton: Princeton University Press, 2004), 21–22.

84. Janet L. Dotterer, Millersville, Pennsylvania, to Susan Hill, Gettysburg, October 15, 2004, e-mail.

85. Quoted in Mary Spotten Groff, "Elsie Singmaster, Pennsylvanian" (master's thesis, University of Maine, Orono, 1934), 47.

86. Robacker, *Pennsylvania German Literature*, 153.

87. Singmaster, *Magic Mirror*, 3–4. Singmaster gave examples of each form of speech: "'Wir haben einem Studenten!' cried Frans Huber" (High German); "'Ach, mir hen en student!' John Lichty laughed" (Pennsylvania German); "'I bet it gives a student again!' scolded Jesse" (Pennsylvania English); "'Hark!' said Ida Conrad. 'We have a college student!'" (English).

88. Donald Radcliffe Shenton, "Contemporary Fiction on the Pennsylvania-Germans," *Allentown Morning Call*, July 3, 1943.

89. Kohler, "Elsie Singmaster and the Regional Tradition," 15.

90. Crow, "Introduction," in Crow, *Companion to Regional Literatures*, 1.

91. Karen L. Kilcup and Thomas S. Edwards, "Confronting Time and Change: Jewett, Her Contemporaries and Her Critics," in Kilcup and Edwards, *Jewett and Her Contemporaries*, 13.

92. Crow, "Introduction," 1–2.

93. Josephine Donovan, *New England Local Color Literature: A Women's Tradition* (New York: Frederick Ungar, 1983), 110.

94. Singmaster, "A Man in the House," in *Bred in the Bone*, 85, 275.

95. David Walbert, *Garden Spot: Lancaster County, the Old Order Amish, and the Selling of Rural America* (New York: Oxford University Press, 2002), 9.

96. Richard Ohmann, *Selling Culture: Magazines, Markets, and Class at the Turn of the Century* (London: Verso, 1996), 29.

97. Theodore P. Greene, *America's Heroes: The Changing Models of Success in American Magazines* (New York: Oxford University Press, 1970), 171–72.

98. Quoted in Frank Luther Mott, *A History of American Magazines, 1885–1905*, 5 vols. (Cambridge: Belknap Press of Harvard University Press, 1957), 4:546.

99. Jan Cohn, *Creating America: George Horace Lorimer and the Saturday Evening Post* (Pittsburgh: University of Pittsburgh Press, 1989), 10. Lorimer served as editor of the popular magazine from 1899 to 1936 and as publisher from 1932 to 1934.

100. Ohmann, *Selling Culture*, 1–10, 15.

101. Ferris Greenslet, Singmaster's editor at Houghton Mifflin, was an associate editor at the *Atlantic Monthly* from 1902 to 1907, before becoming literary advisor and director at Houghton Mifflin in 1910. The *Atlantic* became part of Houghton Mifflin when the publishing house merged with Ticknor and Fields in 1878.

102. Foote, "Cultural Work of American Regionalism," 31.

103. Ohmann, *Selling Culture*, 252.

104. Singmaster, "Does It Pay?" *Current Literature*, October 6–10, 1930, 17.

105. Frederick S. Bigelow, *A Short History of "The Saturday Evening Post," an American Institution in Three Centuries* (Philadelphia: Curtis, 1927), quoted in Cohn, *Creating America*, 5–6, 189.

106. Singmaster, *A Cloud of Witnesses* (Cambridge, Mass.: Central Committee on the United Study of Foreign Missions, 1930), 9.

107. Mott, *History of American Magazines*, 4:698.

108. Quoted in ibid., 4:769.

109. Salme Harju Steinberg, *Reformer in the Marketplace: Edward W. Bok and the Ladies' Home Journal* (Baton Rouge: Louisiana State University Press, 1979), xvii.

110. Mary Ellen Zuckerman, *A History of Popular Women's Magazines in the United States, 1792–1995* (Westport, Conn.: Greenwood Press, 1998), 138.

111. Singmaster, "A Student of Languages," *Woman's Home Companion*, October 1927, 75.

112. Douglas, *Terrible Honesty*, 27.

113. Nolt, *Foreigners in Their Own Land*, 3–4.

114. Carmen Birkle, "Home Away from Home: The Construction of Germany and America in Elsie Singmaster's 'The Lèse-Majesté of Hans Heckendorn,'" in *How Far Is America from Here? Selected Proceedings of the First World Congress of International American Studies Association, May 22–24, 2002*, ed. Theo D'haen (Amsterdam: Rodopi, 2005), 395.

115. Nolt, *Foreigners in Their Own Land*, 3–4.

116. The Bach Festival celebrated its hundredth anniversary in 2007. The Bach Festival Choir performs Bach's Mass in B Minor each year during the first two weekends in May on the campus of Lehigh University. The work was first performed in Bethlehem on March 27, 1900, at the Central Moravian Church. The location changed to Lehigh University in 1912.

117. Elsie Singmaster Lewars, "The Pennsylvania Germans," c. 1936, Archives of Christ Lutheran Church, Wentz Library, Lutheran Theological Seminary, Gettysburg, Pennsylvania.

118. Richard N. Current, review of *I Speak for Thaddeus Stevens*, by Elsie Singmaster, *Pennsylvania Magazine of History and Biography* 71 (1947): 294.

119. Dayton Kohler, "Elsie Singmaster," *Bookman*, February 1931, 621.

120. Singmaster, *Martin Luther: The Story of His Life* (Boston: Houghton Mifflin, 1917), 72.

121. Frederick K. Wentz, ed., *Witness at the Crossroads: Gettysburg Lutheran Seminary Servants in the Public Life* (Gettysburg: Lutheran Theological Seminary at Gettysburg, 2001), vii.

122. Singmaster, *The Book of the United States* (New York: George H. Doran, 1926), 315–16.

123. Greenslet to Lewars, January 9, 1923, folder 21, bMS Am 1925, Houghton Library. Greenslet proposed that Singmaster would receive 10 percent of the first ten thousand sales and 15 percent of any additional sales.

124. Reader's notes, November 15, 1937, bMS Am 2030, E9272, ibid.

125. Kent to Lewars, December 28, 1940, folder 26, ibid.

126. Kent to Lewars, April 9, 1942, and May 28, 1942, ibid.

127. Reader's notes, February 15, 1933, D8716, ibid.

128. Reader's notes, March 13, 1924, C1952, ibid.

129. Willa Cather, "Willa Cather Talks of Work," in "The Kingdom of Art: Willa Cather's First Principles and Critical Statements, 1892–1896," ed. Bernice Slote, quoted in Terry Heller, ed., "Sarah Orne Jewett Text Project," Coe University, 1997–2005, http://www.public.coe.edu/-theller/soj/ess/cather-2.htm.

130. D. B. W., "Recent Fiction," *New Republic*, January 6, 1926, 198.

131. The four volumes are *1616–1781, 1723–1797, 1787–1830*, and *1835–1860*.

132. Lewars to Kent, September 9, 1942, folder 16, Houghton Library.

133. "Current Fiction, *Katy Gaumer*," *New York Times*, March 14, 1915.

134. J. K. Singleton, "New Novels," *New Republic*, June 27, 1923, 130.

135. Review of *Keller's Anna Ruth*, by Elsie Singmaster, *Saturday Review of Literature*, September 18, 1926.

136. Review of *Ellen Levis*, by Elsie Singmaster, *New York Times Book Review and Magazine*, March 13, 1921, 19.

137. "From Pennsylvania Soil," *Bookman*, May 1926, 350.

138. "Dr. H. C. Sherman Receives Columbia Award," *New York Times*, March 11, 1936.

139. Review of *When Sarah Saved the Day*, by Elsie Singmaster, *Pennsylvania-German*, December 1909, 633–34.

140. Preston A. Barba, review of *I Speak for Thaddeus Stevens*, by Elsie Singmaster, *Allentown Morning Call*, July 12, 1947.

141. "Our Leading Dutch Writer," editorial, *Allentown Morning Call*, October 1, 1958, 14.

142. Albert G. Hofammann Jr., "Elsie Singmaster Wrote of Dutch," *Allentown Sunday Call-Chronicle*, July 11, 1965.

143. "Elsie Singmaster Visits Allentown; Tells Hosts She Hopes Penna. Germans Will Never Change," Singmaster family scrapbook, Macungie Historical Society.

144. "Elsie Singmaster Will Be Here to Autograph Books," *Allentown Chronicle*, ibid.

145. Grace K. Nadig, Philadelphia, to Singmaster, Boston, November 15, 1940, copy in author's possession.

146. Barba, review of *I Speak for Thaddeus Stevens*.

147. Preston A. Barba, "To Our Readers," *Allentown Morning Call*, June 16, 1956.

148. Reader's notes, December 15, 1938, bMS Am 2030, G1719, Houghton Library.

149. Lewars to Kent, May 14, 1940, folder 14, ibid.

150. Lewars to Kent, June 5, 1942, folder 15, ibid.

151. Henry S. Borneman, Philadelphia, to Elsie S. Lewars, Gettysburg, January 25, 1943, Pennsylvania German Society Archives, Kutztown, Pennsylvania.

152. Dorothy Canfield Fisher, review of *A High Wind Rising*, by Elsie Singmaster, n.d., typewritten copy by James Arthur Singmaster in author's possession.

153. Joseph Wood Krutch, "Old and New," review of *Bennett Malin*, by Elsie Singmaster, *Nation*, August 30, 1922, 214.

154. Malcolm Cowley, *After the Genteel Tradition: American Writers, 1910–1930* (Carbondale: Southern Illinois University Press, 1936), 12–18.

155. Donna M. Campbell, *Resisting Regionalism: Gender and Naturalism in American Fiction, 1885–1915* (Athens: Ohio University Press, 1997), 23.

156. Frank Norris, "A Plea for Romance Fiction," *Boston Evening Transcript*, December 18, 1901, quoted in ibid., 4.

157. Cowley, *After the Genteel Tradition*, 13.

158. Norris, "A Plea for Romance Fiction," 5.

159. Campbell, *Resisting Regionalism*, 5.

160. Ibid., 51–55.

161. Douglas, *Terrible Honesty*, 217–53.

162. James Arthur Singmaster Jr., interview.

163. "More American Chronicles," review of *Ellen Levis*, by Elsie Singmaster, *Nation*, April 20, 1921, 596–97.

164. Review of *The Hidden Road*, by Elsie Singmaster, *New York Times Book Review*, June 10, 1923, 18.

165. D. B. W., "A New Oasis," review of *Keller's Anna Ruth*, by Elsie Singmaster, *New Republic*, July 28, 1926, 289.

166. Singmaster, "My Adventures in Criticism," *Atlantic Monthly*, December 1912, 853.

167. Kohler, "Elsie Singmaster and the Regional Tradition," 17.

168. Review of *Ellen Levis*, *Nation*, 597.

169. "The Mighty Average," review of *Basil Everman*, by Elsie Singmaster, *Nation*, March 27, 1920, 401.

170. Quoted in Campbell, *Resisting Regionalism*, 56.

171. D. B. W., "New Oasis," 289.

172. Catherine M. Prelinger, *Episcopal Women: Gender, Spirituality, and Commitment in an American Mainline Denomination* (New York: Oxford University Press, 1992), 24.

173. Hill, *World Their Household*, 174.

174. Lewars, "Seminary Hymn," *Table Talk*, May 1991, 4.

175. Mrs. Bertram Pickard, "Women in the Modern World," speech given before the Council of Women at the Deaconess Motherhouse, Philadelphia, March 13, 1943, pp. 12, 14, Archives of the Evangelical Lutheran Church in America, Chicago.

176. Dr. F. Eppling Reinartz, "Our Church in This War and in the Post-war Period," ibid., p. 24.

177. Bertha Paulssen, "Facing This Reality," ibid., p. 28.

178. Douglas, *Terrible Honesty*, 219–20.

179. Robert W. Koons, interview by author, February 1998.

180. Michael Kowalewski, "Contemporary Regionalism," in Crow, *Companion to Regional Literatures*, 8.

181. Elsie Singmaster Lewars inherited the three-story colonial brick structure her father had built for his retirement (1924) on the perimeter of the Gettysburg seminary campus.

Gettysburg's residents called the home "the Lewars house" in recognition of its distinguished owner. Lewars's will granted the Lutheran Theological Seminary first option to buy the house and its adjoining property. Today "the Lewars House" is the official residence of the current seminary president, Michael Cooper-White, and his family.

182. Herman Stuempfle, "Eulogy for Elsie Singmaster Lewars," September 1958, copy in author's possession.

183. Anne T. Eaton, "The Changing Art of Writing Books for Children," *New York Times Book Review*, November 15, 1936.

184. Frank Luther Mott, "The Tie to Franklin Was an Inspired Myth," review of *The Saturday Evening Post Treasury*, selected from the complete files by Roger Butterfield and the editors of the *Saturday Evening Post, New York Times Book Review*, October 31, 1954.

185. Frank McSherry Jr., Charles G. Waugh, and Martin H. Greenberg, eds., *Civil War Women* (New York: August House, 1988); Martin H. Greenberg, Charles G. Waugh, and Frank McSherry Jr., eds., *Civil War Women II* (Little Rock: August House, 1997); Elsie Singmaster, *Gettysburg: Stories of Memory, Grief, and Greatness*, introduction by Lesley J. Gordon (Tuscaloosa: University of Alabama Press, 2003). In addition, *Martin Luther: The Story of His Life* was reprinted in 2003, and *Rifles for Washington* in 2005, both by Kessinger Publishing in Whitefish, Montana. And the Macungie Historical Society issued *Katy Gaumer and Other Stories of Millerstown* in 2008.

186. Lindley, *You Have Stepped Out of Your Place*, x.

187. Memo, Mr. Brookes to Mr. Venn, May 29, 1947, "Elsie Singmaster" folder, Houghton Library.

SELECTED

PENNSYLVANIA

GERMAN SHORT STORIES

by

ELSIE SINGMASTER

BIG THURSDAY

Elsie Singmaster published "Big Thursday," with illustrations by Leon Guipon, in the January 1906 issue of *Century* magazine, while she was still a student at Radcliffe College. Her first published story was "The Lèse-Majesté of Hans Heckendorn" (*Scribner's*, November 1905), but "Big Thursday" was the first story for which she was paid, and it first established Millerstown as a Pennsylvania German place and the town's residents as quintessential Pennsylvania German citizens confronting a changing social and cultural environment. The story will have resonance for today's readers, as the Lehigh County Fair still takes place each year in Allentown.

* * *

From Slatington down to Hosensack, from Stinesville across to Centre Valley, Lehigh County was astir, though it was just dawn of a clear September morning. For this—an ecstatic thrill ran down one's spine at the mere mention—this was Fair Week; and, moreover, this was Big Thursday. There were other holidays, of course. Christmas was well enough in its way, and gaily celebrated in the county-seat. Out in the country, however, where purses were not so deep, they did not expect so much from Santa Claus. Fourth of July came in the midst of the busiest season of the year, and only faint echoes of the city's boom of cannon and blare of bells reached the farm. But Big Thursday! It was not alone because of his Jersey or Durham cattle in the sheds or his wife's pies or preserves upon the shelves of the exhibition buildings that the Pennsylvania German looked forward, from September to September, to Big Thursday. It was because he himself was part of the exhibit, he was the fair. He toiled all year on the farm or in the wire-mill or the cigar-factory in order that his family might hold up their heads among their neighbors; and now on this day he meant to lose his own individuality in that of the crowd—the biggest crowd, if you please, at the biggest fair in the finest State in this great and glorious country! If he had consulted the wish which hid itself down in the bottom of his heart, he would have gone to the fair alone. There was the wife, however, who had looked forward to this day as eagerly as he, and there were the children,—six, seven of them,—and there was the grandmother, who had not missed a Big Thursday for years and years. He could not for the world disappoint them, though he did have to engineer their slow progress through the crowd instead of cheerfully elbowing his own way alone. Besides, after dinner he could easily get away to lean on the race-track fence, and with thrills which caught his throat even now watch Prince Alert break the record. And last year he had seen among the signs in the Midway one which read: "Homo Bovino. Walk in! The Greatest Curiosity of the Age!" That creature he meant to inspect. The children were too young to see such things, and the wife—*ach!* she would not be interested. Besides, he could tell her about it afterward. He had caught a glimpse of the Homo Bovino, and was sure that he detected through the boy's thin clothing the straps by means of which hoofs had been attached to his poor crippled limbs.

The great trolley system, which, like a huge octopus, reached from the county-seat far into the next counties, could not, for all its doubling of forces and speed, gather in all those who wished to come. The foresighted started early; they arose at four o'clock, packed their luncheon, and hastened to catch the five-o'clock car, when, lo! they discovered that the whole village shared their prescience. Even the first car was crowded far beyond the minimum of safety. The country through which they sped lay like a vast garden, well watered, well tilled, fertile. Here and there on the hills, a single scarlet beech-limb or faintly yellowed hickory flung out a gay reminder that summer was almost gone. In the fence-corners the asters nodded gently, and the ironweed lifted its head proudly from the lush meadow-grass. There was a faint mist in the lowlands, and the morning breeze blew cool. Otherwise it was still summer.

The cars that day did not run straight to the Fair Grounds, as was their usual custom. Instead, in spite of loud objections, they emptied their passengers at Sixth and Washington streets, in the middle of the city, and twelve squares from the fair. Then with a loud clanging of gongs they started back whence they came, to Emaus and Millerstown, to Siegfried's and Coplay, to East Texas and Egypt, to gather in other waiting thousands.

Presently, in long trains which thundered down from the coal-regions or across from Berks County or "Chersey," came the visitors from other counties, eager to find some flaw in the management which might compare unfavorably with their own fair.

"It ain't so many side-shows like ours," Berks County would remark when once within the gates.

"I'd like to see them beat our record at the races," Northampton would rejoin proudly.

From the coal-regions came the miners. Encumbered with no women-folk or children, with the wages of a month in their pockets, they determined to forget for twenty-four long, glorious hours the blackness and heaviness of their toil. They pinned their return tickets in their pockets, and now for a day of it!

For several hours it seemed as though the fair itself were crowded into the space at the intersection of Sixth and Washington streets. And here, where the great arms of the octopus dropped their prey, in the midst of farmers from her own county, of envious kinsfolk from Berks and Bucks and Northampton, of miners from Mahanoy City, Shenandoah, Centralia, and riot-stained McAdoo, of city reporters who had quarreled among themselves for the privilege of reporting the "Dutch Fair," and of sporting-men who came to see the races, stood pretty Mary Kuhns, the prettiest girl in Miller-stown, a little village ten miles away. And Mary, who was usually accompanied by a train of gallants, was alone, and therefore a little frightened.

Until the evening before she had expected John Weimer, to whom she was to be married the next summer, to be her escort. Then, however, he had come to make his daily call, with a distressed expression on his round and rosy face.

"We cannot go to-morrow in de fair," he announced. "Pop's cousint at Oley he died, an' I must go to de funeral."

"An' miss de fair!"

"It iss no oder way, Mary. We can go Fridays in de fair."

"Fridays! You know it ain't no good Fridays. Were you, den, such good friends wis your pop's cousint?"

"No, I nefer once saw him. But pop he can't go because he has it so bad in his foot, an' mom she can't go because she has to stay by pop, an' it iss nobody left but me."

"Your pop's cousint, an' you nefer saw him, an' you must go all de way to Oley down to de funeral!" Mary's eyes blazed, and she sat up very straight in the rocking-chair.

"Now, Mary," he said soothingly, "you know how it iss wis funerals. We can go Fridays in de fair."

"*You* can when you want. *I* am going to-morrow. It iss me Fridays too slow."

"But, Mary, wis who den will you go?"

"Oh, I guess I can pick somebody up who does not haf to go to his pop's uncle's funeral. I get some one. I can sink already of somebody what would be glad to go, efen if his pop's aunt wass going to haf to-morrow her funeral. Or I can go alone. I sink dat would be, anyhow, de nicest. It iss me anyhow a boder to haf a man always along."

"Mary, when you would go alone in de fair I nefer forgive you."

"I sink I get along," she responded saucily. "Oh, dear, I am getting already sleepy. I sink it iss getting pretty late."

"But, Mary, all de people!"

"Where?" said Mary, as she craned her neck to see out beyond the honeysuckles.

"*Ach*, Mary, don't be so ugly! At de fair, of course."

"What do I care for de people? I am not afraid of people. When I haf trouble, I can ask de police. Dey will be dere, I guess."

"Mary!"

The creak of her rockers suddenly ceased.

"Chohn, tell me once dis: When a policeman's second cousint dies, dare he get off to go to de—"

"You da'sn't go alone, Mary Kuhns! Why, I rader ask Bench an' Chovina Gaumer to take you dan haf you go alone in de fair."

At this Mary rose stiffly. Benjamin Gaumer, who had been one of her own most devoted admirers, had the month before married Jovina Neuweiler; and though Mary was at the time engaged to John, Benjamin's defection had hurt her vanity more than she allowed any one to suspect.

"You can go right aways home," she said. "If you wass de only one in all de world what could go wis me to-morrow in de fair, yet I would go alone."

"Mary—"

But Mary had vanished within doors. He waited for a few minutes in sore distress.

"She had no business to get so mad. I can't help it pop's cousint had to die."

That she would venture to the fair alone he did not for a moment seriously consider. If she were independent like Jovina Neuweiler, he might believe her. But Mary was afraid of Weygandt's mildest cow.

Whether she was braver than he knew, or whether anger and disappointment had bestowed upon her a temporary courage, the next morning found her alone in the great crowd at the county-seat. She wore her best white dress, laundered to a smooth stiffness which would have supported its own weight without the four stiffer petticoats beneath. Although she was uncomfortably cool, she would not for the world have hidden any of the glories of her white dress under the jacket which her mother had bade her take, and which she carried on her arm. A sash of ribbon as blue as her eyes encircled her waist, and the frill of lace around her neck stood out like a little ruff of the Elizabethan period. Under her best hat—a white Leghorn trimmed with buttercups—her fair hair was brushed back as smoothly as its curly nature would allow. On her hands were her white mitts, drawn carefully back from her fingers so that John's ring, a garnet with two emeralds, should show. If the tears did threaten to start when she realized that she was alone, or remembered that she had not told her mother that John was not coming with her, her face wore a most deceptive mask of cheerfulness, so that many older eyes that day gazed with pleasure upon so much youth and innocence enjoying itself.

There had been many Millerstonians on the car by which she came—Billy and Sarah Knerr and their brood of six, Jimmie Weygandt and Linnie Kurtz, the young Fackenthals, and her own brother Oliver and his wife. Mary succeeded, however, in climbing aboard without being seen by any of them.

"Dey will sink it iss mighty funny dat he did n't come along," she said to herself.

As she listened to the gay chatter in the car her spirits rose. One could have a good time even by one's self. Any time that she got tired of being alone she could join the Knerrs or Ollie and his wife. Presently the fields gave place to long rows of suburban houses built close together, with tiny yards, as though there were no wide fields behind them. Their progress through the streets was slow, with long waits on the switches, then a sudden mad dash where there were double tracks. When they reached Sixth and Washington streets, Mary did not follow her fellow-townsmen through the crowd to the other car, but, mounting the steps which led into a store, she stood head and shoulders above the throng and looked out over them. Then she permitted herself an exclamation for which she had often reproved her brother Oliver.

"*Harrejä!*" she said; "it iss no end of people!"

Car after car added its quota to the multitude, then sped with clanging gong back whence it came. Bewildered-looking women pressed their way through the crowd, the balloon-man and the peanut-vender cried their wares at its edge, and round-faced, tanned youths, with bright ties, and flowers in their buttonholes, jostled one another with rough gaiety. Once the sound of a child's cry rang clear and sharp above the din, but was quickly lost in the shouting, the creak of the car-wheels, and the loud bells.

Presently Mary's eyes fell upon a group of men standing near her. She caught snatches of their conversation,—mentions of Prince Alert and Myrtle Peak,—and she watched admiringly the gleam of the huge diamonds in their shirt-bosoms.

"Well, I bet it 'll be the biggest thing this county ever saw," one of them exclaimed. "How much you got on it?"

She did not hear the man's answer, but suddenly the group turned and looked at her. She was not unaccustomed to admiring glances, but there was something about the rudeness of their stare which troubled her.

"I—I sink I go on," she said to herself, her cheeks afire, as she started up the street.

The Fair Grounds lay twelve long squares to the west, but Mary preferred the walk to the wild scramble necessary to secure a seat in a car. Besides, there were many interesting things to see—the shop-windows, the great white bear in front of the fur-store, the huge horse at the saddler's, and the dummies at the tailor shops, which were so natural that once, on a previous visit to the county-seat, she had asked some directions of one and been much astonished that he did not reply. There were also hundreds of people, old and young, by threes or fours or in family groups of six or seven, and many couples, sweethearts evidently, whose air of gaiety sent a sharp stab of envy to Mary's heart.

"He might 'a' come," she thought; "but what do I care? I am hafing chust so good a time as when he wass along."

She bought her ticket at the gate of the Fair Grounds, and then—

"But dis iss me first grand!" she said rapturously at her first glimpse of the enchanted country, bigger, more beautiful, noisier, and more crowded than ever before.

The grounds covered about eighty acres in the form of a square, inclosed by a tall fence. They had originally been covered by a thick grove of trees, half of which had been cut down; and it was there, on the wide, open space, that the chief business of the fair was conducted. There stood the exhibition buildings,—the main building, the agricultural building, the flower-house, and various other frame structures designed to shelter the treasures of the county,—and beyond them the long sheds whence came sounds which made the farmer feel at home at once—the low of cattle, the crow of roosters, and the long *baa-a-a* of sheep. Above them towered the grand stand, and beyond curved the race-track—"the best in the State," if you please, you Berks and Northampton county people. Near the entrance gate lay the Midway, "the size of which, ladies and gentlemen, we cannot guarantee, of course, to be equal to that of the great and only original Midway, but whose quality, we can assure you, is, if anything, superior." It consisted of two parallel rows of tents, their doors, before which platforms had been erected, facing each other, and the ground between beaten as hard as that of the much-vaunted race-track. At one end stood the tent of the famous Georgiana and her company of trained entertainers, "warranted, ladies and gentlemen, not to offend the most refined taste." Across the narrow alley, Penelope,—her manager pronounced her name in three syllables,—the Petrified Lady, exhibited her adamantine charms, and next door Bosco the Wild Man of the Siberian Desert rattled his chains, so that even the crowd outside, who had not money enough to pay the admission fee, could share the horror of his close proximity. The Homo Bovino—a favorite for years— was in his place, and the snake-charmers and the Rubber Man. If one only had money enough to see them all!

In the lower half of the grounds, under the trees, were the shooting-galleries, the merry-go-rounds, the great swings, the tents of the fortune-tellers, and, far beyond them all, stretching its length along the whole side of the great inclosure, a huge bar, where the sporting-man from New York clinked glasses with the Irishman from Hazleton, and the reporter who watched them planned to end his article on the Pennsylvania-German County Fair with this sentence, "The Pennsylvania Dutchman goes to his fair to see and be seen, but the dearest of all to his heart is the mammoth bar, at which, although it extends for the length of two city squares, it is hard to get standing-room."

And over all, from the entrance gate to the race-track, from the cattle-sheds down to that other long shed at the very bottom of the grove, hung Noise like a tangible thing. At a little distance not one of its elements could be distinguished. The cries of the managers of Bosco, of Penelope, of the Rubber Man, the weird fanfare before the tents of the snake-charmers, the shriek of tin whistles, the loud reports at the shooting-galleries, the blare of a band down toward the bar, the bucolic echoes from the cattle- and poul-try-sheds, the blasts of the calliope, the jingle of the mechanical piano at the merry-go-round, the sound of ten thousand voices—all blended into one great vociferation, indescribable, elemental.

It was small wonder that little Mary Kuhns should stand for a moment bewildered. It was hard to decide where to go first. Presently, however, she climbed the steps of the main building and went slowly down the broad aisle. Here hung a quilt composed, so its tag stated, of four thousand, four hundred, and seventy-six pieces, and beside it an elaborate crocheted spread.

There were wax-works, and hair-works, and paper flowers, rolls of crocheted or tatted lace, embroidered doilies, pincushions of unique design—one representing a huge carrot, another a tomato. After admiring them all, Mary hastened on to the food exhibit. There she found Linnie Kurtz's preserved peaches, Savilla Arndt's canned pears, and, standing proudly above them, Jovina Gaumer's cake, five layers high, with an elaborate scroll design in tiny pink wintergreen drops on its white icing. In its side yawned a huge wedge-shaped orifice from which the judges had cut the generous slice from which to test its quality. That it was satisfactory the blue tag, emblem of the first prize, declared.

Mary, however, was not thoroughly appreciative of this evidence of her towns-woman's skill.

"Pooh! what do I care?" she said to herself. "He nefer would 'a' married her when it had n't been for her cake. Now I am going to look once for Ollie's chickens and Chimmie Weygandt's cows."

She found them both, each with a blue tag above their stalls, then she laid her hand for an instant on Bossy's broad face.

"You know me, don't you, Bossy?" she said.

She wandered forth again past the side-shows and the race-track to the cool shadow of the grove, now transformed into one vast dining-room. The tomtoms had ceased to beat, the calliope blew out its last despairing note. Even the fortune-teller, with her prosaic husband by her side, partook of huge hot rolls and frankfurters in the doorway of her tent. The tents of Bosco and Penelope and the Homo Bovino were closed; and did not one's imagination halt before the abode of so much mystery, one might guess that they, too, were dining.

At the eating-stands there were several menus offered. For fifteen cents one could get a huge plate piled with sauerkraut and mashed potatoes; or, for a quarter, a large helping of stewed chicken and three or four waffles. Were one so lacking in discrimination as to care for neither of these delicacies, one might have fried oysters, or sandwiches—ham, chicken, beef, or tongue between thick slices of bread, or oysters or frankfurters between the halves of a long roll.

Mary hesitated for an instant between the chicken and waffles and fried oysters. Of the sauerkraut she would have none. She liked it well enough, to be sure, but one could get sauerkraut any day at home. Chicken and waffles were much more appropriate to high days and holidays, but fried oysters were rarest of all; and presently she sat with a plate of sizzling-hot oysters before her, and a huge saucer of cole-slaw beside the plate. She ate them both, down to the last crumb of oyster and the last bit of slaw. Then

"Why ain't Chohn den here wis you?"

"Ay, his pop's cousint died, an' he had to go to de funeral."

"Could n't you come Wednesdays or Fridays?"

"No."

"Well, could n't he stay away from de funeral?"

"Ay, of course not. Funerals come first, I guess."

"Well, you stay now here by me, an' we watch de races." The woman divined some lover's tragedy in Mary's indignant response. "Den you must find right away your folks. Look out once, you get your nice dress against de fence. See, dey are starting. See once! Look at de funny carts. It iss de brown one what iss de best. My man he saw him race already."

In the excitement she grasped Mary's arm. The roar of the crowd around them settled into a dull murmur, then into silence. There was a false start, then the horses were off again, four of them, almost neck to neck.

"Iss dat all?" cried Mary in bewildered disappointment of something, she knew not what. "Chust horses running?"

"You wait once," said the stout woman. "Twice around iss a mile. Chust watch once how dey fly!"

In a second Mary was holding her breath with the rest. She had never seen a race before, she had no preference among the horses, she knew nothing of the mad excitement of those whose money is staked upon the outcome of the race, to whom victory may mean plenty, defeat ruin. Nevertheless, a strange thrill shot through her, born of the sight of the clean-limbed, glossy-coated racers—which, she began to feel, were vastly superior even to Jimmie Weygandt's Bessie—and the consciousness of the strain and excitement in the crowd about her. In six seconds over two minutes the race was over, and Mary, her cheeks flushed and her eyes shining, leaned out across the fence, hurrahing with the rest.

Presently, when the shouts of the multitude were dying slowly away, she looked around for the stout woman, to find that in some way the crowd had pressed between them. Fearing that the big man might come back and speak to her again, she walked away. The side-shows were deserted except for their proprietors, and she wandered slowly down between the dirty tents. The snake-charmers, deprived of their audience for a while, watched her with curious wistfulness. There was an air of the woodland about her. One thought instinctively of wide meadows and the sound of softly flowing water bubbling from the cool edge of the woods, and of all manner of pleasant country things. The famous Penelope, who now sat in the tent door indulging in a little talk of the trade with her manager, eyed her curiously.

"Seems to me," she was saying, "if I was a man, I would n't be fooled so often. Once let a woman into this tent, and she'd be on to my petrifactions in less 'n no time. Gracious, Bill! Look at this a-comin'!"

Bill turned and regarded Mary as though she were a visitor from another world.

"They don't make 'em like that in New York, do they, Mamie? Can't you just see the hay growin' and hear the lambs bleat?"

"Well, I guess!" responded the fair Penelope. "But that girl ought n't to be wandering round here by her lonely—that she ought n't. I've half a mind to tell her."

The manager grinned. "Set down, Mamie. You 'd be a fine one to march up to that sprig o' youth and beauty and warn her against the ways of the wicked world, now!"

The woman drew the shawl which half concealed her shoulders a little closer.

"Sometime we're going to get out o' this business, Bill. It makes me sick."

"Nonsense!" he rejoined cheerfully. "You 'd be back in a week, Mamie. You know you would."

For the space of a second her eyes followed the white figure. Then she rose.

"Come on, git up and sing your little song," she said with a gaiety that was half real. "There's more galoots a-comin' to see Penelope. Make hay while the sun shines, for there is rain comin', or my name's not Mamie Bates, alias the Petrified Lady."

It was a tradition that Big Thursday was always fine. Now, however, in spite of the fair promise of the morning, low clouds began to gather in the west, hid from the crowds by the grove, and a low rumble, indistinguishable from the thunder of hurrahs, presaged the coming of an unseasonable thunder-storm.

Mary, as oblivious as the rest to the ominous sound, started slowly down through the grove. She had always wished to know what attraction at the lower end of the Fair Grounds drew so many people in that direction, and now she meant to find out. She looked lovingly at the merry-go-round as she passed. The manager had gladly started it at the appeal of a number of young people for whom the races seemed to have no attraction, and it ground out gaily "The Carnival of Venice," while its wooden horses curveted and lions pranced. Mary watched the riders enviously. Last year—

"I sink he need n't 'a' gone to his pop's cousint's funeral," she thought, her lips quivering like a child's. She began, alas! to be tired. She had been walking or standing since seven o'clock that morning, and it was now past four. There was no place to sit down, however, save the beaten, dusty ground, and she walked on down toward the great shed. As she approached it, the multitudinous shouts from behind gave place to another sound, akin yet different—the loud voices of men and women, raised now in heavy laughter, now in shrill dispute. Mary drew nearer. What could they be doing? Suddenly another sound, fainter but as continuous, reached her ear—the clink, clink of glass against glass, and Mary knew. For an instant she was too astonished to move. They did not come and go, these men and women crowded together. They stood and drank and drank, and quarreled or laughed, and drank again. Mary, who, with all her kith and kin, was "strictly temperance," fled, fearful lest the fate of Sodom and Gomorrah should suddenly encompass her. She would go home, straight back to Millerstown. As she passed the exhibition building, the wide, dusty steps, almost deserted, looked so inviting that she sat down for an instant. A man reeled by and she caught her breath in a sob. Suddenly her fright became terror. A stream of something wet and cold struck her in the neck, and she sprang up and looked fearfully around. At her side stood a young man who held in his hand a small squirt from which the water had evidently come.

"What do you mean?" demanded Mary, angrily. "I did n't do you nossing."

For reply, he pointed the little toy at her again. The conviction dawned slowly upon her that he had sprinkled her on purpose. For a second she was speechless.

"W-when Chohn Weimer wass here, you get de worst srashing you efer had, dat I can tell you!"

The boy laughed.

"Or our Ollie or Chimmie Weygandt or Bench Gaumer!"

"You must haf a lot of fellers," he said impudently. "Come on; you be my girl for a while. We go an' get some lemonade wis a straw in it."

Suddenly Mary's deliverance came in the shape of a girl of about her own age, who, squirt in hand, deluged the young man's celluloid collar and purple tie with a well-aimed jet of water. Mary, more horrified than ever, started rapidly away.

The races were over, and she found herself suddenly pressed on all sides by the crowd. If she could only find Ollie, or the Fackenthals, or the stout woman, or some one to take care of her! Her taste of independence, at first sweet, had turned bitter. Oh, to be home getting supper, or sitting on the porch with John! But would John ever care for her again? The Weimers were all easy-going until they were roused. Then look out! Old John Weimer, her John's uncle, had not spoken to his wife for thirty years, although in all that time they had lived in the same house, eaten at the same table. Suppose her John should never speak to her again! At any rate, she would go straight back to Millerstown and tell him that she was sorry. She started toward the wide gate marked "Exit," her aching feet a little less painful now that they were set toward home, and her blue eyes bright again. Suddenly she felt a splash of water on her hand. She glanced around piteously. Why could they not let her alone? Then Mary's eyes, with more than fifty thousand other pairs of eyes, sought the sky. The storm was almost upon them. The loud rumble needed not the sudden hush to make itself heard. She was caught and whirled along in the mad rush for shelter. She tried at first to struggle out to the edge of the crowd toward the exit gate, but she could not move. Once she slipped and fell on one knee, and a man's strong hand lifted her from the ground. She looked up gratefully from under her broad hat, to meet a pair of sharp eyes and a sarcastic smile.

"Where 's your mother, my dear?"

Mary gasped. It was the big man! She ducked her head under the arm of another tall man on the other side, and elbowed her way frantically through the crowd. Her blue sash became untied and trailed behind her; but she heeded it not until, caught under a heavy foot, it held her back; then she gathered it around her. The rain came no longer in huge drops, but in wind-driven sheets which in a moment washed all semblance of stiffness from her hat and set it flapping about her face. She slipped into her jacket, which only made her shiver as it pressed her wet sleeves against her arms. Great red stains from her leather purse marked her white mitts. A woman pinched her arm spitefully as she rushed against her in her mad flight, and once a man swore, but she paid no need. She was afraid to stop; she expected each moment to see that sarcastic smile and hear that smooth voice, "Where 's your mother, my dear?" Suddenly the crowd gave way about her, and she caught a glimpse of the exit. One more determined shove, a ruthless stepping on her neighbor's feet, and Mary was out in the wide street, where thousands of people, rain-soaked and tired like herself, struggled for places in the street-cars. She tried in vain to climb up the steps of a car. As soon as she secured a foothold, she was pushed back. The crowd was no longer a good-natured holiday throng: it was a vast mob of selfish beings, worn out by the day's pleasuring, and angry at the storm which put an end to it.

As she looked about her she was astonished at the bedraggled appearance of the hundreds who started with her down Washington street. The men turned their collars up and their hats down, and thus tramped along in comparative comfort. But the women! Their skirts hung about them limp and soiled, their hats retained not a vestige of the gay jauntiness which had that morning delighted both the wearer and the beholder. One woman, who looked the more bedraggled because her dress had, like Mary's, once been white, tried to make friends with her.

"Dis iss once a surprise, ain't it—dis rain?" she remarked cheerfully. "Haf you den far to go till you get home?"

Mary looked at her, from the dripping roses on her hat to the soiled ruffles above her muddy shoes.

"I sink I do not know you," she responded with dignity.

"Nor I you," the woman answered sharply. "An' when you would see yourself once you would n't want to know yourself."

With which remark, she hurried on, leaving Mary dumfounded. How did she dare to talk to her like that? Was not this her best hat, her best dress, and her new blue sash? All at once Mary realized how she herself must look, and was properly punished then and there for her haughtiness. She had forgotten, in the blessed prospect of getting home, how her hat flapped against her face. She became suddenly aware of every wet stroke. She realized that her blue sash trailed behind her as she walked, and that her white dress was mud-splashed to her knees.

She plodded on. The west wind, which grew stronger as the rain ceased, was cold, even through her coat, against her wet arms; the water which had soaked through her thin shoes made curious noises as she walked. For a while she had lifted her skirts carefully; now she let them drop. They could not be any wetter or more soiled than they already were. In sudden hopelessness, Mary doubted whether she should ever reach Millerstown again.

The street seemed suddenly dark, then there twinkled out at the corner a faint blue light, then farther down another and another. When she finally came to Sixth and Washington streets her fright was augmented by bewilderment. The crowd of the morning seemed to have increased a hundredfold. It was not yet time for the excursion trains to leave, and the visiting thousands lingered here, waiting for any excitement which might befall. The car-despatcher shouted madly at his subordinates, who would not hear or heed; he cursed the people, who stood constantly between the tracks and, overestimating the patience of the motormen, were dragged almost from under the wheels of the cars by their friends.

Tears of relief started to Mary's eyes as she saw on the front of a car about to start the single charmed word, "Millerstown." She started forward and tried to climb aboard. The conductor, however, took her gently but firmly by the arm and moved her down from the running-board.

"No more room."

"*Ach!* take me along—please take me along!" she cried, but the car had gone.

How she spent the next hour she did not know. She was aware that several persons spoke to her as she hung about the edge of the crowd, but she could not remember what they said. Once she thought she saw the tall man coming toward her, but she did not move.

When the next car started, however, Mary was aboard. She knew there had been a wild scramble for seats, and she remembered a curious ripping sound which seemed to come from under the feet of the man next to her, and which probably marked the separation of the ruffles on her gown, but she did not care. She was going home.

The evening wind, damp and cold, sent shivers up and down her arms and across her shoulders. She would die of consumption. As well that, however, as anything else, since John Weimer no longer cared for her.

When they reached the little village between the county-seat and Millerstown, the car was emptied of all its passengers save her. Evidently the other Millerstonians, the Fackenthals, the Knerrs, and the Weygandts, had caught the earlier car. As they sped on, she could tell each foot of the way, though she sat with her eyes closed. The smell of tar at the pipe-foundry, the rush of dampness as they dashed through the little valley which Trout Creek makes for itself in the meadows, the grinding of the wheels as they climbed the slope on the other side, the mad leap of the car as they reached the long, level stretch where the conductor bade the motorman "Let her go," the sickening twist as they turned the sharp curve at the end, the blaze of the flaring bleeder at the furnace, and then—home!

Mary rose stiffly as the car stopped. Her teeth chattered.

"*Ach!*" she thought, "I can nefer again be happy so long as I lif!"

The conductor helped her down. Millerstown had gone to bed. There were lights here and there in the second stories, but beneath all was dark.

"Oh, dear! Oh, dear!" sighed Mary. "If only—"

A pair of strong arms infolded her, and the rest of the sentence was lost in a sob.

"*Ach,* Chohn!" was all she could say over and over again. Then: "But how could you get so soon home from your pop's cousint's funeral?"

"I did n't stay for de funeral," he said. "I went, an' I came wis de first train back. It made me sick. I wass so afraid because you might go alone in de fair, Mary. And de train wass late, an' I only chust got here. I haf been worried crasy, Mary. Were n't you scared, all alone?"

For answer she laid her cheek against his hand.

"I nefer, nefer, nefer will again do anysing what you say I da's n't," she answered.

THE VACILLATION OF BENJAMIN GAUMER

Courtship and marriage in the Pennsylvania German village take center stage in this story, first published in the March 1906 issue of *Century* magazine, with illustrations by Leon Guipon. Still single and enrolled at Radcliffe College when this story appeared in print, Singmaster playfully contemplated the balance of power in Ben's relationship with Jovina Neuweiler. Pennsylvania German food plays a role in Ben's courtship. Singmaster once received a letter from a reader who offered an in-kind payment for the author's good writing. It read, "I've been reading your account of Pennsylvania *schnitz und knep*. I can't make it, but I can make good mayonnaise and am sending you a jar."

* * *

"When I wass young—"

"Dat wass a good many years back, Sarah," interrupted old Peter Gaumer, ungallantly.

"When I wass young," Sarah Arndt went on,—"and dat was n't so many years back as when *you* wass young, Pit Gaumer,—de girls had more spunk as dey haf nowadays. Nobody would 'a' taken it from a feller dat he went one Saturday wis one girl and de next wis anoder girl."

"Perhaps de girls wass more anxious to get de fellers den as dey are now," said Peter, slyly.

"Nosing of de kind," old Sarah answered sharply. "It wass dat dey had more spunk."

"Well, who has n't now no spunk?" queried Peter, balancing a little more comfortably on the hind legs of his chair as he leaned against the tree in front of the Fackenthals' house. "Sit once down on de bench, Sarah, an' tell us from dese girls what haf n't no spunk."

Sarah sat down on the wide bench. She was a little old woman with sharp black eyes, which peered forth uncannily from under her black silk sunbonnet.

"Why, it iss Chofina Neuweiler and Mary Kuhns what are me too soft. Benj Gaumer he—"

"Now look a little out, Sarah! Benj iss my nephew."

"I don't care what he iss. He goes wis bos de girls."

"Well, I gif him right. Two girls are for sure better dan one, Sarah."

"Well, I sink it iss a sin an' a shame. When I wass Mary, I srow him ofer, or make him pretty quick srow Chofina ofer; or when I wass Chofina, I do de same sing. He would n't go twice wis anoder girl when he had once started to keep company wis me, dat I can tell you! We will easy see which one has de most spunk."

"Perhaps he don't know yet for sure which one he wants."

"Den I gif him notice he must pretty quick find out, dat iss what I would do." Old Sarah rose with a nimbleness which belied her seventy-five years, and went briskly away, and Peter gazed meditatively up the street to where, on the Neuweilers' door-step, sat Jovina, the daughter of the house, with his nephew, Benjamin Gaumer, by her side.

Benjamin was in reality the most miserable young man in the Pennsylvania-German village of Millerstown; for Benjamin halted between two opinions, or, to speak more correctly, between two girls, and though most of his waking thoughts for a year had been devoted to an effort to decide between them, he seemed to grow each day farther from a solution of the difficulty.

Mary Kuhns was the prettier of the two. She was short and plump, with light, fluffy hair, blue eyes, and a skin which no amount of exposure to the wind or sun could harm. Her voice, as Benjamin often said to himself, was "like old man Fackenthal's pigeons what coo so pretty." The women, alas! called her "flirty," which, translated into the masculine vocabulary, meant that direct glances were not the only method by which Mary beheld her fellow-man. She was so short that she could stand under Benjamin's outstretched arm, and he often remembered with delight how she fled to him for protection when Weygandt's old mooly looked at her in the lane. He had encouraged her with shameless deceit to think the mild beast dangerous, and she clung to him helplessly. Fortunately, he was not at hand the next day to see her walk through Weygandt's meadow, where there were thirty cattle, and switch them, even savage old Tom, with a willow switch as she passed.

There were times when Benjamin was positive that Mary was his choice. Then he grew hot with jealousy of John Weimer and Jimmie Weygandt, to whom she freely dispensed her favors, and he made up his mind that, before another day passed, Mary should be his. But—and in this hesitation lay his undoing—before he decided finally, it would be well to see Jovina once more.

Jovina was not pretty, except for her dark eyes. She was tall and spare and sallow, and her hair was a dull brown. Jovina, however, could cook, and for that reason her popularity was equal to Mary's. Plain cooking is not counted much of an accomplishment in Millerstown, for every woman is a good plain cook. There were a few, however,—Jovina, Savilla Arndt, and Linnie Kurtz,—in whose skilful hands cooking had become a fine art, and Jovina perhaps excelled all the others.

"Chofina can bake sirty-sefen kinds cake," her mother claimed proudly. "And she need n't look once in de receipt-book. She can make, of course, pancakes an' funnel-cakes an' *schwingfelders* an' waffles, besides. De sirty-sefen means fancy cakes."

Besides this, Jovina could make yeast-beer and root-beer and half a dozen fruit-vinegars. Her chicken and waffles, her *schnitz und knöpf*, her *latwerk* (apple-butter), were the envy of all the other women. Her soap was always the whitest, her dried peaches and corn were the most tasteful, her liver-pudding, sausage, and *pan-hass* (scrapple), the best in the village. Was it any wonder that the delicious flavors of the products of her skilful hands veiled for a while Mary Kuhn's saucy face and dimmed the tender glances of her blue eyes?

Had Benjamin been more sophisticated, he might have ascribed the duality of his love-affairs to the naturally polygamous instincts of man. So advanced a theory, however, had not yet become part of Millerstown's ethics. Each man was expected to love, cherish, and, in many cases, obey one woman, be she sweetheart or wife. Girls were allowed, on account of their natural fickleness, to change their minds. Any masculine wanderings from the narrow path of single-hearted devotion, however, were considered evidences of woeful weakness of character. Hence Benjamin, who had once shared Millerstown's old-fashioned opinions, and who had no new theories with which to console himself for his inconstancy, was thoroughly miserable.

"It iss n't any oder way about it," he would say despairingly to himself. "I must pretty soon decide. When I don't, den John Weimer or Jimmie Weygandt will perhaps get her. But perhaps it iss n't *her* what I want, but Chofina. An' den when it *iss* Chofina, she iss pretty spunky, an' perhaps she won't haf me when I put it much longer off."

As he ate Jovina's crullers and molasses-cake, he looked with eager anticipation down a long line of years during which crullers and "fine-cake" should be his daily fare. When he had thoroughly satisfied his hunger, he decided to ask her to be his. Then, as he ate still more, he began to think that perhaps he had better see Mary once again before taking so irrevocable a step. Mary's eyes were so blue, and there was such an alluring dimple in her chin! Mary was always so sweet-tempered, and Jovina—well, Jovina had a mind of her own.

Ten minutes on the Kuhnses' dim, vine-shaded porch with Mary by his side convinced him that it was not Jovina that he wanted at all. Poor, desolate Jovina, she would probably be heartbroken when she heard he was to marry Mary, but that, of course, could not be helped.

In another ten minutes he had again changed his mind; for Mary gave him a piece of chocolate-cake, "which I myself baked," she explained. Now Mary's was the exception which proved the rule of Millerstown's good cooking. Even everyday necessities, such as pie, bread, and fried potatoes, grew into strange things in her hands. When she attempted anything as ambitious as chocolate-cake, the result was sad to behold and worse to taste. At the first bite, Benjamin's lips puckered over a huge lump of baking-soda, and he said fervently to himself: "*Nay, bei meiner Seele! Des du ich net!*" ("No, by my soul! This I will not do!") Again the star of Jovina was in the ascendant. Should he ever get the taste of that soda out of his mouth? Certain delicious crullers suggested themselves as an antidote, and firmly convinced that "good cooking iss more dan good looks, for cooking lasts, and looks don't," he determined to seek Jovina the next day and offer her his heart and hand.

Jovina, however, to whose ears had penetrated some gossip concerning her willingness to share the attentions of her lover with another, was, naturally enough, in a bad humor, and the sharpness of her voice and the angry flash in her black eyes reminded Benjamin by force of contrast of another voice which was always soft, and other eyes in which he never saw aught but tenderness. Mary Kuhns was the girl who should be the future Mrs. Benjamin Gaumer. Mary, however, again fed him cake, with results disastrous to her prospects.

Thus it went on all the long summer. Millerstown did not for a moment appreciate Benjamin's situation, and undertook to tell the girls plainly what it thought. For its pains it got only a laugh from Mary and a scathing "It would be a fine sing for Millerstown when de folks would learn once to mind deir own business," from Jovina. Evidently the girls did not purpose to take any one into their confidence. No one thought of admonishing Benjamin. He had always been too ready with his fists to make that an inviting task.

The girls, meanwhile, who lived near each other on Church street, continued to be good friends.

Then one day Mary, coming out of Jovina's gate, met Sarah Arndt. The old woman greeted her with a sly smile.

"Well," she began, "did n't she do you nosing?"

"Who?" Mary asked in frank amazement.

"Ay, Chofina."

"Why, of course not. Why should Chofina do me anysing?"

The old woman laughed shrilly.

"Sure enough! You need n't act as when you did n't know what she said from you and Benj."

"From me and Benj?" A faint color began to show on Mary's cheek.

"Yes. She said dat you wass trying to get Benj Gaumer away from her, and dat she would settle you once."

"What will she do?" Mary spoke in angry haste.

"I don't know; but you better look a little out."

"I guess I can take care of myself; you can tell her dat once." Mary slammed her own gate defiantly.

That evening old Sarah stopped for a moment at the Neuweilers' to tell Jovina's mother that Mary said that she "would 'a' srown Benj long ago ofer, only she liked to tease Chofina." Both Jovina and Mary might have known better than to believe Sarah's tales, but the subject of their common lover had, through long teasing, become a sore point. So Mary walked by Jovina one day on the street without speaking to her, only to realize a second later that her trouble was unnecessary, as Jovina had turned her head the other way. After this there was openly declared rivalry between them for Benjamin's attentions. Whether they wanted his love was another question. Mary was just as cordial to John Weimer and Jimmie Weygandt as she was to Benj, and whether Jovina would ever really accept him was doubtful.

"Perhaps he gets after all left," said old Sarah. "Perhaps Mary will take one of de oders, and perhaps Chofina will at last get her spunk up and not haf him. When I wass young, girls had more spunk, dat iss what dey had. No man could fool so long round and yet mean nosing by it."

Meanwhile poor Benjamin grew more puzzled as each day went by. Mary's smiles seemed to grow more winning and her eyes deeper, and Jovina's "fine-cakes" lighter and more delicious. Then suddenly, almost without realizing it, he was engaged.

One Sunday evening he went to see Jovina, assuring himself, as he walked up Church street, that Jovina was the girl for him. His last call on Mary had not been very satisfactory. She had seemed less confiding, less sweet than usual, and had several times spoken sharply to him.

"She has also a temper," he said to himself. "I sink I take de cooking."

He did not find Jovina on the front door-step, where she usually received him, and, wondering a little, he opened the gate into the side yard and went around to the back porch to inquire of Mrs. Neuweiler whether her daughter had gone away. To his surprise, he found Jovina herself, in a new and most becoming pink dress, rocking vigorously back and forth in the rocking-chair.

"I sink you are fixed up pretty fine for de back porch, Chofina," he commented, gazing admiringly at her.

"Why, Benj?"

"Why, you ought to be sitting out front where de folks can all see your fine new dress."

"I am not fixed up for de folks," said Jovina.

Benjamin's mouth opened in astonishment. That coquettish remark from staid Jovina, who often harshly criticized Mary Kuhns for "making de men sink too much from demselves!" Jovina, who had yielded to an unaccountable impulse to be "flirty," blushed suddenly and becomingly.

"Shall we den go out front," she demanded with asperity.

"Well, I guess not," said Benjamin, firmly, as he sat down on the step at her feet. "I sink we will stay here—anyhow, a while. Your dress iss for sure fine!"

At this Jovina, who usually "gafe him a mousful" when he began to flatter, smiled sweetly.

"Look a little out; you might make me vain," she said.

"I guess it iss no danger, Chofina. Do you want to go dis efening in de church?"

"*Ach,* I don't know. Do you?"

"No."

"Well, den, I guess we won't go."

Benjamin gasped. Was Jovina actually making an effort to please him? Not once during the evening did she show any of her "spunk." She agreed with everything he said. Usually they had long and heated discussions about religious matters. It was just the time when the "New Baptists" were leaving the "Jonathan-Kuhns Baptists," and Jovina, who went, did not agree at all with Benjamin, who stayed. It was quite by accident that Benjamin introduced the subject this evening. He had such an exhibition of Jovina's temper the last time they discussed it that he might have known better than to try again. This evening, however, Jovina only said sweetly:

"I sink it would perhaps be better when we would talk from somesing else."

Whereupon, with all doubts driven from his mind, Benjamin proposed, and was immediately accepted.

"When shall we den get married, Chofina?" he asked.

"Oh, I sink I can be by Sursday all ready. I haf chust dis week made me dis new dress, an' I will buy me a coat an' hat."

"But, Chofina, I sought it took much longer to get ready to get married!" he exclaimed in surprise and consternation.

"It does not take so long of course as when we were going to housekeeping for ourselfs. We will, of course, lif here wis mam and pap. An' you haf dis new suit to get married in."

"Yes, b–b–but—" this mad haste took away his breath—"dis is me pretty much of a hurry. No—no—Chofina,"—he saw her figure straighten in the moonlight,—"I did n't mean nosing by it! I meant—I meant—could we get a minister so soon, Chofina?"

"I sink it would be a good sing when we would go ofer to New Chersey. Den all de busybodies in Millerstown need n't know nosing about it beforehand. I heard you say once dat when you got married dat would be de way what you would do. Besides, we need ofer in New Chersey no license."

"Yes, but—"

"I will of course tell mam and pap, and you can tell Wednesday efening your mam. Den we can slip easy Sursday morning away."

So occupied was Benjamin with his own thoughts that he scarcely knew how the rest of the evening passed. Finally he bade her good night and went home.

"It iss me too much of a hurry, dat iss what it iss," he said miserably to himself. "It iss n't dat I don't want to get married, or dat I don't want Chofina; but—but dere iss Mary Kuhns."

The old puzzle rose like a specter to harass him.

"Perhaps it wass only in my mind dat Mary wass de last time ugly to me," he thought. "Perhaps she wass a little chealous from Chofina. She iss ten times so good-looking as Chofina. Chofina iss me too homely."

He forgot Jovina's pretty new dress and the flush on her cheek. He knew now, once for all, which he wanted: it was Mary. He could feel the touch of her little hand and see the coquettish gleam in her soft eyes. And poor Mary! What would she do if he should marry Jovina? Perhaps it would break her heart and she would die, and he would be to blame. Mary was such a little girl! She was not big and strong like Jovina, who was almost as tall as he. What should he do? He could not go and tell Jovina that he had been mistaken. In the first place, she might hold him to his promise, and there would be an awful scandal, which would effectually put Mary beyond his reach. On the other hand, she might angrily release him, and he did not wish to break with her entirely. That would mean that he would *have* to take Mary. Of course he wanted to marry Mary, but he did not want to be driven to it.

His round and rosy face dropped in such doleful lines when he looked in the glass in his room that it made him almost sick with pity for himself. All night Jovina, tall, dark, and inexorable, seemed to stand beside his bed.

Nor was he any less miserable on the eve of his wedding. He had seen Jovina only once. Then she was very sweet to him, and there was a soft flush on her cheek. He began to feel easier. The same afternoon, however, he passed Mary on the street, and the alluring tilt of her chin sent him back into despair. He could scarcely attend to his work in the cigar-factory. The boss frowned, and the boys chaffed him gaily.

"You act as when your mind wass away some place. Perhaps it iss ofer by Mary, or perhaps Chofina. Which one is it anyhow, Benj?"

Benjamin frowned only a trifle less darkly than John Weimer, who said, "*Esel!*" ("Donkey!") under his breath.

When Benj went home for supper on Wednesday, a big plate of crullers occupied the place of honor in the center of the table.

"Chofina Neuweiler gafe dem to me," his mother explained. "I wass once ofer dere a little while dis afternoon. My! but Chofina iss a good cook. Don't you sink so?" She looked at him inquiringly, but his mouth was full and he did not answer. "I belief perhaps she iss going somewheres off to-morrow."

"Why do you sink she is going somewheres off?" Benjamin had not yet announced the fact of his approaching marriage. That would be the first decisive step, and he hesitated to take it. Now, however, he realized that the time had come when it could no longer be put off.

"*Ach,* nosing; only her mam said to her somesing about 'when you come back, Chofina,' and I sought perhaps she wass going somewheres off."

Thereupon Benjamin announced that he and Jovina proposed to journey the next day to New Jersey to be married. His mother, who had never liked Mary Kuhns, expressed her approval; and, buoyed by this and the memory of her crullers, he went to see Jovina in a fairly cheerful frame of mind. They planned to make the journey by trolley, starting at five o'clock in the morning. He decided not to notify the men at the shop that he was not coming, but to let his mother send the boss word after he had gone. It would be a good joke on Millerstown.

As the evening wore on, and Jovina seemed to prefer long silences to conversation, his cheerfulness waned. He saw John Weimer go swiftly past in the dusk and a furious jealousy added to his soreness of heart. He did not want to marry Jovina Neuweiler; he wanted to marry Mary Kuhns. Jovina noticed his gloom, but whether or not she suspected its cause, there was a solemnity about her good night which warned him that his choice was irrevocable.

He needed neither the alarm-clock nor the sound of his mother's voice to arouse him the next morning. Indeed, he was awake long before it was time to get up, and he was not sure that he had slept at all. He ate so little breakfast that his mother was frightened.

"You will feel bad when you do not eat somesing, Benj. Come now; here is some raisin-pie."

He silently shook his head. The unaccustomed splendor of his Sunday clothes worried him, and there was something about the exceeding tightness of his high collar which reminded him of the other yoke he was about to assume. He stole through the streets to the Neuweilers' more like a thief than a prospective bridegroom, and, avoiding the boardwalk, went around to the back door upon the grass. Jovina met him at the door, the bright pink of her dress reflected in the glow of her cheeks.

"Say, Benj," she began, "you go a little ahead down to de trolley, an' I will come a little behind. Den when de folks see us dey will not know dat we are wis each oder."

Thus admonished, Benjamin sped away with a sudden lightness of heart. The evil day was postponed for a few minutes at least. When Jovina met him down on Main street, however, his despair again overwhelmed him. The next time he saw that spot he would no longer be free. No longer could he live his own life. No longer could he join the boys in the gallery of the church on Sunday evenings; he would have to sit with Jovina. No longer could he dash gaily around the Copenhagen ring at the Sunday-school picnics, winning a kiss for a forfeit from every girl whose hands he could slap. He would have to stay close by Jovina now. And, worst of all, nevermore could he join the gay group on Mary Kuhns's doorstep; nevermore could he take her walking or trolley-riding. Nevermore could his hand linger caressingly on hers as he bade her good night; nevermore would her glances at him be aught but straightforward and direct. He was back for the moment on the Kuhns's porch in the summer dusk, and Mary was laughing as she tried to get her hand away. Benjamin smiled.

"Benj!" He came back to the awful present with a start. This was not dusk;

it was dawn. The girl at his side was not gentle Mary; it was tall, stern Jovina—Jovina, whom he was about to marry!

"Well?" he answered dully.

"Don't you see den de car!" she exclaimed.

He raised both arms in a wild signal to the motorman, and the car, speeding toward them like a Juggernaut, stopped with a great grinding of wheels.

"It would haf been a fine sing when we had got left!" commented Jovina as they climbed aboard.

As they passed Sarah Ann Mohr's, that good lady was just opening her front door. Benjamin ducked his head, hoping she had not seen him. Jovina, however, gaily waved her hand, and, as Benjamin looked back, he beheld Sarah Ann, her fat arms akimbo, the light of knowledge beaming in a broad smile on her cheerful face. Their engagement was announced.

As they sped past the creamery, the farm-wagons with their shining cans had begun to drive up, and again Benjamin bent his head. Jovina, however, sat all the straighter, proud in the consciousness that she wore a becoming new dress and that she was going to be married. There was little conversation between them. She called his attention to Jimmie Weygandt as he started around his wheat-field, scythe in hand, to mow the first row before the reaper; and Jimmie, who neared the fence as they turned the corner by his fields, waved his hat and shouted. Jovina's "Hello Chimmie!" was the only answer he received. Already Benj could see him seated by Mary Kuhns's side on the porch, dark in the shadow of the honeysuckles. The more his face darkened, however, the more cheerful did Jovina become. She hummed a hymn as they dashed on, she admired the goldenrod flaming into splendor in the fence-corners, and presently she slid along the bench toward Benj.

"It hardly seems true dat we are going to be married, does it now?" she asked.

"No, it don't," he said quickly. Was Jovina beginning to have doubts as to the wisdom of their proceedings? "Are you sure it iss den for de best, Chofina? Are you sure we haf not den hurried ourselfs too much? Do you sink we had perhaps better go back?"

"No, indeed, Benj! I am sure," Jovina interpreted his questions as the effort of a doubting lover to assure himself of her affection.

"You will den nefer repent?"

"Nefer, Benj; nefer. I—I haf lofed you dis long time; I—" Jovina's remarks were suspended while she grabbed for her hat, which threatened to blow off in the blast created by the tremendous speed at which they dashed through the street of the next village—"I wass not fery happy for a long time till I found it wass I and not Mary Kuhns what you lofed."

Benj groaned. Was it right for a professing Christian—a Johnathan-Kuhns Baptist at that—to enter into an agreement in which the other party was the victim of a delusion? Would it not be better to break the fact to Jovina that it was not she whom he loved best, but Mary? Again, however, his old doubts assailed him.

"If I do dat, den Chofina will nefer look at me again. Suppose I should den want her! An', besides, if Chofina wants to say dat we wass going to get married, and den I would n't, eferybody will belief her; for Sarah Ann she saw us going off in de trolley. When a fellow an' a girl go off so early in de morning in de trolley, it means dat somesing iss up."

He could not understand how it was that he had happened to propose. He forgot again Mary's heavy chocolate-cake and her coldness to him. Nor did he think of Jovina in her new dress flushing softly as he complimented her.

They reached the county-seat before he was aware. There, even though it was only six o'clock, the town was thoroughly awake. The day seems to begin an hour earlier in southeastern Pennsylvania than in other places. The cars which passed as they waited for the Easton car were crowded with men going to their work down at the wire- or rolling-mills. A little later a crowd of girls and women on their way to the silk-mills and shoe-factories would fill the streets. A man who was sweeping the old-fashioned double porches of the United States House at the opposite corner threw down his broom as he helped the porter carry out the heavy satchels of departing guests of the house, who dashed wildly across the pavement and into a carriage, meanwhile calling to the driver to "Hurry up once or we miss the train!" Already the doors of an establishment at the other corner swung vigorously back and forth. Men pushed them in swiftly, then came out more slowly, wiping their lips. The car-dispatcher, standing in the middle of the tangle of tracks, shouted strident Pennsylvania-German oaths at the motormen and conductors, who in turn answered him as gruffly.

When the lumbering "double-trucker" marked "Easton" swung around the corner from Hamilton street into Sixth, Benj and Jovina climbed aboard and began the second stage of their journey. There was little danger that any one would guess that they were prospective bride and groom. The frowns on Benj's brow did not lift for an instant, and, as time went on and all her efforts at conversation failed, Jovina's face also lost its cheerful expression. Benj gazed mournfully out of the window on one side of the car and Jovina on the other, he with bent shoulders, and she with head high in the air.

It was about eight o'clock when, having left the car at Easton, they crossed the Delaware bridge into Phillipsburg, New Jersey.

"I sink it iss perhaps early yet to go to de preacher," said Benj, after a long silence. "Perhaps we had better take a little walk once. De folks do not get so early up here like in Lehigh County."

"All right," assented Jovina, cheerfully. "I wonder where dese steps go." As she spoke, she pointed to a flight of steps which fell from the street-level.

"We will see once," he answered. She followed him down the steps, which lay along the side of the steep river-bank. At the foot they came upon a little railroad station. The tracks followed the windings of the river along the New Jersey side. Overhead, on another road, thundered the heavy freight-trains back to their own county-seat.

"I sink dis would be a pretty good place to rest," said Jovina as she spied the seats in the little waiting-room. "It iss noisy here, but it iss quiet, too."

She led the way thither, and they sat down. The station-agent eyed them curiously as they waited for half an hour in solemn silence. Then Benjamin arose, and Jovina, who had begun to think that Phillipsburg, even it if were slower than Lehigh County, would by this time be thoroughly awake, prepared to follow.

"You wait here a little," Benj commanded as she gathered up her pocket-book and her gloves. "I will go first out and walk up an' down a little."

"Well, I guess I go wis."

"No; you will get tired. You stay here." There was such sternness in his voice that Jovina sank back. Did he purpose to run away? She determined to change her seat to where she could watch every inch of the little platform. Just as soon as he started up the steps she would find her at his side. She yielded for the first time to her suspicions that perhaps Benj was beginning to repent, and she grew each moment more angry.

"If it wass not for one sing he might go back," she said to herself. "An' dat iss dat by dis time all Millerstown knows eferysing about it. Sarah Ann Mohr she saw us, and besides, I told mam dat by dis time she could tell. Go back and not married, when I start out to get married! I guess not! It iss too late now for him to sneak out of it. If he only knew somesing what *I* know, he might be glad enough. But dat sing I will not tell him—not yet, anyhow. In a half-hour we will be married; den it will be time enough."

In spite of the firm purpose betokened by Jovina's tightly pressed lips and flashing eyes, she was, at the end of a half-hour, still the same Jovina Neuweiler. As Benj walked up and down the platform, he realized that the time for procrastination was past. Each moment his anguish grew more intense.

"It don't make anysing out now what happens," he thought. "I would be willing to do wisout Mary, too, and nefer get married, if only I did n't haf to marry Chofina. I don't care for cooking or nosing. Mam's cooking iss me plenty good enough."

Wild thoughts of flight sped across his brain. There, however, stern, watchful, implacable, sat Jovina. He looked nervously at his watch. It was already after nine o'clock. He expected each moment to see her at the door, beckoning him to follow her up the steps. Presently she appeared.

"Benj!" she called. "What time iss it at your watch?"

He pretended not to hear, and she called the second time in tones which admitted of no misunderstanding.

"I don't know for sure. Wait once; I look." He drew his watch slowly from his pocket.

"It iss somewheres near nine," he said weakly.

"Well?" demanded Jovina.

"Well? well?" he repeated in confusion. "How do you mean wis 'well,' Chofina?"

"I guess you know what I mean. I sink it iss a funny sing when—"

"Chofina, wait once." He interrupted frantically the rush of her speech. "I haf a plan. Wait once a minute, Chofina."

Jovina waited at least five.

"Well?" she said again.

"Why, it says here on de time-table dat a train goes to Riegelsville at nine-sirty. I used to know a preacher what wass preaching dere. Don't you—d–d–don't you—" Benj stammered madly in his excitement—"don't you sink it would be a good sing to go once down dere an' get married?"

Jovina considered the proposition for an instant. The railroad ran down the Jersey side of the river. Had it been the Pennsylvania side, she would have concluded that Benj wished to delay the ceremony until it was too late in the day to get a license. In Jersey, however, they would need no license, hence he could gain nothing by delay. She did not object to satisfying what appeared to be only a harmless whim. It was only nine o'clock, and they had the rest of the day before them.

"But, Benj," she exclaimed, "it will cost to go down to dat place. We haf spent already a good deal money."

"What do I care for money!" he said with reckless prodigality. "We haf safed on de license."

"Haf you got de tickets?"

"No; wait once. I get dem." He vanished swiftly into the station. As he waited for his change, he looked back. There stood Jovina in the doorway.

Her hat cast a shadow across her face which to him appeared like a deep scowl.

"*Ach*, I'm coming!" he said hurriedly. Had it begun so soon as this, that she would watch him every minute? The cheerfulness caused by the prospect of a delay vanished instantly. He pictured Mary at his side. How differently she would have acted!

It never occurred to him to help Jovina up the steps of the car. He climbed up himself and sank despairingly into the first seat, half of which was already occupied, whereupon Jovina, who followed close at his heels, seized him by the arm.

"Are you den not right?" she demanded, and he rose and followed her to a vacant seat. Presently she called his attention to a strong odor of mint which seemed to envelop them.

"It iss a powwow doctor lifs along here," she explained. "Sarah Ann Mohr told me once from him. Lots of folks come from Beslehem an' Nazares an' lots of places in Norsampton County ofer. He gifs much medicine, an' it smells of mint."

Benjamin, however, plunged in despair, heard not a word. Nor did the conductor's loud "Riegelsville! Riegelsville!" make the least impression upon him. He did feel, however, Jovina's clutch upon his arm.

"It iss Riegelsville," she said. "Come on!"

Benjamin came. Now at last his bachelor days were ended. He made, however, another brave effort.

"I sink perhaps dat preacher has mofed away."

"It don't make nosing out when dat one has mofed away. I guess dere iss anoder."

Jovina kept her hand on his arm till, having left the station, they followed the other passengers toward the dark opening of a covered bridge.

"Wh–where are you going?" he queried.

"Can't you see de town iss ofer here? We must pay first toll, I guess. De town iss on de oder side of de bridge."

Benj paid, forgetting for once in his life to count the change. When they stepped again upon solid ground, he suddenly halted.

"Chofina!" he almost shouted, "we are again in Pennsylfania. It wass de rifer what we crossed."

"Well, what of it?"

"We can't get married in Pennsylfania wisout no license."

"Den we go back to where we come." Her voice was terrible in its sternness. Was this his little game? Benj, however, had never before been within a dozen miles of Riegelsville, and knew nothing of its topography. He regarded this as a special interposition of Providence in his behalf.

"But, Chofina, it would not bring good luck to go back to a place for a second time to get married."

"We are going to Phillipsburg to get right aways married. Dat iss what we are going to do." To Jovina the only ill luck which could possibly befall was further delay. "Come on; it iss pretty soon perhaps a train back." Again she laid her hand on his arm. "Come on. But what iss now de matter?" For Benj had suddenly stopped at the opening of the bridge.

"I—I haf—I haf lost my pocket-book!"

"Well, you must 'a' dropped it here. Come on; let us look once. When did you last haf it?"

"I don't know," he almost wailed. "I paid de tickets an' de toll from some loose change what I had. I might 'a' lost it efen in Millerstown already. How will we den get home, Chofina? I haf only a few cents loose change any more."

For a few minutes they searched diligently.

"It ain't here," said Benjamin. "*Ach!* what will we do? Where are you den going, Chofina?"

Jovina had started toward the station.

"Come on!" she said.

"But I haf no money! We can't walk."

"You haf de tickets, anyhow, to Phillipsburg. We can sit in de station till de next train comes."

"But we can't walk from Phillipsburg to Millerstown, I guess."

"Benj Gaumer," she commanded, "dere iss one way, and only one, what you can get home besides walking. Dat way I will tell you when we get to de station." Thereupon Benjamin followed her.

"I haf plenty money of my own," she announced; "but I don't take no strange fellows trafeling round wis me. I would take a fellow if I wass married to him, and no oder kind; dat I can tell you, Benj Gaumer! You need n't say nosing now. When we got to Phillipsburg once it will be den time enough."

For the next hour he sat silently beside her. He slipped his hand surreptitiously into one pocket after the other, but no purse could he find. He listened greedily to the clink of silver in Jovina's pocket-book as she changed it from one hand to the other. Certainly she moved it around oftener than was necessary. There was a north-bound train in an hour, and again he left her to climb unaided to the car. Again her "Chust smell de mint, Benj!" as they passed Raubsville fell on deaf ears, and it was necessary for her to remind him forcibly that they had reached their destination.

He followed weakly behind her up the long steps, in the embarrassed helplessness of the man with empty pockets. When they reached the top she paused.

"Well?" she said grimly.

Benjamin looked up the street, then down, then he thrust his hands wildly into his pockets. The two minutes that had passed since his last investigation had not served to create a purse. Then he capitulated.

"What for a preacher, Chofina?" he asked.

"So long as dere ain't no New Baptists nowhere but in Millerstown, I don't care. But no Menisht (Mennonite) an' no Casolic (Catholic) an' no Chew! Whatefer oder preacher you can find dan dose, I don't care."

"Wh–where den will I find him?" he asked.

She cast upon him a glance of withering scorn.

"Go in dat store an' ask!" He followed the direction she indicated.

"De drug-store?"

"Yes."

The clerks looked slyly at one another as Benj entered the store after a moment's frantic struggle to push in the door which was marked "Pull."

"Where iss a preacher?" he demanded wildly.

"The second house from the corner on the next block, sir."

"Sank you." Benj started out, but came speedily back.

"He ain't for sure no Casolic?" he queried.

"No what?"

"No Casolic."

"Oh, Catholic you mean! No sir."

"Nor yet a Menisht nor a Chew?"

"A what? He is a clergyman of the Lutheran Church."

"Sank you."

"He's harder hit than most," a clerk remarked as Benj joined Jovina on the opposite corner. "Look at 'em; they're going the wrong way."

He rushed to the doorway and called loudly, whereupon Jovina stood still, while Benj moved on a few paces.

"You're going the wrong way!" he shouted. "The preacher lives up the other way."

Jovina seized Benj by the arm, and the clerk went back to the store.

"I'm afraid I've spoiled sport," he laughed. "The poor chap won't get away from her again."

When they reached the preacher's door, Jovina herself asked if he were at home and, upon being answered affirmatively, motioned Benj to precede her. The maid, whose dancing eyes gave testimony that she understood their errand, invited Jovina to walk up-stairs and lay off her hat.

"No, I won't need to lay off my hat. I can be married in a hat."

Was this another scheme of Benj's to get away? Had he mysteriously communicated with this saucy girl, and was she trying to aid him?

"Not much does she get me away!" Jovina said to herself. "I am a little too smart for dese New Chersey ones."

The maid ushered them into the preacher's study, and he rose as they entered.

"You wish to see me?" he asked smilingly. "From Pennsylvania? Ah, I understand. Yes, I can perform the ceremony immediately."

He asked them various questions. The only objection he had to his present pastorate was the fact that it lay in a town which was a veritable Gretna Green, and he was not always sure that the persons he married were truthful about their age or their residence. In this case, however, his mind was more at ease. In the first place, they were certainly both of age, and, in the second, the clothing of the groom, in which he was evidently not thoroughly at home, and the bride's gay and beruffled attire, were too conspicuous to have been donned for an elopement. As he turned from Jovina to Benjamin, however, he began to be puzzled.

"If this young woman were apparently as unwilling to be married as this young man," he said to himself, "I should feel it my duty to decline to marry them."

Benjamin's replies, however, though wanting in spirit, were correct as to the letter, and presently he and Jovina were pronounced man and wife.

As the preacher shook hands with them, Jovina slipped a dollar bill from her hand to his own.

"He lost his pocket-book," she explained.

"But—but, my friend, I can't take a fee from you!"

"*Ach!* dat don't make nosing out," she said calmly. "He will chust haf to pay it back again."

At this the preacher bowed, his chin deep in his collar. He went with them toward the door. When they reached the hall, the maid paused for moment with her dusting, and Jovina looked at her sharply. Had she been listening? Had this saucy little thing heard Benj's gruff replies? Was she laughing at them? Jovina turned toward the preacher.

"You must excuse him because he don't seem so anxious," she explained loudly. "It iss n't as he don't want to get married; it iss because—because—"

Jovina was not an habitual prevaricator, and invention was difficult—"it iss because he has new shoes an' he has it so in his feet. Good-by, *Para* (Pastor)."

Then Jovina looked haughtily at the pretty maid,—Jovina, who herself had lived out one summer at the Weygandts', where she expected to be treated as one of the family,—and waving her hand majestically, issued her commands:

"Will de serfant-girl open de door?"

Blissfully unconscious of the laughter to which master and maid yielded as she seized Benj again by the arm, she walked briskly down the street.

"I sink it would be nice when we would take de steam-cars home," she said. "We haf come by de trolley. We can walk back across de bridge to Easton."

"All right." Had she proposed an air-ship, Benj would have been equally satisfied. If she chose to waste the difference between the trolley fare, which was fifteen cents, and the railroad fare, which was fifty, well and good. She carried the pocket-book, and she had promised to get him back to Millerstown. She bought some bananas and soft pretzels, and they ate their dinner as they crossed the bridge. When they reached Easton they found that they had just missed a train, and it was almost dark when they reached their own county-seat. They had scarcely spoken a word. Jovina, from whose stern eyes the sharpness had vanished, glanced occasionally at Benj with an expression curiously like wistfulness around the corners of her mouth. Benj, however, paid no heed. He mounted the train at her suggestion and rose to leave it at her word; but he had no will of his own. It simply "made nosing out" what happened now. When they reached the corner from which the Millerstown cars started, they found that again they had missed a car. Thereupon Jovina suggested that they take a walk on Hamilton street, where suddenly the faint twilight gave place to the blaze of electric lights. It was she who asked the shouting car-despatcher what time the next car departed for Millerstown, she who piloted the way across the crowded street, she who bought a bag of peanuts from the Italian at the corner. Then Benj gave the first sign that he still possessed an interest in life, for he munched them greedily. He was hungry—not, however, for peanuts or bananas or pretzels, but for boiled cabbage and pork and schnitz-pie. He realized suddenly that he wanted schnitz-pie more than he had ever wanted anything in his life. And, alas! his mother seldom baked it! It was at Jovina's alone that he had ever got enough schnitz-pie. Suddenly he drew a deep breath. He was henceforth to live at Jovina's! The black clouds which hemmed him in brightened. It was true that they were still so very gray as to be almost black;

but Jovina, had she only known, had good reason to take courage. He remembered for the first time to help her into the car, and as he sat down beside her he noticed that she wore her pink dress. A loud shout from the rear suddenly drew his attention.

"Well! Well! Look once in front dere! Chust married, fellows! Hello, Benj!" It was Billy Knerr and the young Fackenthals. At their gay sally every one in the car grinned broadly, and Benj blushed like a girl. Another penalty for being married! The sense of his own misery surged over him again. Jovina was to blame for this. He looked around at her and for an instant her own glance, tormented, pitiful, pathetically unlike Jovina, held his own. That instant something new was born within him—a sense of possession. He rose to his feet and looked angrily back at his fellow-townsmen.

"You fellows had better shut up once!" he called. "It shows mighty poor manners to yell at a lady in de street-car! An', what iss more, any one what does it will settle wis me!"

So amazed were they, and so thoroughly convinced that he meant what he said, that they were instantly silent.

The streets of the county-seat and the long, ugly rows of suburban houses were soon left behind. Then they sped out into the summer darkness, where the lights were gleaming in scattered farmhouses.

"Are you cold, Chofina?" Benj asked suddenly, as the cool evening breeze blew through the car.

"N–no," she answered, startled by his solicitude. "But I am tired."

"An' I, too."

Suddenly Jovina began to tremble.

"No, it ain't dat I am cold. It iss somesing else. It iss somesing dat I must tell you, Benj. I haf known it sometime already. It—it—iss—it iss dat—"

"Well?"

"It iss dat Chohn Weimer will some one of dese days marry Mary."

"Mary? Mary who?"

"Why, Mary Kuhns."

"Chohn Weimer marry Mary Kuhns!" He laid his hand heavily on her wrist. "How do you den know dis?"

"Chohn told me himself, an' it iss for sure true."

John Weimer marry Mary Kuhns! Mary Kuhns, whose steady suitor he had been for three years! Now all Millerstown would say that she had thrown him over for John. A fierce anger against her swelled within him. What right had she to treat him like this? Then at last the morning of Benjamin's content dawned.

"But—but—"

"But what, Benj?" prompted Jovina in a voice thick with suppressed tears.

"Wait once," he said, his forehead wrinkled in a frown, his grasp on her wrist growing each moment tighter. "But Chofina, it wass I what srew Mary Kuhns ofer, and not she me."

"Of course it wass," said Jovina.

"Chovina, did you haf de wedding-day so soon because of Mary's also getting married? Did you sink folks would say she srew me ofer? Did you do it den for me?"

"Of course I did," said Jovina.

His clasp this time closed on Jovina's hand. Her own, however, was suddenly drawn away.

"Chofina!" he exclaimed, "do you turn away from me?"

"No—no; it ain't dat, Benj. I haf somesing else to tell you, Benj."

"Wait once, Chofina. It iss almost time to get out. Den you can tell me."

He helped her down tenderly. Billy Knerr called after them something about a serenade they would have the next evening, but they paid no heed as they started up the dark and silent street.

"Now, Chofina, what iss den dis foolish sing what worries you?"

"It iss dis, Benj," she sobbed: "it iss your pocket-book. I picked it up on de bridge, and I haf had it all de day. *Ach!* Benj, what will you do?"

"You haf den had it all day!" he repeated dully. "Why, Chofina, if I had not lost it, it might be dat we would not haf been yet married!"

"I knew it—I knew it! I knew it all de time!" she exclaimed wildly. "Den you don't lofe me a bit! It would make nosing out to you when I wass dead!"

For the fraction of a second Benj considered. As he had said, if he had not lost his pocket-book they might not have been married. Then how Millerstown would have laughed! And now—

"Chofina," he whispered, "it iss all right. Don't you cry a minute. I am not mad ofer you, Chofinily; I am glad. Listen once. If we wass not already married, dey would all say dat she srew me ofer, and dat you wass second choice. Now we haf a good one on her!"

"But, Benj, are you sure you don't lofe her no more?"

"I nefer lofed her," declared Benjamin, sure of his mind at last; "an' now I hate her!"

THE COUNTY SEAT

*I*n "The County Seat" (*Atlantic Monthly*, May 1908), the up-and-coming Oliver and Susannah Kuhns and their children, Oliver and Louisa, move to Allentown in search of a more sophisticated and varied life. Here Singmaster explores the question of how Pennsylvania Germans adjust when they encounter life beyond their village. Singmaster's own family moved from Macungie to Brooklyn in 1887, and then to Allentown in 1890. Elsie's father served as pastor of St. Paul's Lutheran Church, Allentown, from 1890 to 1900, and her novel *The Magic Mirror* is set in Allentown.

* * *

"I and Ollie and the children are going to—" Susannah Kuhns bent over the salad dressing which she was stirring on the stove as though it, for the moment, took all her attention. Meanwhile, she watched her guest, stout, placid Sarah Ann Mohr, from the corner of her eye. Then she brought out the rest of the sentence with a jerk,—"are going to move."

"T–to m–move!" exclaimed Sarah Ann. "When, Susannah? Where will you move? Why?"

Susannah straightened her back, so that it reached the perpendicular and passed it.

"We are going to move to Allentown. I am sick of Millerstown. Millerstown is too slow and too dumb and too Dutch."

"But you will get homesick."

"Homesick! For why should I get homesick? I have my man and my children by me. It is no one in Millerstown I care for."

"Ach, Susannah!" Sarah Ann's eyes filled with tears. She was accustomed to Susannah's tempers, but she had never seen her in such a mood as this.

Susannah poured the dressing over a bowl of crisp endive and set the empty pan in the sink with a slam.

"Oliver is sick of working at the furnace. He will go back to his carpenter trade, and in Allentown he will get two dollars a day. And my children will talk English, and when they are through with the school, they can work in the factory."

"But your things will get broken when you move."

"Pooh, that is nothing. I will just get new ones."

"But who will lead the singing in the church?"

"I don't care."

"Won't you never come back?"

"Never to live."

"But *why* do you go?" Not even a plague could have driven Sarah Ann from Millerstown. "You have here your nice house, and it is where you have always lived, and—"

"I hate it," said Susannah. Then she went to the screen door. "Dinner!" she called.

Sarah Ann rose as the two children, Oliver and Louisa, came in.

"But you won't be here for the Sunday-school picnic or the Christmas entertainment."

Little Louisa answered, her fat cheeks almost cracking with scornful laughter.

"We can go every day to a Sunday-school picnic or a Christmas entertainment in Allentown."

"Don't you sass Sarah Ann," said their mother sharply. "This afternoon you are both to help me."

For the next few days, Sarah Ann went back and forth from her own house to the Kuhnses, with tears in her eyes. Susannah gayly declined her help. She scrubbed the floors, she whitewashed, she washed and ironed and packed. Her husband helped her with the heavy things, and in the intervals of work, wandered miserably about.

"Do you want to move to Allentown, Oliver?" Sarah Ann asked him.

"Yes," answered Susannah. "He does."

Susannah sang while she worked. She had led the singing in the Evangelical Church since she was a girl, but she would sing there no more. There were great churches in the county seat, churches with stained-glass windows and crowds of people, where they would want her to sing. Then cross, unwilling Oliver would be glad they had moved.

Nearly all Millerstown came to the station to say good-by. Susannah told them again and again how glad she was to leave, and they listened to her silently. She seemed already like an alien.

"I should not be surprised if it is by and by no one at all in Millerstown," she said laughingly. "Millerstown is too slow."

The eyes of the other women met. They thought Susannah Kuhns had lost her mind. Sarah Knerr joined them just before the train pulled out.

"You forgot your soap-kettle, Susannah," she said breathlessly. "I ran all the way to tell you. It hangs yet in the back-yard."

"I am not going to take it," answered Susannah.

"How then will you boil your soap?"

"I ain't going to boil soap. I buy my soap."

"And won't you make apple-butter, and won't you butcher?" gasped someone.

Susannah did not deign to answer. She looked back as the train started. It would have been a relief to jump up and down in her seat as the children were doing. Oliver told them sternly to "shut up and sit still," but they were too excited to obey.

The crowd at the station in Allentown seemed to their unaccustomed eyes great enough for a holiday or fair week. Susannah could hardly follow Oliver, with Louisa hanging from one hand, and Ollie trying to escape from the other.

"Mom!" he shrieked every few minutes. "Look once here!"

At the big skeleton of the Powers building, Oliver stopped them.

"There is where I shall work at two dollars a day," he said.

In spite of himself there was pride and excitement in his voice.

A little farther on he stopped at the opening of a narrow street.

"It is here where we shall live."

"I see where," screamed little Ollie.

Their goods were being unloaded before the door of a tiny frame house.

"I too," echoed Louisa.

Oliver unlocked the door and let them in.

"It is not a nice house," said Louisa.

"It *is* a nice house," reproved her mother sharply. "It is while it is not yet fixed up that it don't look so fine." Then she waved back her husband, who came into the room with a roll of carpet in his arms. "Don't bring it in yet. Did you think I should put down carpet when the house is not yet cleaned?"

"But I must go Mondays to work, and Sundays it is no working, and I can only help to-day and to-morrow."

Susannah looked at him.

"Do you mean I should put down the carpets before it is everything washed up?" she asked.

"No," he answered, meekly. "But you shall wash this room first, and then I can move the things right aways in."

"Begin at the bottom to wash the house!" gasped Susannah. "And go up! I guess not. I begin at the top, like always."

She went upstairs and looked about her. She could not suppress an exclamation of horror. Then she went to the head of the stairway.

"You shall just come up once and see how dirty it is here," she called. "It will be dinner till I make the garret done."

"But the things? Shall they stand all the time out?"

"You can watch them so it don't anybody carry anything off," she replied. "I—" The rest of her sentence was lost in the sound of a stiff scrubbing-brush, pushed swiftly across rough boards.

In an hour, Ollie tiptoed softly to the bottom of the garret stairs.

"Mom," he called, in a wild whisper. "Come down, come down!"

"What is the matter?" asked Susannah in fright.

"The police have got Pop."

Susannah sprang to her feet, upsetting the pail of water. Little Ollie got nimbly out of her way as she flew.

"They'll take him to jail," he cried.

"Oliver!" called Susannah, "I am coming."

When she reached the front door she saw Oliver nervously moving the boxes. A policeman had paused in the middle of the street for a last word.

"They must be off in half an hour," he said.

Husband and wife scarcely spoke until the things were safely inside.

"This awful thing shall not come to Millerstown," said Susannah. Then she thrust a broom into Oliver's hands. "Go out and sweep a little off."

Susannah clattered back into the garret. Brisk worker as she was, it was dinner-time before she finished.

"I tell you it is clean for once," she said proudly, as they sat on the boxes, eating the lunch which Sarah Ann had put up for them. The children had begged to take theirs out on the back step, but she would not let them. "And have all the neighbors know what we are eating! I guess not."

"But at home, they know always what we have for dinner," said Louisa.

"This is home," corrected their mother sternly.

After dark, they put up two beds by the faint light which came in from the arc light outside. They had no oil for their lamps and they were afraid to light the gas. The children were already asleep on a pile of carpet, and did not wake when they were put to bed.

An hour later, Susannah lay down beside her sleeping husband. There had been one rug which she had not been able to clean before she left Millerstown, and she had taken it down into the yard and had beaten it there. She closed her eyes with a great sigh of relief. Then she sat up. What was this noise? She was conscious for the first time of the rush of trolley-cars, the roll of carriages, the tramp of feet. Somewhere in the neighborhood a band was practicing. She jumped with fright at the sound of the church clock striking eleven.

"We must get used to it," she said to herself. "It cannot be so quiet here like in Millerstown."

She was not to get used to it that night, however. She tossed and rolled, determining that she would not hear the clock strike again, then listening and waiting for it. She grasped her husband's arm in terror, when, toward morning, half a dozen men sat down on the doorstep to finish a noisy argument.

It was dawn when she fell asleep. The milk-carts and market-wagons had begun to come in from the country, and rattled noisily by, and for a while she was conscious of them in the midst of her drowsiness. Then, slowly, they faded away.

She woke to wonder uneasily where she was. The first stroke of the church clock recalled her to herself. It was five o'clock, and she must get up. No, it was six. How had she happened to sleep so long? And Oliver was asleep. She laid her hand on his shoulder. As she touched him, the clock struck again. Seven! It could not be.

"Oliver!" she called.

"Yes, yes," he answered crossly.

Then, deliberately, the clock struck eight.

She lay staring, until the stroke had died away. To sleep until eight o'clock on a day like this, when on ordinary days she got up at five!

All morning she worked feverishly, only stopping to comfort Ollie, who came in crying because some boys had struck him.

"Nobody would hit me in Millerstown," he wailed. "I don't like it here. We don't get nothing good to eat."

"You just wait once till to-morrow," his mother consoled him. "Then we go in the church and the Sunday-school, and I make a good dinner."

Susannah was growing impatient. She could not find places for her furniture. The kitchen was so narrow that the old-fashioned settle which her mother and grandmother had owned could not go there at all. Where would Oliver rest when he came home tired? And where would the children play? Besides, her fire would not burn.

She grew more and more surprised as the hours passed, that no one came in to help. When people moved in Millerstown, everybody helped. She thought with a proud catch in her throat of the morrow. Then her neighbors would be glad enough to know her. Then they would go to church, and she would be invited to sing in the choir. She hummed the first line of "Ein feste Burg," then burst into song, her high, shrill soprano dwelling on the notes as long as she could hold them. By the time that she reached the second stanza, there was a rap at the door. She answered it quickly. A little girl stood on the step.

"My mother says you shall please stop singing. She wants to sleep. She takes a nap in the afternoon."

"Takes a nap!" repeated Susannah, her astonishment for the moment holding her wrath in check. "Is she sick?"

"No, but she takes a nap. And you shan't holler."

She looked up impertinently as she went off the steps.

"'Ein feste Burg ist unser Gott,'" began Susannah as loudly as she could, before the door closed. Then she saw across the street the blue coat of the policeman, and thought better of it. They would see. Hollering, indeed!

She looked with proud satisfaction upon her family when they were ready for church the next morning. The house, too, was in fairly good order, although there were many things yet to be done. It did not occur to her to touch any of them to-day. She had never heard of any one working on Sunday. Her eyes widened with astonishment as she listened to the quick strokes of a hammer in the next house.

When the Millerstonians visited the county seat, they went invariably to St. Peter's Church. There the morning service was still held in German, there was a German prayer-meeting, and a German Bible class. Susannah would have preferred to go to an English church, but Oliver would not hear of it.

The usher showed them to seats well toward the front. The children stared round the great church. Once when a purple gleam from the rose-window fell on little Louisa's dress, she gasped with delight. Her mother had no eyes for anything but the organ and the choir. The organ seemed large enough to be a church itself. She saw with astonishment that there were only four singers in the choir. Surely they would be glad to have her.

She joined in the singing with a heartiness which made those near her turn their heads. She was pleasantly conscious of their attention.

Afterwards the preacher spoke to them in the vestibule. He hoped they would come regularly to church. They would be glad to have the children in the Sunday-school and their father and mother also.

"She will sing in the choir," said Oliver proudly. "She sang always in the choir at home."

The preacher hesitated for a second. Susannah's singing had reached even to him.

"It is very kind," he said. "But we have a quartette. We pay them."

"I don't ask any pay," said Susannah quickly.

"But you see these people are engaged for the year," explained the preacher. "Their voices are trained. They—"

"But she would be willing to sing along with them," persisted Oliver "Would n't you, Susannah?"

Susannah's face had grown very red, and her black eyes snapped. She had always been quick to take offense.

"No," she said sharply. Then she seized Oliver by the arm. "Come on home." There were tears of vexation in her eyes. "He might 'a' said right aways he did n't want me," she said.

She would not go with Oliver and the children to Sunday-school in the afternoon, but she went with them afterwards for a walk. She did not enjoy it. There was no place to go. In Millerstown they went to see either her parents or Oliver's parent, and always stayed for supper.

The children were restless and uneasy all the evening. There was no place to sit outside but the doorstep, and Susannah would not let them sit there for an instant. It was too close to the woman who said that she "hollered," and to the woman who put down her carpets on Sunday. In the morning she would take them to school, then they would have more to interest them.

Oliver started away at six o'clock. The county seat had not yet grown so English that it had forgotten its habit of early rising. Then Susannah called the children and gave them their breakfast. At eight o'clock she took them to school. Little Louisa cried as she came away. She had heard the whispered "Dutchy" from the girl in the next seat, and she did not dare to pinch her as she would have pinched Sarah Knerr.

Nor did Ollie like his seat-mate any better. He hailed him, also, as "Dutchy," and when Ollie, who was braver than Louisa, kicked him, he told the teacher, and Ollie spent the rest of the morning on the platform.

His mother declined to listen to their complaints. She had spent all her patience on the stove. What would Millerstown say if it knew that she burned her pies on the bottom and that they were raw on top? She had swept the pavement three times, and still it was dusty.

Worse than all, however, had been the insult she had received from the lips of an impertinent resident of the county seat. She had discovered that with the limited storage-room in the house, they would have no place to keep one of her greatest treasures, a large feather-bed. She was trying to decide what to do with it when there came a rap at the door. The young man to whom she opened it told her that he had come to buy old clothes, old furniture, old anything.

"It is here a bed," she answered slowly. It would be hard to part with it, but it would doubtless yield the price of a new lounge for the parlor.

The young man stared at it. He had never seen a feather-bed.

"I might carry it somewhere on a vacant lot," he said. "I'll carry it away for a quarter."

For an instant Susannah could not speak. Then,—

"A vacant lot!" she repeated. "Had you never no grandmother what had such a bed? My grandmother she made it herself, out of her own feathers. What for a bed did your grandmother have, then?"

The young man put his head on one side. Whether he resented the implication cast upon his grandmother, or whether he merely desired to be sarcastic, it was hard to tell.

"How would you like to sleep on somebody else's grandmother's dirty old bed?" he asked, and was gone.

"You lie!" cried Susannah after him. It was not exactly a logical response to anything the young man had said, but Susannah did not care. It showed her wrath and defiance.

It was small wonder that she had little patience for the children's complaints.

"You will just have to get used to it," she said to little Louisa. "I cannot be always fighting."

Little Louisa burst into tears.

"I want to go back," she wailed.

"Louisa!" began her mother; then she stopped, staring at the doorway. Her husband, whose lunch-pail she had packed that morning, and whom she had not expected to see before night, stood before her. He looked pale, and sick.

"What is the matter?" she faltered. "Have you got it somewheres, Oliver?"

He sat down on the nearest chair. "He wants I should work on such a scaffold what hangs out of the window. I fall and break my neck. I won't break my neck for nobody. He said I could go."

Susannah looked at him, helplessly.

"But if you don't work, how shall we get along?"

He shook his head but did not answer.

"What shall we do, Oliver?" she repeated.

Little Louisa looked up at her, her fat face swollen with crying.

"Mom—" she began.

"Be quiet," said her mother.

Oliver lifted his head.

"Perhaps, Susannah, if we—"

"Be quiet," said Susannah to him, also. "I am thinking."

"Listen, Mom!" Ollie began to dance up and down. "Let us go—"

"You hold your mouth, or I send you to bed," said Susannah. She stood in the middle of the little kitchen, her arms akimbo, a frown above her black eyes. No one would ever have thought that she was really in the choir-loft of the Millerstown Evangelical Church, looking down into the admiring eyes of Millerstown, which, gasping, let her take all the high notes alone.

"Louisa," she said sternly, "if you are quiet and Ollie is quiet and you Pop is quiet, we will go back."

THE OLD RÉGIME

*S*ingmaster believed that education was essential for a productive life, and she often encouraged young readers to be attentive students. This story, which appeared in the October 1908 issue of the *Atlantic Monthly*, features Millerstown's youth, but it may be based on a personal experience that Singmaster described in "My Adventures in Criticism" (*Atlantic Monthly*, December 1912). "I appeared before a school-board to protest against the retention of an old school-teacher," Singmaster wrote in that essay. "I recounted in as mild language as I could the objections to him, held not only by me, but by two long-suffering generations." To Singmaster's chagrin, the teacher was not dismissed but was reinstated at a higher salary!

* * *

It was the opening day of the Millerstown school, already two weeks after the usual time. The Virginia creeper along the pike was scarlet, the tall corn in the Weygandt fields—tree-high, it seemed to the youngest children—rustled in the cool September wind, and above, the blue sky arched, immeasurably distant. It seemed good to be getting back to winter tasks. The fields and hills were not quite so friendly as they had been a week before.

For generations there had been a wild scramble for seats on the first day of school. The earliest comers had first choice, and the triumph of having secured a "back seat" was not entirely shattered by the later and punitive shifting which befell them.

No one but the teacher could unlock the front door. There was another way to get in, however, through the dark cellar, where at recess Oliver Kuhns played "Bosco, the Wild Man, Eats 'em Alive," as his father had done before him, then up through a trap-door to the schoolroom. Lithe, swarthy Oliver was usually first, then the two Fackenthals and Billy Knerr and Jimmie Weygandt and Coonie Schnable. Coonie might be found bartering his seat to a later comer on as good terms as he could make.

This morning, as usual, it was the rear seats which were at a premium. Ollie Kuhns flung himself into one, and the next three boys followed. Then there were no more "back seats." A wail arose. Coonie Schnable, the stingy, offered five cents and was jeered at; Jimmie Weygandt offered five cents and a new knife and was more courteously denied.

"*You* don't need a back seat," Oliver assured Jimmie. "But if Coonie sits where Teacher can see him, he gets licked like sixty."

Coonie grew pale under his summer's tan.

"He don't like my Pop, nor none of my family," he said.

"My Pop says he used to lick them till they couldn't stand," offered Ollie cheerfully. "But he learned them. My Pop would 'a' had him back this long time if the others would."

The older of the Fackenthals took from his pocket a short tin tube. Plastered on it was a ball of putty.

Little Ollie laughed. He threw himself back in his seat, his feet on the desk. It was only seven o'clock and the teacher would not be there till eight.

"You just try once a putty-blower!" he warned. "You will easy see what you will get!"

Twenty years before, the children's fathers and mothers had gone to "pay school." It was before the establishment of the public-school system, and the pay-school was kept by Jonathan Appleton, of New England origin and Harvard training. Why he had come to Millerstown no one knew. It never occurred to Millerstown that he might have displayed his learning to better advantage in a larger and more cultivated town. They regarded the thirty dollars a month which he was able to earn, as a princely salary for a man who spent his summers in idleness and knew nothing about farming. Jonathan seemed to like Millerstown,—at least he stayed for twenty years, and married a Millerstown girl, little Annie Weiser, who adored him.

"You might 'a' had Weygandt," her mother mourned. "For what do you take up with a *school-teacher?*"

Little Annie only smiled rapturously. To her Jonathan was almost divine, and her marriage a beatitude. Like most perfect things, it was also short-lived. Two years after they were married, Annie died.

In another year, Jonathan lost his position. By that time the Millerstown school was free, and to the minds of many Millerstonians there was good reason for changing.

"Here is Jonas Moser," said William Knerr. "He is a Millerstown boy. He has gone for three years already to the Normal. He has all the new ways. They have there such a model school, where they learn them all kinds of teaching. The Normal gets money from the state. We pay our taxes. I think we should have some good of this tax-paying. We did n't pay nothing for Teacher's schooling. And he is pretty near a outlander."

"Boston isn't outland!" said Oliver Kuhns. "And Teacher" (Appleton was to retain the title, if not the position, till the day of his death) "Teacher is a good teacher. He learned all of us."

"He whips too much."

Oliver laughed. "I bet he whipped me more than all the rest put together, and it never did me no harm. I am for having an English teacher like him. Jonas Moser don't talk right yet, if he is a Normal. I don't want my children taught Dutch in the school."

Appleton laughed when he heard they were talking of electing Jonas Moser.

"Nonsense!" he said. "Why, Jonas Moser can't teach. His idioms are as German as when he left, his constructions abominable, his accent execrable."

"But they say he has methods," said Oliver uneasily. "They taught him in such a model school."

"Methods!" mocked Appleton. "A true teacher needs no methods."

"Yes, but–but—" Oliver stammered. Jonas Moser was leaving no stone unturned to win votes. It was as though he had learned electioneering also at the Normal. "But could n't you say you had anyhow *one* method? He has books about it. He brought them to the school-board."

"Nonsense!" said Appleton.

When he found that they had elected Moser, he was at first incredulous, then scornful. He said that he was going away. But he did not go. Perhaps he was too old or too tired to find another position. It might have been Annie's grave which kept him there.

When, at the end of the year, Jonas Moser resigned, half of Millerstown wanted Appleton back. But there was another Millerstown boy ready to graduate at the normal school, who claimed his turn and got it. He resigned at the end of a month, giving his health as an excuse. It was true that he looked white and worn. Unfortunately for the children's disciplining, he did not tell what anarchy had reigned. It might have been, however, that the school-board suspected it.

"We will now try a Normal from away," said William Knerr. "These children know those what we have had too well."

Presently Appleton's scorn was succeeded by humility. He applied for his old position and was refused. It would have been an acknowledgment of defeat to take him back. He grew excited, finally almost vituperative.

"Your school is a pandemonium," he shouted, his black eyes gleaming above his long, white beard. "The children are utterly undisciplined. They learn nothing. They are allowed to speak your bastard German in the schoolroom. They have no manners. You have tried seven teachers. Each one has been worse than the last."

"Well, anyhow, the children ain't beaten black and blue," said William Knerr sullenly.

"Beaten black and blue!" repeated the old man. "Oliver Kuhns, did I ever beat you black and blue?"

"No, sir," answered Oliver heartily.

"Or you, James Fackenthal?"

"No, sir." James Fackenthal was burgess and he sometimes consulted with Appleton about the interpretation of the borough ordinances.

"Or you, Caleb?"

"No, sir."

Then he whirled round upon Knerr.

"And you I never whipped half enough."

It was, to say the least, not conciliatory. The eighth "Normal" was elected.

After the ninth had come and gone, they engaged a tenth, who was to come in September. On the opening day, he did not appear. Instead came a letter. He had decided to give up teaching and go into the life-insurance business. Oliver Kuhns pointed out the fact that the letter was dated from the town whither the last teacher had gone.

"I guess he could n't recommend Millerstown," Oliver said.

"I know another one," said William Knerr. "He lives at Kutztown. I am going to-morrow to see whether I can get him."

Oliver Kuhns rose to his feet.

"I make a move that we have Teacher come back to open the school, and stay anyhow till the Normal comes," he said.

Ten minutes later, he was rapping at Appleton's door.

Appleton had been reading by candlelight and his eyes blinked dully.

"The school board wants you to come back," said Oliver tremulously. "You shall open school in the morning. We are tired of the Normals. We want you shall learn our children again."

The old man took off his spectacles with a wide sweep of his arm. Oliver seemed to see the ferrule in his hand.

"I shall be there. But I do not *learn* the children, Oliver, I *teach* them. Write it on your slate, Oliver, twenty times."

Oliver went off, grinning. The old man could joke. He had expected him to cry.

The teacher was up as early as the children the next morning. He dressed with care, looking carefully at one shirt after the other. Finally he chose one whose rents would be hidden by his coat and waistcoat. Then he donned his high hat.

All Millerstown saw him go, his coat-tails flying in the breeze, his hat lifted whenever he caught the eye of curious watcher behind house-corner or syringa-bush.

"Good-morning, Miss Kuhns!—How do you do, Miss Kurtz?—Not coming to school, Miss Neuweiler?" Such ridiculous affectation had always been his. He had called the girls "Miss" before they were out of short dresses.

The children, too, saw him coming; not Oliver and the Fackenthals or Billy Knerr, because they did not dare to leave the seats they had chosen, but the rest of the boys and all the girls.

"His coat-tails go flipperty-flop in the wind," giggled little Katy Gaumer. "We never had no teacher with a beard before."

"He looks like a Belsnickle," laughed Louisa Kuhns. "I ain't going to learn nothing from such a teacher."

Thus had they been accustomed to discuss the various "Normals."

Ollie bade Louisa sharply to be still.

"You ain't going to behave that way for this teacher," he said. Then he swung his feet down to the floor, describing a wide arc through the air. The other three boys did the same, and there ensued a wild scramble from window to seat.

"This is my seat!"

"No, my things are already on it."

"My books are in that there desk."

"It don't belong to neither of you."

"Give me my pencil-box."

"This is my slate!"

The roar of sound had not lessened when the door opened behind them. They did not hear him come in, they would probably not have heeded if they had. Then, suddenly, Coonie Schnable, quarreling with a little girl over a pencil-box, was bumped firmly into a seat, and Daniel Wenner into another.

By that time, after a moment of wild rushing about, peace reigned. Each seat was occupied by a child, every voice was silent, every eye fixed upon the front of the room.

This was a new way of opening school! Usually the Normals had said gently, "Now, children, come to order." They had never begun by seizing pupils by the collar!

Teacher walked to the front of the room, and laid his hat on his desk. He was smiling pleasantly, and though he trembled a little, the light of battle was in his eye.

"Good-morning, children."

With one accord, they responded politely. None of them had been taught the manners which he had "learned" their parents, but perhaps they had inherited them.

Teacher did not allow a minute for the respectful silence to be broken.

"We will have the opening exercises. We shall sing,—

"Oh, the joys of childhood, roaming through the wildwood,
Running o'er the meadows, happy and free.

"And remember to say *joys, j-o-y-s,* not '*choys.*' Who starts the tune?"

"We did n't sing last year because the boys always yelled so," volunteered Louisa Kuhns, anxious to be even with Oliver.

"To the corner, Louisa," said Teacher grimly. "Next time you want to speak, raise your hand."

It was a long time since a pupil had obeyed such an order as that. Nevertheless, Louisa found her way without difficulty.

"Now, who can start this tune?"

A hand went up timidly.

"I guess I can, Teacher."

"Very well, then, Katy. Ready."

Teacher stood and watched them while they sang. Then he read a chapter from the Bible. His predecessors, having respect for Holy Writ, had long since omitted that part of the opening exercises. There was not a sound till he had finished.

"Oliver Kuhns, are you in the first class?"

Ollie raised a respectful hand.

"Please, Teacher, my Pop is Oliver. I am Ollie. Yes, I am in the first class."

"In what reader are you?"

"We are nearly through the Sixth Reader."

"We will go back to the beginning. Second class, where are you?"

Katy Gaumer lifted her hand.

"We are in the middle of the Fourth."

"You also will go back to the beginning. Third class, come up to the recitation benches and take a spelling lesson."

Teacher opened the third-class spelling book at random.

"Elephant," he began. "Tiger." He laid the book down. "Why don't you write?"

The class sat as though paralyzed.

"We are n't that far," ventured Katy.

"It is the second lesson in the book," said the teacher. "Go to your seats and prepare it."

It was a sad morning for the Millerstown school. In the bottoms of their haughty hearts the children still cherished a faint desire to do well. Appleton's angry amazement at their ignorance mortified them. They felt dimly, also, that he was grieved, not, like the Normalites, because he had to teach such unruly children, but for the sake of the children themselves. There was not a sound in the room, except the impatient movement of a foot when the correct answer would not come.

After recess Katy Gaumer raised her ever-ready hand.

"Please, Teacher, I think we know our lessont."

"Lesson, Katy. You may come out." A diligent scratching responded to "elephant" and "tiger."

"Jagu—" began the teacher, then suddenly paused, his face pale. At the door stood a strange young man. Behind him came William Knerr and Oliver Kuhns. William advanced bravely into the room, Oliver remained miserably at the door. If he had only told Teacher that he was only engaged temporarily! But he had not dreamed that William Knerr would find a teacher so soon.

Appleton saw that resistance was useless. At William Knerr's first word, he passed the spelling-book politely to the young man, and walked toward the door.

"I could n't help it, Teacher," said Oliver, as he and William Knerr went out.

Teacher turned to look back. He seemed to take the measure of the Normal with a glance of his keen black eyes.

"May I stay and visit your school?" he asked humbly.

"Certainly," said the young man jauntily. What an unprogressive school-board this must be, who would tolerate such a teacher, even as a substitute! "Do you teach Phonetic Spelling?"

"No," answered Teacher, as he sat down. "Just plain spelling."

"Oh!" said the young man. He saw also that the copy had been put on the board in a fine Spencerian hand. That would have to be corrected. His Model School taught the vertical system.

"Elephant," he began.

"We have already spelled elephant," said Katy Gaumer saucily. "And tiger."

The Normal smiled at Katy. He had determined to make the children love him.

"Jagu—" he began. But it seemed that jaguar was not to be pronounced. A ball of something soft and wet sailed past the Normal's head. He pretended not to see. Inwardly he was debating whether the moral suasion recommended by his text-book was the proper method to apply. He decided to ignore this manifestation.

"Jagu—" There was a wild clatter from the corner of the room. A pencil-box had fallen to the floor.

"Jagu—" began the Normal again.

There was another crash. The Normal saw with mingled relief and regret that the old white-bearded man had slipped out.

"Boys!" he cried nervously.

"Boys!" mocked some one in the room.

The Normal started down the aisle, realizing, not without some fright, that the time for moral suasion was past. He thought it was Oliver Kuhns who had dropped one of the pencil-boxes.

"Go home," he commanded sternly.

The children were startled into absolute silence. Hitherto, even the Normals had tried to keep their inability to control the school from the knowledge of Millerstown. This one would send them out to publish his shame. Billy Knerr laughed.

"Go home with him," commanded the teacher.

There was a wild roar of sound. Every child was shouting, the little girls and all. Oliver and Billy sat firmly in their seats. They did not propose to be cheated of any sport.

"Boys!" began the Normal. Then he became desperate, incoherent. "If you don't go out, I'll get somebody in here who will go out."

There was another shout, and the boys sat still.

"Well, stay where you are, then," the Normal commanded. "But you must obey me."

He wished that the old man would come back. There was something about the stern glitter in his eye which made it seem impossible that he could ever have tolerated such wild uproar as this. He did not guess that the old man was still within call. If he had walked to the window, he might have seen him, sitting on a low limb of the apple-tree, grimly waiting.

It is not necessary, and it would be painful, to describe the last half-hour of the morning session of the Millerstown school. Those who have plied putty-blowers and thrown paper wads and dropped pencil-boxes and given cat-calls will be able to picture the scene for themselves. Others will not credit the most accurate description. When the Normal went down the path at noon, he was consulting a time-table. Unfortunately for any plans of escape, William Knerr met him, and instead of going to the station, he went over to the hotel for his dinner.

"He is coming back," said Ollie Kuhns.

As Ollie prophesied, the Normal did come back. But he did not come alone. William Knerr was with him, and the burgess and Danny Koser and Caleb Stemmel, all members of the school board, and, all but William, bachelors, ignorant of the ways of children.

The Millerstown school was not to be thus overawed. Billy Knerr behaved well enough, for his father's eye was upon him; but a frenzy seemed to possess the others. What did Oliver Kuhns care for the burgess and Danny Koser? They were neither his mother nor his father. What did Katy Gaumer care for Caleb Stemmel? There was a chuckle from the back of the room, and a quick turning of Directors' heads. Every eye was upon a book. Perhaps, thought the Directors, they had imagined the chuckle.

The Normal announced that they would continue the lesson of the morning.

"Elephunt," he began, forgetting his normal-school training.

"It is el-e-*phant*," corrected Katy Gaumer.

"*Tiger*," said the Normal in a terrible voice. There came a howl from the back of the room. It sounded as though the beast himself had broken loose.

The Normal laid down the book. "Learn your own children," he said hotly. "I resign."

He walked down the aisle and out the door.

The laughing children looked at one another.

"He walked in one piece away," squealed Katy Gaumer, in delightful Pennsylvania German idiom, so long unforbidden in the Millerstown school. Then Katy looked up at the Directors, who gaped at one another.

Perhaps she wanted to show how quickly feminine decision can cut the knot of a masculine tangle, or perhaps, woman-like, she welcomed a firm hand after months of liberty.

"Teacher's setting in the apple-tree," she said. "I can see his coat-tails go flipperty-flop."

THE ETERNAL FEMININE

*S*ingmaster suggests in "The Eternal Feminine" (*Lippincott's Monthly,* July 1910) that the hard, stingy Pennsylvania German character of Helen Reimensnyder Martin's stories is the exception to the rule in the village community. Published just two years before Singmaster married Harold Steck Lewars, this story depicts a marriage between the spineless Susan Ehrhart and her mean husband, Samuel. Singmaster resisted writing sentimental romance stories—"profitless mush," she called them—that wasted the reader's time. She hoped her stories would build up the reader's mind.

* * *

Susan Ehrhart stood at the kitchen sink, washing dishes and crying. Her tall, muscular figure shook, the tears ran, unchecked, down her face, and the little house was filled with the sound of her voice. She cried as one who knows no shame, as if she did not care if all Millerstown or all Lehigh County or all the world heard her.

"I am going right home to my Mom."

She listened for an instant, as if expecting a response; but none came, unless the regular tap, tap, tap, of a shoemaker's hammer somewhere in the neighborhood could be called an answer. Indeed, as she listened, it seemed to lose for a second its regularity and become animate, telegraphic, intelligible. The taps became shorter, they rose in a crescendo to a single loud stroke, then they went on evenly. It was as if they said:

"I don't care if you do."

Susan finished her dishes, dried her hands, and put on her sunbonnet and shawl. Then she opened the door and went out.

"I am going right aways home to my Mom," she announced to the quiet night.

The taps went on evenly. Susan walked across the yard to a little shop.

"I am going right aways home to my Mom."

When there was still no verbal answer, she lifted her hand and beat, not upon the door, but upon the wooden wall beside it. She heard the wild clatter of a thousand shoe-nails falling to the floor, as the boxes toppled from the shelf within, then an angry exclamation.

Without going in, she went out the road toward Zion Church. It was not long after sunset, and there was still a faint gray light in the west, against which the roadside trees stood out dimly, and by which Susan, if she had cared, might have picked her way through the mud. The cold March wind blew upon her back. As she plodded along, bowed and bent, she looked like a work-worn peasant. She might have posed for Millet. But in free, Pennsylvania German America, it was not necessary to suffer her wrongs silently. As she went she cried aloud:

"I am going right aways home to Zion Church to my Mom."

A stranger coming to Millerstown and meeting Sarah Ann Mohr or old man Fackenthal, or indeed almost any one of her citizens, would have said that the Pennsylvania Germans were kindly, hospitable folk, a little given to gossip, perhaps, but possessing in the main many more virtues than faults. Any one who met only Samuel Ehrhart, on the other hand, would be likely to say that the Pennsylvania Germans were sordid, parsimonious, and disagreeable. Samuel's character was enough to prejudice the observer against his whole race.

How he had won Susan, no one in Millerstown knew. She was not handsome, she had stooping shoulders and a long thin face, and she was six inches taller than her husband. But surely she must have had at least one better chance! And, lacking that, would it not have been better for her to stay forever in her father's house? Samuel's aunt had looked curiously at her as she stood before the stove in Samuel's kitchen, manufacturing a delicious meal out of the small rations which Samuel allowed.

"Susan," she said, the words bursting from her as if they could no longer be restrained, "Susan, what did you want with Samuel? Did you like him?"

Susan did not answer. Instead, she had looked down at Samuel as he came in from the shop. He might have been a tenderly loved child or a treasured jewel. Then she looked at his aunt as if words were powerless to express her emotion. To Susan, Samuel was then still the most wonderful person in the world.

"Like him!" her eyes seemed to say. "Who could help liking him?"

Samuel had gazed uneasily at his aunt as he came in. She rose at once.

"Never mind, Sammy. I'm not going to stay for dinner. Don't you think it!"

"*Ach,* but won't you stay once?" urged Susan. "That is—"

Samuel's aunt saw the swift frown of disapproval, and the bride's amazement, then her prompt and tender look of obedience. This time her voice was sarcastic.

"Don't be frightened, Sammy. I'm going home."

Millerstown watched the couple for a month with wonder and amusement. Then Elias Bittner reported to old man Fackenthal that they had quarreled.

"What about?" asked old man Fackenthal.

"About insurance. Susan, she has been paying on insurance eight years already, and Samuel, he won't pay no more because he says it is nothing in the Bible from insurance, and he don't believe in making money off of dead bodies."

Old man Fackenthal laughed.

"Samuel would n't give nothing for the graveyard fence because it don't say nothing in the Bible from graveyard fences. Don't he know he will get the money after Susan is dead?"

"He says he don't trust no insurance company."

"But she will lose all the money she has already paid in."

"Well! It is n't his money."

"What did Susan do?"

"She cried and went home to her Mom. But Ellie Benner says she don't believe she said anything to her Mom, or her Mom would n't 'a' let her come back. Her Mom is spunkier than she. Ellie says Susan must just 'a' told her Mom that she came home to visit once a little."

Three times Susan had gone home. The second time it was because Samuel scolded her for inviting her former "company girl" to stay overnight.

"Do you want to land me in the poor-house, with company all the time?" asked Samuel.

The third quarrel arose when Samuel accused her of having pared the potatoes wastefully.

"I saw your potato-peelings in the bucket," he scolded. "Don't you know how to peel potatoes better than that, say!"

Each time, as Millerstown suspected, Susan had not told her mother the real reason for her coming. She cried loudly when she started; but it was three miles to Zion Church, and one may cry away the worst of griefs in that distance. By the time her journey was over, she always thought better of her rage.

Samuel was not at all disturbed. He never doubted that she would return, and in the meantime she was being fed at her father's table, and his own supplies would last longer. He thought sometimes that Susan ate a great deal, but he consoled himself by remembering that she worked a great deal also. He did not believe that this last quarrel was any worse than the others. It had begun when Susan suggested buying flower-seeds for the garden.

"Flower-seeds!" cried Samuel.

"Why, yes. A few such sweet-peas and sturtians, and a few others to it yet. They only cost five cents a package."

"Five cents! Think of the flour you could buy till you have a few packages!"

Susan reluctantly yielded.

"Well, I guess I can get a few seeds from my Mom—if she kept any this year. She thought once she would buy her altogether new ones."

"I don't like flowers," declared the surly Samuel. "They take up too much room; they are only a nuisance. And think of all you could do while you are working at flowers!"

"But I must have my flowers, I must have my flowers!" Susan had a way of insisting over and over upon things when she was excited. "I cannot get along without my flowers. I must have my flowers."

Samuel looked up at her.

"You are not now any more at home," he reminded her. "You will not have any flowers."

"It won't cost nothing," pleaded Susan.

"Yes, it will. It will cost room and time. I know how it goes with flowers."

Susan burst into tears. There never was a human being who cried more easily than Susan.

"I am going home to my Mom. I am going right aways home to my Mom to Zion Church to stay."

Samuel thought of the supply of pies and cakes.

"You can go," he said.

Susan's mother was just winding the clock as she walked into the kitchen. Every one else in the house had gone to bed. Mrs. Haas was a short, enormously fat woman, who in spite of her breadth looked younger than her daughter.

"Why, Susan!" she cried. "My, but I am glad to see you! But where is your man? And what is the matter that you are crying?"

Susan's woes burst at sound of the kind voice.

"I come home to stay always," she wailed. "Please let me stay always. He is mean to me. He will not let me have flowers, he would not let me have any company girl overnight, he will not pay the insurance that Pop paid always for me, he—"

Mrs. Haas sat heavily down in the kitchen rocking-chair.

"*Um Gotteswillen!*" she cried. "Is it true?"

"Yes, it is true," sobbed Susan. "It is all true. When I came home before, it was each time something wrong. I thought I would try it again. But now I cannot try it again."

"No," said her mother firmly; "I guess you will not try it again. I guess I and your Pop can keep you. You can go now to bed, Susan, in your own bed like always, and I will bring you a little garden tea, and to-morrow we will go and fetch your things."

Samuel looked up calmly from his shoemaker's bench the next morning when Susan came in. He had not expected her back so soon.

"Well?" he grinned.

He heard Susan's answering sob, then a sharper voice. Susan's portly mother pushed her away into the shop.

"I thank the Lord I have this chance to tell you how mean you are, Samuel Ehrhart," she said. "We are here to fetch Susan's clothes. No mean, stingy man need take care of my children, that is all I have to say, and my children need n't work for such a mean, stingy man."

"B–but—"

Mrs. Haas would not let him go on.

"I and Susan are going to get her things. You can come along to see that we don't get anything of your trash."

Samuel got awkwardly to his feet, dropping the shoes from his leather-aproned lap. He forgot that he had carefully arranged a patch, economically cut from a tiny bit of leather, and that it would be difficult to get it into position again.

"B–but—" he began.

Mrs. Haas slammed the door and was gone. His shoe-nails fell clattering to the floor, but he did not hear. He grew suddenly pale. He knew Susan's value. He had never dreamed that it would be possible to live so cheaply as they had since her advent. She did not only her own work, but she was beginning to wash and clean for the neighbors. He had looked forward to the day when she would become as much of a wage-earner as himself. Perhaps it would have been better to let her have a few flowers. He followed Mrs. Haas over to the house.

Susan sat by the kitchen table. He saw with relief that she was still crying. Susan would be easy to manage.

"Susan—" he began.

Susan's mother appeared at the door of the cupboard with a sauce-pan in her hand.

"Oh, you came to watch, did you? Well, this is Susan's. You can't say it is n't, for I gave it to her."

Samuel stood in the doorway, fingering his apron.

"Susan—" He began again.

Mrs. Haas thrust the sauce-pan beneath his nose.

"It is Susan's, or is n't it Susan's?"

"Yes," he faltered; "it is Susan's."

"Well, then," said Mrs. Haas. She added it to a pile of pans and dishes on the table. "You'd better look a little over those things. Perhaps it is some of yours there." Her eyes dared him to claim any of them. "Now I am going upstairs. Come, Susan."

But Susan did not move. She was too spent with grief. Her mother patted her arm.

"Then stay right there, Susan."

Samuel's eyes brightened. He swiftly determined to say a few things to Susan. But they must be said to her alone.

"Susan," he began, "you can have—"

Mrs. Haas's foot was on the step. She heard the whisper and looked back. She saw that the least bit of Susan's cheek was visible.

"You come with me," she commanded Samuel sternly. "I don't want it said that I took any of your things. I guess I know what I gave Susan when she got married, and I don't believe she got much since, but you come once along and see."

Samuel went with a backward glance. He grew each moment more terrified. He thought that he might promise her more than the flowers. She might keep some of the chicken money.

Mrs. Haas opened the door of the closet in Susan's room. She held up a red petticoat.

"I suppose this is Susan's?"

Samuel was too perturbed to smile.

"Perhaps Susan don't want her things taken away," he ventured timidly.

Mrs. Haas refused to see his meaning.

"I don't know why you would want any left here," she said scornfully. "You could n't wear them. You may be saving, Samuel Ehrhart, but you are not that saving. Is this Susan's?"

"Y–yes," stammered Samuel. The article in question was Susan's hat.

"And this?" It was Susan's best dress.

Samuel had edged toward the door.

"I have something to tend downstairs," he explained. "I must put the draught on for dinner."

"All right," answered Mrs. Haas promptly. "I will go along with you. Here, you can take these clothes of Susan's, and I will take the rest. You can put them on the table, with the other things, then we can pack them in the wagon."

"You might—might—st–stay for dinner."

Mrs. Haas's laughter echoed through the house. "To dinner! When you would n't have Susan's company girl overnight. I guess not!"

Samuel reluctantly picked up an armful of clothes, the familiar gray wrappers and blue skirts. They were so long that they trailed behind him down the steps, and his mother-in-law bade him sharply to gather them up.

Susan had apparently not moved. But the fire was burning brightly, and the tea-kettle was bubbling. Samuel's eyes brightened. Susan's mother also saw the steaming kettle.

"Susan, help me to carry these things to the wagon," she commanded sharply.

Susan lifted her long, tear-stained face. She was crying again like a child, without any attempt to wipe away the tears.

"*Ach*, Mom," she wailed. "I do not think I am going along with you home."

Mrs. Haas paused, confounded. She stood still, her arms round the bundle of clothes, which was as large as herself.

"Not going along with me home!"

"No, I think I will stay here, Mom."

"You 'think you will stay here, Mom'!" In her amazement she repeated her daughter's words.

"Yes," said Susan. It might have been Samuel's evident fright and repentance which moved her, it might have been the touch of the familiar tea-kettle. "I think I will stay here, Mom."

The bundle of clothes slid from Mrs. Haas's arms!

"You said he would n't let you have any flowers!"

"Yes, Mom."

"You said he scolded you for peeling the potatoes too thick!"

"Yes, Mom."

"You said he made you give up the insurance what your Pop paid, always, so you could have something when you are old!"

"Yes, Mom."

"Well, then! Are you crazy?"

Samuel came a step nearer. He still held his bundle; the wrappers and petticoats trailed again about his feet.

"You can have the flowers if you want to, Susan. And you can have a quarter—*ach,* I mean a half of the chicken money, Susan, and—"

Mrs. Haas cut him short.

"Do you believe him, Susan? Do you believe him for a minute?"

Susan hesitated. His words sounded sweet in her ears, but she could not say that she believed them.

"Then come home," commanded her mother, stooping to pick up the clothes.

Susan hid her face in her arms.

"I can't go home, Mom. I can't help it. I know he is mean, Mom. But I can't help it! The whole trouble is—I—I—like him!"

And, with a final wail, Susan took off her sunbonnet, and sought her gingham apron, hanging upon its accustomed hook.

THE SQUIRE

*I*n "The Squire" (*Atlantic Monthly,* September 1910), the imposition of worldly culture and village meddling make divorce seem inevitable for a young Millerstown couple. The author asks how far the squire, the village patriarch, might go to protect Millerstown from the influence of outside values. At a time when urbane sophisticates belittled rural Americans, Singmaster portrayed the Pennsylvania German village ethos sympathetically. Esther Forbes in the *Boston Evening Transcript* remarked that Singmaster, like the devoted Pennsylvania Germans she clearly admired, was "attractively sturdy in her mental attitude" (July 3, 1926, book section).

*   *   *

The squire was a bachelor, and lived alone in his house; therefore he was able to use the parlor and dining-room for offices. The parlor contained only a pine desk, a map, hanging "at" the wall, as Millerstown would have said, and a dozen or so plain pine chairs. The law was administered with scant ceremony in Millerstown.

The squire sat now in the twilight in his "back" office, which was furnished with another pine table, two chairs, and a large old-fashioned iron safe. He was clearly of a geographical turn of mind, for table, safe, and floor were littered with railroad maps and folders. The squire was about sixty years old; he had all the grave beauty which the Gaumer men acquired. Their hair did not thin as it turned gray, their smooth-shaven faces did not wrinkle. They all looked stern, but their faces brightened readily at sight of a little child or an old friend, or with amusement over some untold thought.

The squire's face glowed. He was going—his age, his inexperience, the certain disapproval of Millerstown notwithstanding—he was going round the world! He would start in a month, and thus far he had told no one but Edwin Seem, an adventurous young Millerstonian who was to leave that night for a ranch in Kansas, and whom the squire was to visit on his own journey. For thirty years he had kept Millerstown straight; there was no possible case for which his substitute would not find a precedent. Fortunately there were no trusts to be investigated and reproved, and no vote-buyers or bribers to be imprisoned or fined. There were disputes of all kinds, dozens of them. There was one waiting for the squire now in the outer office; he shook his head solemnly at thought of it, as he gathered up his maps and thrust them back into the safe, that precious old safe which held the money for his journey. He had been thirty years gathering the money together.

The law might be administered in Millerstown without formality, but it was not administered without the eager attention of the citizens. Every one in the village was on hand when simple-minded Venus Stuber was indicted for stealing, or when the various dramatic scenes of the Miller-Weitzel feud were enacted. This evening's case, Sula Myers *vs.* Adam Myers for non-support, might be considered part of the Miller-Weitzel feud, since the two real principals, Sula's mother and Adam's mother, had been respectively Sally Miller and Maria Weitzel.

The air was sultry, and rain threatened. The clouds seemed to rest on the tops of the maple trees; it was only because the Millerstonians knew the rough brick pavements as they knew the palms of their hands that there were no serious falls in the darkness. They laughed as they hurried to the hearing; it was seldom that a dispute promised so richly. There was almost no one in the village who could not have been subpoenaed as a witness, so thorough was every one's knowledge of the case.

Already the real principals faced each other, glaring, under the blinding light of the squire's hanging lamp. It made no difference that Millerstown listened and chuckled or that the squire had taken his seat behind the pine desk.

"When it don't give any religion, it don't give any decent behaving. But God trieth the hearts of the righteous," said Mrs. Myers meaningly.

She was a large, commanding woman, who had been converted in middle life to the fervent sect of the new Mennonites, and young Adam had been brought up in that persuasion. Except for his marriage, young Adam had been thus far his mother's creature, body and soul.

Sula's mother, Mrs. Hill, was large also. She took off her sunbonnet, and folded her arms as tightly as possible across her broad bosom.

"There is sometimes too much religion," she said.

"Not in your family, Sally," rejoined Mrs. Myers, her glance including not only Mrs. Hill and Sula, but all their sympathizers, and even Caleb Stemmel, who was supposed to be neutral.

Caleb Stemmel belonged in the same generation with the squire; his interest could be only general. Caleb did not see Mrs. Myers's scornful glance; he was watching pretty Sula, who sat close by her mother's side.

Sula looked at nobody, neither at her angry mother beside her, nor at her angry mother-in-law opposite, nor even at Adam her husband, sitting close by his mother. She wore her best clothes, her pretty summer hat, the white dress in which she had been married a year before. Even her wedding handkerchief was tucked into her belt.

Sula had been strangely excited when she dressed in the bedroom of her girlhood for the hearing. There was the prospect of getting even with her mother-in-law, with whom she had lived for a year and whom she hated; there was the prospect of seeing Adam's embarrassment; there was another reason, soothing to her pride, and as yet almost unacknowledged, even to herself.

Now, however, the glow had begun to fade, and she felt uncomfortable and distressed. She heard only dimly Mrs. Myers's attack and her mother's response. Immediately Mrs. Myers told Mrs. Hill to be quiet, and Mrs. Hill replied with equal elegance.

"You will both be quiet," said the squire sternly. "The court will come to order. Now, Sula, you are the one that complains; you will tell us what you want."

Sula did not answer; she was tugging at her handkerchief. The handkerchief had been pinned fast, its loosening took time.

"It was this way," began Mrs. Myers and Mrs. Hill, together.

The squire lifted his hand. "We will wait for Sula." He looked sternly at Mrs. Hill. "No whispering, Sally!"

Sula's complaint came out with a burst of tears.

"He won't support me. For three months already I did n't have a cent."

"All this time I supported her," said her mother.

"She had a good home and would n't stay in it," said Mrs. Myers.

The squire commanded silence again.

"Sula, you were willing to live with Adam's mother when you were married. Why are n't you now?"

"She—she would n't give me no peace. She would n't let him take me for a wedding-trip, not even to the Fair." She repeated it as though it were the worst of all her grievances: "Not even a wedding-trip to the Fair would he dare to take."

Mrs. Hill burst forth again. She would have spoken if decapitation had followed.

"He gave all his money to his mom."

"He is yet under age," said Mrs. Myers.

Again Mrs. Hill burst forth:—

"She wanted that Sula should convert herself to the Mennonites."

"I wanted to save her soul," declared Mrs. Myers.

"You need n't to worry yourself about her soul," answered Mrs. Hill. "When you behave as well as Sula when you're young, you need n't to worry yourself about other people's souls when you get old."

Mrs. Myers's youth had not been as strait-laced as her middle age; there was a depth of reminiscent innuendo in Mrs. Hill's remark. Millerstown laughed. It was one of the delights of these hearings that no allusion failed to be appreciated.

"Besides, I did give her money," Mrs. Myers hastened to say.

"Yes; five cents once in a while, and I had to ask it for every time," said Sula. "I might as well stayed at home with my mom as get married like that." Sula's eyes wandered about the room, and suddenly her face brightened. Her voice hardened as though some one had waved her an encouraging sign. "I want him to support me right. I must have four dollars a week. I can't live off my mom."

The squire turned for the first time to the defendant.

"Well, Adam, what have you to say?"

Adam had not glanced toward his wife. He sat with bent head, staring at the floor, his face crimson. He was a slender fellow, he looked even younger than his nineteen years.

"I did my best," he said miserably.

"Can't you make a home for her alone, Adam?"

"No."

"How much do you earn?"

"About seven dollars a week. Sometimes ten."

"Other people in Millerstown live on that."

"But I have nothing to start, no furniture or anything."

"Your mother will surely give you something, and Sula's mother." The squire looked commandingly at Mrs. Myers and Mrs. Hill. "It is better for young ones to begin alone."

"I have nothing to spare," said Mrs. Myers stiffly.

"I would n't take any of your things," blazed Sula. "I would n't use any of your things, or have any of your things."

"You knew how much he had when you married him," said Mrs. Myers calmly. "You need n't have run after him."

"Run after him!" cried Sula. It was the climax of sordid insult. They had been two irresponsible children mating as birds mate, with no thought for the future. It was not true that she had run after him. She burst into loud crying. "If you and your son begged me on your knees to come back, I would n't."

"Run after him!" echoed Sula's mother. "I had almost to take the broom to him at ten o'clock to get him to go home!"

Adam looked up quickly. For the moment he was a man. He spoke as hotly as his mother; his warmth startled even his pretty wife.

"It is n't true, she never ran after me."

He looked down again; he could not quarrel, he had heard nothing but quarreling for months. It made no difference to him what happened. A plan was slowly forming in his mind. Edwin Seem was going West; he would go too, away from mother and wife alike.

"She can come and live in the home I can give her or she can stay away," he said sullenly, knowing that Sula would never enter his mother's house.

The squire turned to Sula once more. He had been staring at the back of the room, where Caleb Stemmel's keen, selfish face moved now into the light, now back into the shadow. On it was a strange expression, a hungry gleam of the eyes, a tightening of the lips, an eager watching of the girlish figure in the white dress. The squire knew all the gossip of Millerstown, and he knew many things which Millerstown did not know. He had known Caleb Stemmel for fifty years. But it was incredible that Caleb Stemmel with all his wickedness should have any hand in this.

The squire bent forward.

"Sula, look at me. You are Adam's wife. You must live with him. Won't you go back?"

Sula looked about the room once more. Sula would do nothing wrong—yet. It was with Caleb Stemmel that her mother advised, it was Caleb Stemmel who came evening after evening to sit on the porch. Caleb Stemmel was a rich man even if he was old enough to be her father, and it was many months since any one else had told Sula that her hat was pretty or her dress becoming.

Now, with Caleb's eyes upon her, she said the little speech which had been taught her, the speech which set Millerstown gasping, and sent the squire leaping to his feet, furious anger on his face. Neither Millerstown nor the squire, English as they had become, was yet entirely of the world.

"I will not go back," said pretty Sula lightly. "If he wants to apply for a divorce, he can."

"Sula!" cried the squire.

He looked about once more. On the faces of Sula's mother and Caleb Stemmel was complacency, on the face of Mrs. Myers astonished approval, on the faces of the citizens of Millerstown—except the very oldest—there was amazement, but no dismay. There had never been a divorce in Millerstown; persons quarreled, sometimes they separated, sometimes they lived in the same house without speaking to each other for months and years, but they were not divorced. Was this the beginning of a new order?

If there were to be a new order, it would not come during the two months before the squire started on his long journey! He shook his fist, his eyes blazing.

"There is to be no such threatening in this court," he cried; "and no talking about divorce while I am here. Sula! Maria! Sally! Are you out of your heads?"

"There are higher courts," said Mrs. Hill.

Millerstown gasped visibly at her defiance. To its further amazement, the squire made no direct reply. Instead he went toward the door of the back office.

"Adam," he commanded, "come here."

Adam rose without a word, to obey. He had some respect for the majesty of the law.

"Sula, you come, too."

For an instant Sula held back.

"Don't you do it, Sula," said her mother.

"Sula!" said the squire; and Sula, too, rose.

"Don't you give up," commanded her mother. Then she got to her feet. "I'm going in there, too."

Again the squire did not answer. He presented instead the effectual response of a closed and locked door.

The back office was as dark as a pocket. The squire took a match from the safe, and lit the lamp. Behind them the voices of Mrs. Myers and Mrs. Hill answered each other with antiphonal regularity. Adam stood by the window; Sula advanced no farther than the door. The squire spoke sharply.

"Adam!" Adam turned from the window.

"Sula!"

Sula looked up. She had always held the squire in awe; now, without the support of her mother's elbow and Caleb Stemmel's eyes, she was badly frightened. Moreover, it seemed to her suddenly that the thing she had said was monstrous. The squire frightened her no further. He was now gentleness itself.

"Sula," he said, "you did n't mean what you said in there, did you?"

Sula burst into tears, not of anger, but of wretchedness.

"You'd say anything, too, if you had to stand the things I did."

"Sit down, both of you," commanded the squire. "Now, Adam, what are you going to do?"

Adam hid his face in his hands. The other room had been a torture-chamber. "I don't know." Then, at the squire's next question, he lifted his head suddenly. It seemed as if the squire had read his soul.

"When is Edwin Seem going West?"

"To-night."

"How would you like to go with him?"

"He wanted me to. He could get me a place with good wages. But I could n't save even the fare in half a year."

"Suppose"—the squire hesitated, then stopped, then went on again—"suppose I should give you the money?"

"Give me the money!"

"Yes, lend it to you?"

A red glow came into Adam's face. "I would go to-night."

"And Sula?" said the squire.

"I would—" The boy was young, too young to have learned despair from only one bitter experience. Besides, he had not seen Caleb Stemmel's eyes. "I would send for her when I could."

The squire made a rapid reckoning. He did not dare to send the boy away with less than a hundred dollars, and it would take a long while to replace it. He could not, *could not* send Sula, too, no matter how much he hated divorce, no matter how much he feared Caleb Stemmel's influence over her, no matter how much he loved Millerstown and every man, woman, and child in it. If he sent Sula, it would mean that he might never start on his own journey. He looked down at her, as she sat drooping in her chair.

"What do you say, Sula?"

Sula looked up at him. It might have been the thought of parting which terrified her, or the recollection of Caleb Stemmel.

"Oh, I would try," she said faintly; "I would try to do what is right. But they are after me all the time—and—and—" Her voice failed, and she began to cry.

The squire swung open the door of the old safe.

"You have ten minutes to catch the train," he said gruffly. "You must hurry."

Adam laid a shaking hand on the girl's shoulder. It was the first time he had been near her for weeks.

"Sula," he began wretchedly.

The squire straightened up. He had pulled out from the safe a roll of bills. With it came a mass of brightly colored pamphlets which drifted about on the floor.

"Here," he said. "I mean both of you, of course."

"I am to go, too?" cried Sula.

"Of course," said the squire, "Edwin will look after you."

"In this dress?" said Sula.

"Yes, now run."

For at least ten minutes more the eager company in the next room heard the squire's voice go on angrily. Each mother was complacently certain that he was having no effect on her child.

"He is telling her she ought to be ashamed of herself," said Mrs. Myers.

"He is telling him he is such a mother-baby," responded Mrs. Hill. "She will not go back to him while the world stands."

"The righteous shall be justified, and the wicked shall be condemned," said Mrs. Myers.

Suddenly the squire's monologue ended with a louder burst of oratory. The silence which followed frightened Mrs. Hill.

"Let me in!" she demanded, rapping on the door.

"This court shall be public, not private," cried Mrs. Myers.

She thrust Mrs. Hill aside and knocked more loudly, at which imperative summons the squire appeared. He stood for an instant with his back to the door, the bright light shining on his handsome face. Seeing him appear alone, the two women stood still and stared.

"Where is he?" asked Mrs. Myers.

"Where is she?" demanded Mrs. Hill.

The squire's voice shook.

"There is to be no divorcing in Millerstown yet a while," he announced.

"Where is he?" cried Mrs. Myers.

"Where is she?" shrieked Mrs. Hill.

The squire smiled. The parting blast of the train whistle, screaming as if in triumph, echoed across the little town. They had had abundance of time to get aboard.

"He is with her, where he should be," he answered Mrs. Myers, "and she is with him, where she should be," he said to Mrs. Hill, "and both are together." This time it seemed that he was addressing all of Millerstown. In reality he was looking straight at Caleb Stemmel.

"You m–m–mean that—" stammered Mrs. Myers.

"What *do* you mean?" demanded Mrs. Hill.

"I mean,"—and now the squire was grinning broadly,—"I mean they are taking a wedding-trip."

THE BELSNICKEL

y the time this story was published (*Century* magazine, January 1911), the Singmaster family had lived in Gettysburg for ten years and the author had completed her education at Radcliffe College. "The Belsnickel" revisits the Pennsylvania German village of Singmaster's youth and probes the meaning of ethnicity in a country where the freedom of self-determination often led young people away from their roots. The values Singmaster cherished from her early years included "an appreciation of good music, a love of nature, a high regard for scholarship, a kindliness toward fellow human beings, a relentless devotion to duty, a sense of humor, a respect for integrity of character, a keen delight in the church, and an unwavering faith in God" (Mary Spotten Groff, "Elsie Singmaster, Pennsylvanian" [master's thesis, University of Maine, Orono, 1934], 49).

*   *   *

The Millerstown school, crowded almost to bursting, seemed to spend itself in one great sigh as the teacher rose to open the Christmas entertainment. It was the first elaborate entertainment for many years; it was the first English entertainment in the history of Millerstown. Teacher and pupils had meant its character to be a surprise, but fate had overruled their plans. There was only one person in the crowded room who did not know the title of every speech, the name of every song; only one who had not participated in some detail of the excited, almost agonized preparation. That person was the guest who sat upon the platform.

Katy Gaumer, than whom none had a better right, first told the secret. A week earlier, she stood in the Millerstown store, a scarlet "twilight" on her head, scarlet mittens on her hands, a scarlet shawl about her shoulders. Her thin legs, in their black stockings, completed her resemblance to a very gorgeous bird; she seemed, with her quick motions, her waving of her grandfather's newspaper in the faces of her audience, about to fly at them. Caleb Stemmel was speaking dolefully. Caleb Stemmel seldom spoke in any other way.

"Nothing is any more like it was when I was young."

"It is perhaps a good thing," answered Katy Gaumer, with the pertness of thirteen.

"We had entertainments that were entertainments—speeches and candy and a *Belsnickel*. We went to trouble; but these teachers, bah!"

Katy Gaumer had no love for the teacher, but she hated Caleb Stemmel. Katy's loves and hates were as decided as all the rest of her emotions.

"We are going to have an entertainment that will flax any of yours, Caleb Stemmel."

"Yes; you will get up and say a few old Dutch pieces, then you will go home."

"Well, everything was Dutch when you were young."

"Yes; but now things should be English. But you are too lazy. You will be pretty much ashamed of yourselves this year, that I can tell you."

"Why this year?"

"Because a visitor is coming."

"Pooh! What do I care for a visitor?"

"This is one that you care for!"

Katy was already half-way to the door, her black legs flying. She turned now, and went back.

"Who is it?"

Caleb Stemmel liked to tease.

"Don't you wish you knew?"

Katy Gaumer stamped her foot. She had respect for age in general, but not for Caleb Stemmel.

"If you don't tell, I'll snowball you when it gives a snow once," she threatened.

Caleb Stemmel did not answer until he saw that Danny Koser was about to tell.

"It is a governor coming," he said slowly.

Katy Gaumer drew a step closer. No eyes of tanager or grosbeak could have shone blacker against scarlet plumage.

"Do you mean—do you mean that Uncle Dan is coming home?"

"Yes; your gran'pop he was here this afternoon, and he told us. And what will the governor think of Dutch Millerstown?"

Once more had Katy reached the door at the other end of the long room. She had a habit of forecasting her own actions: she could see herself pounding at the teacher's door, then racing to her grandfather's, her heart beating, beating, beating, her whole being in the glow of excitement which she loved, and of which she had little enough. Now she stopped, her hand on the latch. The secret must be told; only by the aid of all the fathers and mothers in Millerstown could the entertainment be made adequate. There was no reason why she should not have the pleasure of the first announcement.

"We are going to have an English entertainment, Caleb Stemmel," she cried. "We have been practising for a month already. Aha, Caleb Stemmel!"

Outside she paused and stretched out her arms. There was not a soul in sight. She looked up the street and down; she could see the last house at each end of the village, and then the quiet country. The street-lamps were not lighted. Why should they be, to dim the light of the heavenly moon which hung above the Weygandt farm? Ten minutes ago she had been only little Katy Gaumer, with lessons learned for the morrow, bedtime hours off, hating the quiet village, and bored with life; now she was Katy Gaumer, the grandniece of one of the great men of the world. If he would only help her, she might be anything—*anything!*

There was no one at hand to remind her that she was only one of twenty-odd grandnieces and nephews, and that a governor, after all, was not such a great man, since he had at least forty-five peers, and that there were even higher offices in the land. No Millerstonian would have so discounted his hero. Daniel Gaumer had made his own way and had achieved success. To this small relative he was greater than the President of the United States. If she could do well, if all the children did well, if some one would only say to him that it was largely her effort which made the entertainment a success, what might he not do for her! She might go to a higher school; he might make her father and grandfather send her; he—

But Katy never stopped to dream. She would prove to be a very good woman or perhaps a very bad one, but she would never be a lazy one or a mediocre one. With an excited gasp, she ran down the street.

The teacher said not a word of reproof for her betrayal when she gasped out her news. He was in Millerstown for only a few months, substituting for a friend and waiting for something to turn up. He was also a Pennsylvania German, but he would as soon have been called a Turk. He had changed his name from Schreiner to Carpenter, and the very sound of Pennsylvania German was unpleasant to him. He knew far better than any one in the village Daniel Gaumer's greatness. He sat now by the table, listening to Katy, their eyes meeting for the first time in entire friendliness.

"I told it because I knew, if Uncle Dan was coming—"

"He is your uncle!"

"My pop's uncle," explained Katy, proudly. "I never saw him. I knew, if he was coming, they would have to know their pieces better. Ollie Kuhns he won't learn his unless his pop thrashes him a couple o' times; and Jimmie Weygandt he won't learn his until the very last minute unless his mom makes him, and then he will stick anyway, perhaps; and they won't let us have the church organ to practise beforehand for the singing unless they know; and everybody must practise all the time the words they can't say. I *had* to tell."

"Exactly," agreed the teacher. His face was solemn; he felt as though he were to appear before the State Board for an examination. He realized that these were things that he would never have thought of. He blessed the inspiration which had suggested an English entertainment, he blessed this energetic child who had persuaded the others to take part. "Sit down, Katy."

It gave Katy another thrill of joy to be thus solicited.

"Not now. I am going to my gran'pop's; then I'll come back."

Now, on the afternoon of the entertainment, there was an air of excitement both within and without the school-room. Outside, the clouds hung low; the winter wheat in the Weygandt fields seemed to have lost its brilliant green; there was no color on the mountain-side, which had been warm brown and purple in the morning sunshine. A snow-storm was brewing, the first of the season, and Millerstown rejoiced. Millerstown believed that a green Christmas made a fat graveyard.

The school-room was almost unrecognizable. The walls were in reality brown, except where the blackboards made them still duller; the desks were far apart, the space from the last seat, where the ill-behaved preferred to sit, to the teacher's desk, to which they made frequent trips for punishment, seemed interminable. This afternoon, however, there was neither dullness nor extra space. The walls were hidden by masses of crowfoot and pine, brought from the mountain; the blackboard had vanished behind festoons of flags and red bunting. The children were so closely crowded together into a quarter of the room that one would have said that they could never extricate themselves; into the other three quarters had squeezed and pressed almost all the fathers and mothers of Millerstown. Grandfather and Grandmother Gaumer were there, the latter with a large and mysterious basket, which she directed Katy to hide in the cloak-room, the former laughing with his famous brother. "Mommy Bets" Eckert, a generation older than

Grandfather Gaumer, was there; and there were half a dozen babies who cooed and cried by turns, and at whom misanthropic Caleb Stemmel frowned. Not another soul could have crowded in.

It was Katy who showed them to their seats, her cheeks redder than her red dress, her motions more bird-like than ever. Only she seemed able to keep her eyes from the platform, where the great man sat; only she seemed able to think. For Katy the play had begun. Was he not here? Had he not smiled at her? Was he not handsome and friendly, like Grandfather Gaumer? Were not her dreams coming true?

Katy knew her part as she knew her own name. It was called "Annie and Willie's Prayer." It was long and hard for a tongue which, for all its striving, could not yet say *th* and *v* with ease. But Katy would not fail, nor would Adam, her little brother, who lisped through "Hang up the Baby's Stocking." If only Ollie Kuhns knew "The Psalm of Life" and Jimmie Weygandt "There Is a Reaper Whose Name Is Death" as well! They had known them this morning—known them so well that they could say them backward—but would they know them now? The children's faces were white; the very pine branches seemed to quiver with nervousness; the teacher tried vainly to remember English speech which he had carefully composed and memorized. As he sat talking with the stranger, he frantically consoled himself with the recollection that examinations always terrified him; but that he was always better in a few minutes.

Once he caught Katy Gaumer's eye and tried to smile. But Katy did not respond. She saw plainly enough what was the matter with him, and prickles of fright went up her backbone. His speech was to open the entertainment. Suppose he should fail! Katy had seen panic sweep like fire down the ranks of would-be speakers. If he would only let her begin, *she* could not fail!

But the teacher did not let her begin. No such simple way out of his difficulty occurred to his paralyzed brain. The stillness in the room grew more deathlike; the moment for opening came and passed; Katy Gaumer, now in her seat, gazed at him sternly; and still he sat helpless.

Then suddenly light flooded his soul. Why should he say anything at all? He would call on the stranger. It was perfectly true that a visitor's speech was never known to come anywhere but at the end of an entertainment. The teacher thought of that, but he did not care. The stranger should speak now, and thus set an example to the children. Hearing his easy English, they would have less trouble with *th* and *v*. Color came back to the teacher's cheek; only Katy Gaumer realized how terrified he had been. So elated was he at his deliverance that he introduced the speaker without stumbling.

Daniel Gaumer had spoken for at least two minutes before the shock of surprise reached the brains of his hearers. The children looked at him, refusing to believe their ears; fathers and mothers nudged each other; the teacher's mouth opened. Only Katy Gaumer sat unmoved, and Katy was too much astonished to stir. The distinguished stranger had been away from Millerstown for thirty years; he was a graduate of a university; he had honorary degrees; the teacher had warned the children to look as though they understood him, whether they understood him or not; and now the distinguished stranger did not even address them in English, but spoke Pennsylvania German!

It came out so naturally, he seemed so like any other Millerstonian standing there, that they could hardly believe that he was distinguished or even that he was a stranger. He said that he had not been in that schoolroom for thirty years, and that if any one had asked him its dimensions, he would have said it would be difficult to throw a ball from corner to corner. And now he could almost reach across it! He remembered Caleb Stemmel, and called him by name, and asked him whether he had any little boys and girls there to speak pieces, at which everybody laughed. Caleb Stemmel was too selfish to care for any one but himself. He talked as though he were sitting behind the stove in the store with Caleb and Danny Koser and the rest. And then—the teacher's face flushed, the bright color faded from Katy Gaumer's cheeks, the fathers and mothers nudged each other once more— *he said he had come a thousand miles to hear a Pennsylvania German Christmas entertainment.*

He said that it was necessary, of course, for every one to learn English,— it was the language of their country,—but that at Christmas-time they should remember with pride that no nation in the world felt the Christmas spirit like the Germans. It was a time when everybody should be grateful for his German blood, and should practise his German speech. He had been looking forward to this entertainment for weeks; he had told his friends about it; he knew that there was at least one place where he could hear "Stille Nacht." He almost dared to hope there would be a "Belsnickel." If old men could be granted their dearest wish, they would be young again. The entertainment, he said, was going to make him young for one afternoon.

Then the great man sat down, and the little man rose. The teacher was panic-stricken once more; He was furious with himself for having called on Daniel Gaumer first; he was furious with Daniel Gaumer for thus foolishly upsetting all his teaching; he did not care, he said to himself, whether the children failed or not. He announced "Annie and Willie's Prayer."

It seemed for a moment that Katy herself would fail. She looked back into the teacher's eyes. He could not have prompted her if his life had depended on it. He glanced at the program in his hand to see who came next.

But Katy had begun. She bowed to the audience, she bowed to the stranger,—she had effective, stagy ways,—and then she began. To the staring children, to the astonished fathers and mothers, to the delighted stranger, she recited a new piece. They had heard it all their lives; in fact, many of them knew it by heart. It was not "Annie and Willie's Prayer," it was not even a Christmas piece, but it was as appropriate to the occasion as either. Katy knew this also like her own name; it was the way Katy Gaumer knew everything. It was "Das alt Schulhaus an der Crick," and the translation compares with the original as the teacher's Christmas entertainment compared with Katy Gaumer's:

> To-day it is just twenty years
> Since I began to roam;
> Now, safely back, I stand once more
> Before the quaint old school-house door,
> Close by my father's home.
>
> I 've been in many houses since,
> Of marble built and brick;
> Though grander far, their aim they miss,
> To lure my heart's old love from this
> Old school-house on the creek.

Katy Gaumer's eyes did not continue to rest on the visitor's face. There were thirty-one stanzas in her recitation; there was time to look at each one in her audience. At the fathers and mothers she did not look at all; at Ollie Kuhns and Jimmie Weygandt and little Sarah Knerr, however, she looked hard and long. She was still staring at Ollie when she sat down— staring so hard that she did not hear the applause, which the stranger led. She did not sit down gracefully; she hung half-way out of her seat, bracing herself with her arm around her little brother, and still staring at Ollie Kuhns.

The teacher forgot to announce Ollie's speech, but no one noticed. Ollie rose, grinning. This was all a beautiful joke to him. He knew a trick worth two of Katy's. Did he not know a piece called "Der Belsnickel," a description of the masked, fur-clad creature who in Daniel Gaumer's day had brought cakes for good children and switches for the *nixnutzige*? Ollie had terrified the children a thousand times with his representation of "Bosco the Wild

Man." It was a simple thing to make them see a fearful Belsnickel before their eyes.

And little Sarah Knerr, did she not know "Das Krischkindel," which told of the divine Christmas spirit? She had learned it last year for last year's Sunday-School entertainment; she said it now with exquisite and gentle painstaking. When she was through, the teacher rose as though hypnotized and went to the organ. There was an advisory hum from Katy Gaumer, to which the teacher listened with irritation. He had some sense. There was, of course, only one thing to be sung, and that was "Stille Nacht." The children sang, and their fathers and mothers sang, and the stranger led them with his strong voice.

Only Katy Gaumer, fixing one of the remaining performers after the other with her eye, sang no more after the tune was started. There was Coonie Schnable. She said to herself that he would probably fail, anyhow; it made little difference whether his few unintelligible words were English or German. Coonie Schnable was always the clown of the entertainment; he would be of this one also.

But Coonie did not fail. Ellie Shindler recited a German description of "The County Fair" without a break; then Coonie Schnable rose. He had once "helped" successfully in a dialogue. For those who know no Pennsylvania German it must suffice that it was a translation of a scene in Hamlet. For the benefit of those who are more fortunate the translation is appended. Coonie now recited all the parts.

Hamlet: Oh, du armes Schpook!
Ghost: Pity mich net, aber geb mir now dei' Ohre,
    For ich will dir amohl eppas sawga.
Hamlet: Schwetz rous, for ich will es now aw hera.
Ghost: Und wenn du haresht, don nemsht aw satisfaction.
Hamlet: Well, was is 's? Rous mit!
Ghost: Ich bin dei' dawdy sei' Schpook!

To the children, everything which Coonie did was funny, and their fathers and mothers laughed with them. The stranger seemed to discover still deeper springs of mirth; he laughed until he cried.

Only Katy Gaumer, stealing out, was not there to see the end. Nor was she at hand to speed her little brother Adam, who was to close the entertainment with "Hang up the Baby's Stocking." But Adam had had his instructions. He knew no German recitation,—this was his first essay at speech-making,— but he knew a German Bible verse which his Grandmother Gaumer had taught him: "Ehre sei Gott in der Höhe und Friede auf Erden, und den Menschen ein Wohlgefallen" ["Glory to God in the highest, and on earth peace, good will toward men"]. He looked like a Christmas spirit himself as he said it, with his flaxen hair and his blue eyes, as the stranger might have looked fifty years ago. Daniel Gaumer smiled at him as he passed, then gathered him to his knee.

Suddenly little Adam screamed and hid his face against the stranger's breast; then another child shrieked in excited rapture. The Belsnickel had come! It was covered with the dust of the school-house garret; it was not of the traditional huge size,—it was, indeed, less than five feet tall,—but it wore a furry coat,—the distinguished stranger leaped to his feet, saying that it was not possible that that old pelt still survived,—it opened its mouth "like scissors," as Ollie Kuhn's piece had said. It had not the traditional bag, but it had a basket,—Grandmother Gaumer's,—and the traditional cakes and apples were there. It climbed upon a desk, its black-stockinged legs and red dress showing through the rents of the old, ragged coat, and the children surrounded it, laughing, begging, screaming with delight.

It was then that the stranger joined his brother at the back of the room, asking who the Belsnickel was. He did not realize how large a part Katy had had in the entertainment; he knew only that custom selected the most capable and popular scholar for that delightful office. Katy's grandfather called her to him, and she came slowly, slipping like a crimson butterfly from the furry pelt, which the children seized upon with joy. She heard her grandfather tell his brother that she was "Abner's little girl," and her eyes met the stranger's bright gaze. She hesitated in the middle of the room and looked at him. A consciousness of kinship warmed her heart, then a smothering joy. He, too, had hated Millerstown, or he would not have gone away; he, too, loved it, or he would not have come back. He would understand her, help her. He understood even now, for stooping to kiss her, he hid her nervous, foolish tears from Millerstown.

THE SUFFRAGE IN MILLERSTOWN

*I*n *The Book of the United States* (1926), Singmaster chides her beloved country for its reticence in granting female citizens the right to vote, but when this story was first published (*Saturday Evening Post,* March 16, 1912, with illustrations by Charles de Feo), women's suffrage was a controversial issue at both the national and the international level. Singmaster was thirty-two when she wrote "The Suffrage in Millerstown," and she knew first-hand, through the popularity of her stories, the authority that came of having a public voice.

* * *

There are few women in Millerstown who take naps or who lie down in the daytime. It is safe to say that no woman, unless she was seriously ill, ever lay down for a whole afternoon; it is absolutely certain that none but Lizzie Kerr ever spent a whole afternoon—and that in November—reclining upon an outside cellar door.

It was not a position which Lizzie chose for herself. In the first place, she had no time for this extraordinary proceeding. When one has a husband and seven children, the youngest less than a year old, and when one is the only woman on a farm where there are fourteen cows, twenty pigs and a few hundred chickens, that need constant attention, one should be busy every moment. In the second place, Lizzie found the position exceedingly uncomfortable. Lizzie was very large and she was accustomed to rest upon a feather bed—not a hard board. Besides, it is apt to be a little cool on the first Tuesday after the first Monday in November; and besides, it is neither dignified nor decent to slam a cellar door upon one's husband and then lie down upon the door.

Of all this Lizzie was thoroughly aware. Her hands were clenched; she answered the muffled voice from beneath her with a voice utterly unlike her own; at the sound of her baby screaming in his cradle in the kitchen she put her hands over her ears; at thought of her bread-sponge running over the bowl and her pies burning in the oven, she groaned. She did not cry, however, though she looked like a tender-hearted person to whom tears came easily. Occasionally she lifted herself into a half sitting posture, but almost immediately lay down again, feeling it safer to distribute her weight over as many of the flimsy boards as possible. She meant to save Alpheus from committing a great wrong, but she did not wish to crush him to death.

The baby screamed himself to sleep, and woke and screamed again; a stranger, passing in a buggy, asked whether she was ill, and receiving her lying answer that she liked to sit on the cellar door, looked at her as though she were a lunatic; the prisoner commanded, argued, cajoled, pleaded—she grew colder and colder, stiffer and stiffer. However for the sake of the morals of Millerstown, for the sake of her husband rushing to ruin, for the sake of her poor children threatened with destruction by the demon rum, Lizzie Kerr continued to embrace her martyrdom. Once she tried to sing Cold Water is the Children's Friend, but she did not get beyond the first line.

An hour ago she had been standing by her kitchen table working her bread, an entirely suitable and becoming occupation for the mother of seven, and Alpheus had faced her as he drew on his husking mittens. Alpheus was a little, energetic man, for whom his wife had great admiration. He was smart; his brothers looked up to him for counsel; the men at the store listened to him with respect; he read the newspapers learnedly and recounted marvelous tales of extraordinary things—of French people making a Christmas dinner on camel's meat, of women demanding the ballot and battering policemen and being battered in turn by them, of evil men blowing up bridges with dynamite. He could argue with the preacher; he could read both English and German. Until yesterday she had been proud to be his wife. She was richer than he—the farm was hers, inherited from her father; but she had been proud to marry so smart a man. Until yesterday she had been content to know no law but his will; until yesterday she had concerned herself with nothing outside her natural sphere. Now, interfering where she had no business, rushing into a situation of which she knew nothing, governed by ridiculous prejudice and feminine ignorance, she had made a fool of herself.

"I was yesterday in the store, pop," she had faltered when she could fill her lungs with enough breath to speak.

"Yes—well?" answered Alpheus. "What then?" He stared at Lizzie suddenly with some alarm; he had never seen her look like that. "Do you feel bad, mom? Do you have it somewhere?"

Lizzie leaned upon the bread-sponge which rose in great billows about her round arms. With her rosy cheeks and her bright smile, Lizzie was an attractive person—a person to whose company it was good to return after a day's work; but now Lizzie did not smile.

"They talked about the election, pop. They said that Moser was temperance, pop, and Steiner was for the taverns. I said you wouldn't vote for Steiner for the world; and then I came home—and he was sitting here and talking, pop. I—"

Alpheus was annoyed and disgusted.

"Pooh!" he said as he started for the door.

Lizzie was before him, however. She moved with more agility than one would have expected in a person of her size. Bits of dough clung to her fingers; her face was scarlet.

"You are a church member; you have all these boys to bring up. How will you bring up these boys if there is a saloon in every house, pop? How—"

Alpheus was more agile than Lizzie; he dodged past her and closed the door. Then, walking briskly across the meadow to the cornfield, he laughed. Women were good for some things, of course; but they had no minds. Lizzie had no mind or she would realize that the temperance question had absolutely nothing to do with this election. Steiner might occasionally take a drink—that was none of the world's business. He was the candidate of Alpheus' party; he had great respect for Alpheus and the influence Alpheus had over his brothers and several illiterate voters; he would bring them good roads and prosperity. It was foreordained that Alpheus should vote for him. Lizzie was crazy!

Contented with himself, amused at his wife, Alpheus worked on. Presently he began to pity Lizzie. He decided that he would explain things to her that evening. He was really very fond of her.

After a long time Lizzie roused herself from the apathy in which she worked to go to the cellar for the baby's milk. The cellar was across the yard; under its slanting door was a steep flight of steps; below, in the cool dampness, stood a dozen brimming crocks of milk.

"I ought to make butter," said Lizzie as she drearily contemplated them. "I am behind with everything. Nothing will ever be right with me again. Oh, my soul!"

Then slowly Lizzie climbed the steps and heated the milk and filled the baby's bottle. Her tears dropped upon him as he lay sound asleep in his cradle. She was disgraced in the eyes of her friends; she was disappointed in the idol of her soul.

It seemed three hours—it was really but one—before Alpheus returned from the cornfield. It was not yet two o'clock and the polls did not close until six; but he said to himself that his brothers might wish to vote early or Steiner might not think him sufficiently concerned. He came whistling across the meadow. At sight of the open cellar door he turned his steps toward it.

"Mom," he called into the depths, "I am going now to town."

There was no answer; Alpheus went toward the kitchen.

"Did you know you left your cellar door open, mom?" he asked.

Lizzie was standing by the table, where he had left her. Whether the cellar was open or closed made no difference to her.

"Pop," she began, trembling; at which Alpheus remembered.

"When I come home I will talk to you," he said indulgently. Then he patted Lizzie on the shoulder.

Lizzie began to plead.

"Ach! pop, don't vote for Steiner—please, pop!"

"Of course I will vote for Steiner!"

"When you have little children, pop? What if they come in the tavern, pop?"

"*Geh mir aweck!*—Get out!"—mocked Alpheus. "You make me laugh!"

"He takes drinks, pop. And the people in town, they said—"

"I don't care what they said." Alpheus finished washing his hands at the sink. "Where is my other coat?"

"Ach! but, pop, you can talk with me a little about it, I guess. I am dumb—but I am not so dumb, pop. I—"

Alpheus slid rapidly into his coat. Then he applied the brush and comb which lay on the little rack by the door. Then Alpheus could not resist a foolish but overwhelming temptation.

"I must be there early," he said importantly. "I always mark the tickets for a couple o' fellows."

"What!" cried Lizzie. Sometimes Alpheus read to her accounts of election frauds and subsequent investigations. In her confusion, it seemed that he, too, was about to commit fraud. The foundation of Lizzie's world was shaken.

"Goodby," said Alpheus cheerfully.

The baby in the cradle began to cry. Alpheus turned back to his wife.

"Shall I fetch you a little milk?" he asked as tenderly as though he spoke to the baby.

Unable to answer, Lizzie started to follow him. She meant to tell him that she had brought the milk and that the baby had the bottle; but her voice choked. She was shocked; she was hurt; she was—though she did not suspect it—furiously angry at Alpheus' superior airs. When she reached the door he had vanished down the cellar steps and she followed across the yard.

Then, suddenly a great, new, overwhelming emotion filled Lizzie Kerr's soul. Never in her life had she done a violent thing. She had disciplined setting hens; she had spanked her children; but it had been done after deliberation, it had been done with dignity. This was done without consideration, without forethought. She leaned over and lifted the slanting cellar door and closed it upon the little man within. Then, partly from pure weakness, Lizzie Kerr, mother of seven, of great size, lay down upon the door.

The first frantic sound that rose from within added the reproaches of a tender heart to Lizzie's already overwhelming emotions.

"Mom!" called Alpheus. "Mom! Somebody is shutting me in the cellar! Lock yourself in the kitchen, mom, and then lock yourself in the upstairs, mom! And holler like sixty!" His first thought was for her. It was with bursting heart that Lizzie answered.

"I am shutting you up, Alpheus. It is Lizzie. Nothing is after me. I am sitting on the door."

"What!" screamed Alpheus shrilly.

"I must talk to you about this, pop, before it goes any farther." Lizzie's voice became more clear. She did not weep—her tears seemed to be forever dry. She prayed for eloquence; she thought of the people in the Bible who had been given tongues of fire. "You see, pop, it is this way: The people say that Steiner has parties and that the people drink. It is not raspberry vinegar, pop, or yeast beer—it is real beer in bottles from the tavern, pop. They sometimes have some of this cha'pagne-water. Suppose these poor little children should get some, pop! Suppose little Lizzie should stay out late in the night, pop; and suppose little Alpheus should come home yelling and hollering, pop! Suppose—"

The cellar door quivered.

"Get up!" ordered Alpheus. He spoke as he might have spoken to his horse or his dog. Lizzie had never heard that tone addressed to her. Her cheeks flushed, but still she spoke gently.

"Will you promise to vote for Moser, pop?"

"Get up!" commanded Alpheus again.

"Will you promise not to vote for Steiner, pop?"

"Get up!" ordered Alpheus, more furiously.

"Will you promise not to vote for anybody, pop? Will you stay here with me? Will you—"

"Get up!" said Alpheus in a terrible tone.

For a few minutes there was silence. The door shook slightly again; but

Alpheus, though strong, was short—he could get no purchase on the door. Then motion, as well as sound, ceased. Indeed, actual physical paralysis was no more numbing than the sensations that filled the breast of Alpheus. Had the barn fallen upon him and bade him lie still, he could have been no more amazed. Presently silence was succeeded by a more furious burst of anger. He would vote for whom he chose; now he was absolutely determined to vote for Steiner—nothing would keep him from it! If she had not acted the fool he might have listened to her; but he was the boss—nobody could make him do what he didn't want to do.

Poor Lizzie did not answer. Indeed, she did not hear half he said, for another sound penetrated to her ears and filled her with dismay. Presently, when he paused for breath, Alpheus heard it also.

"Your baby is crying!" he shouted. "Go to it!"

Lizzie was wringing her hands. The baby should have gone to sleep at once and slept for hours. He had a bottle and he was comfortably fixed. Had he broken the bottle and cut himself? Was something after him—the cat, perhaps? Had—

"Your baby is starving!" said Alpheus. "Shall a mother sit on a cellar door while her baby is dying?"

"He is not starving," said Lizzie. "He has his bottle; and, anyhow, he could go without a little while and not starve. He—"

"Then something is after him," declared Alpheus. "He will die then—"

"He will not die while he is yelling like that," said Lizzie hoarsely. Oh, if only she only had him in her arms! "That's a mad yell, pop. He is only cross. Oh, say you will not vote for Steiner!"

"I will vote for Steiner!" shouted Alpheus. He remembered suddenly Peter and George, depending upon his advice, and the incompetents expecting him to mark their tickets. He shook the door. "Let me out! Get up!"

"No!" said Lizzie. "No, pop, I cannot."

Fortunately the day was only cool and not cold; fortunately the sun shone directly upon Lizzie's bed; fortunately no one passed but the one stranger; fortunately it did not occur to Alpheus to pretend a fall down the cellar steps, or to remain silent and simulate death, or to take any other means of adding to Lizzie's agony of mind.

He told her he was cold; she advised him to get as close to the cellar door as he could and reminded him that he had a means of escape. He recalled to her her promise to obey; she put him in remembrance of her long years of obedience and suggested the Higher Power, to whom one owed a higher obedience. She quoted Bible verses at length; she reminded him of moral truths and precepts that have little to do with elections. In some strange, unconscious way, Lizzie had allied herself with those unaccountable lunatics known as reformers. Alpheus was certain now that she was crazy. He reproached her with her presumption in setting forth her opinions; and then another dam broke in the long-checked current of Lizzie's mental processes.

"The farm is mine!" said she. "I do half the work. I guess I can have some say, Alpheus."

She had not called him Alpheus for years. It was as though she chose to ignore all the relations of duty and affection that bound them together. Alpheus remembered the smashed windows of London, the dismay of London's mighty men.

"Lizzie," said he weakly, "what will my children think when they see me penned in the cellar?"

"Will you promise not to vote for Steiner?"

"No!" roared Alpheus. "Get up!"

Thus the long afternoon passed. The baby ceased crying and slept, and waked and cried again, the boards under the baby's mother grew harder, the air colder; but Lizzie still lay upon the cellar door.

At length, now, with infinite patience, Alpheus explained to her the political situation. Steiner had nothing to do with the taverns.

"Except drink in them!" said Lizzie with a new quickness of thought.

Steiner would bring them good roads.

"But he is a bad man!" said Lizzie. "It is better to have bad roads. Will you promise not to vote for Steiner?" she asked.

"No!" shouted Alpheus. "Get up!"

It was half-past four when the children came home from school. Alpheus, the oldest, was twelve; Lizzie, who was next to the baby, was five; they were the most obedient children that ever lived. Their mother had risen now to a sitting posture. Seeing her, they hurried up the lane.

"You are to go to your Aunt Sally," she said. "You can go to Aunt Sally till six o'clock."

The children stared at her and at each other; then they trotted off. Only little Alpheus looked back.

"Why do you sit on the cellar door, mom?" he called.

"Because I like it," said Lizzie.

From the earth beneath came a reproving voice.

"Ain't you ashamed, mom, to lie to children! Ain't you ashamed?"

"Will you promise not to vote for Steiner?" asked Lizzie with the same deadly monotony.

"No!" yelled Alpheus. "I won't."

After a long time the clock in the kitchen struck five. The sound reached the cellar. In an hour the polls would close.

"That was six o'clock," said Alpheus.

"It was five," corrected Lizzie.

It seemed to Lizzie, shivering without, and to Alpheus, shivering within, that hours passed before there was another sound. Then Lizzie spoke once more:

"Will you promise not to vote for Steiner?"

To her amazement Alpheus returned a prompt "Yes."

"W–what?" faltered Lizzie.

"I said 'Yes,'" repeated Alpheus. To Alpheus' shame, be it said, Alpheus did not tell the truth. An expedient had occurred to him. If he could only get to the polls in time!

For all her weight and stiffness, Lizzie almost sprang from the door. It was at once lifted and Alpheus thrust up his head. Then he bounced out.

"You dare not make a man promise something when you have him penned up!" he shouted. "It says so in the law. I am going to vote. I—"

Alpheus paused. Up the lane came the children.

"What time is it?" Alpheus demanded furiously of his wife.

"It struck six already," she said heavily; "I thought I would give you another chance to do right, Alpheus."

"What!" began Alpheus—then paused.

Seeing the wild-looking creature before him, Alpheus was suddenly appalled. The recollection of his wrongs, of Steiner's probable rage, of his own little, unshepherded political flock, vanished from his mind; he saw instead those wild, window-smashing Londoners.

"Mom," said Alpheus, "are you going to parade like—like those others? Will you vote, mom?"

Solemnly Lizzie returned his gaze. She was stiff and sore in body and mind; she was a stranger to herself.

"I do not know yet what I will do," said she ominously.

Alpheus was distracted with fright. It would have made no difference to him now if Steiner had been plunged into the sea. He tried to take Lizzie's unwilling hand; he called to the children to "Come quick to mom!" Then he rushed into the kitchen.

"See, mom!" he cried. "Here is the baby—the little baby, mom! It cries for you, mom! See!"

Thankful for the fierce screams with which the baby resented being torn from his bed in the midst of sleep, Alpheus bore him forth and placed him in his mother's arms. Then, as the amazed and terrified children surrounded her, Lizzie returned—for the time at least—to woman's sphere. With a loudness which inspired a like demonstration from all her frightened offspring and made Alpheus declare that hereafter he would do everything she liked and nothing she did not like—with a heartiness that branded victory as a not unmixed satisfaction—poor Lizzie wept.

ZION CHURCH

*I*n "Zion Church" (*Atlantic Monthly*, March 1913), Singmaster examines the effects of economic growth and ethnic diversity in the predominantly agrarian Pennsylvania German Lehigh Valley. A minister's daughter and a church leader, she imagined how the balance of power in her fictional congregation might be altered by demographic change. Her character Matthias Lucas, whose once absolute power in Zion Church's congregation is questioned by the new congregational council, retaliates in a criminal way. This tragic story is timeless.

* * *

Beautiful Zion Valley is an oval plain with hills surrounding it like the sides of a cup, and with a winding stream following the line of its longest diameter. In the centre of the valley, with the graveyard and the winding stream at its back, and opposite it and across the road the house of Matthias Lucas, stands Zion Church. The house of Matthias Lucas is old; it was built, as the German inscription above the door bears witness, by Matthias's grandfather in 1749. Below the name and date, carved in the stone, are the words, "God bless all those who go in and out."

The church is a magnificent one for a farming community. It is built of gray stone, its style is Gothic, and its spire, a hundred and ninety feet high from the base to the golden ball at its top, seems to rise higher than the hills. The great church room measures fifty feet from the floor to the apex of the arched ceiling. There are no frescoes; the walls are gray; the straight pews and the strange high pulpit with its winding stairs are dark walnut; the woodwork of the high galleries is painted white. The windows are clear glass; they were kept bright at first by Matthias Lucas, who, after he had given the church, became for love of it its sexton; they are polished now by the women of the devout Pennsylvania German congregation. From some of the windows, one may see straight into the leafy hearts of old oak trees; from others one may look through thinner foliage out across the surrounding farms to the hills. From the distance, the gray mass of Zion Church dominates the landscape like the cathedral of Chartres upon the broad plain of France.

Zion Church is rich; she owns the broad stone house and the five farms of Matthias Lucas. She has no debt; her paint is always shining; the grassy lawn about her is always smoothly trimmed; her graveyard, whose mounds are covered with myrtle or lily-of-the-valley or clove-pink, is set with straight white stones on which no moss is allowed to gather.

Many of the graves are interesting to the antiquarian. There are several of Indians who were converted by the preaching of the first pastor, and there are many with German inscriptions. The inscriptions which are carved to-day are English; sometimes, added to those already on a tall monument, they form a record of the transition from one language to another. The grandmother of the Arndts was recorded, "Sarah Arndt, *geboren* Peterman"; their mother was described as "Ellen Arndt, daughter of Rudolph Hummel"; above the grave of their young sister-in-law, who died a year ago, is written, "Elizabeth Arndt, *née* Miller." The Pennsylvania Germans have become cosmopolitan indeed! But the inscriptions on the Lucas graves are all German. Even Matthias, the last of his family, died before any one dreamed that the residents of Zion Valley would learn English.

It is three generations since Matthias Lucas in his middle-age cursed the congregation and the church and almost God himself, and went no more to service.

The Kirchen Rath (church council) met one winter evening, as it had met since the days of Matthias's grandfather, in the Lucas kitchen, an appropriate place, since, like his father and his grandfather, Matthias managed the affairs of the church. The second building in which the congregation worshiped had become unfit for use, the plans for a new church lay spread before the council on the old oak table. The members of the council, which had been in session from seven o'clock until midnight, had been arguing, and they were tired.

Then rose Matthias Lucas angrily from his chair. He was about forty years old, a man of powerful build and with a fine, ruddy color from working in the fields. He had inherited wealth from his father, and he was steadily adding to it. He meant to give largely to the new church, which was his own as much as was his great stone house or his farms or his wife and child. Devoted, generous, stubborn, Matthias Lucas might have said with conviction, "I am Zion Church."

"Who will have to build this church?" he demanded hotly, in his sonorous German speech. "Who will have to give most of the money? I will! Whose people gave the land in the beginning but mine? This—" Matthias laid his hand on one of the papers spread out before him—"this is the way it is to be."

The point under discussion was a minor one, some small difference in the height of the steeple, or in the work required on the foundation, a point on which there might easily be two opinions, both of them right. Matthias Lucas might have yielded, but he was stubborn and he had not been accustomed to having his judgments questioned. On the other hand, the church council might have yielded, but it had been looking at plans for five hours, and as far back as the mind could reach it had been domineered over by a Lucas. When the vote was taken, there were seven votes against Matthias and none with him.

Still standing, Matthias had his say.

"You will build the church alone, then. Not a penny will I give."

Peter Arndt rose and faced him. The candle-light made two bright spots of their white faces in the great, low room with its brown, raftered ceiling and its black shadows. The members of Zion Church were not rich. All the low arable land of the valley belonged to the Lucases, and the fine ore deposits on the higher, poorer farms lay still unsuspected and undisturbed beneath the ground. The loss of the contribution of Matthias Lucas would be calamitous. But Peter Arndt faced him bravely.

"Then we will build it alone."

Tired of their long meeting, certain that to-morrow Matthias would think better of his foolishness, the other seven members of the church council untied their horses from the fence along the lane and rode home. Matthias laughed when they had gone.

"Build it alone!" he mocked. "Not while the world stands! They will build it my way, or they will not build at all. They have no money."

Matthias was right; without him Zion Church was not able to build. The old church was patched up and services were held there for ten years. Matthias, sitting in his front room on Sunday mornings, watched the congregation assemble, but did not join them. He listened in stubborn silence to the admonition of the preacher, he continued to contribute to the preacher's salary, but into the church he would not go.

"I will not risk my life in that old shell," he declared to his wife. "It will come down on their heads. When they are ready to build, let them come to me and we will build."

But the church council did not come to Matthias. Presently, his wife and his only son died of smallpox, and, since even this isolated Pennsylvania valley had begun to observe quarantine, their bodies were carried directly from the house to the burying-ground, without the customary service in the church. Thus Matthias did not have to break his word.

Aghast at the sorrow which had come upon Matthias, the members of Zion Church visited him and shed more tears than did the stern man sitting in his grandfather's armchair in his lonely kitchen. When the funeral was over, he went about his work as though nothing had happened. The preacher added admonition to his consolation, he besought and then commanded Matthias to return to his church. But Matthias's heart was not softened; it was then that he cursed Zion Church and said that as God had forsaken him, so had he forsaken God.

Almost at once, as though to add to his bitterness and anger, the walls of the new church began to rise. The deep ore-beds had been opened; great blast furnaces had sprung up through all the Pennsylvania German counties. The members of Zion Church had been saving their money in anticipation of building; now, as they began to sell their ore, they added to their original plan. They had for their church a spirit of mediaeval devotion like that of the builders of Amiens; they would erect the finest building in many days' journey.

Of their plans, Matthias would hear nothing. Again the preacher visited him; humbly the church council asked his forgiveness, and explained that all the details of their plans had changed; they had rejected their own plans as well as his. But he would not listen.

"You think you can cajole me," answered Matthias grimly; "but not a penny shall you have unless you come back and sit in my kitchen and vote to build the way I want it."

The walls of the new church rose rapidly, and Matthias from his window opposite, and from his farms and gardens, watched them rise. Sometimes he smiled.

"They will never pay for it," he assured himself with satisfaction. "Those who were fools enough to build for them will not get their money."

Presently the church was completed. By the day of dedication, the pastor had promises for all the money needed.

From his lonely house, Matthias watched the final preparations. It was October, the season of harvest-home, and into the new church were carried great sheaves of wheat and the tallest stalks of corn. Presently, when Peter Arndt drove up with his wagon loaded with fine apples and pears and vegetables, Matthias crossed the road to speak to him.

"You are my tenant," said he, harshly; "nothing from my land is to be taken into the church."

Without answering, Peter Arndt drove away. Matthias's old friends had begun to be afraid of him.

There was to be communion at the morning service, and it had been ten years since Matthias Lucas had gone to the communion-table. If his heart ached and his lips hungered for the token to which he had been accustomed from his childhood, he comforted himself with hate. He sat behind his bowed shutters and watched the congregation of Zion Church rejoicing in its new possession. He saw the children come to practice for their exercises, he saw flowers being carried by the armful until the cemetery looked like a great garden, and his heart hardened the more within him. He said now that they had cast him off, and he believed what he said. He realized fully, with intolerable pain, that they could do without him.

That night, complete from floor to spire, fresh from the careful hands of its builders, decked with the fruits of the field as a token of thankfulness to God, with the white communion-cloth spread already on the altar, Zion Church, waiting for its consecration, burned to the ground.

Matthias Lucas's maid-servant gave the alarm. The rosy light, reflected from the flames against the wall of the barn and thence into her attic room, wakened her, and she went, screaming, to pound at Matthias's door. By that time the church was a mere shell about a roaring furnace. The paint and varnish were fresh, and they, with the dried leaves and grain of the decorations, fed the flame to so fierce a heat that the walls fell outward with a great explosion.

From his window, Matthias Lucas watched. He heard the screams of his servant as she rushed down the road, he heard the panting of runners as they came in answer to her call, he heard cries of frantic inquiry and wild sorrow. He knew from whom each sound came; he could tell the voice of each of his old friends, who loved their church as they loved their souls: of Peter Arndt, and John Lorish, and James Bär, and many others. The silver communion service was in the church; Peter Arndt had to be restrained by force from rushing into the flames to find it. Watching them, listening to them, Matthias felt that he was almost like God Himself.

"They will come back to me!" he cried. "They owe this money, they will have to pay it, the law will make them, and they still have no church. They will come back to me!"

When he had had his breakfast and had looked after his stock, he went into his parlor and sat down by the window. His heart felt strangely warmed; he spoke gently to his weeping servant.

"It will be built up," he assured her, to comfort her.

Soon after nine o'clock the congregation began to gather. There were many from a distance who had not heard the dreadful news; as they came over the hill, they drew rein in horror, and then urged their horses on. Matthias could hear their cries and the galloping feet of their horses. A few who drove to the very ruins before they saw that their church was destroyed, sat dumbly, making no effort to dismount from horse or wagon.

"They will have to ask me to help them now," said Matthias again to himself, a strange peace in his heart.

But no one crossed the road to Matthias's house. The men tied their horses and gathered about the preacher, the women sat on the grass in the graveyard in the warm sunshine; they were helpless, homeless, distraught. From group to group went his weeping servant, telling what she knew of the fire.

Presently Matthias saw that they were going to hold a service. The older people found seats on the flat tombstones, the younger ones stood about. There, within that low stone wall, all the congregation of Zion Church was gathered, and there was crying such as had often accompanied the laying-away of the mother of little children, or of the strong man, dying in his youth. Only one of the living members was not present—Matthias Lucas, who waited in his house across the way.

Through the open window, Matthias could hear the preacher's voice, broken, trembling; he could see the preacher's hands, lifted in petition.

"'Lord,'" cried he, "'Thou hast been our dwelling place in all generations!'"

To Matthias, it seemed that the agonized plea was lifted to him. Then, with sobs and cries, the congregation tried to sing;—

> Ach, Gott, verlass mich nicht,
> Gieb mir die Gnadenhände!
>
> Oh, God, forsake me not,
> Thy gracious hand extend me!

Involuntarily Matthias Lucas sang with them the words which he had learned at his mother's knee,—

> Thy Holy Spirit grant;
> And 'neath the heaviest load,
> Be thou my strength and stay,
> Forsake me not, O God!

They were in trouble, these foolish, headstrong people, but he would help them. He would not wait for them to come to him; he would go to them. Matthias rose from his chair.

But, as the members of Zion Church sang, a change came over them. The hymn rose as it had risen many times before from that solemn place, at first a cry of misery. But presently its tone changed. The God to whom they cried had sustained them always when they called upon Him thus; He would sustain them now. Their voices strengthened and became calm; the great music of the choral rose above the blackened ruins and floated out over the fields and hills to heaven itself. They dried their tears and took heart.

Then they drew closer together, and the preacher's clear voice, cheering and encouraging them, penetrated to the old stone house, where in his wealth and his bitterness, Matthias listened.

"We will begin to rebuild to-morrow," announced the preacher. "God will bless us. We will take promises now. I will give a year's salary, if you will help me by sending me things from your gardens."

Immediately the offerings began, and steadily they went on. The debt was to be paid, a plainer building was to be erected at once, the congregation of Zion Church was equal to its trouble. They did not call upon Matthias, they did not think of him. Close to the graves of his wife and child, they made their plans; without the fold, alone, holding to his chair for support, stood Matthias in his desolate house.

Then, Matthias went slowly out of the door and across the yard and the road to the churchyard.

"Listen to me!" he cried. "I have something to say."

He pressed close to his old friends as though he were pursued by a terror from which they must defend him, and they, thinking that he was smitten by disease or madness, drew away in fright. The minister went toward him, and the girl who had stayed in his house because she had loved her mistress and her mistress's child.

"Listen to me!" he cried again. "I will build you a church, a church of stone, to last forever, with a great spire. You shall have my farms to endow it perpetually. Do not draw away from me! You must let me do it, or I will die! *For in the night, I came over with a candle and set fire to the church you built without me!*"

A SOUND IN THE NIGHT

*S*ingmaster's friends remember her disdain for alcoholic beverages. Four years after the enactment of the Volstead Act, Singmaster published this regional story about the Improved Mennonite Shindledecker sisters' support for prohibition (*Saturday Evening Post,* January 19, 1924; reprinted, with illustrations by Elizabeth Shippen Green, in *Bred in the Bone*). Singmaster believed she could comment safely on controversial social issues from the margins of Pennsylvania German literature.

* * *

I

Betsey Shindledecker and her sister Tilly sat opposite each other at a large quilting frame which filled half their kitchen. Betsey was tall and stout, and to her round, benevolent countenance the transparent Mennonite cap with its narrow black strings gave an aspect of saintliness. Her dress was of soft gray chambray, made with a full skirt and close-fitting waist and over her bosom was folded a large neckerchief of gray chambray. Tilly, who also wore the Mennonite garb, was older and taller, and somewhat stooped. When she walked across the kitchen she had the appearance of one bending to watch her own steps, and the black ties hung perpendicularly from her cap. She had a thin face and an alert, nervous expression, as though she listened constantly for the approach of something which was unpleasant, if not dangerous. The sisters were members, not of the main body of the Mennonites but of a small and very strict offshoot called the Improved Mennonites.

The Shindledeckers needed no quilts; in ancient painted chests in bedrooms and attic were enough to last their lifetime and the lifetime of several large generations after them. There were quilts of woolen material put together in squares and diamonds and oblongs, and there were quilts of muslin in all patterns known to Pennsylvania Germandom. There was none of silk, because taste and conscience opposed the use of silk. There was one in which tiny circles of calico had been joined together, the lacy result being ornamental rather than useful. There was one which had in it twelve thousand half-inch squares. Even the white material between the colored patches which formed the design was cut into squares and sewed together. The quilting was a marvel of neatness and exactness. There were intricate circles, sprays of flowers, animals and, loveliest of all, graceful feathers.

In the rooms with the painted dower chests stood old beds, some of them four-posters, tall chests of drawers and washstands with pitchers and basins of brown pottery. In the room over the kitchen, which the sisters shared, the basin had upon its brim two perching doves which held in their bills a little cup for soap. All the sheets and towels in the house were homespun. The sheets were broad, with a seam down the middle; the towels were five times as long as they were wide, with loops at the top to hang over wooden pegs in the doors, and fringe wrought of the material at the bottom. Upon them borders were embroidered in cross-stitch, sometimes conventional designs, sometimes the name of the long-departed maker, sometimes a little verse or motto. The kitchen cupboard was of walnut, and so were all the chairs and tables. The Shindledeckers were slow people, unmoved by changing fashions.

The Shindledeckers were naturally shy, and the trait had been cultivated until the two surviving members seldom went from home except to meeting. They tilled their garden in the early morning and sent their milk to the creamery by a neighbor, who also did their errands at the store. Only trespassers upon their property could draw them from the house and into conversation. When hunters threatened the rabbit that came to their porch each winter evening for an apple, or the squirrels that lived in their woodland, Betsey especially became bold as a lion and drove off the marauders with loud and truculent speech.

The fields were oftener trespassed upon than the woodland, in the center of which was one of the deep pits called sink holes, which are common in the limestone country. It was said that before the time of the oldest man living, a farmer quarrying limestone had suddenly sunk from sight with his wagon and two horses, and that the surrounding earth was not firm. The pit had long been filled by a subterranean spring, and was supposed to be bottomless. Round it was a close growth of magnificent trees, the summer haunt and the spring and fall resting place of all the native and migrant birds, which knew no terror of the black pool.

Regardless of completely equipped beds and chests filled to bursting, when the Shindledeckers felt each fall the impulse to quilt they set to work, and the quilt now stretched taut upon the frame bade fair to excel in beauty all those made by themselves and their mother, grandmothers and great-grandmothers. Upon a foundation of creamy unbleached muslin had been appliquéd wreaths of roses mixed with sprays of pale-blue larkspur. The designer of the chintz from which they had cut the delicate and beautiful pattern was an artist rare among designers. Under each green leaf and rose or blue petal a tiny bit of padding had been placed so that the wreaths seemed to lie upon the creamy surface. The spaces between were laid out in a feather pattern in blue chalk, to be followed by thousands of tiny stitches, and then brushed or washed off.

As they worked the sisters could look out in three directions—back into the woodland, to the right up a white road which mounted the hills, and to the left across beautiful fields toward the city of Lanesville. By pressing their faces to the windowpanes and looking sidewise they could see the little meeting-house across the road where they attended services on Sunday morning and Wednesday evening. The rooms at the front of the house were kept closely shuttered, except at the time of fall and spring cleaning, and the approach of visitors could not be discerned until they pounded at the back door. Visitors had to pound; it was not until they had thus proved the seriousness of their intentions that Betsey answered. Tilly would never have answered though the very roof clattered about her ears.

The sisters enlivened their pleasant work with song. Tilly had a high soprano and Betsey a basslike alto. They sang the hymn book through, Tilly elaborating with really skillful runs and quavers the theme as sung by Betsey.

This morning the view was beautiful beyond words to describe. The color in the woodland at the back of the house was startling in its brilliancy of red and yellow, and the color on the distant hills mysterious in its rose and purple. The winter wheat was green and in among the shocks of corn lay piles of brilliant yellow ears. There was not a cloud, not a disturbing breath of air; the loveliness made one's heart ache.

"Sometime we'll make us a quilt with such autumn leaves," planned Tilly. "We'll get samples and samples and samples, till we find the right one."

"Yes, well," agreed Betsey, looking at her sister with admiration.

Tilly was artist and poet, though she had no suspicion of it herself.

"I think the brown cow is so nice in the sun," she said, looking out upon their little field. "She gets sort of a orange color on her rough back."

"And the chickens, also." Betsey looked out the opposite window, pleased to be able to add an observation. "But you," she said, suddenly looking under the quilting frame—"you don't match nothing, you old gray one."

A large cat walked out and approached the door. He was an unresponsive beast and his dignified and indifferent behavior was the joy of their lives. They insulted him, but they adored him, and Betsey moved at once to let him out. She was five years younger than Tilly and it was fitting that she should wait upon the cat.

"He thinks we're going to sing."

"Well, let's begin," laughed Betsey.

An hour passed in music and another in silence and the morning waxed more and more brilliant. It was time that Betsey rise and put the potatoes on to boil, but she could not bear to interrupt the steady setting of her tiny firm stitches. A scratching at the door brought her to her feet.

"The proud one has come back."

"If he'd only earn his keep! If he'd only catch once one little field mouse!"

This was nonsense; Tilly could not bear to see anything caught.

Betsey opened the door, saying contemptuously, "So you want in now, do you? You think I've nothing to do but wait on you?"

The cat entered slowly, his tail in the air. Something else came in with him, a faint sound, and Tilly raised her head and stayed her needle as though sewing were a noisy process.

"Listen!" she cried.

Betsey did not say "Where?" or "What?" She stood breathless. Without doubt, footsteps were approaching.

Instantly, as one would throw out one's arm to save one's self from a fall, Tilly drew down the nearest shade and then rose and crossed the room and drew down the others. Betsey had by this time softly slid the bolt in its socket. There was a knock, courteous and a little apologetic; she stood motionless. There was another, firmer and more insistent; she still stood motionless. There was a third, thundering, irritable, and she opened the door about two inches. The two men standing without, Dan Webber from the creamery and a Lanesvillian whom Betsey did not know, peered into a black cave.

"Good-morning, Betsey," said Dan.

"Good-morning," answered Betsey.

"Good-morning, too," said the stranger as though he were frightened. He was a small and astonishingly timid-looking person.

"Good-morning to you," said Betsey with a twinkle in her eye.

Dan Webber stood first on one foot, then on the other as if waiting to be invited in, though he knew perfectly well this was an unfounded and ridiculous expectation.

"We want to see you once a little."

Betsey remained silent. She was here, she could be seen—at least her nose and the buttons on her waist and a long narrow section of her capacious apron could be seen.

"That is, we want to talk to you a little."

Betsey still said nothing. She could be talked to as well as seen.

"It's important," said Dan.

Betsey waited.

"This is what we're after," explained Dan, looking angrily and helplessly at his companion: "We want to find out if you're for wet or for dry."

The Shindledeckers did not read newspapers and the inquiry was bewildering. The door moved in Betsey's hand, not away from the frame but toward it.

"For wet or for dry?" she repeated in her deep voice.

"Are you for liquor or against liquor?" asked Dan plainly.

"Am I for liquor?" The narrow opening acted as an amplifier for Betsey's words. "Am I for liquor?" She answered oratorically—something grand and spectacular was lost in Betsey—"Am I for the devil?"

Dan took a step nearer the door.

"I knew you ladies were all right. Now this is the way things are with us: Our constable is no good and we want to elect Peters here. There's something wrong going on in this neighborhood. At Unionville there's a distillery and a bonded warehouse, and this these here bootleggers are emptying little by little. They're making thousands of dollars, perhaps millions. They must travel along this road or the back road—there's nowhere else to go—and if we had a good constable he could catch them. What we want you ladies to do is to help us."

"Help you?" repeated Betsey.

"Vote for Peters," said Dan.

"It's against my religion," said Betsey. "I wouldn't vote for anything."

"It's only coming to the schoolhouse and dropping a little paper in the box."

"No, sir." Betsey shook her head violently. First one ear could be seen, then the other. "We plain people are not for voting."

"Lots of plain people are going to help us."

"Then they're wrong," declared Betsey. "I won't vote. *Nix cum rous* with voting."

"Will your sister?" asked Dan, trying to be patient.

"She less than I." Betsey quoted from the beautifully wrought sentiment on a hand-woven and embroidered towel: "'Little and unknown, prized by God alone,' is what we ought to be in this world. I would sooner die than vote."

Betsey closed the door.

The two men looked at each other, then they stamped off the little porch and out the path. From the front they gazed at the substantial close-shuttered house.

"*Esel!*" said Dan furiously.

"*Kelver!*" said Peters still more furiously.

"*Verrickt!*" said Dan.

"*Narrisch!*" said Peters.

They meant that the Shindledeckers were donkeys, calves, fools and lunatics. They stamped down to the white road, looked angrily across at the sedate meeting-house which to their thinking bred these creatures, and, winding up their machine, chugged furiously away.

Within, Betsey stood still in the darkness until she heard across the wide space and through the thick door the loud sound of departure; then she said, "You can come out now."

Tilly returned from an inner room. Her shyness was really a disease; she was pale with terror.

"What did they want?"

Betsey raised the thick shades and the bright sunshine streamed in.

"They want us to come and vote for a constable so he'll arrest the people that are stealing liquor at Unionville."

"I thought all the liquor was poured away!"

"There's some left," said Betsey grimly. Betsey was less innocent than Tilly.

"What do they do with it?"

"I guess they sell it."

"But that's wicked!"

"Yes," agreed Betsey. "But I will not vote."

"No," said Tilly. "That's not right either."

They returned to their work, but their day was spoiled; the roses and larkspur had lost their lovely color.

"They travel along this front road or the back road with it," explained Betsey.

"I don't see why all the people don't get out and tie a rope across the road and catch them," said Tilly.

"They're afraid," answered Betsey. "They're cowards. This Peters who shall be constable is not one to catch anybody."

II

The two Shindledeckers went to bed early. In the middle of the afternoon they had left their delectable occupation of quilting and had gone to husk corn. They divided this work into many short periods so that it might not stiffen their hands, but this afternoon they decided to do a long stint and complete the task. When night came they were tired. They went a second time to the chicken-house to be sure that all was secure and they prepared the bed for their haughty cat with more than usual care. It must not be supposed for an instant that they found life dull. Life was interesting, romantic, and exciting. To-day it had been too exciting for comfort; it disturbed them to hear of wickedness and crime. In their minds liquor was the root of pretty much all the evil in the world. Their consciences troubled them; they believed they should have listened more patiently to the creamery man; but on the other hand they did not believe it right to vote.

"The Government ought to burn up such a place," said Betsey as she laid her smooth head on her pillow. "Why should they leave such a place to tempt wicked people?"

"That's true," agreed Tilly, who, being older, covered her head with a neat cap.

"I don't need liquor," declared Betsey.

"Nor I," said Tilly.

"I never even saw any that I know of."

"Nor I," said Tilly.

"I guess we ought to go to sleep. It's nine o'clock."

"Yes," agreed Tilly. "I wish we could get a whole width done to-morrow. I'm going to get up early."

"Good-night," said Betsey.

"Good-night," answered Tilly. "My, the moon is bright!"

"Yes," said Betsey, trying first one side, then the other. "Perhaps that's the reason I'm so restless."

At ten o'clock Betsey rose and looked out the window. At once Tilly sat up in bed.

"What's the matter?"

"Nothing."

"Did you hear something?"

"No, I just wanted to look out. Everything is so bright and still. Were you asleep?"

"No," said Tilly. "I thought once I heard a noise."

"I guess it was the gray one walking round," said Betsey as she climbed back into the high bed.

She had never been more wide awake and she would have liked to talk about the gray one, but she thought Tilly ought to sleep. But Tilly was not inclined to sleep, though she lay motionless for an hour.

"Betsey," said she as the clock struck eleven, "are you awake?"

"Yes," answered Betsey. "I haven't closed an eye."

"I thought I heard a noise," said Tilly.

"What kind of a noise?"

"Something outside the house."

Betsey rose again and went to the window and raised it a few inches. She then knelt down with some creaking of bones and laid her ear to the aperture.

"It's nothing," she announced. "The bunny's sitting down on the grass. He's better than a watchdog."

"Yes, well," said Tilly. "I'm sorry I got you out."

"It's all right," said Betsey amiably.

She lowered the window and went back to bed, but still she could not close her eyes. She wondered whether Tilly was asleep; there were a hundred things she would like to talk about. She heard the clock strike twelve and then one.

Tilly was awake; she sat up as though released by a spring.

"Betsey!" she cried in a hoarse whisper.

"Yes!" Betsey sat up also.

"Did you hear that?"

"I felt it," said Betsey in amazement. "The bed sort of shook and there was a sort of rumbling."

"Do you think it's an earthquake?"

"No."

"What do you think it is?"

Betsey bounced out like a great rubber ball. She went this time to the window at the rear and lifted the shade and the sash. There was still a slight vibration of the house. Staring into the woods, she remained so long motionless that Tilly crept from bed and joined her. Overhead shone the full moon, before them was the dark wall of trees, and under the trees was the faintest light, not the sifted silver of the moon, but a pale gold. The vibration of the ground had ceased, but there was the throbbing of an engine. Suddenly the light went out and the throbbing stopped abruptly. The two sisters pressed close together.

"What is it?" asked Tilly, trembling.

"I don't know," said Betsey.

"I believe I've heard it before," said Tilly. "I thought it was a dream other times, but to-night I was for once wide awake."

"It's in our woods," said Betsey indignantly.

"What do you think it is?"

"It's an automobile."

"What do they want?" Tilly shook like a leaf. This was no ordinary car; it must be a heavy truck, as heavy as the great moving vans which traveled from Philadelphia to Pittsburgh. A fearful suspicion began to dawn in her mind. "What are they doing by us?"

"They're liquor people." Betsey was so far removed from the world that she knew no other name. She ceased to guard her speech, but spoke in a loud tone. "They're in our woods; they're perhaps hiding there."

"Why should they hide there?" whimpered Tilly.

"I don't know," said Betsey in a still louder tone.

"Perhaps it's something wrong with the car," suggested Tilly. "Or perhaps they are just passing on the back road."

"They have no business on the back road," declared Betsey in a voice of rage. "And they're in the woods, deep in, almost as far as the sink hole. I can tell it from the light. I'm going back there."

Tilly was smitten dumb. She stood paralyzed while Betsey sat heavily down on the floor and began to put on her shoes and stockings.

"You're going back to the sink hole now?"

"To be sure I am," roared Betsey in her deep alto. "We'll not have such people on our land. I'll see what this is and if they're liquor people I'll tell them what I think."

With a groan Tilly sat down and began to put on her shoes and stockings.

"I'm not afraid," said Betsey. "You needn't go along."

Tilly uttered another groan, but she continued her dressing. She was speedier than Betsey and she finished first.

"Will we wear our shawls?" she asked in a whisper.

"No," said Betsey, still in her loud tone. "We'll wear our husking jackets to go through the woods." She tramped noisily down the stairs. "You get them and I'll light the lantern."

"Will we go clear in the woods?"

"To be sure. Of course we'll not sneak up on them; we'll let them know we're coming."

Betsey took the lantern from the mantel and stepped out upon the porch. The fields were bright; the yellow piles of corn could be plainly distinguished and it was possible to tell the golden hickories from the crimson oaks. There was not a sound in the world.

"Perhaps we dreamed it," said Tilly. "We were wakeful, and when you're wakeful you get queer ideas."

"No," shouted Betsey, stepping off the porch; "we did not dream it."

Moving heavily, but not slowly, she went along the little path and Tilly followed close upon her heels. In the shadow the gleam of the lantern brightened.

"It's not far," said Betsey in a shout. "It's not farther than the meeting-house." She stood still and drew a deep breath and let it out in a trumpet blast. "We're coming!"

She waited an instant as if for an answer, then she moved forward. The lantern cast monstrous shadows of her and Tilly against the darkness; they resembled dimly an elephant followed by a giraffe.

"I give you warning that we're coming!" shouted Betsey. "You're on our land, whoever you are, and you must give an account of yourself or get off."

She stopped and listened. There was no sound.

"Mind now!" she shrieked. "I'm almost by you!"

"We're surely near the sink hole," wailed Tilly. "Oh, don't let us fall in!"

"We're at the sink hole," said Betsey. "You hold the lantern behind me. The moon shines on the water and I can see better with it alone."

Passing through the low growth which surrounded the pool, Betsey held her extended palm over her eyes and stared. She saw the smooth black surface of the bottomless water and round it the ring of tall and beautiful trees which had shed a few bright leaves upon its surface. As she stared, a little rustle began and a shower of leaves fell. But Betsey was not interested in leaves.

"I see your automobile!" she screamed, addressing the other side of the pool. "I see its front end. I want you to answer me when I talk. You're on my land and you must tell who you are."

Even this stern admonition had no effect. Indignantly Betsey turned and seized the lantern from the hand of Tilly as though it were a staff.

"Are you going round to them?" whimpered Tilly.

"I are!" shouted Betsey, forgetting her parts of speech in her desire to be emphatic. She strode ahead and again Tilly followed on her heels.

The circumference of the sink hole was not large. Betsey shouted a loud

"I'm coming" at the end of every few steps and she had not uttered more than ten or twelve before she found her way barred. She had seen aright; a gray truck, of the variety used by the Army, pointed its nose over the pool. Bound closely upon its load was a thick cover, so that it looked like the Conestoga wagons which her great-grandparents had watched starting on their long journeys to the West.

"Where are the folks that are with this automobile?" demanded Betsey. "I ask you for the last time."

Even this appeal had no effect. Betsey went round to the other side of the truck and stood regarding it. She sniffed the air with a rabbitlike motion of her nose.

"I smell it," she cried. "Don't you smell it, Tilly?"

"I guess so," faltered Tilly. "But I thought liquor always had a bad smell."

"Look there!" cried Betsey.

"Look there!" moaned Tilly at the same moment.

They were pointing at two different objects. What Betsey saw was the rear wheels carefully blocked with large stones; what Tilly saw was an object on the ground.

"They got too near and they couldn't get out," said Betsey. "See, the front wheels have sunk in the bank. I guess they went for help."

"It's a man!" cried Tilly hoarsely. "A dead man!"

Betsey turned the light of her lantern upon a prone figure. She approached and scrutinized it carefully. "He's not dead. It's from him that this loud smell comes."

To the further horror of Tilly, she went close to the quiet, comfortable, and blanketed figure, and laid her hand upon it.

"I want you to get up and go away. I don't want you on my land. Do you hear me?"

The man slept heavily. He was tired and the liquor from the bonded warehouse was powerful. In his confusion he had, as Betsey guessed, driven too close to the sink hole and his disgusted and alarmed companion had gone for help.

Betsey handed the lantern to Tilly.

"Hold it once a little."

"What are you going to do now, sister?" It was only in moments of intense emotion that Tilly used this tender address.

Betsey put her hand under the canvas cover.

"Bottles in boxes," she said when she had explored.

Bending over, she took up a sharp stone. There was a sound of cracking glass, then a still more potent odor in the sweet night.

"Liquor," she said. She took a step toward the slumbering guardian. "I don't care how much your stuff's worth, I'm going to do my duty."

"What are you going to do?" Tilly screamed; she was afraid Betsey might be going to punish the sleeping man with death.

Betsey answered with deeds instead of words. She stooped and began to tug with both hands at the heavy stones which held the wheels.

"It will slide into the sink hole!" cried Tilly.

Betsey worked as if with madness. She spoke with sarcasm as though she had lost her mind.

"You're a smart woman to guess that, Tilly," she said, still shoving the heavy stones.

Suddenly she moved back and stood upright. There was a sucking noise and the truck lurched forward like a cow dropping to her knees. It seemed to stand on end, then it dived and there was a splash. The splash was not loud; the truck seemed to be pulled down quickly as though by a beast reaching upward for its prey. The black water closed; the quickening wind sent down a shower of leaves which rocked on the surface, then were still, like tiny boats at anchor.

"You take the lantern." For some reason Betsey spoke in a whisper. "You go before and I'll come behind."

"I wish we were home," wailed Tilly.

"We'll soon be home," said Betsey. "We'll soon be home and in bed asleep."

III

Betsey finished the morning work while Tilly sat down at the quilt with its delicate wreaths of roses and larkspur. It was election day, but neither realized it. They hoped to turn another fold of the quilt that night, but their stitches were so fine and set with such exquisite care that it was doubtful whether they would reach their goal. It was hard to tell which made them happier, to finish the section they allotted for the day or to have some of it left for the morrow.

There had been a sharp frost, but there was still lovely color in sky and earth. The leaves carpeted the woods, covering all tracks of man and machine. If an investigation had been made it had not extended beyond the sink hole.

"My, I hope we can get a nice autumn-leaf pattern!" sighed Betsey.

Tilly looked up happily.

"It would be my idea to get a pattern with quite small leaves and cut each leaf out and make a quilt like the one with twelve thousands patches, only instead of each little square there should be a little, little leaf."

"That would be my idea." Betsey's cheeks flushed with pleasure.

"And the white part in tiny pieces."

"Yes," said Betsey; "that's what I thought too."

"It would take all winter."

"Yes," said Betsey; "we would work a long time till we got each leaf turned in round the edge. Would we pad them a little?"

"Yes," said Tilly. She turned her bending head toward the door. "Ach, it's some one coming!" she cried woefully. "I think we had enough company to last a while. Why can they not let us to ourselves?"

Betsey put out her hand and slipped the bolt, and rose and pulled down the shades. There came first a courteous knock, then an irritated knock, then a loud and furious thunder.

"I have a car out here," called Dan Webber. "I'd like you ladies to change your minds and vote. Those that aren't on the right side are on the wrong side."

There was no answer.

"If we're all afraid to do something how can we accomplish anything? You ladies are surely not afraid to come and drop a paper in a box! I'll bring you back in fifteen minutes."

There was no answer.

"It's no use," said a second voice. "You're wasting your breath."

Dan shook the door as if in a frenzy.

"I wish I had an axe," he said viciously, not meaning to be heard within, but heard nevertheless.

"*Verrickt*," said the other voice. "Let them be."

"They're not, either," contradicted Dan. "They have their minds. They're just cowards, that's all." He did not care if they heard this remark. He turned and shouted like a pettish child, "Keep your old door locked, you cowards!" and stamped off the porch.

Within the sisters sat motionless until peace and silence rolled back in waves. Betsey answered Dan when she had lifted the shades and let in the sunshine upon the old cupboard and the fine cat and the pretty quilt.

"We'll keep it locked," she said, and sat down to her work. "You may be sure of that."

THE COURIER OF THE CZAR

*L*ike the previous story, "The Courier of the Czar" first appeared in the *Saturday Evening Post* (June 7, 1924) and was also collected in *Bred in the Bone*. It, too, features Betsey and Tilly Shindledecker, who live quiet, simple lives on their farm just outside Lanesville, Pennsylvania. The Improved Mennonite sisters are representative of the rich variety of religious folk in Pennsylvania German culture, and their dignity under duress conveys the author's sympathetic intent. Rural protagonists living at the margins of a more sophisticated world, Betsey and Tilly nonetheless are independent, productive, and contented women. This story won an O. Henry Short Story Award in 1924.

* * *

I

Hearing the clock strike twelve, Betsey Shindledecker opened her eyes. She had not been asleep; she had merely been waiting for her sister Tilly, who lay by her side, to be asleep. At eleven o'clock Tilly had spoken, at half past she had turned from one side to the other; but now for half an hour she had been lying quietly.

Betsey lay blinking and looking round the room. The windows were dim rectangles outlining a sky which was only a little brighter than the black wall; the ancient bureau and washstand and dower chest showed only as indistinct masses. All other objects were lost—the two colored prints on the wall, one of Marianna, one of Juliana; the mirror, the chairs, one draped with the plain Mennonite garb of Betsey, the other with the plain Mennonite garb of Tilly. The two white caps hanging on the tall posts at the foot of the bed were lost, and so were the stripes in the carpet and the gay pattern of the coverlet. It would be impossible for any night to be darker or for any wind to whistle more ominously than the wind whistled at this moment round the corners of the house.

Her mind relieved by Tilly's quiet breathing, Betsey explored with hand and foot. Her foot sought her woolen slippers, her hand the thick flannel gown which hung on the post near her head. Finding both, she stood in a moment slippered and robed. Still Tilly breathed quietly.

Moving slowly, Betsey approached the door. When a board creaked beneath her great weight she stood still a long time; when Tilly sighed she put out her hand to clutch the corner of the bureau and thus to support herself. She grew no more comfortable in mind as she advanced, because the steps would creak far more loudly than the floor, and when she reached the bottom of the flight she would have to speak a reassuring word to the dog and the cat. This was not a new experience; for almost a month she had been stealing nightly from her sister's side.

Compared to the bedroom, the kitchen was bright. The fire shone through the mica doors of the stove and was reflected from the luster ware on the mantel and the brass knobs on the ancient cupboard. The black window-panes formed mirrors, so that there seemed to be many fires. On one side of the room a quilt was stretched on a frame and on the taut surface lay scissors, spools of thread, a little pincushion, two pairs of spectacles and two thimbles. The ground of the quilt was dark and spread over it were multitudes of white spots of various sizes.

Other reflecting surfaces were presented by the eyes of a large gray cat and a large Airedale dog, the one lying on a chair, the other beside the stove. Apparently unsurprised by this mysterious advent in the middle of the night, the cat purred and the dog parted his lips and teeth in a grin, and both having raised their heads, laid them down. They paid no heed when Betsey, touching a spill to the coals, lit the hanging lamp which illuminated brilliantly the quilt and the sewing implements lying upon it. The background of the quilt was blue and the white spots were star-shaped. The Milky Way crossed the surface diagonally and along the edge, and in the dark spaces were set Orion, the Pleiades, Ursa Major and other familiar constellations. Between the stars the quilt was covered with tiny stitches set close together.

Sinking into one of the Windsor armchairs at the side of the frame, Betsey selected a needle from the pincushion. It was not one of the fine needles with which the delicate quilting had been done, but a larger one, and she used it not to sew, but to destroy sewing. Stitch by stitch she ripped the fine work, sighing as she did so. It was clear that that which she ripped was not so even as the section opposite the other chair.

The hands of the clock pointed to half past twelve, and presently to one. Then Betsey exchanged the large needle for a smaller one, and, threading it, began to replace the stitches she had ripped out. Those she put in were as straight as a ruler and as much alike as rice grains.

At three o'clock she rose stiffly. Though her back ached, and though her eyes were heavy and her hands stiff, she was happy; the catastrophe which she feared and against which she struggled was postponed a little longer. Then suddenly she was smitten by terror. She did not exactly hear Tilly move, but she knew that Tilly had moved; moreover, that she was awake. If Tilly spoke she believed she would die of shock. But when Tilly did speak she answered calmly.

"Betsey!" The voice was sharp with terror. "Sister!"

"Yes?" Betsey walked toward the stairway.

"Where are you?"

"I'm coming." What should she say? It would be easy to invent an excuse, but Betsey did not like to lie. "I did not lock the door, Tilly."

"Why, no, of course not! I locked it, like always. Come back to bed!"

"I'm coming," said Betsey.

Her voice was steady, but her heart jumped in her side, and as she grasped the railing to ascend she was aware of her pulse throbbing in her wrist. She felt her way across the room and lay down, slippers, gown and all. She was trembling, not only because she was frightened but because she was cold.

"I had a queer dream," said Tilly drowsily. "I dreamed I could not see any more to sew straight."

"Are you awake?" asked Betsey sharply.

Tilly did not answer. Did she speak from a dream or from full consciousness?

II

Hearing the clock strike twelve, Betsey opened her eyes. It was harder to open them to-night than last night, and last night it had been harder than the night before. It was the twenty-eighth night she had wakened at twelve o'clock and had gone faltering down the stairs.

Beside her Tilly lay quietly, her breathing that of a child. The sky was black outside the rectangle of the window and there was again an uneasy whispering round the frame. The old furniture showed only vague outlines.

"I can't do this forever," said Betsey to herself. "I'm getting thin and I'm getting so tired I can't wake on time, and then what will happen?"

Her exploring foot sought her slippers, her exploring hand sought her bedgown. Anxiety made her nervous; she held her breath to listen. But Tilly slept sweetly.

"If I'm no more so heavy the boards won't creak so under me," she thought as she felt her way across the room. "*Ach,* but I'm tired!" She repeated the word mentally with each step—"Tired, tired, tired!"

In the kitchen there was the same glow of the fire, the same loveliness of light and shadow. The Maltese cat lay on his chair, the Airedale dog lay before the stove. Each lifted his head and each settled himself and closed his eyes. The starry quilt had advanced a little farther; a new section was set with two varieties of stitches, one short and regular, the other long and irregular.

Betsey found her large needle and sat down heavily. She ripped one stitch, then another. The point of the needle caught in the material and made little marks. She bent lower and lower. Were her eyes also growing dim? She picked out another stitch and another; then her forehead touched the belt of Orion, her hand lay quietly upon Ursa Major.

After a long time she became conscious of some impending disaster. Was she hurt and helpless? When she opened her eyes and saw Tilly standing by the quilting frame power was restored to her and she sprang up. Tilly stood tall and bent in her gray bedgown. Saying nothing, she looked at the quilt, then at her sister, then at the quilt.

"What is it?" she asked at last. "What do you make alone here in the middle of the night?"

Betsey stood paralyzed.

"You're ripping out my sewing and doing it over. That's how it gets always all right by morning. Isn't it so, Betsey?"

Betsey did not answer.

"You think I can't see any more?" demanded Tilly.

Betsey said not a word.

"No, I can't see any more." Tilly answered her own question. "This long time already I have trouble. I can't see to sew. I can't see to read. Sometimes I can't see you. I've twice stepped on the cat and once on the dog. If I don't step on them all the time it's because they get nice out of my way. They know me. I'll give up sewing. You'll have enough trouble with me yet, Betsey, without ripping out my crooked stitches. Now come to bed."

Betsey looked at the clock. The hands pointed to half past four.

"It's not worth while to go to bed. I'll get dressed ready to milk, and I'll watch for Herr when he comes to fetch the milk and I'll say he shall tell Doctor Landis to come to us. He'll cure you, Tilly. He'll surely cure you."

III

The clock ticked solemnly. It was now eight o'clock, now nine. Soft flakes of snow had begun to fall; the sky seemed to stoop lower and lower. Tilly sat at the end of the settle, her elbow on the arm, her hand supporting her bending face, a finger pressed upon each eye. Now and then a tear rolled down her cheek.

"It's not that I'm crying," she explained angrily. "It's that my eyes water."

"Yes," answered Betsey. Betsey was the only moving object except the pendulum of the clock. The dog and cat lay motionless but alert. Even the cupboard and the mantel and the starry quilt seemed to be alert and waiting. "It's ten o'clock," cried Betsey at last. "Why, then, does he not come?"

"He has perhaps a great many sick ones."

Betsey looked up the road and then down.

"You can't see far in the snow," she explained.

"Is it snowing?" asked Tilly.

Betsey turned from the window and looked at her sister.

"Do you ask because you want to keep your eyes covered, or is it that you can't see?"

"I want to keep my eyes covered," answered Tilly. Tilly did want to keep her eyes covered, but it was because she believed that if she uncovered them she could not see. "I sewed perhaps a little too late last evening. If you want to sew, sister," she said heroically, "then sew."

"I don't need to sew," replied Betsey. "He's coming. He has his buggy, not his auto. I guess he's afraid the snow will get deep for him. He's driving his Minnie horse, the yellow one. She's a good horse; they say when sometimes he's tired and falls asleep she takes him home. I would rather have a good horse than an auto. He's stopping at the gate." Betsey's voice grew shrill, the dog and the cat lifted their heads, the furniture seemed to stir as though that for which they all waited was now imminent. "I don't believe he'll hurt you, sister."

Doctor Landis tied his horse and came up the path, a stout, ruddy-faced man with a short, bristling mustache. He walked heavily, carrying his medicine case in one hand and a book in the other. He was a worldly Lutheran and a great reader.

"He's carrying his book," said Betsey. "He forgets he has it, I guess. If he would read the Bible, how fine that would be!"

Tilly did not answer. The water which streamed from her eyes burned like fire.

Doctor Landis brought in with him a breath of cold air and the pleasant odor of drugs. The room seemed to brighten, Tilly's spirits rose and Betsey felt so relieved that she sank upon a chair. Doctor Landis laid his medicine case and book on the settle and pulled off his gloves. He was able to speak the fluent Pennsylvania English of his generation, though he preferred the Pennsylvania German of his ancestors.

"Well!" he exclaimed. "Did I bring that wicked book along? I have no wife and no child, and I'm not a smoker, and I must have something to fill in the time in this healthy place. It's twenty years since I was in this house. Now what's the matter with the eyes, Tilly?"

"They burn me and ache me." Tilly pressed her fingers against the lids. "I can't see any more."

"You mean you can't see me?"

"I can see you if I take my hand away; but I can't see to sew."

Doctor Landis bent above the quilt. He made an inquiring sign to Betsey, pointing first to the quilt, then to Tilly. Betsey nodded and he completed the pantomime by shaking his fist at the starry sky.

"Now let's see these eyes." He sat down beside Tilly on the settle, and she put out her hand on the other side. It touched the book which he had laid there and she clutched it and held it as though it were a rope flung to a sinking swimmer. "Open your eyes," commanded the doctor.

As Tilly obeyed with agony, the hot flood became hotter. She could see the doctor's face, but nothing beyond it, not even Betsey standing at his elbow.

"It's worse to-day than yesterday," she said, as though that lightened the seriousness of the case.

"And worse yesterday than day before, I dare say," mocked the doctor. "Yet you kept on sewing?"

"We had the starry quilt to finish," explained Tilly. "I thought when the starry quilt was done I'd rest my eyes, and then it would also be soon time to work in the garden."

The doctor lifted the lid of Tilly's right eye, then the lid of the left. Tilly could not suppress a groan, at sound of which Betsey trembled from head to foot. The doctor rose heavily.

"Have you any black muslin, Betsey?"

Betsey took a roll from the cupboard drawer.

Standing by the table, the doctor folded a thick bandage and laid white gauze upon it; then he turned to Tilly, a bottle and a medicine dropper in his hand.

"Watch me, Betsey. See? Like this, four drops in each eye, night and morning."

"Oh! Oh!" moaned Tilly.

"Keep your eyes tight shut. Now I'm going to bandage them with a black bandage. If for any reason you have to remove it you're to do it in a dark room."

"Must my eyes be tied shut?" gasped Tilly.

"They must, indeed." The doctor stood at the table spreading salve on the white gauze. "Put fresh gauze on, Betsey, and fresh salve, night and morning."

"For how long?" faltered Tilly.

"A week from to-day I'll be back to look at them."

"A week!" cried Betsey. "Must she keep them covered for a week?"

Smitten dumb, Tilly said nothing; she merely lifted the doctor's book and opened it as if to read and thus prove that this was a bad dream.

"A week at least," said the doctor. "Then we'll see how they are. Too much quilting, Tilly. How old are you?"

"Only sixty-five," answered Tilly. "And I have good spectacles. I bought them from such a peddler twenty years ago."

"I'll bet you did," mocked the doctor.

He came across the room, holding the bandage as a child might hold a cat's cradle, and tied it tight round Tilly's eyes.

"Not a whole week!" wailed Tilly.

"A whole week," said the doctor, pulling on his gloves. "Betsey can surely amuse you for a week."

IV

It was nine o'clock in the morning and the Shindledecker kitchen was in order for the day. The cow had been milked hours ago, the dog and cat had been fed, the human beings had eaten their breakfasts, the dishes had been washed, and a dozen doughnuts, four pans of rusks, three pies and one cake had been baked. At the window sat Betsey, a mass of blue star-dotted material on her lap. The starry quilt was out of the frame, and she was putting in the hem. Outside, the rain poured upon the sodden earth. From within the landscape looked inexpressibly dreary, but when the door was opened, there came in the smell of spring.

Tilly did not sit at the window, nor was there sewing in her lap; she sat in the corner of the settle and her hands were empty. The black bandage remained across her eyes.

"First it was a week," she said despairingly. "Then another week and another week, and now yet another week."

"I have a feeling that next time it will be different." Betsey spoke in the strained voice of one determined to be cheerful.

"I have no such feeling," answered Tilly. "I feel that he will come and come and come and that I will sit and sit and sit. If it was only something in the world to do!"

"I'll read to you," offered Betsey.

"I know the Bible from beginning to end," declared Tilly. "I've read it every day since I was little. I don't believe it is meant that we shall get stale on it. And the hymn book, that I not only know but I can say it and sing it from the beginning to the doxology, both German and English. And the Martyr Book—that I know too. I know all about how they were persecuted and driven out and sent to prison and beheaded. I know how one of the brethren was burned with an iron. You can't catch me on the Martyr Book. And the almanac—that I know also."

"We could sing," suggested Betsey. Her voice had a heartbroken quality. Her heart was breaking.

"Sing!" mocked Tilly. "Sing! When I'm blind!"

The clock ticked on and on, the rain fell steadily, silently upon the earth, audibly upon the roof of the porch, noisily through the tin spouting. Another sort of rain fell quietly from Betsey's eyes upon the starry quilt. Tilly did not cry; the consequent physical agony was too keen.

"If I could only do something for you!" mourned Betsey in her heart.

"You can do something for me if you will," said Tilly, as though she could see into Betsey's heart.

"What can I do for you?" asked Betsey eagerly.

"There's a book in this house," said Tilly. "The doctor left it the first time. I guess he forgot it. When he said I must have my eyes tied shut I looked quickly at it. I could not read the reading, but I saw the picture. It was a picture of an old woman kneeling, and a sword was pointing at her and a man was standing with a whip over her. Her back was bare and her breast was bare. I must know what happened to that old woman. Will you not"—Tilly's wheedling voice besought, pleaded; she knew but too well how much she asked—"will you not read me that book, Betsey?"

"Where is the book?" asked Betsey, to gain time.

"Hidden in the upstairs," confessed Tilly. "I hid it. I was afraid he would ask for it. I hid it first in the churn, then I carried it in the upstairs."

"He did ask for it," said Betsey. "He said did I see such a book laying round. I told him no."

"I heard you," acknowledged Tilly. "It was before I took it to the upstairs. I was then sitting on it. Will you read me that book, Betsey?"

"I cannot," wept Betsey. "Anything else I'll do for you. But that is the world's book."

"You'll not find out what became of that poor old woman with the sword pointing at her and the whip coming down on her?" Tilly's voice was hard.

"No," wailed Betsey. "I can't. It's to resist temptations such as this that we're given strength. We have done our duty all our lives; let us not now break our rules when we're old."

The rain fell soddenly, the tears of Betsey fell steadily, Tilly sat motionless and blind on the settle.

"The cat is getting all the time fatter," said Betsey, achieving a brief composure.

There was no reply.

"But the dog gets a little thinner now that he goes so often out rabbit chasing."

There was no answer.

"Sister," said Betsey, "won't you talk to me?"

"I have nothing to talk about," said Tilly. "Dogs, cats, rabbits, baking, rain—how sick I am of all these subjects. I would like something new to talk about. I'd like to know what became of that poor old woman with the sword pointing at her and the whip held over her. I'd like to talk about her."

"It's a book of the world's people," said Betsey. She buried her face in the starry quilt. "I can't! I can't!"

V

The sun rose at six o'clock and its earliest beam, shining in the face of Betsey, woke her from sleep and to the consciousness of a leaden heart. It was Sunday, and all her life until a few weeks ago she had wakened cheerfully on Sunday. She enjoyed the rest from labor, she loved to go to meeting, she loved all the day's peace and opportunity for meditation. The meeting-house stood across the road, and there had never been a rain so heavy or a snow so deep that attendance was impossible. A few times there had been no one else there but William Hershey, and once even William had not been able to get through the drifts on the mountain road, but the sisters never missed.

Betsey waked now with no sense of peace or assurance. She repressed a groan as, turning, she looked at the bandaged head on the pillow beside her. Six weeks had passed since the doctor's first visit, but Tilly's eyes were still useless. She slept quietly and her mouth below the black cloth was not unhappy. The blind are said to resign themselves more quickly than the deaf; perhaps Tilly had resigned herself. Or, her fate still hanging in the balance, she may have felt hope.

Betsey had not only her acute and tender anxiety about her sister to trouble her; she had a sin to remember and a cruel penance to look forward to. She had committed an offense and this morning she meant to confess it in meeting.

"I can be a sinner," said she, weeping. "But a hypocrite I cannot be. I can't look them any more in the eye over there."

Slipping carefully from bed, she went about her work. Tilly slept late, and it was well that she did; her cruel hours of conscious darkness were that much shorter. Betsey opened the kitchen shutters and let in the horizontal sunshine; then she shook down the fire, and slipping into her working-jacket, took her milk pail on her arm. The morning was not cold: the day which had dawned was to be like a day of May dropped accidentally into March. Tulips and hyacinths were pushing up through the soil of the garden, buds were swelling, the woodland back of the house had begun to have a look of misty purple as the twigs and little branches changed color. Spring had always meant a foretaste of Heaven to Betsey. How strange it was to have an aching heart!

Tilly slept on and on. Betsey prepared the breakfast, and still she had not come. She stole upstairs and looked at her, and realized after a moment of panic that she was asleep and not dead.

Pushing the breakfast to the back of the stove, she sat down with her Bible. But she could not read. The Book lay strangely in her hand, the words looked unnatural, there was no sense of comfort from touch or sight.

At nine o'clock, when Tilly had not waked, Betsey stole to the room once more and got her Sunday dress, and returning to the kitchen, put it on. The devil tempted her to make an excuse of Tilly's blindness to stay at home, but she resisted him. He seemed to whisper in her ear; she saw his smile, his horns, his cloven hoofs.

"Don't go this morning," he advised. "Go next Sunday. This morning the meeting will be large. William Hershey will be there with all his family;

you don't wish those little children to hear you make confession. Elder Nunnemacher will be there, and you have always stood well before him. Perhaps next Sunday he will have to go elsewhere. The Stauffer sisters will be there—think how astonished they will be! And the Erlenbaughs and the Lindakugels and the Herrs and the Schaffers—all will be amazed. Wait, Betsey, wait!"

"No," said Betsey aloud to the empty room. "I'll not wait. I'll leave my poor sister to find her way down, but I'll not wait."

Walking to the foot of the stairs, she called up to Tilly.

"It's time for me to go to meeting, sister. Can you eat your breakfast alone, do you think? It's everything ready."

"Yes," answered Tilly. "Or perhaps I'll lay till you come back."

"Yes, well," said Betsey. "You can call the dog to you."

Betsey shuddered—she had told a lie; it was not quite time to go; only William Hershey had driven up to the meeting-house, and he came early to make the fire. But she dared not wait.

On the porch she lingered and breathed in the sweet air. If she could only breathe enough, perhaps she could ease her heart. But contemplation of Nature could not heal sin; that was certain as the sin itself. She went slowly down the path to the gate, and across the road and into the meeting-house. William Hershey was putting coal into the stove; Mary Hershey sat with her baby in her arms; little Amos and little David walked sedately about.

"Good-morning," said William. "How are you, Betsey, and how's poor Tilly? We're coming soon to see you."

"She's not good," answered Betsey, selecting a seat.

She did not smile at the children or answer William's announcement of his visit; she merely turned her face to the wall and sat motionless. Her black bonnet hid her eyes, her stout shoulders were bent, her woe was so apparent that the members entering happily from the morning sunshine were cast down. Was poor Tilly, indeed, doomed to blindness?

Elder Nunnemacher did not appear and William Hershey preached a short sermon. He selected his subject for the benefit of Betsey, pointing to the joys of Heaven as a reward for the sufferings of earth, not dreaming that Betsey believed herself shut out of Heaven. Her heart sank lower and lower, her lips trembled, she could scarcely restrain herself from crying out. She knew that everybody was looking at her and feeling sorry for her, and the devil tempted her again through self-pity.

"You have nobody in the world but Tilly. You're not rich. You have no husband and no children. Life has cheated you. Take what pleasure you can. Show some spirit. Don't make a fool of yourself."

"I will make confession," said Betsey in her soul.

"Wait till after the hymn, anyhow," advised the devil.

"No," said Betsey. As William finished she rose slowly. "I have something to say," she announced in a muffled tone.

In the silence which followed Betsey looked at the floor. The Shindle-deckers never spoke in meeting; they never spoke to any one who did not first speak to them; they almost never went from home and they never willingly admitted strangers to their house. There was, their friends believed, no one in the world so shy. And here was Betsey on her feet. All sorts of wild notions flew through their astonished minds. Was Tilly dead and had Betsey lost her reason?

"I must confess my sins," declared Betsey in a stronger tone. "I have done wrong. I have done what is forbidden among us. I have read a worldly book. It's a large book with pictures, called 'The Courier of the Czar.'" "The Courier of the Czar" was only a secondary title; upon the real name, "Michael Strogoff," Betsey did not dare to venture; as it was, she pronounced "Czar" in two syllables, the first K. "It was called 'The Courier of the K-zar.'"

She was heard not with disapproval but with stupefaction; her audience did not understand what she meant. They knew the Bible and the hymnal, and some of them knew the Martyr Book; but they knew no other literature. They did not know the word "courier" nor the word "K-zar."

Betsey saw their stupefaction.

"A courier is a messenger," she explained. "He's one that carries messages and goes on errands. A K-zar is a king."

Still all the Hersheys and Erlenbaughs and Stauffers looked at her blankly.

"It's a story," she went on. "We have stories in the Bible and stories in the Martyr Book. But we know all the stories in the Bible and the Martyr Book by heart. This is a new story. This man is to carry a message for the K-zar to his brother, who's in a city with enemies all round it. He must go three thousand miles through enemies and forests and across great rivers. The Susquehanna is nothing to those rivers. A wicked man, Ivan, catches him; and in order to make him tell who he is he takes his mother and puts a sword in front of her and is going to whip her, and when she shrinks from the whip the sword will pierce her. That's what Ivan does. It's like you read in the Martyr Book when they burned the people and drowned them. Then when this courier defended his poor mother this Ivan burned his eyes with a hot sword and made him blind." Betsey's tongue failed her on this word; she repeated it, and her effort produced a prolonged and tragic sound—"b-l-i-n-d!"

"But he went on and on, and a young girl helped him. They find a good young man who is their friend, and this Ivan has had him buried in the sand up to his neck and big birds get after him and he dies. They come at last to the place where he is to give his message to the brother of the K-zar and they are floating on an iceberg down the river, and there are springs of something like coal oil near the river, and it's on fire, and they're floating on the ice in the midst of the fire."

Stupefaction continued, but it was now not the stupefaction of amazement but of enchantment. Betsey told her story well, and every eye was fixed upon her; every pair of lungs was either full of air or empty of air; inhalation and exhalation had ceased. Betsey, alas, ceased also.

"That's as far as I have gone," she said, exhausted. "But I'm going to finish this book. I'm going to finish it this afternoon, on the Sabbath, whether or no."

Now eye met eye, color came back into pale cheeks. The prevailing expression was one of excitement touched with horror. Betsey remained standing; she seemed about to leave; as though, willing to bear the consequences of her crime, she would excommunicate herself and depart. Only William Hershey was able to reason. He rose slowly, his gentle bearded face turned toward Betsey. Were there tears in William Hershey's eyes?

"Betsey," he asked slowly, "do you do this for your poor sister?"

Betsey seized the back of the bench before her. She looked smitten, as he looks the secret of whose heart is discovered.

"Don't blame Tilly," she said. "The doctor says she must be yet for a long time in the dark. She knows the Bible and the Martyr Book and the hymns, and now her mind has to work all the time on itself."

"You're reading this to her?"

"I'm reading it aloud," said Betsey stubbornly. "If she listens I can't help it."

"Sit down," bade William gently and commandingly. "It's here something that this sister must decide. She must do what she thinks is right. Let us sing Number Thirty-Seven."

But Betsey was not through.

"I like this reading," she confessed wildly. "I don't feel wicked in my sin. It makes me feel good; it sorts of clears out my soul. I would rather read than quilt. And we have fifty-eight quilts. Many times Tilly and I wept over the poor martyrs; why should we not weep over these poor others? Our forefathers fought with wolves where this meeting-house now stands. The Hersheys were in it, I'll bet, and the Stauffers and the Erlenbaughs—all had to fight with wolves and Indians. I forgot to say that when this poor courier of the K-zar and the young girl were floating down the fiery river the wolves got after them. They—"

William Hershey was alarmed; he despaired of Betsey's reason. He started Hymn Number Thirty-Seven.

VI

The stewed chicken and the mashed potatoes and dried corn and slaw and cherry pie which composed the Shindledecker dinner were consumed and all evidences of the meal removed. The cat lay on his chair; he slept, then woke and looked about, then slept again. Betsey went to the porch to hang up the dish towels and the dog came back with her. He had an expectant air, and when he lay down he did not rest his head on his paws, but kept it high. Below her black bandage Tilly's mouth looked happy. Betsey was pale, but she too looked happy. Tilly's head turned, following her sister as though she could see. She looked impatient.

Betsey opened the door of the kitchen cupboard and got out a book. The doctor knew now where his book was, and he had promised Tilly to bring her others by the same author. One was called "From the Earth to the Moon," another "Twenty Thousand Leagues Under the Sea." But Tilly knew there was no book like this in the world and she meant to ask Betsey to read it again, and perhaps again. Her necessity knew no consideration for others; she would take all the blame for Betsey's sin, if there were blame; but Betsey must read.

"I'm ready," she said. The smile on her face was beatific.

Betsey opened the book. Ignoring one of the unities, the author had brought the villainous Ivan into the foreground of the narrative. Himself disguised as the courier of the Czar, he had entered the besieged city and was about to betray it. Upon him, in a room of the grand duke's palace, having escaped the burning river, came the real courier led by his faithful maiden. In terror, Betsey laid the book upon her knee.

"Now everything is at an end," she warned her sister. "Remember, he cannot see, and here is this wicked Ivan, who can see. What can he do?" Her face was pale. "You must be prepared, sister."

Tilly clasped her hands.

"Go on," she commanded. "I'm ready."

Betsey's eyes traveled down the page.

"Oh, sister!" she cried sharply.

"What is it?" asked Tilly.

"Oh, listen!"

"Go on!" urged Tilly.

"'Ivan uttered a cry,'" read Betsey. "'A sudden light flashed across his brain. "He sees!" he exclaimed. "He sees!" and like a wild beast trying to retreat into its den, step by step, he drew back to the edge of the room.'"

"He's not blind, then?" gasped Tilly. "But it said he was blind!"

Betsey read on.

"'Stabbed to the heart, the wretched Ivan fell.'"

"But how—"

Betsey lifted her hand for silence. Here were medical words she could not pronounce, but she could give the blessed sense of what she saw.

"Listen once! When they held the hot sword before his eyes, Tilly, he was crying to think of his poor mother and his tears saved his eyesight."

"Oh, I am thankful to God," cried Tilly. "Oh, read that part again, dear sister."

Betsey looked out the window; she needed, suddenly, a wider view than she could get across the kitchen, broad as it was. She looked out the window to the east, then out the window to the west. She rose and walked first to the one, then to the other.

"Oh, do read it again!" besought Tilly. "Just once, sister. I'll ask for no more. Oh, please!"

Betsey gazed out as though at some strange phenomenon. There was a truly strange phenomenon to be seen.

"Oh, I would like to hear it again," begged Tilly. When Betsey did not answer she was terrified. "Why don't you speak to me, Betsey?"

Another person spoke for Betsey. The door opened and the two Stauffer sisters came in. They were about the same age as the Shindledeckers; and like them, one was tall and stout and the other tall and thin. From under their black bonnets they looked out, at once eager and guilty and excited.

"We came—" began one, and looked at her sister.

"We came to see how that fine man got through," finished the sister. "We came to see if he is yet alive. It's surely no sin!"

Betsey stood looking at them and then out the window. Utterly bewildered, Tilly sat turning her bandaged face first in one direction then in the other.

"Spare your wraps," invited Betsey pleasantly. She looked across the fields to the south and saw Eleazar Herr approaching with his long stride, and down the road to the east and saw six Erlenbaughs walking in procession, and up the road to the west and saw William Hershey's heavily laden buggy. If she was not mistaken, Mary was in it, and the baby and the little boys.

Her heart swelled; William's approach removed her last lingering sense of wrong-doing. It had been delightful to have Tilly hang upon her words; it had been thrilling to hold the Improved New Mennonite congregation spellbound; now she would have both pleasures in one. She would make these people sad and then how happy! The muscles of her arms tingled as though preparing for dramatic gestures.

"Wait once a little," she said, addressing Tilly. "Then I will begin again in the beginning."

THE AMISHMAN

"The Amishman" first appeared in the *Ladies' Home Journal,* with illustrations by E. F. Ward, in April 1925; it was also collected in *Bred in the Bone* later that year. While she describes the particular look and customs of the Amish people in this story, Singmaster also connects their land and lifestyle to America's first-generation agrarian society. Singmaster distinguished among various sectarian dress and practices. She always referred to the Pennsylvania Germans, never to the "Pennsylvania Dutch," which she saw correctly as a misnomer for Pennsylvanians of German descent. When a reviewer of her book *A High Wind Rising* (1942) referred to the Pennsylvania Dutch, Singmaster wrote in a letter to the editor that his mistake was "enough to make a historian's hair stand on end."

* * *

I

Martin Ebersole stood in the corner of the lofty markethouse in Lanesville. Beyond him was stall after stall, presided over by Amish and Mennonite, Conservative or Progressive, Dunker or River Brother, each in his distinctive garb, or more worldly Lutheran or Reformed, all thrifty, shrewd, substantial. Some of the plainest Mennonites had come in the most beautiful cars, the most retiring Amish owned the richest farms in a county which produced food and tobacco higher in value than the gold of Alaska.

Up and down surged the crowd, the poor and the comfortably off and even the rich, who preferred to do their own marketing, counting the bruises from the huge baskets carried by their fellows less painful than the eating of poor cuts of meat. Here a young woman, painted, idle and useless, bought ready prepared the necessities of life, contemptuous of the stoutness and plain apparel of the woman who sold; here a bride and groom shopped together for the first time; here a parsimonious husband kept watch upon his wife. There were plain people among the customers as well as among the merchants, and they were as shrewd in buying as their fellows in selling.

Martin, who was an Amishman, had a thick, curling, silky beard, though he was only twenty-three; his hair, cut square across his forehead, waved almost to his shoulders. His large eyes, long at the corners and heavily lashed, were like dark agates in color and his complexion was white and pink. His suit of thick gray wool, worn to a beautiful softness, was home-made, the short coat held close round his body with hooks and eyes, the high-waisted trousers fastened after the fashion of sailors' trousers.

His stock was depleted, but there was still at least one sample of each of the commodities which he and his mother, Mahala, had packed into his wagon. Worldly people used automobiles, but to the truly Christian they were forbidden, and a drive of three hours on a cold morning was far less of a burden than the consciousness of wrongdoing. The Ebersoles knew the commercial value of variety, and Martin had remaining before him one pie, a few dishes of potato salad, a few picked eggs and pickled beets, a half-pound pat of butter, a few pasteboard cups of soft cheese, a little bag of noodles, one bunch of watercress and one of cultivated poke. His stock had been smaller than usual because to-morrow meeting would be held at his mother's house and she had reserved all her baking for the dinner.

Martin was thinking of his appearance; he wished that he had let his mother cut his hair as she suggested. Two strange women, pausing arm in arm, were thinking of his appearance also and one said in amazement, "What a curious and beautiful creature!" Fortunately he did not hear; beside mentally bemoaning his unshorn condition, he was anxiously watching the door. It was time for him to marry and he had picked out his mate. He did not know her name, but he knew her and all her alluring ways, as she waited at the Brunstaetter baker stall across the aisle. She was late this morning; usually she came at seven to relieve Brunstaetter who then went home for his breakfast, and it was nine, and she had not arrived. She was a thin girl with the most beautiful red cheeks and redder lips and yellow hair. She had earring on her ears and a chain upon her neck and a watch upon her wrist and a bright word for everybody. She was of the world's people, but that did not trouble Martin. For love of his father, his mother had left the straight sect of the New Mennonites for the straighter sect of the Amish; his bride would love him equally well.

The two women looked at Martin for a long time, not so much deliberately as abstractedly; then they took a few halting, absentminded steps and looked at Lizzie Funk and her daughter Sallie in the next stall who were also

Amish. Lizzie was about forty years old, but unless one caught the lively flash of her black eyes or got a glimpse of her brown hair, one might suppose her sixty or eighty. The stiffened sides and the little cape of her black bonnet hid her curling hair and her smooth pretty neck. Beneath the bonnet was a white cap with inch-wide ties tied under her chin. The style of her clothing was prescribed but she was permitted latitude in color and her waist and skirt and shawl-like neckerchief were dark purple and her apron was dark red. This morning she was in a gay mood; she enjoyed the bustle of market and she also enjoyed a brief independence of her husband, Israel, who believed that man was divinely appointed to rule.

About Sallie's age there could be no mistake. Plump, quick-moving, and pink-cheeked, she could not be twenty. Her bonnet too was deep, but a tendril of bright hair drifted out over the edge; it had a little cape, but she bent her head and then her white neck showed; it hid her face, but she tipped back her chin and then one could see that her eyes were blue. She was smiling at this moment at thirteen-year-old Isaac Herr, at sight of whom the strange women clutched each other. Isaac wore long trousers and a little short coat, fastened like Martin's with hooks and eyes. Against a broad, flat hat, set on the back of his head, spread an aureole of flaxen curls. His cheeks were pink, his eyes blue.

"Adorable angel!" said one of the strangers.

Hearing this impulsive remark Sallie pouted. There was nothing remarkable about this baby of an Isaac, though she had seen idiots staring at him before; Martin Ebersole was far handsomer. Yet if they had called Martin an adorable angel, she would have hated them.

The stock of Lizzie and Sallie was far larger than that of Martin. Here, in addition to food-stuffs, were hooked rugs and braided rugs and paper flowers. As agent for a green-grocer they sold spinach, beans, tomatoes, lettuce and strawberries from the South. Three dressed chickens remained of a dozen, and they had one live bird, a huge gander tied to the front of the stall, a burlap bag fitted closely round him. He quacked, and brave women patted him as they went by.

It must not be supposed that because Sallie brought rugs to market she had none at home. Fifteen quilts, all the rugs she would need for a house, sheets, towels and pillow-cases lay in her dower chest. In a sense the rugs she sold lay there also, in the form of goldpieces in a little bag. There were two bolts of goods, one of white cotton, one of gray wool and these she often pictured made up into garments designed not for her, but for a tall, plump, young man. It was too bad that the beautiful eyes of that young man, traveling from the door to Brunstaetter's stall and back to the door and back to

Brunstaetter's stall, should avoid the familiar blue eyes of Sallie and seek the unfamiliar and perhaps dangerous gaze of a stranger. To-day, however, Sallie did not mind; she had a secret joy.

At the Brunstaetter stall, toward which Martin looked in vain, bread was piled in Alpine heights. All ordinary breads were here, plain white bread and whole wheat bread and rye bread and brown bread and raisin bread, and cinnamon buns and doughnuts, and all other breads, strange to the rest of the world, but familiar to Southern Pennsylvania, Schwenkfelder cake, crumb pie, "rivvel" cake, rich "hutzel" bread, "kaffee krantz" and "mondel krantz," and even bitter "saffron bread." The more common varieties were made in large quantities in the bakery, but the essentially native products were brought in in small lots by an accomplished and rapidly diminishing race of expert cooks.

At a quarter past nine, Martin began to grow desperately uneasy. His rolling eyes gazed now at the door, now at Brunstaetter's stall, but they did not see his love. Soon he would have no excuse to linger. Besides, many duties waited him at home; in early May every moment counted.

At half past nine he glanced in a moment of anguished inadvertence at the Ebersole [sic; she means Funk] stall. He avoided whenever possible both the eyes of Lizzie who looked at him with the natural resentment of a mother who sees her daughter neglected, and of Sallie who looked at him with tenderness which was equally unwelcome. At present they had no thought for him; having breakfasted at half past three, they were now eating sandwiches made of rolls and fried ham and egg. It was necessary for them to open their mouths wide and the motion expressed all the honest pleasure which they felt. Instead of satisfying his own sharp hunger with one of the similar sandwiches prepared by his mother, Martin scornfully compared their method of eating with the delicate ways of the baker's clerk. She ate only ice-cream cones, and how daintily she licked the sloping sides!

At quarter to ten Martin's love had still not come and he strained his eyes over the crowd. He should be carrying out his baskets and packing his wagon and making ready for his successor. He saw that Lizzie Funk had taken her sharp eyes to the stall of her sister at the far end of the market, and much as he disliked Sallie's unconcealed interest in him, he leaned across the barrier.

"The baker has this morning a new clerk," he said, believing with masculine stupidity that he succeeded in hiding his anxiety.

A wave of color flooded Sallie's face. Her bonnet was pushed back and her eyes shone. Sensible and clever as she was, she believed that she concealed her rapture at being addressed, and her deeper rapture in the news she had to give.

"She isn't here any more."

"Where is she?" asked Martin.

"In Philadelphia," explained Sallie. "She has a place there. She takes the tickets in such a moving picture."

To Sallie, and it should be to Martin also, the moving picture was taboo. Sallie looked down, suddenly unable to hide her bliss. The girl was gone and gone forever; Philadelphia was as distant as Cairo.

"In Philadelphia!" To Martin Philadelphia was as distant as—let us say—Paris.

"Yes," Sallie joyfully hastened to give all the information she had. "I heard them say it is close by the railway, called the Palace."

"Called the Palace," repeated Martin. Something seemed to gnaw his plump side and he pressed it with his hand.

"Yes," Sallie repeated the wicked word. "The Palace."

"Close by the railway," said Martin.

"Yes," said Sallie, as though that, too, were wicked. Then from her fool's paradise, she spoke again. "I don't believe it's a nice place."

Martin withdrew to the other side of the stall. Sallie believed that it was because he saw her mother coming and the brief interview seemed stolen and therefore sweeter. Martin withdrew, however, for quite another reason; he was dizzy with love and hate, love for the baker's clerk and hate for Sallie, who dared to speak lightly even of the place where the baker's clerk worked. For an instant he leaned against the wall, then he began to pile plates together and to put glasses and cups into small baskets and small baskets into large.

"I should 'a' made up to her," he said dully. "I should this long time already made up to her."

Having packed his wagon, he sat in meditation until an irate farmer, desiring his place, yelled at him to move on. He drove abstractedly down the narrow street, his heavy hooded wagon a menace to traffic, then out into the treeless, fertile country. The winter wheat was green, buds were swelling, tobacco plants were set out under white covers, ornamental shrubs bloomed in door-yards, daffodils and tulips shone in the sunshine, and the first really warm air of spring fanned his virgin cheek.

He drove on and on, until at the end of ten miles he left the Lincoln Highway and entered a by-road. At its end he came upon a settlement of truck farmers. The houses were of stone and white-washed, the yards and fields were in perfect order, the fences were white and the gates bright blue, and a wooded hill threw all into beautiful relief. One house stood out as largest and tidiest of all and there Martin drew rein. The door opened and stout Mahala hurried down the path. She wore a white cap tied beneath her chin, a brown dress, a red neckerchief, and a bright blue apron. Her step was vigorous, her expression that of good-nature and contentment. She was extraordinarily loquacious, but she did not demand a response to all her remarks.

"Well, Martin!" she cried. "What happened you? You're late and it's planting time and meeting is to-morrow!"

Always economical in the use of words, Martin made no answer. Mahala began to lift down the baskets and set them on the grass. From the open door came the delicious odor of spices and fresh bread, and now from within, now from without, came Mahala's voice.

"You sold everything—that's good. I have all my things baked already for to-morrow. I bet there'll be a lot of people here if it gives a good day. We'll move the benches in this evening. I don't like to leave everything always till Sunday morning. I don't think it's right. I guess the people grabbed the fresh things. Were Lizzie and Sallie there?"

Moving away, Martin pretended not to hear. Nor did Mahala wait for an answer, her question being purely rhetorical.

"Sallie's the best cook I know for one so young. I believe she can do everything her Mom can do and more too it yet. I believe—"

Martin moved farther away; this song he had heard until he was sick of it. Reaching the safe seclusion of the barn he stood still and addressed the echoing spaces.

"I should 'a' made up to her this long time," he said again slowly. "Now on Monday I'll go after her."

II

Martin opened the door of the farmhouse and stood looking out. He was dressed in a black suit, made in the same fashion as his week-day gray, but some of his archaic beauty had departed under the maternal shears. Before him and near at the hand there was a beautiful sight. Outside the blue gate stood a slender and perfectly symmetrical young pin oak and amid its delicate leaves flitted at least thirty yellow salad birds. On a strip of grass a few dandelion heads had gone to seed and the birds hopped back and forth from the grass where they feasted, to the low branches where they piped a roundelay of praise for their breakfast. Apple blossoms scented the clear air, tulips lifted their proud heads. If Martin had walked to the corner of the house and looked back at the woodland he might have seen a myriad shades of green, from the pale grayish tone of young oak leaves, through bright poplar to dark pine and spruce, all interlaced by the white of dogwood and the red of maple buds.

The kitchen, living-room, and best bedroom, opening into each other by broad doors, were prepared for meeting. The old cupboard and tables of simple and beautiful design were sound and unmarred as on the day, a hundred and fifty years before, when they left the hand of a skillful Ebersole. Back of the doors hung long towels of homespun embroidered with little flowers and initials, and on the bed was an elaborate quilt of the "Lost Rose in the Wilderness" pattern. All the Ebersole chairs stood in regular rows and beside them were benches, brought from their storage place in the barn. Mahala was prosperous, hospitable, and devout, and the meeting was frequently held at her house. The rag carpets were beautifully woven and the hooked and braided rugs lying upon them showed the same fine workmanship as those manufactured by Sallie Funk. On a little shelf in the corner stood a large Bible, a copy of the Martyr Book which related the heroic story of persecutions, and a few German hymn books.

In the out-kitchen, neatly ranged on a table and carefully covered, were pies and loaves of bread and cake enough for forty people, a freshly opened crock of apple-butter, jars of pickles and preserves and two boiled hams, and on a smaller table by the stove vessels and materials for making a large quantity of coffee. Cooking would not begin for a long time, as the meeting which would open at nine o'clock, would not close until after twelve.

Martin had not moved to the doorway to observe the beauty of nature, he had moved thither to get out of hearing of his mother's voice. But the voice followed him and the words were clear and plain. Mahala had been moving briskly about since five o'clock and her tone grew weary.

"I must have help, I can't get along any more as I did. Either that or we'll have to give up market and that would be a great loss. My feet hurt and my legs hurt and my arms hurt and sometimes I'm so tired I can't tell if I'm going or coming and I can hardly get undressed to go to bed at night."

Martin was not remiss in that he offered no sympathy; the most quick-spoken person would not have got a word in.

"I don't like to hire. My Mom never hired and I don't like to hire. They had to hire at Good's and she stole their gold and stood on the cat. You can't hire anybody that's fit, anyhow, or that knows anything—nobody but Yankees. They're all shussles, that's what they are. Our good girls are either yet at home or else they get married, they don't hire out, and no outlander would I have. They don't bake, they don't snitz, they don't can, they buy their soap. Words fail to tell what they don't know."

Martin bit his lip; but before he could enter a word in defense of outlanders, Mahala went on.

"One ought not to postpone marrying. It doesn't look right and our religion is against it. I was sixteen when I married. I heard—" The sharp note in Mahala's voice changed; it was now not irritable, but anxious. "I heard it said that Good's boy is making up to Sallie Funk. That would be a proud match for the Goods. Sallie will have her Pop's farm, while she's the only child and she's a Number One worker. It wouldn't wonder me if she had many chances. The one that gets her is lucky, that's what I say."

Martin stepped down on the grass. He had determined to announce his intentions to his mother when meeting was over, and he would not tell her now. He was terrified lest she might suddenly abandon her indirect method for a plain question, "Why don't you take Sallie?"

His flight was promptly checked; the carriage of Israel Funk drawn by two stout horses, was coming up the road with Israel on the front seat, tall, stout, bearded like a prophet. Beyond were brethren and sisters on foot and in buggies. Martin did not know which was harder, to listen to his mother, or to look into the cold eye of Israel, the sharp eye of Lizzie, and the tender eye of Sallie.

One by one the carriages drove to the front of the barn. No one would leave before afternoon, and the horses were unhitched and stabled. Martin met the guests at the front door, and shook hands with each one. Moving soberly, speaking gently, dressed in their home-made garb, that of the adults black for Sunday, that of the children exactly similar in design, but of gay color, they showed no trace of the ardor and courage which had brought their forbears thousands of miles across land and sea.

The Herr family, to which beautiful Isaac belonged, consisted of father, mother, four sons, three younger than Isaac and all equally beautiful, and a baby daughter of six months. Her dress was blue, her little neckerchief red, her little apron and bonnet pink, her tiny shoes and stockings black. Beneath her bonnet was a little white cap tied with white ties like her mother's. She was clothed in still another garment, the love of her kin, who could not keep their eyes from gazing at her. The Herr family had been established in Pennsylvania by two brothers, who in 1720 constructed a little cart in their ancestral home in Switzerland and putting thereon their invalid mother, drew her to the coast and there took ship. In Philadelphia they constructed another cart and drew her to the banks of Mill creek, where, near a spring which she selected and loved, these her descendants still lived.

The three aged Bowman sisters had a grandfather many times removed who was sent to the galleys because he would not go to war. The sisters dressed exactly alike and though there was considerable difference in their ages, they had come to look exactly alike.

Israel and Lizzie and Sallie Funk entered, last of all. They had a distant grandfather who was burned at the stake because he insisted upon the comforting sacrament of baptism as an adult after he had once been baptized as a child. Israel spoke of himself as being one of "the tame people," but in his eye and that of his wife there was suddenly an inflammable spark. Israel gave Martin a stern, grave, open glance; Lizzie gave him a quick flash, Sallie gave him no glance at all. Her happy mood still held; she believed that she was entering what was to be her future home.

The mothers with little children sat in rocking-chairs, the other worshipers on stiff chairs or benches. Israel was the preacher, and he opened the service with a long prayer, the burden of which was a plea that the young brethren might remain true, that they might not become lukewarm in the faith or careless in their observance of the rules of the congregation, and especially that they might set their affections upon godly young women of their own religion. Israel had not been trained in the art of public prayer and in addition to petitions he presented a description of the dangers of worldly marriages, prefacing each long sentence with an explanatory, "Thou knowest, O Lord." He alluded frankly at last to a specific case. "Thou knowest how our brother was reasoned with, O Lord," said Israel. "Thou knowest how his folks did their best to save him. But he wandered away, and was seen in Thy house no more."

A long German hymn followed the prayer and then Israel preached a sermon upon the same subject. Martin suspected correctly that the wandering of his eyes had been observed. Israel preached for an hour and half; then other brethren took briefer turns, another hymn was sung and the meeting was over. All the little children had slept and all wakened hungry, but smiling. The aroma of coffee filled the air and the food was ready to be carried in. Martin moved about busily, relieved to have occupation. He did not look toward Sallie and with sinking spirits she refrained from helping Mahala whose chief assistant she usually was. Mahala's spirits sank also; she believed that Martin had let Sallie slip through his fingers and that she was unhappy because Amos Good was not at the meeting.

Late in the afternoon Martin put on his old clothes and carried the benches to the barn and completed his chores. The last of the women who had helped his mother had gone and all was in order. Supper was placed on the table and he sat opposite Mahala whose face was white with weariness and disappointment. Having eaten hungrily, he wiped his mouth and rose and pushed back his chair.

"I'm going to get married," he announced.

Mahala looked up amazed. She did not dare to ask, "Is it Sallie?" or to say, "Of course it's Sallie!" she approached the matter indirectly.

"She's well brought up," she said with satisfaction which was still a little uneasy.

"Yes," said Martin. Of course his love was well brought up!

"She's a first class cook."

"Of course." How else when she lived where baking was done daily?

"She shall bring all her things here," went on Mahala practically. "But she can save them, while I have plenty. It will be convenient in every way."

Her cheeks grew bright and her speech quickened and Martin moved toward the door. He hated to deceive. To-morrow when he brought the stranger home his mother would be reconciled at once; compared to Sallie she was a rose beside a cabbage.

"To-morrow I'm going to see her. I'm going in the morning. I must have the mare shod and I can attend to both."

"To-morrow!" cried Mahala. "When we have so much work? Why didn't you go along home with them to-day?"

Martin answered with one foot on the doorsill.

"It wasn't suitable."

"I always thought she was the one," said Mahala. After all, a day's absence was a small matter if it ended in making Sallie Funk her daughter-in-law. But Mahala was still a little uneasy.

"It would be awful to be yoked with an unbeliever," she called after him.

"Yes," agreed Martin promptly. "Awful."

He spoke honestly; his love would become a believer.

"I'll give you a good infare," called Mahala.

"Yes, well," said Martin.

III

Martin stood in the Lanesville station, a huge dark shed in the center of the city. It was seven o'clock in the morning and the train which would take him to Philadelphia was due at seven ten. He had left his horse and buggy at a livery stable to which a blacksmith shop was attached. He wore his black suit and his broad-brimmed hat and his face was pale. He had spent almost four dollars for a round-trip ticket to Philadelphia, and four dollars was not lightly laid out. He expected to bring the baker's clerk back with him and if she had no money he would have to pay her fare also. But he supposed that like the Amish girls she would have a little pile of gold tucked away.

Even here, where the plain people used the trains, Martin was an object of interest. As the Amish were not students or readers so they were not travelers. They had all they needed for salvation in their Bibles—why seek farther? They had all they needed for daily sustenance in their homes or near by—why travel? The Dunkers and Mennonites were less strict and their garb less noticeable and Dunkers and Mennonites and worldly people alike looked astonished at Martin's height and his smoothness of skin and plumpness of body and thickness of beard. Several traveling men circled round him, inspecting him now from this side, now from that.

The train came to a stop with a jerk as though it too were astonished and the engineer stared out of the window of his cab. Alighting passengers stopped short and departing travelers moved slowly, so that conductor and brakeman hurried them along, their own heads turned sidewise to keep Martin in sight. In the market, beside the Herrs and Brunstaetters and Bowmans and Hickenliebers, Martin had not seemed to be such a curiosity, but each step which took him away added to his strangeness.

Without knowing how noisy the car had been a few moments before, Martin could not realize the suddenness and completeness of the change as he entered. There are noisy as well as quiet Pennsylvanians, and Martin had encountered a noisy group. These were women, a delegation of "Ladies of Gibraltar" going to Philadelphia to join in a national convention. Doubtless there are quiet as well as noisy Gibraltarians, but this was a hilarious variety. It may have been that their gayety had nothing to do with their being Gibraltarians, but only with the fact that for a day in their hard-working, middle-aged lives they were free and happy.

The silence which fell upon them as Martin appeared was broken by a snicker as he proceeded down the aisle. Ignorant of the sensation he created he selected a seat near the back of the car and in front of the single male occupant, a sour-looking misanthropic man. The conductor came for his ticket at once, being unable to wait longer to look at Martin again and as he punched it he winked boldly and unguardedly at the cross man. Several Ladies of Gibraltar felt suddenly a profound thirst which took them to the rear of the car.

By this time Martin was looking at the women in astonishment. They should be at home, cooking, baking, milking the cows, and on this morning in particular doing the family washing. His mother was washing and so were Lizzie and Sallie Funk and all the other women he knew. What sort of

husbands permitted this dereliction and what sort of sons raised no protesting voice? Here was woman in a new aspect.

Martin looked out of the window at the beautiful fields, then back into the
car, then out the window. He was interested in agriculture, but he was still
more interested in the strange sight within. Presently he suffered an acute
shock. He felt a slight touch—one of the skittish creatures was beside him!
He turned toward the window, blushing brilliantly.

"Good-morning," said the newcomer brightly.

Martin did not answer. The stranger was neither persistent nor over-bold,
and reproved by Martin's aspect, she gave a little laugh and rose. Martin realized now that everybody was looking at him and outraged, he glued his eyes
to the pane. The man behind him leaned forward and spoke in a snarl.

"Licentious Amazons!" said he.

Martin's limited vocabulary included neither of these words and he
thought the stranger was speaking in a foreign tongue. Suddenly the Gibraltarians began to sing; then one of them made a foolish speech, then they
sang again. They laughed and called to one another, and two gayer and
younger than the rest, ran up and down the aisle. Martin's face grew red,
then pale, then red.

It was necessary to change trains at West Philadelphia and stepping
down Martin was still amazed. Here were more women, moreover they
were black women! Lanesville had a small colored population and Martin
looked upon occasional visitors to market with interest. They were industri-
ous people who carried baskets but these were as idle as the Gibraltarians.
For an instant he clung to the step, then he was engulfed in the black sea
and stood trembling. He saw a large badge bearing a legend, "The Ladies of
the Egyptian Lodge," he met hundreds of eyes. All were staring at him and
it did not occur to him that he was staring at them, now at a tall, slender
mulatto whose almost straight hair was bobbed, now at an enormous black
woman who must have weighed two hundred and fifty pounds. Eyes seemed
to devour him; he felt as though he were about to fall victim to some strange
enchantment, and in terror he turned his back and faced a long train of
Pullman cars. From every window eyes peered out at the tall Biblical figure
towering above the black faces. Half the passengers believed they saw An-
ton Lang of Oberammergau, then visiting America, the other half could not
guess what they saw.

When his train came, Martin stepped aboard trembling, and the Ladies
of the Egyptian Lodge crowded after him. The remaining journey would
take, he understood, only a few minutes and he sat with shut eyes. Against
his eyelids he saw a picture, a white house set against a lovely wood, a

bright blue gate, a pin-oak tree with a flock of yellow birds, like animated blossoms, a garden with sprouting onions and beans and peas and corn. Against the background he saw the yellow-haired girl. Would that he had her safely there, and how happy she would be to be there!

For an instant his gaze dwelt upon the magnificence of Broad Street Station, then his eye fell from the lofty roof to a table set outside one of the swinging doors which led to the inner waiting-room. Round it were gathered a dozen women in uniforms and approaching it were scores from the train he had left and from other trains. Above it was raised a banner.

THE MOTHER ROCK

BIDS

THE LADIES OF GIBRALTAR

WELCOME

Bewildered Martin looked about. It was a world of women! What had become of all the men? Were they at home doing the work of their wives and mothers? Happily he saw an official in uniform and him he approached with a question.

"Where is the Palace?"

The official stared dumbfounded.

"We have no palaces in this neighborhood."

"I mean a place where they have such moving pictures."

"Oh!" said the official. "Go down those steps and when you get to the street turn to your right and walk a block and you'll see the Palace. Are you a show man?"

"No," said Martin, outraged once more.

"What are you?" The official walked by Martin's side.

"I'm a Christian," answered Martin with dignity.

Outside Martin stood still. Lanesville had a few good-sized buildings, the court house was large and there were handsome churches, but there was nothing to prepare the mind for these towering edifices. He looked up Chestnut Street which seemed like a tunnel. He gazed shuddering at William Penn—what giant creatures had mounted him upon that lofty tower? Suddenly jostled, he looked down. Four young girls insisted upon walking abreast upon the crowded sidewalk. One of them had yellow hair—he turned and looked after her. But his girl was a modest girl!

Before the Palace he stood afraid to lay hold upon his bliss now that it was so near, and as he stood he stared. The film being shown was advertised by many pictures and he did unconsciously what he felt no temptation to do at home. The far from original theme of "Out of the Depths" made possible the representation of opium dens and drinking places from which the pure-minded and unscathed companion of evil men eventually rose to be wife of the prime minister of England. Her position of honor was all the more astonishing to Martin, since as she ascended she seemed to shed her clothes.

For an instant he was tempted to flee, then love and tenderness restrained him. He longed for the yellow-haired girl with a double longing; he wished to rescue her as well as to possess her.

Trembling he stepped inside the door. The activities of the Palace ceased at midnight and began at nine in the morning. It was now half past ten and the heroine was approaching the moment of her apotheosis. But Martin did not think of the apotheosis nor see the sumptuous fittings of the lobby, nor hear the triumphant sound of the Schubert Marche Militaire played thunderously on the organ as the prime minister and his wife descended the grand stairway; he saw only a bright yellow head in a glass enclosure.

He approached slowly and looked down, and the girl looked up and shoved a ticket toward him. As she did so her hand halted and she blushed scarlet. She was chewing gum and her jaws remained slightly parted. She had deliberately encouraged the rolling of Martin's eyes and she knew instantly that she was the object of his visit. She was grateful for the case that enclosed her, from which if necessary she could escape backward into the body of the house. The entering patrons, all of them women, were looking at him and in a moment they would be looking at her.

"Ticket?" she said sharply.

Martin blocked the window.

"You know me," he said tenderly.

"No," answered the girl decidedly. "Take your ticket and move on."

"It can't be that you don't know me!" Martin spoke in pure bewilderment. Was it day before yesterday's hair-cut which had so changed him?

"Of course I don't know you," declared the girl.

"I stood across from you in market," he explained. "Don't you know me now? Martin Ebersole."

The girl looked terrified. The queue of women was lengthening.

"I never saw you in my life. You must move on."

From somewhere in the long line floated an exclamation, "A sort of water buffalo," which Martin heard as little as he had heard the ardent tribute to his good looks in the Lanesville market. He accepted his dismissal instantly; he was not one to conduct a marriage by capture. Besides, the girl was a liar! He stepped out of the Palace and stood along the curb. He could not remember where he was or why he had come.

His first conscious apprehension was of a row of legends which deco-
rated the line of lamp-posts bisecting the broad street. They read

WELCOME

PHILADELPHIA

BIDS

THE LADIES OF GIBRALTAR

WELCOME

He saw suddenly the work of the world remaining undone while women,
young and old, black and white, attended conventions and moving pictures.
Then he saw again the lovely woodland and the farm and the white house
and the blue gate and the garden—and they were empty. He did not remember that he had the best mother in the world; he had no one, he was alone.

He looked up at William Penn and down at the thick traffic and up again
at William Penn and he went briskly toward the railroad station, observed of
all men, and stepped abroad a Lanesville train. It was long past the time for
his noon meal and he was weak with hunger. He did not recognize it as
hunger, he believed it to be heart-ache. But if it was heart-ache it suggested
a strange picture. He saw suddenly and with crystal clearness a market table
laden with good things, a live gander which seemed to smile a good-natured
though somewhat silly smile, a round face tipped back, a pair of blue eyes, a
pair of red lips opened to receive a large bite of roll and fried ham and egg.
Here was industry, here was modesty, here efficiency! Thank Heaven he
could reach Lanesville at three o'clock and there would be ample time before
night to admire these virtues at first hand.

IV

It was ten o'clock when Martin turned from the Lincoln Highway into the
pleasant by-road. The moon was shining and all the sweet-scented world
was still. His mare stepped briskly; those who denied themselves automobiles were entitled to good horses. The mare pranced; she had stood almost
all day, first restlessly and unwillingly in the strange livery stable in Lanesville, then in the more home-like stable of Israel Funk. She was anxious
now to be in her own stable and to whinny to her companions.

Martin let her choose her pace at considerable risk to his life. He was not
exactly responsible, he seemed to have awakened from a long, strange dream
and he was still dizzy. When the horse stopped before the stable he sat for a

few seconds in the buggy until she kicked the door and seemed about to kick the buggy. Then he stepped down, sniffing the cool and scented air. Here there was not only the odor of apple blossoms but the odor of onions and the one was as sweet as the other. There had never been a more promising season since he had begun to take note of seasons.

He unhitched slowly, stopping now and then as if he were still in a dream. A more retrospective and introspective person might have been trying to account for his unnatural infatuation, but Martin being practical, thought only of the blue eyes and plump and affectionate arms of Sallie. Why remember uneasiness and wickedness and unhappiness in the midst of peace and joy? He stood motionless in the darkness until he was roused by a sharp "Martin!" and saw a short round figure dimly outlined in the doorway. It was not quite familiar, the head was dark. But it was his mother, strange as she looked even to her son without her little white cap.

"What is wrong, Mom? Why are you up so late?"

"Why are you up so late?" asked Mahala. Her voice was thin and strained— she had not only done a part of Martin's work along with her own but she had imagined many terrible disasters. His long absence was unaccountable. She thought of him as rejected at Funks' and wandering about despairing. She thought that perhaps there was some one else and he was losing his soul and breaking her heart.

"I had her shod," he explained. "Then I went to Funks'."

"Then it is to be Sallie!" said Mahala. Her question was really a cry, impelled involuntarily by relief and happiness.

"Why, of course," said Martin positively and a little impatiently. "Who else should it be?"

FRAU NOLTE

*T*he setting for this story (which appeared in *Century* magazine in December 1925) is the Bach Festival in Bethlehem, Pennsylvania. In an address she gave in 1936, Singmaster described the annual performance of Bach's Mass in B Minor as the "loftiest achievement of the Pennsylvania Germans," adding, "There [in Bethlehem] many classical German compositions were given their first American performance . . . the singing of Pennsylvania German children has frequently raised the musical standard of a community."

*   *   *

I

When the train stopped at South Bethlehem Frau Nolte stepped down heavily and stood looking about with eager, searching eyes. An express which would have arrived in ample time for the Bach Festival was at this instant leaving New York, but she had preferred to come early, so that she might have the long hours of the journey on a way-train entirely to herself, to rest, to brood, or even to change her mind and return.

Having carried out her intention, she had at the least two hours to spare. In the grounds round the Moravian Church in the heart of the city where the festival was to be held were ancient stone-floored buildings in which lonely or bereaved women were spending their last days, and a cemetery, carpeted with thick turf, roofed by soaring elm-trees, and set with flat gravestones in long ranks. She wished to walk about there, to feel the thick grass under her tired feet, to lift her eyes to the vaulted tracery of leaves, so incredibly near the sky, to hear the first thin notes of the summoning trombones from the church tower, to prepare her soul for that which she hoped to find.

For the crowd she cared nothing; it she could ignore, forget, look through or over. Twenty years ago she had come here with a party of musicians, herself a soloist, and they had not walked in the graveyard, or thought of it except in sentimental appreciation of its romantic quietness; they had stood in front of the church, watching the arriving throng, hailing persons whom they knew, prosperous, happy, and deeply amused at this American ambition to sing Bach. The ambition was laudable, but it was funny none the less. However, though the orchestra was uneven and the conductor used what she called "tricks," the mass had been "not so bad," assisted as the chorus was by Lange's bass and her alto. She had told the conductor so with the passion which enlivened all her utterances about music. She spoke in German, her deep voice vibrating, her bosom heaving.

"It is not he! He is stiller, quieter, more spiritual, less robust, more perfect, thinner; one might say, less emotional. You put yourself in. He never put himself in even in his own music; that we may be sure of. You are going the wrong way!"

She would have liked to sing again, though from the increasing patronage of the festival she was certain that the director had kept on in the wrong way. But the pay was small and her price was large, and in May she usually went to Germany to visit her family.

Now she had ceased to sing. War had almost ruined her; had she been in the fatherland she could have suffered little more. Her sisters with whom she had expected eventually to live were dead, literally of the deaths of their sons on the battle-field. Her savings, sent back to help them, were swallowed up. She had given lavishly, certain of being able to earn more. A singer of German songs, a teacher of German methods, an exponent of German traditions, she had always retained her German name, even her German title; she had wished to be called "Frau" rather than "Madame." She had remained Germanic without realizing how expertly she had been "used," how royal honors had been not so much a tribute to her music as a reward for a more subtle, half-unconscious service.

Naturally, her concertizing days ended abruptly, her pupils dropped away; no other eventuality could, she understood perfectly, be expected. She had been a few years ago famous, sought after by managers, her name printed on the programs of débutantes, "pupil of Nolte," her purse full. Now she was forgotten or avoided, and she had barely enough to live on.

Her hatred of her enemies was no less keen than her resentment toward her fellow-countrymen, and sharper than both was her bitterness against the cruelty of mere existence. Her joy in life had been intense, her good spirits unfailing, but now joy was unknown, and depression unbroken. She had had a robust religion which allowed for human defections and provided for their forgiveness, but it did not help her. She had lost God utterly; when she tried to think of Him, she remembered the battle-fields.

The number of her friends had decreased to almost none. Many had died; some had become Americans, had even changed their names; others had found her lukewarm in the cause of the fatherland. A few years ago she could have summoned fifty persons, not so much to accompany as to attend her to Bethlehem, but now there was no one. She could not summon the dead; she would not invite the newly made Americans, who would probably be afraid to be seen in her company; and she would not risk the mockery of the loyalists.

"Bach in America! Ludicrous!" They would imitate with shrill sounds the thin voices.

It was best to come alone to hear this loftiest achievement of the human mind; the mass was, indeed, more than human. It did not merely express its incomparable text; it elaborated, commented, insisted, now delicately, now positively, now fervidly. All its treasures had not yet been discerned; it was inexhaustible, profound. Youth could adore it but not understand it; age could come to it assured of new bliss. It was more wonderful than any prose or poetry; it remained fresh when almost all other music had grown stale. If she could fill her soul with it once more she would be fed for the remaining weary days of her journey.

She did not expect to hear it well sung, or even tolerably sung, but it would comfort her none the less; they could not altogether ruin it. The conductor gave it in its entirety; he had respect for the composer to that extent. She winced at the thought of the solos for which she had so long ago prepared herself with careful pains; it was not easy music, this!

II

Her heart-beats quickened as, having inquired the way, she stepped out into the sunshine. She had eaten her lunch on the train, and she could forget the needs of her body. She was a forlorn-looking figure; of that she was aware. Her dress bought long ago for afternoon concerts was untidy and out of fashion; her shoes were down at heel. Her hair was gray, and she bothered with no confining veil. One person in a thousand, looking into her eyes, would have read there the record of love and pain and aspiration and despair, felt with the intensity of genius. One person out of a thousand would have adored her, listened to her least word, waited upon her. The others would have avoided her, drawn away from her.

She found the hill steep; she did not remember the hill. She took a program from her bag and studied it; she was following the directions exactly. The festival was held no longer in the Moravian Church, but in the University Chapel on the hillside. She had known this, but she had forgotten it. She went on, though now she walked more slowly.

"*Ich bin alt!*" she said half ruefully, half smilingly. "I am at last old!"

She was startled to see the size of the chapel. She had taken for granted that the festival had been transferred to a smaller building, that its audience had finally dwindled as might have been expected. But this was a large building! She approached the doorway and looked in, and then went slowly down the central aisle. In the apse, tiers of seats had been built up for the chorus and the orchestra; the director, standing under the screen, would have them all before him with the organist to his right. She reckoned the number of seats at a glance; the chorus was greatly enlarged, and if one were to judge by the seating capacity, augmented by hundreds of extra chairs, the audience had trebled instead of having decreased. All was dim and cool and in readiness. A breeze blew softly across the transept, and the fronds of palms set round the pulpit moved gently.

Frau Nolte looked at her ticket and found her seat. She would rest a while. She was a Lutheran, and churchly architecture and appointments pleased her. Bach had been a Lutheran, too, and he realized man's need for ceremonial beauty. She liked to sit here alone, though her heart ached no less, lay no less heavily in her side.

But she did not sit long; her heart, though it was heavy, was not quiet. She began to wonder why she had come, why she had risked an unpleasant impression, why she had not taken her score and sat at her window in some rare hour when the cursed talking-machines—Frau Nolte's vocabulary was adequate—were silent, and reconstruct the music for herself. The thrilling "*Kyrie,*" the up-piled "*Sanctus,*" the pleading "*Agnus Dei*"—her "*Agnus Dei*"—she could reproduce them all in her own soul. Here there would be a hundred details to offend.

Rising she went down the aisle to the door. Ushers had arrived, programs were being arranged on tables, and a few pedestrians and automobiles were entering the campus. All proceeded slowly, gravely, pilgrimwise. It was one o'clock; the sun had passed the meridian, and the shadows were slightly elongated. Under the trees and close to the high walls little groups began to collect and to look toward the church tower.

Frau Nolte stood for a moment on the steps; then she moved away. It was long since she had faced the eyes of men and women, and she realized that she no longer did it unconsciously; she believed that she seemed to stare, and she knew that the curiosity with which they looked back at her was no longer a tribute to her fame—ah, how like a breath on glass was fame!—but astonishment at her appearance. She was strange looking; she knew that. Her body had shrunk, and her departing flesh had left her skin in pendent folds.

On a flight of marble steps which led to a higher level of the campus she sat down. The shadow of a dense, drooping tree was creeping slowly across it, but the stone was still warm; she felt it gratefully with her hand. When one is poor and alone, one avoids illness. She sat leaning a little forward, her arms folded on her knees. A gardener knelt beside the steps and began to trim the edges of the grass with his shears. She looked at him idly; then her glance sharpened.

"You are a Saxon," she said in German.

The gardener lifted his head quickly.

"*Ja*," he answered without thinking. Then he corrected himself, "I am American."

He moved away without completing his work.

"He does not mean to compromise himself," said Frau Nolte.

She watched the thickening crowd. It was still only ten minutes after one, but hundreds besides herself had decided to come early, to enjoy the beautiful scene, to feel the delight of anticipation, and to hear the preliminary music from the tower. Frau Nolte had keen eyes, and she was confident that she recognized a dozen figures. There was Mme. Tesla, a soprano, stout, smiling, her hair at present a pale yellow, her eyebrows dark, her gown pink and white. With her was Dane Carter, an alto, whose real name was Lucia Wohlgefallen, tall and thin, and dressed in black with glittering sequins. The two did not love each other, but they set each other off.

"The sky and the trees and the grass betray them," said Frau Nolte to herself. Her smile was purely humorous; it held for the moment no bitterness.

There was a short, plump man in a white waistcoat,—at sight of him Frau Nolte's hand lifted an imaginary bow,—Zwemer, and with him his wife, little Lida Venable, slender, eager, ambitious, chaste, a true artist. One would like to have a talk with them afterward!

She saw figures grown tiresomely familiar in concert-halls, men who had often visited her behind the scenes, hopeful of a sentence or two which would lengthen the articles upon which their bread depended. One could have written their articles for them if one wished, paying oneself subtle compliments. She wondered whether they would know her. If they did, they would say, "In the audience were Tesla and Dane Carter and Zwemer and Lida Venable"—"and Nolte"? She knew perfectly well that they would not.

She saw a group of women in black dresses and bonnets, with little white ties under their chins, deaconesses, whose tranquillity she envied. Still other hundreds of visitors arrived on foot and in cars and took their places on the green lawn and looked upward.

Then, sweet and far away, Frau Nolte heard the sound for which she longed. The trombone players had come into the tower; they lifted their instruments and began. She heard the strains of a choral, familiar since her babyhood, "*Schmücke dich, O liebe Seele,*" and a crowd of memories rushed upon her. Tears came into her eyes, and she wiped them away again and again. She was afraid for an instant that she was going to sob.

III

When she looked up, a car had come quietly to a stop in the drive at the foot of the steps. It held a single passenger, a young woman, who stepped out and dismissed the chauffeur. She glanced at Frau Nolte and took a seat at the opposite end of the broad step, and, glad to forget for an instant the music which hurt her almost intolerably, Frau Nolte looked in her direction. She was of medium height, and she had a clear skin and brown hair. Some one had dressed her daringly; Frau Nolte's eyes were held. Her skirt was dark brown and accordion-plaited, her blouse creamy lace; and over it there was a short, sleeveless jacket which diminished cunningly the breadth of her shoulders and the depth of her chest. The jacket was green satin, the brightest, springtime green. The colors were those of dark, newly turned earth, of dogwood blossoms and new leaves.

Frau Nolte's gaze swept over her again in pure pleasure. She saw that her hands were ringless, her heels low, her flesh modestly covered. She looked, Frau Nolte thought, ready for life. She half wished that the girl would speak to her, but she made no effort to bring it about.

When the chorals were played, the crowd went into the church. Their advance was slow, reverent, deliberate; they might have been approaching a eucharistic service. But Frau Nolte sat still. When the last of the throng had entered, the girl beside her rose and said smilingly, "Are n't you coming?" and, receiving a shake of the head, went on her way. She walked erectly; one gathered from her step as one did not from her seated figure an impression of physical strength, of reserves of power. Suddenly she turned and came back, looking at Frau Nolte with bright, keen eyes.

"Have n't you a seat?"

"I prefer to stay here," answered Frau Nolte abruptly. Then she repented her curtness. "There are many doors and windows. The general effect will be heard."

The silence on the hillside deepened; the tall trees seemed to interpose a barrier between the noises of the world and some lovely manifestation which impended. A moment ago the air had shimmered in the sun; now, in the changing light, it became liquid. A bee buzzed near-by and then away; his departure seemed to be the last detail of preparation. In a moment Frau Nolte's desire was gratified. A voice cried, "*Kyrie!*"—no, it was many voices. They called again, "*Kyrie, eleison, eleison!*" Then flutes and oboes took up the air and began to weave a spell.

For an hour Frau Nolte sat motionless. The gardener tiptoed back to his unfinished work, saw her, and stepped quietly away; late-comers stole into the church; the shadows lengthened, creeping over her, but still she sat with her chin on her clasped hands. She acknowledged with amazement that she had been wrong; she said with a vague consciousness of a scriptural connection that good had come out of this Bethlehem. A mighty instrument had been created, more delicate than any stringed choir, more responsive than any flute, more profound than any great organ. The faults which she had noted long ago were the faults of youth, of inexperience; now they had vanished. The music swelled gloriously; it died away so delicately that it was impossible to tell whether it had thinned to nothingness or whether one's own fancy had concluded the attenuation. A great edifice built itself magically and then resolved itself, abruptly, now element by element, into its parts. Certain renderings might have been changed, but it would have been merely to make them different and not more perfect.

But Frau Nolte was not satisfied. When the "*Amen*" was sung and the first part finished and the audience streamed out of the church doors, she left her seat and climbed still higher on the sloping campus and walked about in a shadowy place between two buildings. At each turn she saw again the church, the towering spire, the old trees, the lawns, the throng of people. The members of the orchestra had found comfortable places in the shade; some lay at full length on the grass; the chorus massed itself before a photographer against a sunny wall; there was constant motion, and now and then an exclamation or a laugh. The shadows grew still deeper, the sky loftier, the foliage richer, and there seemed to float about, like thin trailing clouds, the echoes of the heavenly music. Frau Nolte laid her hand again across her aching heart. She walked restlessly; she looked still older, still more tired. She had expected to be healed, but her anguish of spirit had quickened, music had failed her, her journey was vain.

When the trombones had played again and the audience streamed back, she returned to her place on the step, quite too cool now in the shadow. She understood her case; she had come not to hear music but to find God, and He was not here. He was nowhere. Her faith was dead; even Bach could not quicken an extinguished fire. She would rest a little; then she would go home. She had now, she said, nothing.

Suddenly she heard uttered a single word; the tenor pronounced it, the bass repeated it, alto and soprano took it up; it was reiterated again and again. There were other words, but she heard it alone, "*Credo*," and again mockingly, "*Credo*." Rising, she lifted her hands as though to shut out the sound. They believed! There was nothing to believe.

She spread out her hands in a gesture of defiance. She would drink the cup to the dregs. She would go down into the church, she would hear every sound, she would give the music every chance with her. There was still the "*Crucifixus*"; let it break her heart if it could! There was a bass solo, to her one of the most marvelous of the numbers, dry, dogmatic, gratifying the ear with beautiful positive endings, "*et unam sanctam catholicam et apostolicam ecclesiam.*" Once she had smiled responsively at its convincingness; there was even humor in it; she would hear that. There were also the "*Sanctus*," the "*Hosanna*"; she would give them earnest attention; let them convince if they could!

She went down the hill, her old-fashioned skirt trailing. She believed that she was altogether defiant, but in reality she was afraid. To have life end thus, aridly, with one's memories defaced, one's heart broken, one's hopes blasted! She found her place and sat down heavily. No one looked at her, and she looked at no one. She sat frowning, trying to check her heavy breathing. She would stay until the "*Hosanna*" was finished; then before the alto soloist sang the "*Agnus Dei*" she would come away.

But despite her determination, when the "*Hosanna*" was finished, she sat still, her mind in turmoil. She knew the music thoroughly, but its volume and passion bewildered her. Before she could move, the violins began their delicate prelude, and from behind a screen of palms, against the background of white-clad sopranos, a dark head was suddenly lifted, and the girl who had sat beside her on the steps rose and stood with her hands clasped.

In the silence, which seemed the deeper for the delicate music, leaped a new emotion, tearing her heart: jealousy, tigerish, sharp, cruel. She belonged to an era which was past, and the feet of youth were at the door, alert, presumptuous, beautiful, and hateful. Her lips curled; she leaned forward, recalling everything, her own decline, the fate of her kin, even, resolutely, her loss of faith. Her heart filled with evil impulses of scorn, of rage, of mockery. She meant to set them free, to will upon presumption its just punishment, to be somehow avenged. She meant to avenge not only herself, and the misfortunes of her kindred, but the woe of the world. She bit her lips, trying to be silent until she could think what she must do. If the prelude had lasted another moment, she might have committed some madness.

But the girl began to sing, and Frau Nolte sank back, bewildered by a fresh emotion. It seemed to her that she herself was singing; here was her controlling of emotion, here her inflections. "*Agnus Dei, qui tollis peccata mundi, miserere nobis.*" As she had studied long ago she had translated the words mentally into her own tongue: "*O Lamm Gottes, der Du trägst die Sünd' der Welt, erbarm Dich unser!*" She recalled her piety, her ardor, her humility.

Then, suddenly in contrast, she felt the scorching, illuminating flame of rage and knew at once the source of her wretchedness, the obstacle between her and her Creator, the stone which sealed her heart. She stood at a parting of the ways; on one side destruction beckoned, on the other waited peace. She knew that she must choose instantly.

She began broken-heartedly to pray; she put hatred away, jealousy away; and as she did so, she ceased to be wretched. A flood of happiness overwhelmed her; she forgot that she was old. She found that which she had sought; she believed that she was immortal.

The girl finished her song and the chorus rose. "*Dona nobis pacem*"—one might have peace if one wished; it was very simple; one needed only to cleanse one's heart and to ask. Frau Nolte sat relaxed, her hands laid lightly in her lap, fixing upon her soul the impressions of the vaulted roof, the stained and storied windows, the waves of tremendous sound, the girl's deep and lovely voice, all the details of the feast which had been spread. It was not probable that she would come again; this would have to last her till she died.

IV

The church emptied quickly; twilight was approaching, there were friends to be greeted, there was enthusiasm to be expressed in full voice and not in churchly whispers, there were trains which would not wait. The chorus went hurrying, happily; the smiling girls passed close to Frau Nolte, one clasping her tired throat dramatically, a pair leaning upon each other in exhaustion which was only half assumed. There were young girls and gray-haired women, and boys and middle-aged men, musicians and university students and clergymen and steel-workers' daughters. They would have a few weeks' rest; then they would begin once more, patiently, diligently, obediently, their magnificent creation. Frau Nolte smiled back at them; she would have liked, in a moment of Germanic impulsiveness, long since inhibited, to hug them. A need for some one to speak to became imperative.

Then some one was provided. A young woman sat down beside her; she saw the apple-green jacket, the creamy blouse, the dark skirt, which suggested the corner of a newly plowed field against blooming woodland. She felt a hand laid on hers.

"You are Nolte!"

Frau Nolte smiled at the girl's breathlessness.

"Well, if I am?"

"Do people know that you are here?"

"I hope not."

"Don't you want them to?"

"No."

"The director would rather have you here than all the rest put together."

Frau Nolte shook a protesting head.

"I came to hear the singing. I used to sing your part. I sang it better. But after a while you will sing it better than I."

The girl lifted Nolte's hand and held it against her breast.

"I came here as a little girl long ago, and I heard you. I copied you. I have worked *terribly*."

Frau Nolte nodded, as though this were nothing.

"Of course. One must. So did he." She spoke with passion. "He used to wake at midnight and steal from his brother's cabinet the music which was denied him and copy it. He put out his eyes that way. You have read about him?"

"Everything."

"You play the piano?"

"Yes."

"The organ?"

"A little."

"You know your harmony?"

"Yes."

Frau Nolte nodded approvingly. She felt her hand taken in a closer clasp.

"You ought to tell me all you know. Where do you live? May I come to see you?"

Frau Nolte smiled, like a wise, humorous old man.

"You're laughing at me!" cried the girl ruefully.

"No, indeed. You can find me in New York. My name is always in the musical directory." She turned and looked at the girl. She had spoken of one essential, work; there was another.

"Are you married?"

"No."

"Have you a lover?" She made no excuse; the girl expected none. A shadow passed over her face; her lips trembled.

"He is dead."

"Ah!" Frau Nolte nodded as though she were not surprised. "Cherish his memory, but love your life!" She slid down suddenly into the pew as a man slides when he wishes to say something at his ease. "Bach, now; think of him! married twice, twenty children, difficulties of all sorts, struggles, battles, disappointment, weakness, anguish—because of them he can lift us up. Live; don't forget that!"

She rose, holding the girl's hand.

"Come to see me, and we will talk. I will scold you a little, but I will praise you more."

They went down the aisle together, and at the doorway looked back. The vaulted roof vanished in shadow, but, beneath, bright streaks of color from the declining sun crossed almost horizontally. Mystery filled the dim apse; it seemed as though the Host, removed for some sanctifying purpose, had been put back upon the altar.

Frau Nolte went down the hill. She was tired and a little stiff, but her thoughts were not upon her body, worn by sixty strenuous years. She remembered the young singer and wondered whether she would come; there was a promised pleasure! She remembered her many pupils; she was in their souls, whether or not they wished her there. She thought with gratitude of the director who had recreated this marvelous music; she sympathized with his happiness, his incomparable satisfactions, his hopes. But she believed that to-day the music had signified more to her than to him because her need had been greater.

She thought of the graveyard on the other side of the town, so still, so blessed. She was too tired to walk thither; she would sit here in the station and remember the arching trees and the last strains of the music. It seemed to her that life was good, that everything was provided for, that a solution of all problems was certain. She began to beat time gently and to hum in her deep voice. She could never, she believed, be unhappy again.

Presently she nodded her head in solemn affirmation. She paraphrased unconsciously the thought of a poet, but it was none the less truly her thought.

"The others may guess," said Frau Nolte. "But the musician knows."

WILDFIRE

P ennsylvania German powwowing came to the public's attention in 1928 when an alleged powwow doctor was murdered in the Pennsylvania German region of the state. Singmaster wrote an article called "Pennsylvania Witch Doctors Openly Casting Their Spells" for the Sunday edition of the *World* (December 16, 1928). The article distinguished clearly between folk powwow practices and witchcraft. In "Wildfire," first published in the *Saturday Evening Post* (March 30, 1935) with illustrations by Rico Tomaso (and collected in *The Saturday Evening Post Treasury* [New York: Simon and Shuster, 1954]), Singmaster sought to contextualize the waning yet still influential use of powwow doctoring in the Pennsylvania German community.

* * *

I

Mrs. Kalkbrenner rose at six o'clock, put on her clothing in the dark, took her shoes in her hand and went softly down the back stairs into the kitchen, her broad body almost filling the narrow space. She went silently—the stairs were padded with thick rug carpet—and she went carefully—her neighbor, Mrs. Lentz, who was only a little larger, had pitched head-first down a similar stairway and had to be dragged out by four strong men. Mrs. Kalkbrenner's daughter Helen, a graduate of the Teachers' College and herself a teacher, used the front stairs; Mrs Kalkbrenner never did.

The kitchen was very cold, but to Mrs. Kalkbrenner it was not uncomfortable; in fact, the icy linoleum felt pleasant enough through her thick stockings. She snapped on the electric light, put on her shoes, donned a brown gingham allover, shook the grate of the stove, opened the lower door, adjusted the chimney draft for a quick fire, descended to the cellar and treated the furnace in the same fashion, returned and stepped into the out-kitchen, whose walls were not brick, but boards. Here stood another stove, in which a fire was laid, but not lighted. She applied a match, and instantly paper and wood flamed, and now the room filled with the odor of burning kerosene in which a stick or two had been soaked. She replaced the lid, pulled over the fire box a boiler filled with water, glanced at the tubs, in one of which clothes were soaking, said, "So!" and went back to the kitchen.

From this stove issued promising murmurs and cracklings. Mrs. Kalk-brenner opened the solid door of a tall wooden cupboard painted gray and built like a secretary, in two parts. On the lower shelf of the upper section stood plates and cups and saucers; on the second, cans of coffee, oatmeal, rice, raisins, spices and other commodities. She took down the can of coffee and reached into the cupboard in the lower section for the pot.

Then, suddenly, she cocked her head; in the front room upstairs Helen was moving about. She crossed the kitchen and, taking from the wall a little mirror, moved with it under the electric bulb. Her eyes were brown, and so was her smoothly parted hair; her cheeks were full and round. She did not look at her eyes or at the parting of her hair; she looked at a red spot beside her nose. The skin was slightly raised and purplish red. She touched it with the tip of her finger—a space the size of a half dollar was hard.

She hung the mirror back on its nail, measured coffee and water into the pot, added the shell of an egg, and cooked two strips of bacon. Usually she ate four strips and two eggs, but this morning her good appetite failed her. When, fifteen minutes later, Helen came down the front steps and back into the kitchen, she called through the closed door from the outkitchen:

"I ate already. You cook you two eggs."

Helen was like her mother in being short and round-faced, but she was slender and her color was very bright. A slight frown was becoming habitual; she grieved for her father, who had died six months ago; she worried over the closing of the bank where the family funds were deposited, and the two cuts in her salary. She was constantly worried and irritated by her mother.

"What's the use of getting up to wash in the middle of the night?" she demanded, soundlessly, of the closed door. She was inaccurate—dawn was brightening the window.

In the outkitchen, Mrs. Kalkbrenner spoke also. She was enveloped in steam; it was that, she thought, which made her a little lightheaded.

"Whatever happens, one must wash and iron," she declared. "One thing I know—it's no boil. No boil would lay me so out."

Helen ate her breakfast; then she washed the dishes which her mother had left and her own; then she entered the steam-filled outkitchen. Mrs.

Kalkbrenner was rubbing on the board clothes which were not soiled. The rising sun shone through the window, gilding drops of condensed vapor.

"Don't hang the clothes outside," begged Helen.

"I always hang outside if it don't rain."

"Why, mother, what have you on your face?"

"*Ach,* just such a little outbreaking."

"It's almost zero, mother."

"I guess I have a coat and gloves and a head shawl and gums," Mrs Kalkbrenner bent over her tub. "Let me be!" said every stroke. "Let me be!"

Helen did not close the door behind her, and Mrs. Kalkbrenner left it open. She heard Helen moving about upstairs making the two beds. She came down into the sitting room and packed fifty examination papers into her brief case. Then she put on her hat and coat before the mirror in the hatrack and pulled on her galoshes. She called good-by and went out the front door. Mrs. Kalkbrenner stepped quickly into the kitchen and through the hall into the parlor; there she peered through the curtains in the bay window, watching Helen until she turned a distant corner. Suddenly she sobbed.

Returning to her washtubs, she rubbed several garments for the second time. She rinsed, she blued, she wrung. Finally she put on her coat, her head shawl, her thick cotton gloves and her overshoes, and, opening the door, carried the basket down the icy boardwalk. The air stung her nostrils and stiffened her face.

"It's the cold," she thought. "Not that the spots get bigger."

By eleven o'clock the clothes were frozen into a condition sufficiently dry, and she brought them in and folded them for ironing.

"If it gave something to lie on, I'd lay me a little down," she thought. Instead she slept heavily in the kitchen rocking-chair. When she woke, she tried in vain to eat. The hard spot on her cheek was larger; as she placed the ironing board, she avoided looking into the mirror.

All afternoon she hoped that Annie Getzendaner would come in. Annie was a smart little woman who belonged to her church and was her best friend. But Annie did not appear. She finished ironing, put the clothes away, cleaned the ashes from the outkitchen stove, and put coal on the kitchen stove. Not until then did she look into the mirror. At what she saw she cried out, "*Gott im Himmel!*"

She went slowly upstairs, carrying a pitcher of hot water. She undressed, bathed, put on her warm nightgown and got into bed. Then she got out and opened the heavy lower drawer of her old-fashioned bureau and lifted the white cloth which covered its contents. A stranger might have thought that a dead woman lay there. Mrs. Kalkbrenner was not frightened; these were merely the underclothes, shoes, and stockings for her burial. Petticoats, underbody and shoes were arranged as they would some day be on Mrs. Kalkbrenner; on top lay a pair of stockings and a folded chemise. All the undergarments made by hand and trimmed with crocheted lace.

She pressed her palm down on the chemise. Inside lay a soft cylinder— five ten-dollar bills in a roll; her precious treasure, saved toward her coffin. Having satisfied herself that it was there, she got back into bed and drew the covers to her chin. Her face was swelling so that soon her head would be a perfect sphere. The hard space was much larger, the ghastly red was deeper and greater in area.

"Surely, Annie will come," she thought. "Surely, she'll come soon and she'll fetch her."

By "her" Mrs. Kalkbrenner did not mean Helen; she meant the pow-wower, Mrs. Mary Haller, a widow, famous far and wide, who could exorcise the evil spirit which had inflamed and hardened her skin and set her head throbbing and her body burning. Mrs. Haller lived at the opposite side of the city, in a three-story brick house which she had earned by exorcising evil spirits. Three times three times she laid her hand on sore joints or on a hard spot in one's side, and three times three she pronounced magic words. Her magic was not evil, it was good; each formula concluded with the names of the Trinity. Doctors hated her, some educated people laughed at her, but with her fine house filled with gifts and a bankbook filled with entries, she did not need to care what anyone thought or said. She dared ask no money, but money she received, sometimes in large amounts, and money she naturally preferred to bowls, chop plates and glass pitchers with red or yellow or green tumblers to match; even to radios and self-playing pianos, which were the gifts of fools. It was true that she had not cured the cholasma, popularly called "liver spots," which darkened large brown areas on Annie Getzendaner's little face, but she was treating her, and Annie expected a cure.

"I'll pay her good money," thought Mrs. Kalkbrenner. "Ten dollars from what I saved toward my burial." She began to mutter, "Annie! Annie!"

II

Mrs. Kalkbrenner lay unpillowed on her bed. On Monday, returning from school at half past four, chilled through in spite of her youth and her warm clothing and her quick step, Helen had heard her mother muttering. Now it was Friday morning, and Mrs. Kalkbrenner's cheeks and chin were so swollen that she could not rest her head on the thinnest pillow. In narrow spaces between cloths soaked with a solution prescribed by Doctor Zinzer showed her skin, here fiery red, here purple. She was constantly drowsy and in pain; in the afternoons her temperature climbed as high as 105.

Like her mother's temperature, thought Helen, mounted Doctor Zinzer's bill and the deduction from her salary for a substitute. She could not pay a trained nurse; thus far she had nursed her mother night and day. Friends and neighbors brought food, but erysipelas was contagious and as long as she could manage alone, she would accept no further help.

In the daytime, Mrs. Kalkbrenner moaned; in the evening she muttered or called, "Annie! Annie!" as though Annie might be downstairs. Annie, Helen explained, was in Reading, nursing a sick brother. Mrs. Kalkbrenner seemed to understand, but in a moment she was calling again.

Now, well-nigh exhausted by the changing of her sheets, she drank milk through a tube. She heard Helen set a chair back against the wall and pull down the shade, and she opened one eye far enough to see Helen gathering bedding in her arms.

"You boil it good?" she asked faintly.

Even with bedding in her arms, Helen went down the front stairs. Her mother heard steps from the hall carpet on the linoleum, then she heard a thud, which she did not interpret as the falling of a human body, worn by labor and lack of sleep.

Helen had been able to let herself down to her knees; then she lay at full length. In another moment the outer door opened and a woman entered, short and thin, with a pointed nose. Her face appeared to be peeling off a summer's deep tan, brown skin and natural skin now queerly divided in area. "Good heavens, girl!" she cried, so loudly that the sound penetrated Mrs. Kalkbrenner's dull ears. "I just this minute heard about your mom."

The voice was lowered; Mrs. Kalkbrenner tried to call, but excitement paralyzed her throat. There was the click of china, the smell of coffee.

"No breakfast!" cried Annie. "Do you think you're made of iron?"

Again Mrs. Kalkbrenner tried to call. Tears scalded her eyelids. She heard quick steps climbing the stairs, crossing the matting.

Annie stood beside her bed. "My God, Sabina! I could 'a' come sooner home!"

"I thought it was all up," whispered Mrs. Kalkbrenner.

Annie bent over the bed. "Wouldn't she fetch her?"

"I didn't say anything. It would be no use."

Annie continued to bend over the bed; she was protected against contagion and other evils. "I'll get her here," she promised.

The tears dried on Mrs. Kalkbrenner's hot cheeks. Annie and Helen talked in the kitchen, but she did not try to listen; she was too heavy, too hot, too confused. "Annie!" she began to mutter. "Annie!"

Helen came into the room with a basin in her hand. Unable to endure the whole of her mother's almost obliterated countenance, she removed and replaced the cloths one at a time.

"Mother," she said, "Annie's coming this evening to stay all night."

"So?"

"She wants me to go to the third story to sleep."

Mrs. Kalkbrenner was slow about answering. Thus a prisoner, dulled by incarceration, disease and despair, might struggle to understand plans for her release. She tried to recapture the gleam of hope which she had seen, and failed. "Annie!" she called. "Annie!"

III

It was Monday night at eleven o'clock, and, her head still unpillowed, her face still swollen almost out of human semblance, Mrs. Kalkbrenner lay in bed. Round the electric bulb had been wrapped a piece of red calico, and in the dim light Annie Getzendaner, bent so that she seemed to sew with her nose, was sewing patchwork. There was no sound in the house and to this back room came no sound from the street. In the third story, Helen slept for the third night, a sleep like death.

Mrs. Kalkbrenner opened one eye. She was still confused, but she began to organize her scattering thoughts. She was in pain, there was something very much the matter with her face, she was very sick. She studied the figure under the red light; it was not Mrs. Lentz; she would be afraid to come. It was not Helen. It was brown little Annie Getzendaner! Mrs. Kalkbrenner's heart threatened to leap from her side. She was sick, perhaps dying. Doctor Zinzer could not help her, though he came daily, but Annie could bring help.

"I have the wildfire, like my mom once had," she thought. "Annie said she'd sure fetch her." She tried to speak, but her lips were stiff. She reached out and tapped the head of the bed. Instantly Annie laid down her sewing. "Will you fetch her?" murmured Mrs. Kalkbrenner.

Annie bent close. "Listen, Sabina," she whispered earnestly. "She's been twice here and tonight she'll come for the last time. You're getting better."

Mrs. Kalkbrenner turned her head a half inch and rolled her aching eyes toward the next room.

"Helen sleeps in the third story. The doctor gives her something. In the mornings I must call her, she sleeps so heavy. Soon the powwower will come, Sabina. *Ach,* she's here, Sabina!"

Annie tiptoed into the hall and down the back steps. Only intently listening ears could have heard the clicking latch of the outer kitchen door, the muttered words, the slight scraping of the iron shovel in the coal bucket, the careful steps on the back stairs. Sabina heard them all; through a narrow slit between her eyelids she watched the door. Her eyelids fluttered; she seemed to be sinking to unfathomable depths.

Mrs. Haller entered the door and crossed the room. She was tall; to Mrs. Kalkbrenner she looked gigantic. She had not taken off her coat or hat; she carried the kitchen shovel, on which was a little heap of faintly glowing coals. She placed herself on one side of the bed and Annie stood opposite. She spoke in Pennsylvania German in a deep grumble:

"Wildfire, I banish you: depart, wildfire, in the name of Father, Son and Holy Ghost."

She handed the shovel across the bed to Annie, who brought it back round the foot, and returned to her place to receive it again and once again.

Mrs. Kalkbrenner lost all sense of time and space. When she woke, Annie was sewing patchwork under the red light. She tapped on the bed and Annie bent over her.

"Couldn't you lay once a little down in Helen's room?"

"I guess I could. I'll first get your milk."

Mrs. Kalkbrenner sucked the milk through a tube. "It tastes good," she murmured. "I'm better."

"To be sure, you are!" said Annie.

IV

"I never heard that it could come right back," said Mrs. Kalkbrenner tremulously.

She sat in the kitchen rocking-chair; Annie Getzendaner stood before the stove, carefully turning slices of breaded veal. The skin of Mrs. Kalkbrenner's round face had a yellow cast; when she bathed, shreds of skin peeled off. Nowhere was it purplish red or hot and hard to the touch. Round the waist of her dark blue calico dress was tied a white apron; she wore a becoming white collar, her hair was evenly parted and smoothly brushed. She had lost fifteen pounds, but had recovered at least five.

This was the first time in seven weeks that she had been up all day. It was true that she had not come downstairs till ten o'clock, and that Annie had come in to get dinner and look after the fires, but far as it was from her normal living, it was vastly better than lying in bed all the twenty-four hours, her flesh burning, the threat of death hanging over her.

On the window still lay a letter addressed to Helen, left by the postman after she had gone. In the corner was printed, ARTHUR M. ZINZER, M.D.; inside was a single half sheet of paper containing a little printing and a few words and numerals. Mrs. Kalkbrenner knew what it was; she had addressed the writer in her own mind. "I didn't tell you to come," said she. No doubt Annie's sharp eyes had seen it.

Annie turned from the stove. "I knew a woman who was well a week, then it took her again. She had it first on the outside; when it came back it went through her nose in her throat and choked her. I heard of another; and with her it went backwards through her hair and at the neck it struck inwards and upwards to the brain. She, too, trusted foolishly in doctors."

The possibility of a return of the erysipelas was terrifying; for the moment Mrs. Kalkbrenner could not contemplate so great a disaster. "It's still cold, if February is almost through," she remarked feebly.

Annie lifted the breaded veal to a platter and the boiled potatoes one by one into their dish.

"It's too cold for you to go and pay her," she said. "I can pay her for you."

Mrs. Kalkbrenner walked unsteadily to the table. She ate veal and potatoes and slaw and warm apple pie.

When they had finished, Annie washed the dishes and put on her hat and coat.

"I'd pay her soon," she advised. "It's a good deal over a month since she was here."

"This evening I'll have it for you," promised Mrs. Kalkbrenner. Agonized, she saw herself unfolding her chemise and extracting one of the ten-dollar bills. "What should I give her?"

"You must decide," said Annie. "She was three times here in the middle of the night in zero weather, and this isn't weak like doctor's medicine."

The day was dull, and when the door closed, it seemed as though twilight were at hand, though it was only one o'clock. Mrs. Kalkbrenner rested her head against the back of the chair; then she went slowly into the front hall and up the front steps, helping herself with both hands on the banister. She knelt on shaky knees and pulled open the heavy drawer. There lay her burial clothes, there her folded chemise. Once, Annie told her, they thought she would die in the night. What would be more natural than for Helen to see that her burial clothes were ready and what more sensible than to use her money when there was need?

She pressed her palm on the soft fabric—there was the little roll. Trembling, she lay down on the bed. At four o'clock she crept down to the kitchen, feeling chilled and terrified.

Helen came in at half-past four, running in on the boardwalk at the side of the house. She had gained none of the ten pounds she had lost and the furrows on her forehead were deepened.

"How are you, mother?" she asked anxiously, her eye instantly upon the window sill.

"So, so."

Slowly Helen took off her coat and hat, and walked into the hall and hung them on the rack. When she came back she sat down by the window and opened the envelope and took out the half sheet. She looked at it and tears came into her eyes. She looked at her mother; Mrs. Kalkbrenner's head rested against the back of her chair and her eyes were closed.

Helen put supper on the table, moving briskly, not with the natural energy of youth, but with the nervousness of exhaustion. Her cheeks were flushed; surreptitiously she wiped away tears.

"I'll get you to bed, mother; then I must run out for a few minutes. Is Annie coming back?"

Mrs. Kalkbrenner held her hand under her chin, her thumb on one side, her fingers on the other, both pressing her throat. She had the look of one choking herself. At this moment she discovered hard glands which had been in her neck since she was born.

"Yes, she is." She rose and walked swiftly toward the hall door, hers the energy of terror. Her throat felt hot and hard.

"Shall I help you, mother?"

"No."

"I'll put the key out for Annie."

Mrs. Kalkbrenner turned on the light in her room and pressed her face close to the mirror. It might be that the darkness was only the shadow of her chin, but the hard lumps were there; they were substance and not shadow. When Annie came, she lay on the bed in all her clothes with the blanket pulled over her.

"In the lower drawer, Annie, in the folded shimmy, is money."

Annie opened the heavy drawer and gathered out the little roll as a bird hooks a worm.

"Will it take all?" gasped Mrs. Kalkbrenner.

Annie counted the bills. Every patient she brought to Mrs. Haller made the cure of her liver spots more certain. "If it's the best you can do, it's all right," she said. "One of the legislatures from Harrisburg had the wildfire and he sent a grand car for her. Five hundred dollars he paid her."

"Feel here," said Mrs. Kalkbrenner.

Annie pressed Mrs. Kalkbrenner's glands. "That's nothing. By tomorrow, now that she's paid, those spots will be soft."

The latch of the kitchen door clicked and Helen came up the steps. She still wore her hat and coat; she was too happy to bear her relief alone.

"I went to see Doctor Zinzer. His bill was only fifty dollars. He was here twenty-five different days and sometimes he was here twice. I had to tell him that my salary for last month went to my substitute and to ask him to wait. He said he would. I hated to do it; he has heavy expenses. He said you made a good recovery, mother."

Mrs. Kalkbrenner glanced at Annie and Annie looked back. "She could have saved her fifty dollars," said both glances. They did not like to be hard on Helen, but she had made the foolish debt, no one else. Mrs. Kalkbrenner leaned out of bed so that she could see the lower drawer—it was safely closed.

"Yes," said Annie, "she sure did—after she got started."

SETTLED OUT OF COURT

*R*ather than take their disputes to the public court system, the Old Order Amish settled problems in private meetings according to established church codes. Amish *Gelassenheit,* based on the biblical model of the suffering servant, emphasizes selflessness, humility, and submission to God's will. Elsie Singmaster openly admired Amish resolve in the face of public criticism. She illustrates the use of Amish judicial practices in this story, first published in the *Saturday Evening Post* (December 1, 1934), with illustrations by Robert W. Crowther.

* * *

At half-past eight on Sunday morning, when the Old Order Amish meeting opened in his father's barn at the top of Dutch Hill near Sorrel Horse, Lancaster County, Daniel Stolz sat on one of the benches placed against the haymow. He was only twenty, but a thick reddish beard spread across his breast; his hair, curling at the ends, covered the standing collar of his black coat. His suit, fastened not with buttons but with hooks and eyes, had been his wedding suit, made by his mother a year ago.

His father, Bishop Stolz, sat near by, dressed in black like Daniel. Gray threads showed in his enormous beard. Beyond sat Daniel's maternal grandfather, Bishop Fornwalt, who was ninety. He was tall and stooped; his white beard was long enough to lie upon his breast, but not thick enough to hide altogether his yellowish-gray chin. His suit was gray.

Daniel bowed his head, but he was not asleep; his hands, large, muscular and calloused, kept up an unceasing motion, which was, however, so slow that it escaped the curious and anxious eyes fixed upon him. His right hand clasped his left, kneading and twisting it as if to crush it or to sever it at the wrist.

The barn was large enough to accommodate all the Old Order congregation; and since the September day was fine, all the congregation were present except for a few very old people and one young mother with a newly
born babe. Parallel with the row of benches on which, along with Daniel,
sat his father and grandfather and the other ministers and older men, ran
six other rows occupied by half-grown boys and women and children. The
bearded men, if they looked straight ahead, saw placid faces, heads coifed
in transparent white, white organdie neckerchiefs and aprons. The dresses
of the older women were dark gray or black; those of the younger women
dark blue or purple or red.

Now and then a young woman lifted a hand to push under her cap a
springy curl, blushing as she did so. The showing of one's hair betrayed
vanity.

The little girls were like flowers—Yohnie Beiler's three in apple green
with white aprons and neckerchiefs and caps; Sam Zook's three in pink;
Noah Zook's four, ranging from one year to eight, in lilac. The boys, large
and small, wore suits like their fathers', made at home and hooked together,
with trousers which ended halfway between knee and ankle. Their hair was
long and unmistakably trimmed round a crock. The very little children had
playthings—a tiny doll, a string of wooden beads, a little box of peppermints,
a four-inch automobile—being Old Order Amish, one might play with automobiles, but not ride in them.

The barn was dim to those entering from the bright sunlight, but to those
within it was bright enough and very pleasant. Shafts of sunlight streamed
through long cracks in the wooden walls and through the narrow apertures
provided for the drying of tobacco. Opposite the mow, which was packed
with hay, on racks almost to the ridgepole, hung thousands of plants cut
only a few days and still green.

Suddenly the little boys and girls ceased to move quietly on their backless
benches, the older folk ceased to glance at one another smilingly. Pigeons
cooed and winged their way from mow to tobacco racks, beneath in the stable a horse whinnied or a cow lowed, in the yard a rooster crowed, but these
sounds were scarcely heard by the congregation. Even Christopher Fischer,
aged ten months, and Jonathan Fischer, aged twenty months—the one on
his mother's lap, the other by her side; both dressed in dark green with tiny
black shoes and stockings—looked straight forward.

Young Bishop Fischer, their father, rose in his place against the mow,
announced a German hymn and himself started the tune; not a choral tune
but a slow chant with three or four notes to each syllable. He was straight

and slender; his bearded face might have served as a model for the face of John the Disciple. He preached for half an hour upon the goodness of God. Besides his voice, there was no sound except the sounds of Nature, not a motion except the flight of pigeons or the lovely sinking of young Christopher's head upon his mother's breast. Christopher's father spoke with passion, as though he spoke directly to someone in his audience.

Daniel Stolz, to whom he spoke, continued to sit with bent head, his hands making the strange motions. His father bent forward a little, so that he might look at him secretly; his brothers, Abraham, Isaac and Jacob, glanced at him and away; several young women, a little past the age when the Amish marry, looked at him and sighed. His mother was not here; she was preparing dinner for the congregation.

"God is always good," declared young Bishop Fischer.

"He is not," answered Daniel in his heart.

"Let us sing Hallelujah, Schöner Morgen," said Fischer.

"I'll never sing again," thought Daniel.

Aged Bishop Fornwalt preached upon the glories of heaven—that is, his climax described the glories of heaven. He began with the creation of the world; he mentioned many names—Adam and Eve, Cain and Abel, Abraham and Isaac, Saul, David, Solomon, Jeremiah and Ezekiel, Hosea and Habakkuk. He listed the disciples and the good women; when he reached the Revelation of St. John, his worn old voice shrilled among the rafters:

"There we'll meet, brethren and sisters! There we'll see our beloved! Ah"—the congregation closed their eyes lest they might look at Daniel—"there to part no more!"

"Heaven is far off," thought Daniel. "It's unreal. I don't believe it gives a heaven. I'll never see them again."

When the sermon was over, the people knelt, facing their benches, and prayed silently. Daniel knelt, but he did not pray. He rose abruptly with the rest and stood facing eastward while Bishop Fischer intoned a long passage of Scripture.

Fischer had preached for half an hour, Fornwalt for an hour; now Daniel's father, also a bishop, preached for three-quarters of an hour. Still the pigeons cooed, quietly young women took their children out, stepping high over the threshold, and silently returned. Bishop Stolz's sermon did not seem too long even after the other sermons. He had a sense of the dramatic and a rich, deep voice. His hearers saw Noah build his ark and the whale swallow Jonah and the Hebrew children clasp hands in the fiery furnace.

Standing, he could not see Daniel, his poor boy, but it was for Daniel that he spoke.

"There's little to win or lose in this life. Life is short, eternity is long. Sorrow endureth for a night, but joy cometh in the morning." In his heart he said, "Daniel, remember life is short. My dear child, you will have them both again."

"Life is long, thought Daniel. "Life is not to be endured. And afterwards is nothing."

An awful thought took shape in his mind—if God had so little regard for human life, why should he, Daniel, have more? There were in the neighborhood several deep, tree-shaded sink holes fed by springs—one on David Zook's property and one behind the house of the Shildledecker sisters. He recalled them as cool, dark, lovely places. There one could find peace.

Bishop Fornwalt intoned a quivering prayer, the congregation genuflected swiftly, smiling inwardly as the aroma of coffee floated across the house yard and the lane and up the barn hill. "Amen!" said Bishop Fornwalt, and all streamed out into the sunshine. Disturbed, the pigeons swept from the shadows into the light and back into the shadows. The sky was cloudless, the air warm. At the foot of the barn hill stood a great summer Rambo tree, its shade perfumed with the odor of ripe fruit.

The cooing of the pigeons and the whinnying and lowing were all drowned by Pennsylvania German chatter. Almost all could speak English, and fairly good English if they wished, but few wished. Moving toward the Stolz houses of whitewashed stone, set in a smooth and weedless lawn and surrounded on two sides with grape arbors, the old folks greeted one another, the middle-aged and young women hastened toward the kitchen to help with the serving of dinner, the little girls took one another's hands, the little boys massed under the laden grapevines.

"Ei, Sally!" Called a voice.

"Well, Bina!"

"*Ach*, let us have the baby once!"

A knot of young men gathered round the truck of the Rambo tree and spoke in a low tone, their hybrid patois almost English:

"*Der young Rebbert hat's widder gemisst; er is g'rad in unser sei stall geflivered,*" said Peter Beiler. "*Wir hen die mules ei'g'spannt un im rous gedragged. Er hat my pap finf thaler gegevva fer de damage.*"

Peter meant that young Rebbert had missed his way again; he had flivvered into the Beiler pigpen and they had to hitch up the mules to drag him out. He had given the elder Beiler five dollars for the damage he had caused.

"He thinks money pays for everything," said John Esch.

"Hush!" warned a voice. "Here comes Daniel."

Daniel walked slowly down the barn hill. He did not see the blue sky, or smell the perfume of apples, or hear the mention of young Rebbert, whose rich father had a country place near by, or the voices which hushed Rebbert's name. He was keenly aware of misery—that was all. For months he had had no appetite and his body was weakened, his mind dulled.

Into the house, to separate tables, went the old men and the old women; then the middle-aged; then the young. The children waited to the last, taking off the edge of their hunger with grapes. The thick-walled house was cool; within fell no direct sunshine.

Each table said silent grace; there was decorum throughout the meal. Mrs. Stolz provided for all the congregation—bread, butter, preserves, pickles and cheese, apple pie, apple tart and schniz pie, platters piled high with grapes, and gallons of coffee.

Daniel ate at the last table, with his mother, his three brothers and the women who had served. They were inclined to be gay, but no one could be gay in poor Daniel's company. Round the barn sat mothers with infants fast dropping off to sleep. One by one, they crossed the hall to a bedroom and returned with empty arms.

When there rose the shrill wail of a very young child, Daniel's cheek quivered and the hand which was lifting his coffee shook so that a few drops fell on the table. His handleless cup was Gaudy Dutch, prized by antiquaries; he was drinking from the deep saucer. When he finished, he stepped across the porch between old men on the benches, past young people scattered on the lawn, in the swing, on the steps of the spring house, and went round the barn.

Row upon row stood the narrow carriages of the brethren, painted gray, a leather curtain taking the place of the dashboard. All the shafts pointed upward, and on the front right-hand corner of each wagon hung the harness. Horses munched their feed from a long trough. Passing through the stables, Daniel climbed the stairs and began to gather hymn books and pile the benches in a corner. He stood still, as though he were listening; then he sat down, his head in his hands.

Back of him spread a murmur of indignation.

"My poor Daniel!" sighed Mrs. Stolz. "It takes the brightness from the day."

"I've talked long to him," said Sarah Esch. "It was my daughter and my grandchild, but I'm older; I can stand things. I'm nearer the end."

Mrs. Stolz and Mrs. Esch looked mournfully at each other; one was very stout, the other very thin and wiry; neither possessed beauty of figure or feature, but both had exquisite beauty of character.

In the yard, Peter Beiler's sister, Anna, spoke in a loud tone: "I'd have the law on Rebbert, no matter what anybody said."

"What good would that do you?" asked another girl. "You couldn't bring Sally and the baby back. And it's against our religion to law."

"Yes, let him go till he kills yet others! He's killed two. Last week"— Anna told about the car in the pigpen.

The brethren began to hitch their restless horses to the little wagons.

"I'd sure like to stay longer; the evening is the nice time and Sister Stolz said we should eat along, but I'm afraid to be after dark on the road."

"It's true. A man came with lightning speed at me this morning. It was well that the horse saw him and slipped quick in the ditch."

The farewells were gay; without Daniel in sight one could forget. Samuel came into the barn calling, "Supper, Daniel! Come, eat! *Wo bist*, Daniel?"

When his father had gone, unanswered, Daniel went down the stairway and across the fields. He was hidden from the house by the barn; he must be alone. The corn was ready for cutting, the shorn tobacco fields awaited his plowing. There had never been a season with sun and rain better pro-portioned. Seeing neither the corn nor the stubble field, he entered a patch of woodland and lay down, his hands clasped above his head. The earth, hard as it was, felt kind. He lay without thought, without feeling.

He woke after a long time, as though he had been shaken by a heavy hand or prodded by a foot. He sat up trembling. It was quite dark; a cool wind carried the dampness of earth and the smell of rotted leaves and rip-ening nuts. As though a voice called, he turned his head sharply. He leaped to his feet and, panting, ran through the woods, across the fields, to a walled inclosure set with white stones. There, on a patch of new grass, he threw himself down, his hands clutching the soil. The earth was not kind, but cruel.

"Sally!" he whispered. "Sally!"

The place was lonely; the sound of automobiles came softened by dis-tance; their lights shone like low stars.

After midnight he rose and staggered out the gate. He did not go home but across the field to the Esch farmhouse where he had courted Sally. He stood looking over the gate at the swing where they had sat, at the barn where they had played bloom-sock after the wedding.

An enormous distorted moon shone with a red light upon the white-washed house and barn. The place looked strange; the house and barn looked like mammoth tombs.

Muttering, he stepped back to the road. He walked with head bent, hearing nothing—neither the murmur of the cars, nor the sounds of the night. Both were lost suddenly in a deafening crash, but still he heard nothing. Glass cracked, wood splintered, metal cracked on stone; he heard only his own thoughts: "Here we traveled, going home so pleasant. She sat with her baby, so sweet. Here I heard her last word. Here—"

The road made a sharp turn, dangerous to those who traveled by motor or on foot; especially dangerous to those who traveled by carriage. Startled, Daniel ceased whispering. In the red light of the distorted moon, he could see lying on its side in the angle of the fence a long, light-colored roadster. A tall boy was walking round as if dazed.

"My word!" said he in a shaken voice. "That was a close one!" He stood still. "Who's here?" he asked sharply. "Answer me!"

"I'm here," answered Daniel.

No light of recognition came into young Rebbert's mind or voice; he had encountered Daniel only once, and that on a darker night than this.

"My word!" he said again. "This is the third time I've missed that corner, if you can believe me. I had an awful accident once; luckily the victims were Conservative Dunkers, or Unimproved Amish, or Old Order Mennonites or something, or my father'd had an awful lot to pay. They don't go to law. He was sore enough as it was—I made mincemeat of the car. Once I went straight through the fence. There are"—the boy laughed hysterically—"there are some Amish called Peachey Amish. Now isn't that a name for a church—Peachey Amish?"

Daniel's hands began their awful motion; his right hand closed on his left; it pressed and twisted.

"They couldn't do anything to me anyhow; I was only seventeen."

Still Daniel kneaded one hand with the other.

"What's the matter?" asked the boy uneasily. "Why don't you speak? Aren't you glad I'm alive? I don't suppose you've got a car. I'll have to get home."

Daniel took a step nearer.

"Oh, we can't do anything with that junk!" laughed Rebbert. "It's time for a new one."

"Are you drunk?" asked Daniel in a sort of awe.

"No!" young Rebbert laughed. "I haven't that excuse. I was drunk the night I ran into the Amish wagon. I didn't know about it—not till they told me the next day. If I had, they'd haunted me. I—what are you going to do? Why don't you speak? Who are you?"

Daniel reached out his left hand; as slick and cold as ice, it slid between Rebbert's collar and the nape of his neck.

"I act for God," he said in perfect seriousness. "I'm going to punish you." His left hand tightened its grip, his right rose and fell, heavy with bone and muscle, heavy with wrath.

"After you stop screaming, I shall give you ten more strokes," he said presently . . .

"Now," he said at last, "I'm done."

Rebbert slipped from his grasp down into the fence corner.

"Get up," ordered Daniel. "A car comes."

The lights on the car were suddenly like moons. Daniel lifted his hand; brakes shrieked and two Dunkers stepped out of the sedan. Daniel was acquainted with both—one was Bishop Yoe, the other Bishop Manweiler. The light of the sedan shone upon the limp figure on the grass. Manweiler bent over it; the bishop, who was more supple, dropped to his knees.

"It's Rebbert's boy," he said. "He's done for himself this time; there's no doubt of that. Did you see him turn over, Daniel?"

"No," said Daniel. "I came along afterward."

"We best take him home." The two men lifted the boy into the sedan. Bishop Yoe sat beside him and held him. "You drive, Manweiler. . . . I suppose you won't ride with us, Daniel?"

Daniel shook his head. Soon the car was only a red light, then it vanished. He entered the woodland where he had sat in the afternoon, and there, unable to recall what had happened, stood waiting for his mind to clear.

Just before dawn he opened his father's gate and went toward the kitchen.

The lamp was burning; his mother sat in her rocking-chair; her face was pale, she seemed to have lost flesh. His father and his young brothers were eating breakfast. Seeing him, his mother cried, "Oh, my child! Where were you all night?"

Samuel Stolz rose. "I was at Esch's and in the cemetery, looking for you." Suddenly, gazing intently, he took on the aspect of a judge behind the bar. "What ails you? What have you done?"

Daniel removed his hat and turned it round and round. "I must make confession."

"To me alone?" asked the elder Stolz, as bishop.

"All must eventually know." Daniel spoke thickly and without much concern. "I came on young Rebbert; again he wrecked his car. It was just where he struck me. He laughed because we don't go to law and because he's only seventeen. What he said made my gall rise. He laughed. It was revealed to me that I should punish him. I beat him. I killed him."

Samuel Stolz sat down heavily; the three boys stared, dumfounded. Mrs. Stolz grew deathly pale; a shade gathered round her mouth.

"Where is he?" asked Stolz at last.

"Yoe and Manweiler came by, and they took him home. They didn't know I killed him; they thought that he was killed in the wreck. Now that I've made confession, I'll go to town and find a policeman and give myself up."

Horror fixed Mrs. Stolz's mouth in a circle; young Isaac caught a sob in his throat.

"Hark!" said young Abraham. "Someone comes in the gate."

The boys twisted in their chairs, watching the door. Mrs. Stolz's mouth closed; she fixed upon her son a look of ineffable love.

"Hide!" cried young Jacob. "*Ach*, Danny, hide quick!"

"Hush with your folly!" ordered Stolz, Senior.

The car stopped, footsteps came up the boardwalk, across the porch. It was not an officer but Bishop Yoe. His broad shoulders almost filled the door; his keen eyes narrowed to points like the facets of a sharply cut stone.

"The boy's all right, Daniel," he said. "We thought you'd be concerned, though he doesn't deserve your sympathy. Samuel, Daniel told you doubtless that he came upon young Rebbert after he had turned over. He's not cut and he has no broken bones, but he's bruised from head to foot. He'll have to lie awhile on his face." Yoe's eyes sought and held the eyes of Daniel. "He was only dead of fright. They want nothing said. One of the hired men fetched the wreck home."

"Thank you for coming," said Daniel.

When the bishop was gone, the Stolzes sat and stood as they were.

"He wrecked his car, then he crawled out and boasted," said Daniel. "I feel that I should give myself up. I had murder in my heart. When I thought I'd killed him I was glad."

"We have nothing to do with man's law," said Samuel. "The brethren will give you a penance."

"Come, eat," begged Mrs. Stolz.

Daniel shook his head and went across the yard, under the fragrant grapes, past the great summer Rambo, up the barn hill. The opposite door was open; through it in the pale dawn he could see the stubble field, ready for plowing. He raised his hands and examined them, lifting them close to his eyes, as though his vision were dull; then he closed them, not fiercely, one upon the other, but slowly, feeling against his palms the smooth handles of a plow.

"I'm better," he thought. "I can work again."

Slow, painful tears ran down his cheeks, vanishing into his thick beard.

THANKSGIVING IS N'T CHRISTMAS

*T*he bounty of the Pennsylvania farmland is reflected in this story, which first appeared in the *Atlantic Monthly* in November 1937. Its protagonist, Mrs. Eichelberger, is a generous Mennonite who represents just one of the many ethnicities that made up American society just before World War II. Singmaster depicts the United States as a nation that welcomes diversity and encourages productivity, founding principles that she believed had made America great. She emphasizes Pennsylvania German contributions to American life through the arts, technology, personal sacrifice, hard work, loyalty, and strong values.

* * *

I

Mrs. Eichelberger was a woman after Benjamin Franklin's own heart—she saved daylight both summer and winter. When, standing at the telephone on Thanksgiving Day, consternation on her face, despair in her voice, she saw Henry Ide's long car enter the lane, it was her twelve o'clock and everyone else's eleven. She laughed excitedly—what a day for Henry Ide to come!

She wore a dark blue dress and neckerchief and a transparent white cap, small and beautifully made. An all-enveloping green gingham apron protected a less voluminous but still large white apron. Her eyes were blue, her smoothly parted hair was dark brown.

She was a Mennonite, but not an Amish Mennonite, and the rule of her meeting did not forbid her rolling her hair a little over each ear. The dark curve of her hair, the bright rose of her cheek, the smooth cream of her neck, gave her a beauty not counteracted by the green apron.

She was looking neither at the telephone nor at the clock, nor at the stove, nor at Pop, sitting at a far window, the Lancaster almanac in his hands, nor at the long table set for dinner and extending pretty well from wall to wall, nor at the kitchen table between the dining table and the stove, laden with vegetables prepared for cooking. She looked through the telephone and the wall to New Holland ten miles away. The fields between her and New Holland, a short time ago covered abundantly with wheat and corn and tobacco, bore now a crop of white which filled the hollows and lay deep on the level. A wind was rising; the smooth surface began to show light arabesques.

The table might well have held her attention, or that of anyone else. On the stiffly starched cloth were laid places for twelve—Pop; John and Melinda and their two older children; Levi and Sally and their older child; David and Ethel; finally, the queer but interesting and attractive outlanders, Mr. and Mrs. Hugger. By "outlanders" Mrs. Eichelberger meant persons not born in Lancaster County.

There was an apparent omission—there was no place for Mrs. Eichelberger. The omission was deliberate—Mrs. Eichelberger would eat after the others finished, not because she was afraid of the number thirteen, but because no one could wait on so many guests and sit at the same time. Melinda and Sally and Ethel would jump up when their aid was required; there was no doubt that obliging little Mrs. Hugger would jump up also when she was needed, or before. But Mrs. Eichelberger would stand throughout.

"For one thing, I can't eat and jump so round," she said. "It shakes me too much up. For another, I know how to do. I had once such a shussle to help; she forgot the salt in the second peas and cut her pie in wedges that would n't cover a saucer. The folks, they thought their Mom was getting old—or mean."

The places at the table were not the only accommodation for Mrs. Eichelberger's family; in the bedroom opening from the kitchen stood two cradles and on the broad bed lay two tiny pillows.

Now, at her twelve o'clock, Mrs. Eichelberger shifted her weight from one foot to the other and leaned her elbow on the telephone shelf. Her feet were, though she would have refused to confess it, a little tired. She had risen at four by her time to prepare for dinner at twelve by her children's time. It put an extra hour into the morning.

She had begun to telephone at her eight, which was Levi's and Sally's seven. They lived far away, almost as far as York County, which was separated from Lancaster by the Susquehanna River. Even at that early hour she had had a little trouble reaching Levi and Sally.

"Hello!" she shouted. "Central!"

Central did not answer.

"Hello!" she called again.

Still Central did not answer. She jiggled the hook. "Hello! Hello!"

"Number?" asked Central briskly.

"I gave it." Mrs. Eichelberger gave it again. When she was excited she could not remember how to shape her lips and protrude her tongue slightly between her teeth to say *th*. "Sree, nine, one, eight."

"Your number?"

Mrs. Eichelberger was always astonished because Central could not remember her number. As she waited she contemplated the table, which even at her eight o'clock and the world's seven was ready for her guests.

"Sally!" she called at last, joyfully. "My, I tried long to get you! Have n't you started yet, Sally?"

"Levi says," said Sally, and that was all that Sally said. In vain Mrs. Eichelberger called. "Perhaps Levi told her to get quick in the auto," she thought, knowing that that was an inadequate explanation for Sally's failure to proceed. "Central!" she called. "Central!"

At her ten o'clock she tried for the third time to get David and Ethel. The turkey was long since in the stove, four pies having yielded their places. The kitchen was scented with the odor of spices and of browning turkey.

"*Ach*, Essle!" she called. The plain people no longer used only Bible names; there was a Doris Zook and a Gladys Ebersole and a Sylvia Kleibscheidel. There would no doubt be Sheilas and Yvonnes presently. Perhaps eventually there would be girls called Freddie and Teddie and Bobbie. It was sorrowful to think of.

Ethel did not mind being called "Essle"—almost everyone called her "Essle," but she hated being called "Asel," which was the pronunciation of *Esel*, German for mule.

"*Ach*, Essle!" called Mrs. Eichelberger, again, rapturously. "Have I then got you?"

It was not Ethel whom she got—it was nobody. She thought of the turkey, a twenty-pounder, of the ham and mashed potatoes and the gravy and the corn pudding and the tomatoes and the buttered beets and the sauerkraut and the bread and the chow—not a dog but a pickle—and the piccalilli and the hot slaw and the spreads and the pies—mince and pumpkin—and the cherry custard.

"Central!" she called, shaking the hook as a dog his bone.

At her eleven o'clock she tried again, frantically, first Levi and Sally, then David and Ethel, then John and Melinda. By this time Pop had come into the kitchen and sat down by the window to study the almanac. He had exchanged his boots for shoes and had shed the old overcoat in which he had tried without success to keep the path to the barn clear. The small area of cheek which showed above his thick beard was burned red by the wind and the stinging snow.

"You can give just so well now as later up, Mom," he said in the metallic tone of the deaf. "It says here the last week in November will contain a period of storm, possibly severe cold and high wind."

"You could a said that before," snapped Mrs. Eichelberger, unreasonably.

Pop said nothing.

"Of course you can't change Thanksgiving because it might give bad weather," acknowledged Mrs. Eichelberger, now sure of her *th*'s. "That's something else again." There was certainly a faint tinkle of the telephone bell—she turned like a shot. "Hello! Hello! Sure it's Mom." She pressed her plump bosom against the shelf. "*Ach,* how it spites me! Hello! Hello! All right! Yes, I hear. *Ach,* no! Hello!"

She turned to face Pop. "John's can't come, near as they are," she announced. "The lane's drifted tight shut. John's thought David's could perhaps get to them. They can't even do that. John says Thanksgiving is n't Christmas, but I am sure put out."

Half an hour later, as Henry Ide's car turned into the lane, Levi's Sally called faintly.

"It's no go, Mom. We started and we had to turn back."

"The others can't come, either," wailed Mrs. Eichelberger. "What will I do with this eatings?"

"The Huggers can come—ain't so?" called Sally.

"Yes, they can. They—" Mrs. Eichelberger interrupted herself. "Sally!" she screamed. "Believe it or not, the Pest is in the lane! He comes in his limousine. It pushes the snow like a plough. He missed the gate by a hair!"

As though Sally's laughter strengthened the current, her voice came clearly. "He's God's gift to you to-day, Mom. And you like him, no matter what you say—you know you do. Thanksgiving is n't Christmas, Mom—we'll be there Christmas. It can't throw two such snows. Let him have the picture and buy yourself such an electric washer. You washed long enough by hand. You do that, Mom!"

"An electric washer! His money would buy no washer, not one tenth part of a washer. I—" Mrs. Eichelberger realized that she was talking over a dead wire. Pop had not heard the roaring of the car, bucking the snow on low gear. "Look once the window out, Pop!" shouted Mrs. Eichelberger. "See what the Lord sent us to eat turkey."

II

Ide, traveling jerkily up the lane, was a tall, broad-shouldered man with a close-trimmed gray beard and gray eyes. His suit was gray and he wore a very dark red tie. He smoked a pipe which gave his mouth a smiling twist. He had spent the early part of his life making machines for the manufacture of ice and he was spending the latter part putting into circulation the money he had made. He liked to help people and he liked to collect mediæval paintings and also Americana of all sorts.

Haverstock, the chauffeur, was tall and broad-shouldered and dressed in a black uniform. He looked not unlike his master and would have looked more like him if Ide had not worn a beard. Ide's sister said that that was why Ide wore a beard—it was simpler than to do without Haverstock. She suggested that sometime they change for the sake of variety.

Wisely Ide sat by Haverstock; on the remote rear seat he would certainly have suffered physical injury. The limousine quivered, it wagged its tail, it dashed ahead as if to mow down the fence, it sped toward the corncrib. It backed, then leaped sidewise; it crouched and sprang. The wheels slid; they spun round, making no progress but sending up fountains of snow.

The gyrations were accompanied by snorts, and these made Ide smile round his pipe. "The dear thing heard us long since," he thought. "I'll bet she's shouting to Pop."

His lips smiled, but his eyes were hungry. He lifted his arm and pressed it against his side. There was no great bulk there, only a thin billfold. "I wonder—will she—at last?"

Mrs. Eichelberger made a frantic dash at the table and began to take off knives and forks and glasses. Then she laughed and set them down in disorder, and opened the kitchen door. The flush on her cheek brightened and deepened; her neck seemed whiter by contrast, her eyes shone.

"*Du liever Friede!* " she cried. The words mean, "Thou dear peace!" They signified, used thus by Mrs. Eichelberger, "Of all things!" "Did you ever!" "In the name of common sense!" She held out her hand. "But you are welcome! And Haverstock!"

Haverstock stepped into the rear of the car, where he began to gather parcels into his arms.

"Are you home to company?" inquired Ide.

"Am I home to company?" Mrs. Eichelberger kept hold of Ide's hand and arm till she had him well within the kitchen. "Look once there if I'm home to company!"

Ide was taken aback. "This is no day for me!"

"No day!" mocked Mrs. Eichelberger. "How else would we eat the turkey—I and Pop and the thin Huggers?" Mrs. Eichelberger burst out with accounts of John and little John and Melinda and Levi and Sally and little Levi and little Sally and David and Essle—there were no *th*'s now. "I phoned till my sroat gave almost out and not a soul can come—not a soul."

"I'd have known better than to come Christmas, but I did n't think of a Thanksgiving party."

"We don't make so much over Sanksgiving," said Mrs. Eichelberger. "But we make always a little somesing."

Ide shook hands with Pop. He liked Pop and Pop liked him. It might be said that Ide liked everybody in Lancaster County. When his sister teased him about his beard he threatened to let it grow like an Old Order Amishman's—unchecked, unpruned, flamboyant.

"It looks as though you expected the whole meeting," he said to Pop in a shout.

"Only our own and two others yet," corrected Pop. "I and Mom are already many times multiplied. By the next generation you can count us by hundreds."

Mrs. Eichelberger made a dash at the oven door and pulled the huge turkey pan out on the lowered lid. "Just in time," she said, basting swiftly.

"That is n't a turkey—it's an ostrich," grinned Ide.

Mrs. Eichelberger counted places. "I and you and Pop and Haverstock and the Huggers," she said. "Six in all."

"The Huggers?" repeated Ide. "And who are the Huggers?"

Mrs. Eichelberger turned to greet Haverstock, who came in with arms laden. "A few oranges, et cetera," explained Ide.

"It's well you brought along a little food once," mocked Mrs. Eichelberger. "Put them down on a chair."

Ide permitted himself a witticism which would have been acceptable from no one else in the world. "The Huggers," said he. "I know the Dunkers and the Foot-washers and the Quakers and the Seventh Dayers, but I never heard of the Huggers."

"These are no religious people," explained Mrs. Eichelberger. "That is, not our religion. I guess they have religion of some kind. They are painters. Hugger is their name—they spelled it for me."

"Painters? What do they paint? Barns?"

"They paint people," answered Mrs. Eichelberger with some asperity. "They are a he and a she. They talk a little queer. They painted Pop and they painted me, but not that we knew it. And they paint cows and they paint woods and the fields and such. And the crick—they painted the crick—you could see the water flowing."

Ide laughed his easy laugh.

"They're nice people," continued Mrs. Eichelberger. "They're not rich people. They live"—she nodded her head toward the west—"they live in the chicken house."

"In the chicken house!"

"*Ach*, it's a big chicken house David built before he was married. No chickens lived ever in it. It has a nice door and windows. He will sometime move it to where he now lives. I put a stove there. They get pretty good along."

"How did they come here?"

"In such a Ford. They just came and they looked in and they stopped the Ford; it lays now back of the barn. It has the taking-off. He works on it sometimes. She says he don't work no faster because he don't want to leave me."

"He shows good sense. Where are their pictures? I'd like to see you and Mr. Eichelberger painted by the Huggers."

Mrs. Eichelberger made a grimace. "They have them. We're not for images in our meeting—you know that. The Ten Commandments are also against them."

Ide looked straight at Mrs. Eichelberger and laughed.

"Go up on the attic if you must," she said. "Your sweetheart's yet there."

"That's the right name for her," laughed Ide. "I love her dearly."

Mrs. Eichelberger shook her head. "She let herself be painted when she was yet worldly. That she would n't a done later."

Ide opened the door of the enclosed stairway. "Haverstock might take some of the oranges and other things down to the Huggers," he suggested.

"Yes, he might," agreed Mrs. Eichelberger. "But he could wait yet a little; then he could help Hugger get her up through the snow."

"Is she sick?"

"No, not sick. But little to plough through drifts."

When the door was closed and the echo of Ide's footsteps died away, Mrs. Eichelberger reopened the door. "Dinner in an hour," she yelled. "Don't be late! And don't kiss her and take the paint off!"

She caught Pop's eye and tapped her forehead and Pop shook his head. "It's good they came," he said. "It'll help get things away."

As though she were stabbing into a feather bed, Mrs. Eichelberger poked her finger toward the stove, on which some of the viands were cooking, then toward the table where others waited to be moved to the stove. "Potatoes," she counted. "Corn, tomatoes, beans,—green and wax,—beets, sauerkraut— all is O. K."

Ide took the second flight of steps slowly as if to come deliberately to a goal of delight. He raised a window shade at the end of the low attic and lifted an old quilt from a large framed oil portrait which stood against the wall. It was he who had covered the portrait, he who had persuaded Mrs. Eichelberger to move it downstairs in summer, away from the burning heat close to the roof. He lifted it and stood it on a chair and sat down in front of it.

The portrait, signed Jacob Eicholtz, was that of a girl of eighteen; she was, Mrs. Eichelberger said, less than twenty when she died. She had dark brown hair like Mrs. Eichelberger's and wide blue eyes and a delicate throat. Her dress was white, and round her neck was a scarf, blue like her eyes. On her lap lay a handful of wild roses—she looked down at them as though bidding them farewell. A hard second glance might condemn the portrait for sentimentality, but no first glance could do anything but adore.

Ide leaned back in his chair and filled his pipe and drew slowly upon it. Mrs. Eichelberger's great-gran'pop must have grieved when his young wife died. Possibly he wore a young, curly, abundant beard, a long coat with tails, a bright shirt, blue or purple or green, finished with a plain band, and a flat high-crowned black hat, but he must have had some engaging qualities to attract so lovely a creature. Ide leaned back farther and clasped his hands at the back of his neck. The attic was cool, but he did not feel chilled.

III

At her one o'clock, which was Ide's twelve, Mrs. Eichelberger opened the stairway door. Six places had been removed from the table, but the table was not shortened. There was exactly the same amount of food to be placed on it—why not leave it as it was? "We shall have for once elbowroom," said she to herself.

Haverstock was here and the Huggers, all hanging their snow-sprinkled coats on the pegs on the door. The wind had risen still more; there were drifts against the fences. Powerful Haverstock had done more than help Mrs. Hugger—he had carried her. The Huggers were slender, dark people, not, Mrs. Hugger to the contrary, very young. They looked worried except when their eyes fell on the turkey or on the Eichelbergers. A city person would have said they were charming people—Mrs. Eichelberger did not know that word. She would have said, and had said, many times, "They are for sure nice!" Their clothes were a little shabby.

Mrs. Eichelberger put her head into the stairway. "Come on down," she called. "Time to give her good-bye."

Ide descended in a dream. He looked at the Eichelbergers and at the Huggers and blinked, as though by so doing he could recover full consciousness.

"This here is Mr. Ide," said Mrs. Eichelberger. "These here are Mr. and Mrs. Hugger."

Ide washed his hands at the sink, then shook hands with the Huggers. He looked a little surprised, but he got no chance to say even "How do you do?" so prompt and voluminous was the flow of Mrs. Eichelberger's speech.

"This man is picture-crazy," said she. "He likes best of anything in the world to sit in the attic and look at my poor great-gran'mom. I never look at her—her neck is too bare. He wants always to buy her; he thinks well of her."

"'Always' is the word," said Ide gloomily. "Twenty times I've been here."

"Sit on the table," invited Mrs. Eichelberger. "When it gives more than six I stand, but to-day I sit."

Pop carved the turkey, Mrs. Eichelberger served the vegetables. The vegetables overflowed the large dinner plates; happily, Mrs. Eichelberger owned many side dishes. There were side dishes in place, both saucers and plates.

"Put your mashed potatoes on such a side plate," she directed, passing the vegetable dishes. "Then the sauerkraut over the top—that's the right way. They get then mixed, yet not altogether mixed."

Ide came out of his brown study into his usual mood of gayety; Haverstock put in a few shy words. Mr. and Mrs. Hugger talked and laughed a great deal, as though they had not for a long time indulged in just this kind of talk and laughter. Their speech was a little odd, not in form or idiom, but in accent. Pop did not talk much; he meant to, and did, eat a great deal, and mastication was difficult. Mrs. Eichelberger talked most of the time; through her speech ran a refrain. "*Ach*, eat!" she urged. "*Ach*, eat!" she pleaded. "*Ach*, don't make me ashamed of my cooking!"

Ide studied Hugger's face from the side—it was slender, dark, beautifully modeled. Hugger's gestures were very unlike Ide's deliberate motions and equally unlike Mrs. Eichelberger's swift jerks of elbow and forearm. His wrist turned lightly; once he lifted his hand and it was as though a bird fluttered. When he talked to Ide or to anyone else he seemed to give all that was in him.

"French," thought Ide. "Strange to find him here."

Turning his head, Hugger met Ide's gaze so squarely that he felt that he must have been staring at Ide. "Mrs. Eichelberger has never told me about her great-grandmother," he said to cover his confusion.

"No?" said Ide. "After I've eaten one more slice of turkey and a spoonful of filling and three pieces of pie, I'll take you to see her."

Mrs. Eichelberger laughed. "He makes free with my house," she said. In her heart a plan was forming. "It's Thanksgiving," she thought. "Thanksgiving is n't Christmas, but I'm going to give him a present. I'm going to give him my great-gran'mom without any money passing. None of my children or grandchildren need a great-gran'mom with such a bare neck."

Ide and Hugger climbed the stairs and after a long time descended. Their voices could be heard meanwhile rising and falling.

"What do you think of that for a Pennsylvania German artist, a copper-smith by trade, untrained except by himself?"

"Amazing!" commented Hugger. "Amazing for anybody. There are faults of technique, many of them, but there she is—to break the heart."

"Exactly," said Ide. "She's often broken mine."

"Are you going to get her?"

Ide shrugged his shoulders. "I've been trying to for fifteen years."

"Does anybody else know about her?"

"It's known that she once existed and then that she vanished."

"How did you find her?"

Ide imitated Mrs. Eichelberger's delightful vernacular. "*Ach,* I chust stopped once by!"

Down in the kitchen Ide reached for his overcoat. "I'm going to Mr. Hugger's house with him, Mrs. Eichelberger, to see his portrait of you."

"I have a milk bucket in each hand," answered Mrs. Eichelberger. "You could well use your time otherwise."

Hugger threw back his head and laughed. The grace of the gesture caught Ide's eye.

"Mr. Hugger," he said, suddenly, "how do you spell your name?"

Hugger laughed a little and flushed. His eye met his wife's and both bestowed a fleeting glance on Mrs. Eichelberger. "H-u-g-e-r," he said.

"Huger!" cried Ide. "Not *Huger!*" He gave the name a pronunciation strange to Mrs. Eichelberger. It sounded like "U-gee"; she was mortified by Mr. Ide's ignorance.

"There was a French artist of that name in whose hands one could safely put old paintings for restoration," went on Ide excitedly. "He was a genius. I've often wished I could find him. He could n't have been your father!"

Mr. Hugger nodded.

"What became of him?" Ide didn't wait for an answer. "The war?"

Again Hugger nodded.

"Were you his pupil? Can you do the same kind of work?"

"I try to."

"Is it that you know Hugger's pop?" demanded Mrs. Eichelberger, agape.

"I know his name well. It is n't a week since I heard him talked about and regretted."

"See, I knew they were somebody!" cried Mrs. Eichelberger.

IV

Ide opened the door and took Hugger by the arm and they went out. The snowplough was chugging in the road, the sun was breaking through the clouds, a rush of pure air filled the room.

"It seems too good to be true!" cried Ide as the door closed.

Mrs. Eichelberger and Mrs. Hugger washed the dishes and Haverstock went out to clear the snow from the porch and the path to the barn. Pop sat by the window, his chin on his breast. When he opened his eyes and saw Haverstock send the snow flying, he smiled beatifically.

The sun was declining when Ide and Hugger came back. Mrs. Hugger saw them coming and called to Mrs. Eichelberger. "They have their arms full of canvases!"

"Good!" approved Mrs. Eichelberger. "He could easy buy half a dozen." But Mrs. Eichelberger was not quite happy—suppose this new art made her present of no value? She was embarrassed when Ide again mispronounced Hugger's name. Ide was an educated man; it was queer for him to make such a mistake. He was excited—that was the reason.

"I'm going to take Mr. and Mrs. Huger back to Philadelphia with me if Mrs. Huger consents," said Ide. "What a day, Mrs. Eichelberger!"

Mrs. Eichelberger hurried to speak. She was a little jealous of the Huggers. "Thanksgiving is n't Christmas," she said. "But I'm going to give you—"

She paused while Ide took out his billfold. It could n't be that Ide, who had such good manners, would offer to pay for his dinner! "Then he need never come back," she thought. "Never in this world!"

Ide laid a green slip on the table. "Let me take her," he coaxed.

Mrs. Eichelberger's lips parted. In absolute stupefaction she bent her head above the green slip. Her *th*'s vanished; it was days before she recovered them.

"Eicholtz was such a coppersmiss!" she gasped. "He made coffeepots and teakettles. He painted pictures, but he painted signs, too. He was well known round here!"

"That's all true," said Ide. "And he was well known a long distance from here."

Mrs. Eichelberger seized Ide by the arm. "But it says sree sousand dollars! I'll give her to you for nosing! I'll—" Mrs. Eichelberger halted. There was a mortgage on John's house and there was to be a third baby at Levi's and she hoped there would soon be a first baby at David's. Also, David wanted to move his chicken house and put it to its proper use, and that was expensive. "I'll—" she said, and stopped.

"Give her to me for nothing!" mocked Ide. "Nonsense!"

"But sree sousand!" protested Mrs. Eichelberger again. "You talked about sree, and I sought you meant sree, not sree sousand!"

"Three thousand," said Ide, pronouncing the *th*'s with care. "That's what she's worth."

"*Du liever Friede!*" cried Mrs. Eichelberger. "My, but Sanksgiving beats Christmas!"

Bibliography of Elsie Singmaster's Works

Elsie Singmaster's writings appeared in print more than five hundred times, mainly in literary journals, popular magazines, church publications, and books. This bibliography lists only the first known periodical publication for each title. An unabridged bibliography is available from the Macungie Historical Society, P.O. Box 355, Macungie, Pennsylvania 18062 (http//:www.macungie.org/).

A dagger (†) denotes Pennsylvania German subject matter.

†"Aaron Ruhe." *Outlook*, August 11, 1926.
"Adam's Queer Bedfellows." *Classmate*, n.d.
†"Adrian." *Bellman*, May 4, 1918.
"Against Orders." *Quest*, June 28, 1941.
"Aged One Hundred and Twenty." *Saturday Evening Post*, March 12, 1927.
†"The Amethyst Flask." *American Junior Red Cross News*, April 1936.
†"The Amishman." *Ladies' Home Journal*, April 1925.
"And There Was Joan of Arc." *Ladies' Home Journal*, March 1927.
"Another Moment." *Classmate*, April 1944.
"The Apple Country." *Woman's Home Companion*, July 1921.
"An Assured Income." *Outlook*, February 7, 1923.
"Autobiographical Sketch of Elsie Singmaster, American Author." In *Authors Today and Yesterday*, ed. Stanley J. Kunitz and Howard Haycroft. New York: H. W. Wilson, 1933.
"An Avian Dread." *Atlantic Monthly*, March 1912.
"The Baccalaureate Sermon." *Youth's Companion*, June 5, 1913.
"A Bad Morning." *Classmate*, May 9, 1936.
"Banker's Morning." *Canadian Home Journal*, January 1945.
Basil Everman. Boston: Houghton Mifflin, 1920.
"The Bathing Beauty." *Collier's*, December 22, 1928.
"A Batter's Lane Ulysses." *Outlook*, December 31, 1919.
"The Battle-Ground." *Scholastic*, February 12, 1938.
"The Battle of Gettysburg." *Outlook*, June 21, 1913.
"Belated Autumn." *Holland's*, March 1922.
†"The Belsnickel." *Century*, January 1911.
†"The Benefactor." *Holland's*, June 1922.
†"Benefits Forgot." *Saturday Evening Post*, April 13, 1912.
Bennett Malin. Boston: Houghton Mifflin, 1922.
"Benny and the Cat's Tail." *Child Life*, December 1936.
"The Bent Twig." *Youth's Companion*, March 14, 1912.

†"Big Thursday." *Century*, January 1906.

"A Biography of Mrs. Claxton." *Ladies' Home Journal*, June 1927.

"The Bird with the Broken Pinion." *Atlantic Monthly*, December 1911.

"Bobby Ravenel's Vocation." *St. Nicholas*, February 1935 (part 1); March (part 2); April (part 3).

"Boneshaker's Farewell." *Boys Today*, n.d.

The Book of the Colonies. New York: George H. Doran, 1927.

The Book of the Constitution. New York: George H. Doran, 1926.

The Book of the United States. New York: George H. Doran, 1926.

"A Boy and a Dog." In *Dog Show: A Selection of Favorite Dog Stories*, ed. Wilhelmina Harper and Marie C. Nichols. Boston: Houghton Mifflin, 1950.

A Boy at Gettysburg. Boston: Houghton Mifflin, 1924.

"The Braggart." *Saturday Evening Post*, December 3, 1927.

†"Bred in the Bone." *Pictorial Review*, November 1925.

†*Bred in the Bone, and Other Stories.* With illustrations by Elizabeth Shippen Green. Boston: Houghton Mifflin, 1925.

"Broken Clay." *This Week*, August 3–4, 1935.

"Brother." *Outlook*, March 7, 1923.

"A Brother's House." *Classmate*, March 28, 1931.

"Buried Treasure." *Target*, August 13, 1932.

"The Buttressed Wall." *Pictorial Review*, December 1933.

"By a Hair's Breadth." N.p., n.d.

"The Case for Co-Education." *Lutheran*, February 27, 1930.

"The Cave-In." *Classmate*, February 24, 1940.

"Centennial Hymn." *Gettysburg Seminary Bulletin*, May 1927. (Later revised and re-named "The Seminary Hymn.")

"Chance." *Pictorial Review*, January 1923.

†"A Charmed Cup o' Fame." *Classmate*, January 1942.

"Cherry Pie." *Ladies' Home Journal*, April 1926.

†"The Child That Was Taken to Raise." *Lippincott's Monthly*, August 1914.

†"The Chimes at St. Peter's." *Youth's Companion*, October 17, 1907.

†"The Christmas Angel." *Pictorial Review*, December 1917.

"The Christmas Guest." *Pictorial Review*, December 1926.

"Christmas in Virginia." *Pictorial Review*, December 1928.

"Christmas on Tinicum." *American Junior Red Cross News*, December 1938.

"The Christmas Tune." *Classmate*, December 24, 1932.

"A Clean Slate." *Outlook*, December 8, 1920.

A Cloud of Witnesses. Cambridge, Mass.: Central Committee on the United Study of Foreign Missions, 1930.

"Commencement." *Holland's*, April, 1923.

"The Connor Charge." *Outlook*, July 9, 1919.

"The Copper Beech." *Youth's Companion*, January 15, 1920.

†"The County Seat." *Atlantic Monthly*, May 1908.

†"The Courier of the Czar." *Saturday Evening Post*, June 7, 1924.

†"The Covered Basket." *Pennsylvania-German*, July 1909.

†"The Cricket." *Ladies' Home Journal*, September 1926.

†"The Crucifix." *Woman's Home Companion*, June 1925.

†"The Cure of Mr. Boyer." *Youth's Companion*, May 4, 1916.

†"The Cure That Failed." *Harper's*, December 1912.

"Daily Themes—How a College English Course Started One Student on a Writing Career." *Scholastic*, November 25, 1933.

"A Day in an Omnibus." *Classmate*, June 7, 1930.

"The Day of Days." *Youth's Companion*, December 23, 1926.

†"The Day of Miracles." *Collier's*, September 22, 1928.

"The Day Will Come." *Classmate*, February 25, 1939.

"The Dear Demented Days." *Collier's*, September 25, 1926.

"The Dear Little Dog." *Target*, March 22, 1941.

"Dedicated to Miss Frances Welles." *Lutheran Young Folks*, March 19, 1938.

†"The Deep Pit." *Saturday Evening Post*, November 12, 1927.

"Descent Is Easy." *Saturday Evening Post*, April 10, 1926.

†"The Desire of His Heart." *American Junior Red Cross News*, December 1939.

†"The Device of Miss Betsey." *Youth's Companion*, February 5, 1914.

"The Diary of Josephine Forney Roedel." *Pennsylvania Magazine of History and Biography* 43 (October 1943).

†"Dinner Was Late." *American Junior Red Cross News*, May 1943.

"The Dodge Bond." *Youth's Companion*, August 17, 1916.

"Does It Pay?" *Current Literature*, October 6–10, 1930.

†"Dorothea." *Harper's*, May 1911.

†"The Dower-Ladies." *Atlantic Monthly*, August 1909.

"A Dream." A Play for the Women's Missionary Society. *Missionary Review of the World*, November 1920.

†"The Dreamer." *Bookman*, January 1923.

†"The Early Bird." *Saturday Evening Post*, June 16, 1928.

†"An Early Spring." *Farmer's Wife*, March 1923.

"An Easter Sunrise." *Youth's Companion*, April 3, 1924.

"An Easy Day." *Ladies' Home Journal*, March 1925.

†"The Eight Hour Day." *Country Gentleman*, October 31, 1914.

"Elfie." *Collier's*, August 15, 1925.

† *Ellen Levis.* Boston: Houghton Mifflin, 1921.

†"Elmina's Living-Out." *Lippincott's Monthly*, February 1909.

Emmeline. Youth's Companion, June 24, 1915 (chapter 1); July 1 (chapter 2); July 8 (chapter 3); July 15 (chapter 4); July 22 (chapter 5); July 29 (chapter 6).

Emmeline. Boston: Houghton Mifflin, 1916.

†"The End of the World." *Collier's*, August 1, 1925.

†"End of the Year." *Saturday Evening Post*, April 13, 1940.

"Escapade." *Saturday Evening Post*, December 15, 1928.

†"The Eternal Feminine." *Lippincott's Monthly*, July 1910.

"Eusebius R. Finds Latent Power." *Classmate*, September 25, 1937.

†"The Exiles." *Harper's*, October 1909.

"The Eye of God." *Saturday Evening Post*, March 1, 1924.

"The Eye of Youth." *Boston Evening Transcript*, September 19, 1917.

"The Face in the Mirror." *McCall's*, May 1921.

†"The Fair." *Woman's World*, September 1937.

"Father's Day." *Youth's Companion*, September 25, 1913.

"The Fiery Cross." *Atlantic Monthly*, October 1926.

"Finis." *Bookman*, August 1927.

"The Fire Tower." *Woman's Home Companion*, May 1924.

†"The Firm Stand of Hans." *Century*, April 1907.

"The Flag of Eliphalet." *Boston Evening Transcript*, May 29, 1917.

"Foreword." *The Battle of Gettysburg: The Battle, the Contestants, the Results*, by W. C. Storrick. Harrisburg: J. Horace McFarland, 1931.

"The Forger." *Pictorial Review*, April 1931.

"Forty Dollars a Foot." *Target*, December 23, 1939.

†"The Fourth of July." *Classmate*, June 28, 1930.

"The Franklin Tree." *Harper's*, December 23, 1937.

†"Frau Nolte." *Century*, December 1925.

"Free as Air." *This Week*, September 1, 1935.

"A Free Saturday: Story of a Susquehanna Flood." In *Yankee Yarns: Stories from the Northeastern States*, ed. Wilhelmina Harper. New York: E. P. Dutton, 1944.

"The Freshman." *Young People*, October 24, 1908.

"A Friend." *Saturday Evening Post*, October 13, 1928.

"A Friend of the Motts." *Classmate*, n.d.

"Garden Week." *Ladies' Home Journal*, December 1936.

"The Gettysburg Assembly." *Lutheran Woman's Work*, November 1919.

Gettysburg: Stories of the Red Harvest and the Aftermath. Boston: Houghton Mifflin, 1913.

†"The Ghost of Matthias Baum." *Century*, February 1909.

"The Gift of the River." *Youth's Companion*, February 21, 1924 (part 1); February 28 (part 2).

"The Glenn Diamond Mystery." *People's Home Journal*, March 1923 (part 1); April (part 2).

"The God in the Machine." *Outlook*, August 2, 1922.

"The Golden Mountain." *Harper's*, December 1918.

†"The Golden Rug." *Woman's Home Companion*, January 1929.

†"The Good Witch." *Collier's*, October 27, 1928.

†"Grandmother's Bread." *Country Gentleman*, April 20, 1918.

†"The Gray Suit." *Ladies' Home Journal*, April 1924.

†"The Great Book." *Allentown Morning Call*, November 19, 1938.

"The Great Day." *Harper's*, November 1907.

†"Great Possessions." *Classmate*, September 25, 1930.

†"Greetings." *Historical Review of Berks County*, October 1935.

"Gunner Criswell." *Harper's*, January 1912.

"The Half-Acre Lot." *Youth's Companion*, May 31, 1906.

"The Hangman." *Bellman*, May 3, 1919.

†"Harrington." *Ladies' Home Journal*, May 1926.

"The Harvest." *Youth's Companion*, August 21, 1913.

"Heat." *Collier's*, August 25, 1928.

"Henry." *Saturday Evening Post*, September 2, 1911.

†"Henry Koehler, Misogynist." *Atlantic Monthly*, November 1906.

"The Hero." *Holland's*, November 1925.

†"Her Own Country." *Lippincott's Monthly*, April 1912.

†*The Hidden Road*. Boston: Houghton Mifflin, 1923.

"The Hide-Out." *Scholastic*, April 14, 1941.

†"The High Constable: A Millerstown Burglar Story." *Outlook*, April 28, 1915.

"Highest Honor." *Portal*, May 25, 1935.

"High Finance." *Saturday Evening Post*, April 24, 1926.

†*A High Wind Rising*. Boston: Houghton Mifflin, 1942.

History of the Women's Missionary Society of the Synod of West Pennsylvania. N.p.: Women's Missionary Society of the United Lutheran Church, 1932.

"His Wife's Money." *Metropolitan,* June 1924.

"Ho, Ho! Said Grandfather." *Lutheran Young Folks,* March 2, 1935.

"The Home-Coming." *McClure's,* June 1909.

"Hookumsnivy." *American Speech,* February 1939.

†"A Household Word." *Youth's Companion,* September 14, 1911.

"The House of Dives." *Bellman,* November 10, 1917.

"I Gotta Idee." *Lutheran Young Folks,* December 22, 1934.

†*I Heard of a River: The Story of the Germans in Pennsylvania.* Illustrated by Henry C. Pitz. Philadelphia: J. C. Winston, 1948.

"I'll Eat the Iron You Make." N.p., n.d.

"The Ill Wind." *American Girl,* October 1924.

†"In Cardigan Square." *Classmate,* December 20, 1936.

†"In Defiance of the Occult." *Booklover's Magazine,* February 1906.

"Indian Captive." *This Week,* May 10, 1936.

"In Jeopardy." *Collier's,* January 12, 1935.

"Introduction." "The Battle of Gettysburg," by Mrs. Jacob A. Clutz. Edited by Elsie Singmaster. *Pennsylvania History* 5 (July 1938).

"Introduction." *Henry William Stiegel: The Life Story of a Famous American Glass-Maker,* by George L. Heiges. Manheim, Pa.: Mount Pleasant Press, 1937.

"Introduction." *A History of Christ's (College) Evangelical Lutheran Congregation of Gettysburg, Pa. 1836–1936,* by Robert Fortenbaugh. Gettysburg: Christ Lutheran Church, 1936.

"In Twelve Hours." *McCall's,* January 1930.

"The Ishmaelite." *Century,* June 1914.

"An Island Is—." *Outlook,* February 19, 1919.

The Isle of Que. New York: Longmans, Green, 1948.

I Speak for Thaddeus Stevens. Boston: Houghton Mifflin, 1947.

"It Was Once a Jail." *Philadelphia Inquirer,* January 1950.

"Jan." *Saturday Evening Post,* July 27, 1918.

"Jerry Church Makes a County." *Pennsylvania Library and Museum Notes,* July 1939.

"Jilted." *Holland's,* September 1925.

John Baring's House. Youth's Companion, July 8, 1920 (chapter 1); July 15 (chapter 2); July 22 (chapter 3); July 29 (chapter 4); August 5 (chapter 5); August 12 (chapter 6); August 19 (chapter 7); August 26 (chapter 8); September 2 (chapter 9).

John Baring's House. Boston: Houghton Mifflin, 1920.

"Journey Home." *Chatelaine,* September 1939.

†"Journey to Onondaga." *Allentown Morning Call,* February 11, 1939.

"Juliet Tells the Truth." *Classmate,* August 13, 1932.

†*Katy Gaumer.* Boston: Houghton Mifflin, 1915.

†*Katy Gaumer and Other Stories of Millerstown.* Macungie: Macungie Historical Society, 2008.

†*Keller's Anna Ruth.* Boston: Houghton Mifflin, 1926.

"The Keys to Heaven." *Holland's,* January 1928.

"A Kind of Lovely Light." *Good Housekeeping,* February 1937.

"A Lady's Word." *Ladies' Home Journal,* August 1927.

"Last Full Measure." *This Week,* May 26, 1935.

"The Last Moving." *Pennsylvania Library and Museum Notes,* July 1938.

"A Late Confession." *Outlook,* May 28, 1919.

"A Late Transplanting." *Youth's Companion,* May 25, 1916.

†"A Lear of Shireman's Gass." *Saturday Evening Post,* April 17, 1926.

"The Legacy." *Delineator,* May 1927.

"The Lèse-Majesté of Hans Heckendorn." *Scribner's,* November 1905.

†"Liesel and the Boy Gilbert." *St. Nicholas,* March 1937.

"The Literary Ambitions of Mary Alice." *Lutheran Young People,* January 5, 1907.

†"Little and Unknown." *Ladies' Home Journal,* December 1924.

"Little Boy Burglar." *Delineator,* February 1927.

"Little Lucy." *Pictorial Review,* December 1929.

A Little Money Ahead. Boston: Houghton Mifflin, 1930.

A Little Money Ahead. Classmate, January 10, 1931 (chapter 1); January 17 (chapter
    2); January 24 (chapter 3); January 31 (chapter 4); February 7 (chapter 5);
    February 14 (chapter 6); February 21 (chapter 7); February 28 (chapter 8);
    March 7 (chapter 9); March 14 (chapter 10); March 21 (chapter 11); March 28
    (chapter 12).

†"The Long Courting of Henry Kumerant." *Lippincott's Monthly,* September 1907.

†*The Long Journey.* Boston: Houghton Mifflin, 1917.

"Looking After Mother." *Girl's Own Paper and Woman's Magazine,* April 1918.

"The Lost Boy." *Lutheran Young Folks,* December 30, 1939.

The Loving Heart. Boston: Houghton Mifflin, 1937.

"Lutheran Institutions in the Battle of Gettysburg and Its Anniversary." *Lutheran
    Quarterly* 43 (October 1913).

"A Lutheran Translator." *Lutheran Woman's Work,* February 1921.

"The Madness of Henrietta Havisham." *McCall's,* February 1920.

†"The Magic Mirror." *Pictorial Review,* November 1921.

†*The Magic Mirror.* Boston: Houghton Mifflin, 1934.

†"A Man in the House." *Saturday Evening Post,* February 9, 1924.

"The Man Who Shot Given." *Good Housekeeping,* December 1913.

†"The Man Who Was Nice and Common." *Harper's,* November 1911.

"Maria Rapallo." *Outlook,* December 20, 1922.

Martin Luther, the Story of His Life. Boston: Houghton Mifflin, 1917.

"Mary Bowman, of Gettysburg." *Harper's,* October 1912.

†"The 'Merry Christian' Tree." *Youth's Companion,* November 30, 1911.

"The Messenger." *Saturday Evening Post,* June 2, 1923.

"Michael's Bargain." *Woman's Home Companion,* December 1934.

†"A Millerstown Prodigal." *Outlook,* February 28, 1914.

†"The Millerstown Yellow Journal." *Atlantic Monthly,* May 1906.

"Mine Luck-Piece." *Outlook,* November 20, 1918.

†"The Miracle." *Booklover's Magazine,* June 1906.

"Miss Adrienne and Clarence." *Pictorial Review,* November 1930.

"Miss Cane on Call." N.p., n.d.

"Miss Glynn." *Collier's,* October 9, 1926.

"Miss Havisham's Madness." *Classmate,* February 11, 1939.

"Miss Pomfret." *Saturday Evening Post,* June 22, 1918.

"Miss Vilda." *Scribner's,* July 1920.

"Mommy." *Pictorial Review,* February 1916.

"The Morning Mail." *Brentano's Book Chat*, January–February 1929.

"The Morrises Always Loved Trees." *Classmate*, August 12, 1939.

"A Mother of Ten." *Youth's Companion*, September 3, 1925.

†"Mother's Girls." *Woman's Home Companion*, July 1917.

"Mr. Brownlee's Roses." *St. Nicholas*, December 1931.

†"Mrs. Barr." *Ladies' Home Journal*, May 1930.

"Mrs. Eveland." *Ladies' Home Journal*, March 1926.

"Mrs. Hunter to the Rescue." *Youth's Companion*, May 23, 1912.

"Mrs. Marconi Climbs the Stairs." *Junior Red Cross Journal*, January 1941.

"Mrs. Pillow." *Saturday Evening Post*, October 5, 1918.

†"Mrs. Weimer's Gift of Tongues." *Lippincott's Monthly*, February 1908.

†"The Music Lesson." *Youth's Companion*, February 28, 1918.

"My Adventures in Criticism." *Atlantic Monthly*, December 1912.

"My County." *Scholastic*, March 5, 1932.

†"My Honest Friend." *Allentown Morning Call*, June 25, 1938.

†"My Mister." *Pictorial Review*, May 1928.

†"Myrtle's Beau." *Saturday Evening Post*, November 10, 1923.

"My Son's Wife, Elizabeth." *Ladies' Home Journal*, December 1938.

"A Narrow Escape." *Portal*, April 30, 1932.

"Neighbors." *Woman's Home Companion*, May 1922.

"Nemesis." *Outlook*, July 18, 1923.

"The Nineteenth of November." *Boston Post Sunday Magazine*, June 21, 1925.

"The Noah's Ark." *Ladies' Home Journal*, December 1920.

"No Friend to Santa Claus." *Woman's Home Companion*, December 1916.

"Nothing Else Counted." *Portal*, February 8, 1941.

"Not on Christmas." *Good Housekeeping*, April 1936.

"November the Nineteenth." *Pictorial Review*, February 1924.

"Now Is the Time." *Portal*, May 25, 1940.

"Of Human Interest in Adams County." Souvenir Program, Adams Sesquicenten-
nial, Commemorating the 150th Anniversary of the Founding of Adams
County, August 30–September 4, 1950. Gettysburg: Adams County Sesqui-
centennial Committee, 1950.

"Oh, Annie!" *American Girl*, October 1923.

"Oh, Be an Angel!" *St. Nicholas*, October 1933.

†"Oh, Harry!" *Saturday Evening Post*, January 31, 1942.

"Old Flo." *Saturday Evening Post*, January 9, 1926.

"Old Mrs. Ferree's Alice." *Today's Housewife*, February 1919.

†"The Old Régime." *Atlantic Monthly*, October 1908.

†"Old Staffordshire China." *Outlook*, February 9, 1927.

"Old Vanity." *Pictorial Review*, August 1919.

†"On Christmas Eve." In *Christmas: An American Annual of Christmas Literature and
Art*, ed. Randolph E. Haugan. Minneapolis: Augsburg Publishing, 1933.

"On Fame's Eternal Camping Ground." McClure newspaper syndicated release in-
sert. *Chicago Tribune*, May 1936.

"On Little Kettle Creek." *Lutheran Young Folks*, April 13, 1940.

"On Such a Night as This." *Household*, March 1935.

†"Open Windows." *Youth's Companion*, May 3, 1923.

†"The Organ at Zion Church." *Youth's Companion*, November 21, 1907.

†"Our Brother." *Saturday Evening Post*, June 5, 1926.

†"Our Illustrators." *Atlantic Monthly*, February 1917.

"Out of the Nest." *Woman's Home Companion*, April 1939.

†"A Pair of Lovers." *Scribner's*, November 1915.

"The Parents of Eloise." *Friend*, March 1942.

†"Peasant Blood." *Saturday Evening Post*, April 28, 1928.

"Penance." *Pictorial Review*, October 1916.

†"The Pennsylvania Germans." N.p., n.d.

Pennsylvania's Susquehanna: Interesting History, Legends, and Descriptions of the "Heart River" of Pennsylvania. Harrisburg: J. Horace McFarland, 1950.

†"Pennsylvania Witch Doctors Openly Casting Their Spells." *World*, December 16, 1928.

†"The Perfectionist." *Outlook*, February 5, 1919.

†"The Persistence of Coonie Schnable." *Reader*, September 1906.

†"The Picture-Taker." *Lippincott's Monthly*, November 1913.

"Piney Wood." *Lutheran Young Folks*, October 27, 1934.

"The Pioneer: Or, a Lover Rewarded." *Collier's*, October 29, 1927.

"The Piper." *Outlook*, March 10, 1920.

"A Place for William." *Youth's Companion*, April 29, 1915.

†"Plain People." *Woman's World*, May 1935.

"Pomp an' Glory." *Saturday Evening Post*, October 9, 1926.

"Poor Thomas." *Holland's*, January 1923.

"The Practice of Writing." *Lutheran Quarterly* 42 (April 1912).

"The Prodigal." *Classmate*, January 9, 1932.

"The Raid." *Saturday Evening Post*, June 2, 1934.

†"The Rebellion of Wilhelmina." *Century*, September 1911.

"Recompence." *Stratford Journal*, December 1918.

"The Red Cross in Adams County." In Percy S. Eichelberger, *Adams County in the World War: April 6, 1917 to November 11, 1918*. Harrisburg: Evangelical Press, 1921.

†"A Red, Red Apple." *Allentown Morning Call*, April 1, 1939.

†"Regina." *Allentown Morning Call*, April 8, 1944.

†"The Reichards' Boarder." *Youth's Companion*, March 9, 1911.

"Release." *Pictorial Review*, June 1918.

"Remember Paoli." *Classmate*, June 27, 1936.

†"The Restoration of Melie Ziegler." *Everybody's Magazine*, May 1907.

†"Retired." *Ladies' Home Journal*, November 1938.

"The Retreat." *Scribner's*, July 1907.

†Review of *The Dutch Country*, by Cornelius Weygandt. *Pennsylvania History* 7 (January 1940).

†Review of *Hex Marks the Spot, in the Pennsylvania Dutch Country*, by Ann Hark. *Pennsylvania History* 6 (January 1939).

Review of *Moccasins in the Wilderness*, by Elizabeth Hawthorn Buck. *Pennsylvania History* 6 (July 1939).

Review of *Notable Women of Pennsylvania*, ed. Gertrude B. Biddle and Sarah D. Lowrie. *Pennsylvania History* 9 (October 1942).

Review of *The Powder Keg*, by Elizabeth Hawthorn Buck. *Pennsylvania History* 8 (April 1941).

Review of *Rifles Beyond Fort Pitt*, by Elizabeth Hawthorn Buck. *Pennsylvania History* 8 (April 1941).

Review of *Sinnamahone: A Story of Great Trees and Powerful Men*, by George W. Huntley Jr. *Pennsylvania History* 13 (April 1946).

Review of *Stephen C. Foster at Athens: His First Composition*, by Elsie Murray. *Pennsylvania History* 8 (July 1941).

Rifles for Washington. With illustrations by Frank E. Schoonover. Boston: Houghton Mifflin, 1938.

"Riley Hears a Voice." *Classmate*, February 8, 1941.

†"The 'Rose-and-Lily' Quilt." *Youth's Companion*, October 2, 1913.

"The Rose-Colored Acacia." *Youth's Companion*, May 26, 1910.

"Sallie." *Gettysburg Times*, n.d.

†"Salt of the Earth." *Ladies' Home Journal*, May 1925.

"Salvadora." *Stratford Journal*, April 1920 (part 1); May (part 2); June (part 3).

"Salvage." *Bellman*, December 28, 1918.

"Sandoe's Pocket." *Woman's Home Companion*, October 1926.

†"Sarah Ann's Deliverance." *Cornell Women's Review*, November 1915.

†"The Saving Grace." *Women's Stories*, June 1914.

"Saving Miss Abigail." *Canary and Blue*, January 1918.

"The Secret Christmas Tree." *Outlook*, December 16, 1914.

†"The Sentimental Journey." *Penn Germania*, September–October 1912.

"Separate Maintenance." *Household Magazine*, June, 1934.

†"Settled Out of Court." *Saturday Evening Post*, December 1, 1934.

Sewing Susie. *Youth's Companion*, April 14, 1927 (chapter 1); April 21 (chapter 2); April 28 (chapter 3); May 5 (chapter 4); May 12 (chapter 5); May 19 (chapter 6); May 26 (chapter 7).

Sewing Susie: A Story of Gettysburg. Boston: Houghton Mifflin, 1927.

"She Is Thy Dream." *Pictorial Review*, April 1935.

"Shelved." *Youth's Companion*, September 11, 1919.

"The Shepherds and the Sheep." *Household Magazine*, December 1937.

"Ships Sailing." *Junior Red Cross Journal*, January 1936.

"Singing Oaks." *Woman's Home Companion*, October 1922.

"Slater Brothers." *Holland's*, February 1926.

"A Slip of the Tongue." *Woman's Home Companion*, June 1930.

†"Sorrel Dan." *Allentown Morning Call*, May 20, 1939.

†"A Sound in the Night." *Saturday Evening Post*, January 19, 1924.

"A Special Providence." *Collier's*, April 13, 1929.

"The Spirit of '63." *Outlook*, July 3, 1918.

†"The Spite Fence." *Harper's*, July 1913.

†"The Squire." *Atlantic Monthly*, September 1910.

"The Steamer Child." *McClure's*, August 1910.

†"Step on the Gas, Pop!" *Country Gentleman*, November 15, 1924.

Stories of Pennsylvania. 4 vols. With illustrations by Alden Turner. Harrisburg: Pennsylvania Book Service, 1937–40.

† *Stories to Read at Christmas*. Boston: Houghton Mifflin, 1940.

The Story of Lutheran Missions. Columbia, S.C.: Cooperative Lutheran Committee, Woman's Missionary Societies, Lutheran Church, 1917.

†"The Strange, Black Stones." *Allentown Morning Call*, January 14, 1939.

"The Strange White Horse." *American Red Cross*, n.d.

†"A Student of Languages." *Woman's Home Companion*, October 1927.

"The Stutterer." *Bellman*, July 8, 1916.

†"The Suffrage in Millerstown." *Saturday Evening Post*, March 16, 1912.

†"The Supply at St. James the Less." *Youth's Companion*, July 23, 1925.

"The Survivors: A Memorial Day Story." *Outlook*, May 26, 1915.

"Susquehanna Saga." *American Heritage*, summer 1952.

"A Sweater for Mabel." *Woman's Home Companion*, April 1920.

"A Swedish Christmas on the Delaware." In *Tales of Christmas from Near and Far*, ed. Herbert H. Wernecke. Philadelphia: Westminster Press, 1963.

†"Sweeney, I Bid Thee Depart!" *Atlantic Monthly*, August 1933.

Swords of Steel: The Story of a Gettysburg Boy. With illustrations by David Hendrickson. Boston: Houghton Mifflin, 1933.

"A Tale Out of Season." *McClure's*, October 1910.

"Temperature 105." *Classmate*, August 1, 1936.

†"Thanksgiving Is n't Christmas." *Atlantic Monthly*, November 1937.

†"Their Great Inheritance." *Lippincott's Monthly*, May 1912.

†"Their Sentimental Journey." *Youth's Companion*, September 5, 1912.

"The Third Generation." *Scribner's*, March 1909.

†"This Dish for You, My Heart Is True." *Allentown Morning Call*, July 30, 1938.

"This Is the Night!" *Classmate*, May 24, 1941.

"Thousand Dollar Daggett." *Lippincott's Monthly*, May 1909.

"A Thousand Dollars." *Youth's Companion*, January 21, 1926.

†"Three Things They Wanted." *Delineator*, June 1930.

†"Till Decoration." *Household Magazine*, May 1937.

"Till He Gets Him a Wife." *Woman's Day*, January 1942.

"The Time to Expand." *This Week*, December 19, 1937.

"Trapped: A Tale of the Southern Mountains." *Outlook*, November 26, 1924.

"Travel Story 1842." *Train, Stage, Canalboat, Steamer*, November 1939.

"True or False." *Classmate*, November 18, 1939.

†"The Truth." *Saturday Evening Post*, March 24, 1923.

"Tumbling Run." *Pictorial Review*, October 1923.

"The Unconquerable Hope." *Atlantic Monthly*, January 1908.

Under Many Flags. Coauthored with Katharine Scherer Cronk. New York: Missionary Education Movement of the United States and Canada, 1921.

"Unfinished Symphony." *Collier's*, March 27, 1937.

"Upstate." *Quest*, October 10, 1942.

†"The Vacillation of Benjamin Gaumer." *Century*, March 1906.

"The Veteran of Seventy-Six." *Outlook*, November 5, 1910.

"The Victor and the Spoils." *Youth's Companion*, February 8, 1912.

†"Virginia's Bandit." *Youth's Companion*, August 1928.

†*Virginia's Bandit*. Boston: Houghton Mifflin, 1929.

"A Visible Return." *Outlook*, September 23, 1911.

"The Visit." *Woman's Home Companion*, June 1923.

"Visit of Lucy Luella." *People's Home Journal*, n.d.

"Visit to Clover." *This Week*, September 5, 1937.

"The Walnut Tree." *Collier's*, January 1, 1927.

"The Ways of the Fathers." *Saturday Evening Post*, July 22, 1911.

"What a Day!" *Portal*, January 12, 1935.

†"What Amelia Wanted." *Literary Cavalcade*, December 1951.

What Everybody Wanted. Boston: Houghton Mifflin, 1928.

"What Everybody Wanted." *Cleveland News Library*, September 22, 1929.

"When a Man Has a Son." *Woman's Home Companion*, June 1918.

†"When Grampap Voted." *Youth's Companion*, October 12, 1916.

†*When Sarah Saved the Day*. With illustrations. Boston: Houghton Mifflin, 1909.

†*When Sarah Went to School*. Boston: Houghton Mifflin, 1910.

†"When Town and Country Meet." *Atlantic Monthly*, September 1907.

"When William Came Home." *Youth's Companion*, August 5, 1909 (chapter 1); August 12 (chapter 2); August 19 (chapter 3); August 26 (chapter 4); September 2 (chapter 5); September 9 (chapter 6); September 16 (chapter 7).

"Who Told on Nina." *Pilot*, February 7, 1942.

†"Wildfire." *Saturday Evening Post*, March 30, 1935.

"The Wind and the Sun." *Classmate*, April 4, 1936.

"Wings." *Pictorial Review*, February 1929.

"A Woman Decides." *This Week*, May 9, 1937.

"Women's Co-Education at Gettysburg College: A Plea for Its Continuance." *Lutheran*, April 15, 1926.

†"The World Turned Upside Down." *Ladies' Home Journal*, April 1928.

"The Yellow Desk." *Delineator*, August 1936.

You Make Your Own Luck. London: Longmans, Green, 1929.

The Young Ravenels. *St. Nicholas*, March 1932 (part 1); April (part 2); May (part 3); June (part 4); July (part 5); August (part 6).

The Young Ravenels. With illustrations by Hattie Longstreet Price. Boston: Houghton Mifflin, 1932.

†"Zion Church." *Atlantic Monthly*, March 1913.

†"Zion Hill." *Country Gentleman*, December 22, 1917.

†"Zion Valley." *Saturday Evening Post*, April 7, 1923.

Index

Page numbers in *italics* refer to illustrations. Publications without parenthetical attributions are by Elsie Singmaster.

Adams County in the World War (Eichelberger), 21
Addams, Jane, 63
alcohol, 20, 42–43
Allentown, 54
American Local Color Writing (Ammons and Rohy), 64
American Red Cross, 21–22
American Women Regionalists, 1850–1910 (Fetterly and Pryse), 41
Amish, 26, 32–33, 35–36, 44. *See also* Mennonites
The Amish in the American Imagination (Weaver-Zercher), 64
"The Amishman," 20–21, 36
Ammons, Elizabeth, 64
Angeli, Marguerite de, 57
Atlantic Monthly, 45–46
attire, *34, 35, 35–36*

Bach, J. S., 14, 50
Barba, Preston, 54–56
Basil Everman, 61–62
"The Battleground," 57, 66
Bayer, Günther, 8
Beaver, James, 26
"The Belsnickel," 46
Bennett Malin, 17–18, 57–59, 61
Bible, 9–10
"Big Thursday," 31–32, 45
"The Bird with the Broken Pinion," 43
Birkle, Carmen, 49, 64
Bok, Edward, 45
The Book of the Constitution, 53
The Book of the United States, 51–52, 53
Borneman, Henry, 55, 56
"Bred in the Bone," 14
Bred in the Bone, 33, 52
Buskirk, Jacob van, 6, 8–9
Buskirk, Lydia van, 5, 8–9

Campbell, Donna, 59
"The Case of Co-Education," 24
Cather, Willa, 52
Century, 46
characters. *See also* literature
  gender of, 41–44
  language of, 32, 36–40
  in local color school, generally, 28
  Pennsylvania Germans as, ix, xii, xiii, xv, 1, 6–7, 13–15, 19, 30
  place as, 30–32, 48–50
  religion of, 13–15
  of Singmaster, generally, ix, xii, 1, 6–7, 13–15, 19, 30
"The Chimes of St. Peter's," 14, 46–47
"The Christmas Guest," 21
cities, 32, 48–50
Civil War, xvi, 66
Civil War Women (anthology), 66
Civil War Women II (anthology), 66
A Cloud of Witnesses, 47
Cohn, Jan, 45
Cooper-White, Michael, 75n. 181
Country of the Pointed Firs (Jewett), 52, 62
"The County Seat," 49–50
"The Courier of the Czar," 14, 15
"The Covered Basket," 14
Cowley, Malcolm, 59
Creating America (Cohn), 45
criticism, 27, 52–62, 65–66, 68
Crow, Charles, 41
cultural transformation, 48–50, 66
Current, Richard, 51
Curtis Publishing Company, 47

D. B. W., 52–53, 62
"The Device of Miss Betsey," 47
dialect. *See* language
Dock, Christopher, 57
"Does It Pay?," 47

Donovan, Josephine, 41
Douglas, Ann, 48
Duff, James H., 57

Ebert, Anna, 24
education, xi, 1, 2–3, 17, 24–25, 25–26
Eggleston, Edward, 27
Eichelberger, Percy S., 21
"The Eight Hour Day," 50
*Ein Jahrhundert aus der Geschichte der Familie
    Zangemeister*, 8
Ellen Levis, 53, 60, 61–62
"The Eternal Feminine," 19

family, 46–47
Faust, Albert Bernhardt, x–xi, xii
feminism, 67. *See also* women
Fetterly, Judith, 41
50 Best American Short Stories, 65–66
Fisher, Dorothy Canfield, 57
Fisher, Henry L., x–xi, xii
Fixing Tradition (Kasdorf), 64
Fleidner, Theodore, 23–24
Fleidner, Zelia, 23–24
Foley, Martha, 65–66
Foote, Stephanie, 29
Forbes, Esther, 1–2, 14, 57
Ford, Daniel, 46
"Frau Nolte," 14, 50
Freeman, Mary Wilkins, 62
Freud, Sigmund, 63

Gage, Matilda, 67
Garland, Hamlin, 27, 29
*The German and Swiss Settlement of Colonial
    Pennsylvania* (Kuhns), x
The German Element in the United States
    (Faust), x–xi
Gettysburg College, 24–25
*Gettysburg: Stories of the Red Harvest and the
    Aftermath*, 66
Gibbons, Phoebe Earle, 26
"The Golden Mountain," 22–23
"The Golden Rug," 36, 48
Gotwald, Luther, 9–10
Green, Elizabeth Shippen, 33, 42
Greenslet, Ferris, 15, 52, 72n. 101
Guipon, Leon, 34

Harbaugh, Henry, x–xi, xii, 26
Harbaugh's Harfe (Harbaugh), 26
Harte, Bret, 27
"Helen Reimensnyder Martin's 'Caricatures'
    of the Pennsylvania Germans"
    (Seaton), 64

Hess, Mary Rice, 56
The Hidden Road, 52, 53, 60
"The High Constable," 19–20, 50
A High Wind Rising, 12, 39, 53, 56–57
Hill, Susan, ix, xiv, xv
history, ix–x, 64
Hofammann, Albert, 54
"Home Away from Home" (Birkle), 64
Houghton Mifflin
    Bred in the Bone published by, 33, 52
    criticism by, 52
    I Speak for Thaddeus Stevens published
        by, 68
    Martin Luther, the Story of His Life
        published by, 13
    as publisher generally, 14, 15, 19, 72n. 101
Howells, William Dean, 27–28, 45

idealism, 50–52
I Heard of a River, 14, 53
illustrations, literary, 34, 35, 53
"In Defiance of the Occult," 37
The Isle of Que, 53
I Speak for Thaddeus Stevens, 51, 52, 54–55, 68

James, Henry, 62
Jewett, Sarah Orne, 27, 41, 52, 62
Johann Bär and Sons, 70n. 30
justice, 44

Kasdorf, Julia, 64
Katy Gaumer, 14, 27, 31, 53
Keller's Anna Ruth, 53, 60–61
Kent, Ira Rich, 19, 52, 56
Kirkus, Virginia, 57
Kohler, Dayton, 40, 51, 53, 61, 65
Koons, Robert, 63
Krutch, Joseph Wood, 57–59
Kuhns, Oscar, x, xi, xii

Ladies Home Journal, 45, 47–48
Lancaster, Bruce, 57
Lane, Gertrude Battles, 47–48
language, 25–26, 28, 32, 36–40, 56
"The Lèse-Majesté of Hans Heckendorn,"
    18–19
Lewars, Adelaide, 69n. 19
Lewars, Harold S., xi, 11, 12, 16, 65
Lewars, Henry, 69n. 19
Lewars, Ralph P., 69n. 19
Lewars, William Black, 69n. 19
Lewars House, 65
liberty, 12, 51–52, 66–67
Lincoln at Gettysburg (Oakley), 57
literary criticism. *See* criticism

"Literary Pilgrimage to Elsie Singmaster" (Forbes), 57
literature. *See also* characters; local color school
  criticism of, 27, 52–62, 65–66, 68
  local color school in, generally, xii, xiv, 2, 26–30
  in magazines, 45–48
  naturalist writing, 59–60
  by Pennsylvania Germans, generally, ix, x–xi
  regionalist tradition in, 29–30, 40–41, 59–60, 63–64
  in Victorian period, 16–21
local color school. *See also* regionalist tradition
  characters in, 28
  language in, generally, 28, 36–37
  in literature generally, xii, xiv, 2, 26–30
  in magazines, 45–48
  Martin, Helen Reimensnyder, in, 26–27, 48
  naturalist writing and, 59–60
  Pennsylvania Germans in, generally, 2–3, 26–27, 30
  realism in, 52–53
  revival of, 63–64
  Singmaster in, xii, xiv, 1, 2–3, 26–27, 30, 37–41, 61–62, 63–64
  United States of America in, 27–30
  women in, 40–44
Long, Harriet C., xiii
The Long Journey, 12, 69n. 19
Lorimer, George Horace, 47
Luther, Martin, 8, 10, 12, 13, 51
Lutheran Church, 7–15, 22–24, 51–52, 63
Lutheran Deaconess Movement, 23–24, 63
Luther's Correspondence, 8

Macungie. *See* Millerstown
magazines, 41, 45–48
The Magic Mirror, 1, 14, 38, 54
"A Man in the House," 43
"The Man Who Was Nice and Common," 26, 39
Martha of the Mennonite Country (Martin), 27
Martin, Frederic C., xiii
Martin, Helen Reimensnyder, xi, xii–xiv, 26–27, 48, 64
Martin Luther, the Story of His Life, 13, 51
Martyr's Mirror (1660), 70n. 30
"Mary Bowman," 66
Mattern, Sarah Ann, 4–5
McPherson, Donald, 25

men, 44
Mennonites, 15, 26, 32–36, 41–44. *See also* Amish
Millerstown
  as a character, 30–32, 49–50
  portraits of, 5, 6, 8, 33, 39
  Singmaster in, xii, 7
"A Millerstown Prodigal," 37
motherhood, 62
Muhlenberg, Henry Melchior, 9, 12
"My Adventures in Criticism," 61

Nadig, Grace K., 54
naturalist writing, 59–60
Nolt, Steven, 49
Norris, Frank, 27, 59
Northrup, Clark, 1

Oakley, Violet, 57, 58
Ohmann, Richard, 45, 46
"The Old Régime," 25
O Pioneers! (Cather), 52
"The Organ at Zion Church," 46–47
"Our Illustrators," 34

Passavant, William, 24
Pastorius, Francis Daniel, x
Pattee, Fred Lewis, 27, 29
Paulssen, Bertha, 63
Pennsylvania German Literature (Robacker), 30
Pennsylvania-German magazine, 26, 54
Pennsylvania Germans
  ancestry of, 1–2, 3–10
  attire of, 34, 35, 35–36
  characteristics of, 6–7, 26, 30, 50–52
  as characters, generally, ix, xii, xiii, xv, 1, 6–7, 13–15, 19, 30
  criticism by, 54–56
  cultural transformation of, 48–50, 66
  education of, 25–26
  Germany-Germans distinguished from, 38
  history of, ix–x, 64
  language of, 25–26, 32, 36–40, 56
  literature by, generally, ix, x–xi
  in local color school, 2–3, 26–27, 30
  in Lutheran Church, 7–15
  religion of, 7–15, 22–24, 51–52
"The Pennsylvania Germans," 50
Pennsylvania German Society, ix–x, xiv, 26, 38, 55, 56
Pennsylvania's Susquehanna, 53, 63
Pennsylvania: The German Influence in Its Settlement and Development, ix–x

Pennypacker, Samuel, 26
"The Persistence of Coonie Schnable," 14
Pickard, Mrs. Bertram, 63
place, 30–32, 48–50
"The Practice of Writing," 22
Prohibition, 20, 42–43
Pryse, Marjorie, 41

Rauch, Edward, 55
realism, 29–30, 52–53, 59–60
regionalist tradition, 29–30, 40–41, 59–60,
    63–64. *See also* local color school
"The Reichards' Boarder," 47
Reimensnyder, Cornelius, xiii
Reinartz, F. Eppling, 63
religion, 7–15, 22–24, 51–52, 62, 66
Rifles for Washington, 52, 53
Robacker, Earl, 30
Rohy, Valerie, 64
Roosevelt, Theodore, 45
"The 'Rose-and-Lily' Quilt," 47
Rosenberger, Homer T., xiv

Sadie (cousin of Elsie Singmaster), 10
Saturday Evening Post, 47
The Saturday Evening Post Treasury, 65
Schoonover, Frank, 53
Schwartz, Mary Lou, 25
Seaton, Beverly, 64
"Seeking Fruitfulness" (Hill), xiv, xv
"Seminary Hymn," 22, 62
"Settled Out of Court," 36, 44
Shenton, Donald Radcliffe, 39–40
Singleton, 53
Singmaster, Caroline Hoopes, 2, 4, 10
Singmaster, Edmund Hoopes, 5, 10
Singmaster, Elsie
    ancestry of, 1–2, 3–10
    characteristics of, 1–2, 25, 50–52, 61–62,
        65–68
    characters of, generally, ix, xii, 1, 6–7,
        13–15, 19, 30, 50–52
    criticism of, 27, 52–62, 65–66, 68
    early life of, xi, 5, 7, 9–10, 17
    education of, xi, 1, 2–3, 17
    education supported by, 24–25
    idealism of, 50–52
    illustration of works by, *34, 35,* 53
    language in works of, 32, 37–40
    last years of, xii, 64–65
    literary career of, xi–xii, xv–xvi, 17–19
    literary influence of, ix, xiii, xiv, 30,
        39–40, 41, 63–64, 65–68
    in local color school, generally, xii, xiv, 1,
        2–3, 26–27, 30, 37–41, 61–62, 63–64

magazines published in, 41, 45–48
marriage of, xi, *11,* 12, 16
in Millerstown, xii, 7
in Pennsylvania German Society, 38
portraits of, *4, 9, 10, 18, 23, 55, 57, 58*
religion of, 7–15, 22–24, 51–52, 62, 66
social involvement of, xv, 21–25
in Victorian period, 16–25, 62–63
Singmaster, Ethyle, 65
Singmaster, Jacob, 68n. 7
Singmaster, James, 4–5, 6, 9
Singmaster, James Arthur, 5, *10*
Singmaster, John, 6
Singmaster, John Adam, 4, 5–6, 8
Singmaster, John Alden
    ancestry of, 3–10
    education and, 17
    marriage of, 4
    as minister, xi, 2, 7, 9–10, 13
    portraits of, *10*
    Prohibition and, 43
Singmaster, John Howard, 5, *10*
Singmaster, Paul, 5, *10,* 43
Singmeister, Carolus, 69n. 7
Skippack School (Angeli), 57
"A Sound in the Night," 14, 42–43
"The Squire," 31, 44
Stanton, Elizabeth Cady, 67
Stevens, Thaddeus, 51
St. Martin, Memmingen (Bayer), 8
St. Martin Church, 8
St. Matthew's Evangelical Lutheran
    Church, 9
Stories of Pennsylvania, 53
Stowe, Harriet Beecher, 27
"A Student of Languages," 48
Stuempfle, Herman, 65
suffrage, 20
"The Suffrage in Millerstown," 20, 43
"The Supply at St. James the Less," 46–47
"The Survivors," 65–66
Swords of Steel, xvi

Thanksgiving, 43
"Thanksgiving Is n't Christmas," 36, 43
Ticknor and Fields, 72n. 101
Tillie: A Mennonite Maid (Martin), xi, xiii
The Tory Lover (Jewett), 62
Twain, Mark, 36

"The Unconquerable Hope," 22
United Lutheran Church in America.
    See Lutheran Church
United States of America, 12, 27–30, 43,
    51–52, 66–67

"The Vacillation of Benjamin Gaumer," 31, 38
Verne, Jules, 15
Victorian period, 16–25, 62–63

Weaver-Zercher, David, 64
Weiser, Anna Maria, 12
Weiser, Conrad, 12, 69n. 19
Weiser, Eva, 69n. 19
Weiser, Frederick S., 69n. 19
Weiser, John Conrad, 69n. 19
Welter, Barbara, 16
Wentz, Frederick, 51
"When Grampap Voted," 47
When Sarah Saved the Day, 50, 52, 54
"Wildfire," 65
Winter, Mildred, 24
Woman's Home Companion, 47–48

women, 16–25, 40–44, 47–48, 59–60,
    62–63, 67
"Women's Co-Education at Gettysburg
    College," 24
Women's Missionary Society, 62
World War I, 13, 21–22, 50, 60

Youth's Companion, 46–47

Zangmaister, Eberhart, 69n. 12
Zangmeister, Eberhard, 8
Zangmeister, Georg Friederich, 4, 8
Zangmeister, Johann Adam, 4, 8
Zangmeister, Magnus, 8
Zangmeister, Phillip, 68n. 7
"Zion Church," 14, 44
"Zion Hill," 37–38

813.52 HILL 2009
Hill, Susan Colestock, 1945–
Heart language : Elsie Singmaster and
her Pennsylvania German wr
ncu

WITHDRAWN